# Unbroken RULES

ELIAH GREENWOOD

This book is a work of fiction. Any references to historical events, real people or real places are used fictitiously. Other names, characters, places, and events are products of the author's imagination, and any resemblance to actual events or places or persons, living or dead, is entirely coincidental.



**Warning: This book is not a dating guide and contains graphic mature scenes and foul language. Read at your own risk.**

ISBN: 978-1-9994390-7-1
Editing by One Love Editing
First printing edition 2019
*Reality Survivor Publishing (Eliah Greenwood)*

*For the people who mess up, but keep trying.*
*Never stop trying.*

# PROLOGUE

## *Haze*
THEN

I used to think police stations were cool.

At least, in the movies. Fourteen-year-old me thought they represented hope: a place where justice was served. But now that I was sitting in one, with my sister's blood drying on my shirt, they weren't cool, or impressive.

They were a fucking nightmare.

"Your parents are on their way, kid," the fifty-year-old-looking officer had said to me, his eyes filled with… *something.* Something I couldn't quite recognize at the time. I remembered seeing it in Vic's mother eyes when she'd asked me if I saw my father often, and I'd said no. I didn't know then that I'd be seeing it for the rest of my life.

This pity.

The pity that crawls up your throat when a fourteen-year-old boy just watched his baby sister bleed to death.

Sure, Tanner, my mother, and my bastard of a father were on their way, but for the past twenty minutes, I'd been alone. Alone, scared, terrified, *empty.*

"We'll find the monsters who did this," one of the police

officers had said to me once I'd told him everything. They thought I wouldn't hear them when they'd whispered, "Most likely the same dirtbags who robbed a couple houses on the south side. We don't think they were trying to kill anyone. Clearly didn't know the kids were home. These two were just in the wrong place at the wrong time."

So, Des was collateral damage? An accident? The unexpected bump in the road of their evil plan?

*Fuck them. Fuck all of them.*

I stared blankly into empty space, thinking of her fingers wrapped around mine before the end. Before she'd closed her eyes and left me behind. Lost. Without her.

Glancing down at my feet, I shivered in my seat, the ice-cold temperature digging into my bones. It was like every good thing, every light, every trace of hope had disappeared from the planet when she had.

Drained, I ignored the furtive looks the officer kept on giving me. They seemed scared. Of what? That I'd snap, lose it, wreck everything? Or did they feel guilty that it wasn't them? That they had this somehow "okay" life compared to the fucking mess that was mine?

They could feel bad for me all they wanted. I knew they'd never really care. Why would they? They didn't know her. They didn't make her laugh, see her toothless smile. They didn't read her bedtime stories or teach her to swim. They weren't the one she came running to when she had nightmares. They hadn't promised to one day stand up to her potential bullies and kick some guy's ass for breaking her heart.

But that's the thing with tragedies. You don't care about the pain until it's yours. You can't cry someone else's tears or fight someone else's battles. And there are no apologies in the world, no sympathetic smiles, no pat on the back that can change the truth—your pain belongs to you and you only.

How ironic that the thing that kills you is the one thing you can't share.

I remember the moment I saw my parents come in. They should've made me feel better but only poured salt into my wounds. The expression in my father's eyes ended me. The hatred. The blame.

I remember Tanner wrapping his arms around me. My mother's eyes were teary. But I knew she wouldn't let herself cry in public. She never had before and sure as hell wouldn't start now. I buried my face into my brother's neck and surrendered to a panic attack. I bawled my eyes out, crying like a baby. I couldn't see, but I didn't want to. I'd never want to. Not if it meant seeing a world without Desiree.

Never, in my entire life, had I cried in front of my father. Showing that kind of weakness had been forbidden to us since we were kids. It was a disgrace in our family. But I didn't care. Because I finally understood. What people said about grief? They were right.

That kind of pain will change you forever.

Not a word was uttered by my dad. Not even a look. Tanner didn't move. He held me tighter. Then, my father muttered something about how I should've been a man. I cried harder.

"We'll fix it, brother, I promise," Tanner whispered as I sobbed. "I'll train you."

I had no clue what it meant at the time. But I couldn't be bothered to think further into it. My glazed eyes swept around the packed and agitated room, and the officer's words echoed in my mind.

*"We'll find the monsters who did this."*

Marcus. His name is Marcus, I'd said.

And I knew, if they didn't find him…

I would.

# ONE
# Fresh Start

## *Winter*
NOW

"How much longer?" my crybaby of a boyfriend whines, laying his head on my shoulder and dragging out a long sigh. Watching the clouds ruin my every chance of catching a view through the window, I ignore the tingling of Haze's breath against my neck and press my cheek to the top of his head. Bouncing his leg like a deprived crack addict, Haze continues to make sleeping impossible for me. He's been at it since the plane took off.

"The flight's two hours and forty-five minutes. We left two hours ago. Do I need to teach you basic math, Adams?"

A smirk stretches his lips, and he hooks a finger in one of the belt loops of my jeans, angling his head so that his mouth hits my ear. "Meet me in the bathroom in five and you can teach me anything you want, baby."

Oh, and he's also been one hell of a tease.

"Why did I ask you to come with me again?" I slap his hand away.

"Please don't pretend like this isn't the happiest day of your life," he laughs and leans back into his seat. As much as I'm tempted to deny his claims, I know he's right. This *is* the happiest day of my life—no matter how much shit I give him for leaving with no luggage, or changing his mind at the last minute, I'm over the moon right now. Haze is coming with me. He's moving to Canada. *Did you hear that, brain?*

I don't think it'll really sink in until I wake up next to him tomorrow.

"What were you thinking getting on a plane with a dead phone?" I mock. He forgot to charge it last night and clearly didn't expect to board a plane this morning. Not that I blame him. We were all exhausted after the day we'd had. No one more than me. *Almost dying will do that to you.* "We have like forty-five minutes left. Try to sleep."

Haze scoffs. "How the fuck am I supposed to sleep with the apocalypse next to my ear?"

I smother a laugh. Next to us is a sixty-year-old-looking woman whose snores are so loud, we jumped in our seats when she started fifteen minutes ago.

"Hey, do you have mints?" Haze glances at the carry-on bag at my feet.

"Sure." I reach for my bag.

As soon as I give him what he asked for, his eyes trail to the woman and her wide-open mouth. We can smell her bad breath every time she exhales.

*Oh my God.*

"Don't you dare!"

He laughs and throws the mint into his own mouth. "You're no fun, Mom."

My eyes divert back to the window. Since we didn't book our flights at the same time, our seats were in completely different sections. Haze wasn't having it. He ended up paying some cranky guy who *absolutely* wanted to keep his seat by the window fifty dollars just to switch seats with him.

"So, what should I expect? Are we going to freeze to death the second we get to Toronto?" he asks, running his fingers up and down my lap.

"What? Of course not. We're in June. The snow *just* finished melting."

"Hold on." He pauses. "You mean there's no snow?"

The look of shock on his face sends me into a fit of giggles.

"Nope. Not until November. What did you think? That we had snow all year long or something?"

"Pretty much, yeah." He shrugs.

"Sure, and we drink maple syrup for breakfast and ride polar bears."

Haze's eyes widen. "No way? That's great. How expensive are igloos this time a year? Rent's not too high?"

I break into laughter at the awful stereotype that came out of his mouth. *Man, this guy needs a lesson on Canada, and he needs it fast.*

"What about your folks? Are they okay with us staying with

them until we find our own place?"

Relief fills me. We haven't really talked about our living arrangements in Toronto although moving in together seemed to me like the most logical thing to do. After all, Haze left his entire life behind *just* so we could be together. I'd hardly see us living separately. I'm glad he feels this way. Because that apartment is not a maybe, it's a must. There's no way Lauren, my oh so sweet mother, will let me live at home, let alone with a boyfriend. She's made it clear before I left for Florida that when I came back, it was time to move out. *You're eighteen now. You're an adult. Time to act like one.*

Harry, the man that I've called my dad my whole life, disagrees, convinced that I'll need all the financial help I can get while I'm in college. I know he'll put up a fight for me, but my mom will probably end up winning. She always does.

"I'm sure they won't mind us staying for a few weeks," I say, the bitter taste of a lie lingering on my tongue.

Truth is, they have no idea Haze is coming.

Simply because they have no idea he exists.

My plan: show up on their doorstep with him and hope to hell they'll let us stay. We only need a place to crash until we move into an apartment that'll preferably be close to my school and the job I have yet to find. I would've told my mom about him given the opportunity, but I can't remember the last time I spoke with her. It must've been at the beginning of my trip. When exactly was I supposed to slide into our nonexistent conversations that I have a boyfriend?

"Okay, so fill me in on your family drama. What's the Kingstons' story?" Haze steadies his elbow on the arm rest and props his chin in the palm of his hand. I smile at his cautious and focused expression.

Crazy to think that, while Haze knows every little stupid detail there is to know about me, he doesn't know much about my life back home. Knowing my favorite color, first pet's name, and favorite band doesn't tell him what's waiting for him once we get off that plane. Yet, he chose to come with me. We've talked about my family a few times in the past. But compared to our conversations about *his* family, we've barely scratched the surface.

"Meh, it's nothing special, really. Mom had me when she was sixteen. She raised me by herself until she met Harry, my stepfather. They got married. He'd just lost his wife to cancer, and he already had a kid of his own, Jaden, who's fourteen now. We're technically not related, but we grew up together, so we consider each other siblings. Then, five years ago, my sister, Maika, was born."

"So, you and your sister share a mother?" Haze asks.

I nod, omitting to tell him that while we were brought into this world by the same woman, that woman treats us completely differently. With Maika, she's this caring, sweet mom. With me? *Don't even get me started.*

"When my Dad got sent to Seattle for his work, my parents

decided to ship me to Maria until I graduated, as you know. My mom followed him, since she'd just been laid off, while Jaden and Maika stayed with their grandma, Harry's mom. They just got back."

"Why didn't you stay at your grandma's place, too?"

"That's the thing. She's not my grandma. She says I'm not her granddaughter since I don't have Harry's blood in my veins."

Haze winces.

"Yep, that's the usual reaction." I crack a laugh.

My stepfather's mother was always narrow-minded. She believes people that get married should spend the rest of their lives together, no matter if they're happy or not. In her eyes, holy matrimony should be sacred and a vow of eternity. She was always against my father remarrying. They didn't talk for years when she first told him she'd never see me as her granddaughter as I came from his second marriage. Harry's dad, on the contrary, is kind and sweet, which, in my opinion, played a big part in his son turning out all right.

Haze reaches for my hand. "And the rest of your family?"

"You already know them. Maria, Kendrick, and Kass. They're all I have on my mom's side."

"What about your mother's parents?"

"They died before I was born. Car crash. My mom said they wanted to put me into the system. They thought she was too young to take care of a baby."

Haze keeps quiet for a while, as though he's trapped in his

own thoughts. Then, he speaks.

"Wow, both our families suck."

I give a faint laugh.

"Tell me about it."

"Can I ask what happened to your biological father? You know… why he isn't around?" His tone hints at how hesitant he is. He's right to be. I usually change the topic whenever someone brings up my sperm donor, but somehow, right now, with Haze's compassionate blue eyes pointed at me, I don't want to.

"I don't know much. My mom said he was one of the bad kids. Came from the wrong side of the tracks. He was nineteen when they met. Then he just took off running the second she told him about me. Like I said, nothing special." A sharp pain cuts through my chest, and my eyes drop to my feet.

*This feeling right here.* That's why. Why I've desperately avoided this moment ever since I could talk.

"Hey, look at me." Haze's voice is low but firm. "Look at me."

I finally do.

"I'm sorry I wasn't there to kick his ass."

Smiling, I reach over to place a quick peck on his mouth, which results in Haze pulling me back in for the real deal. His lips move slowly against mine, but just like every damn time he kisses me, my heart wants to come out of my chest and say hi.

"So, your siblings, cute or monsters?" he asks when we pull away for air.

"Maika is definitely cute. And Jay… He hates everyone. Puberty and all. Last I heard, he wasn't hanging out with the best crowd."

Haze scoffs. "Look at you. Worried about your brother hanging out with the wrong crowd when you're practically dating a criminal."

My mouth drops. "Can you say that any louder?"

"Sure." The bastard clears his throat, "You're worried about your brother hanging out with the bad ki—"

Laughing harder than I should, I slam my hand against his mouth. "Are you insane? Do you want them to think we're trying to hijack the plane?"

As soon as I set his mouth free, his eyes grow as though he's just realized something.

"About that. I forgot the bomb."

I don't think I've ever punched him this hard.

A small gasp erupts next to us.

Great. Snoring lady is awake.

"Ouch," Haze laughs and lifts his hand to his bicep. *I hope that leaves a bruise.*

"He's kidding, totally kidding. He's such a prankster, this one." I turn to the granny and force a giggle. She doesn't bother forcing a smile, judgment creasing her forehead. Meanwhile, the idiot next to me is laughing so hard he can barely breathe.

Note to self: Never bring Haze Adams on a plane.

STUCK IN A THICK CROWD OF travelers, I stand in line and wait for my hideous floral suitcase to come circling around the baggage carousel. We made it to Toronto, and I even managed not to throw my man out the plane window—unbelievable, I know. The airport is exactly the same as I remember, brimming with nervous people rushing to catch their flights. Haze insists on taking my suitcase as soon as it comes to view.

"Anyone here to welcome you home?" he asks and grabs my hand. Shoulders ram into our side as we make our way through the crowd.

"Not that I know of. My parents are out of town with my siblings for the weekend. They're coming back tomorrow morning. My dad called me a few days back to apologize. He would've been here otherwise." I find some comfort in the fact that at least one of my parents cared enough to call.

"Your mom didn't call you?"

"No. She probably had to work."

He scoffs. "Damn right she does. On her priorities."

I chuckle and Haze pulls me closer, feathering my forehead with kisses. Calm seeps into me. Haze is here. With me. In my home country. I still can't believe it. We turn the corner, and all these good feelings come flying out the window when I look ahead of me.

And see him.

My heart drops.

He's standing a few feet away from us. With his hands buried in his pockets and his black hair cascading down his tanned face, he glances around, searching, analyzing. He seems to be waiting for someone.

*No, no, no. Don't tell me that someone's me.*

He hasn't changed one bit, the exact same guy he was when we said goodbye. The promise we made before I left eats at me. I didn't think he'd keep his word. That he'd actually come and pick me up on the day I came back. He made me that promise before we fought. Before I left. Before that night, and most importantly, before I met Haze.

Like he's on a timer, his head snaps up and he notices us. At first, he smiles. Then, he frowns. Because I'm not alone. My first instinct is to run, yet, my feet bring me closer to him. To the guy I didn't think would ever be a part of my life again.

Intending to meet us halfway, the ghost from my past edges his way through the crowd, his footsteps slow but determined. He stops in front of us, and his eyes sway from Haze to me for a few unbearably long seconds.

"Winter, finally."

"Hey," I barely say.

"Who's this?" Haze asks.

I try to speak but the words escape me. Witnessing my struggle, he beats me to it, holding out his hand to Haze.

"Hi, I'm Caleb. Winter's boyfriend."

# TWO

## *Competition*

"Hi, I'm Caleb. Winter's boyfriend."

Haze doesn't make a sound, his eyes jumping back and forth between me and Caleb for a while. His fingers grow tight around mine as he glares at the hand held out to him.

"What the hell?" I reprimand. *He has got to be kidding me.*

The idiot decides he's had his fun and bursts out laughing.

"You should've seen your face."

Haze's shoulders drop with relief.

"You're a complete idiot, you know that?"

"Come on. You show up holding hands with some mystery guy? I had to." Caleb opens his arm for me. "Come here, Kingston."

Haze stiffens up at the nickname. I try to walk into Caleb's embrace, but Haze doesn't let go of my hand—quite the opposite actually; he only holds on tighter—which results in me giving Caleb a very awkward half hug with one arm. He embraces me for a few seconds longer, not giving a single thought to my half-assed hug, and pulls away.

"What's going on?" Haze asks.

"Sorry." I lean back into Haze's frame. "Haze, meet Caleb.

My… best friend."

My brain pauses on the words best friend, but my mouth still says them. I shoot Caleb a look of uncertainty. *Is that okay?* my gaze asks. He nods. It feels so strange calling him that after everything that happened. I'm assuming his presence here means he wants things to go back to the way they were.

"Caleb, meet Haze, my—"

"Her *actual* boyfriend." Haze gives him a smug smile.

"I can't believe you're here." I change the topic. What I really meant to say is: I can't believe you kept the promise we made a million years ago.

"Of course I am. I promised I'd pick you up from the airport, didn't I?"

Haze clears his throat as if to remind us of his presence.

"So… a boyfriend, huh? How'd that happen?" Caleb's eyes travel back to Haze.

"School." Haze feeds him the BS version we tell everyone.

"How long?"

"A while," Haze answers for me again, which makes Caleb uncomfortable, but something tells me that's precisely Haze's intention. He doesn't like him, that much is clear.

"And you didn't tell me?"

"Yeah, I know, sorry."

Caleb acts scandalized, but deep down, he knows exactly why I didn't tell him. We weren't talking. And while I'd love to just pretend like nothing ever happened—the way he clearly intends to—I can't. I'm guessing we'll discuss what happened when we're alone.

"I'm just glad you're home. I missed you."

As he pulls me into yet another hug, my hand slips out of Haze's and Caleb lifts me up, twirling me around. The familiar scent of his cologne tickles my nostrils. He's still using the one I got him.

Caleb and I used to be neighbors. He was that kid your family arranged for you to play with before you could decide if you even liked each other. Our parents became friends before we did, and so, every Saturday, we'd have lunch at his house. My dad and Caleb's would go on and on about the stock market for hours while our mothers gossiped. It became a tradition. Caleb moved out of his parents' house last year, since he's a bit older than me, but we remained close all throughout the beginning of my senior year. Until I left to finish it in Florida, that is.

Sure, Caleb's good-looking. He's half-Filipino, half-Italian, and I've known him to knock many girls off their feet with his dark hair, tan, and soccer player body, but I could never see him in that way. I guess the memory of five-year-old Caleb puking his birthday cake all over my dress ruined it for me. If the friend zone was a country, Caleb would be the president.

"Seriously? I leave for two minutes and that's when you show up?" someone says behind me.

Allie.

Caleb puts me down, and I swivel around, spotting my best

friend in the distance.

"Oh my God!" I run into her arms. She squeals, half laughing, half crying, and suddenly, we're twelve again. I extend my arms out to get a good look at her. She looks stunning—what's new?—with her long auburn hair and green, golden-flecked eyes. Her sun-kissed skin is covered with the adorable freckles she used to despise; they come back every year along with summer. Allie has always been the one with a fashion sense, while I could easily wear a hoodie and sweatpants to a red-carpet event and wonder why people are staring.

"Al, you're here, too?"

"What? Did you think I'd let this guy have you all to himself?" She hugs me again.

I met Allison Gardner, Allie for short, during my freshman year of high school. She was the new girl. We both didn't want to play dodgeball and bonded over our misery in gym class. As Allie and I grew closer, Caleb and Allie did, too. We became this inseparable trio, walking home from school together every single day and hanging out at Caleb's. He didn't hang with us at school—he was way too busy doing stupid shit to impress the cool kids—but when the bell rang, he became one of us.

"I've missed my girl." Allie squeezes me one last time, and we break away from each other.

That's when her eyes land on Haze.

He looks exhausted, wearing a plain white T-shirt and black sweatpants. He didn't have anything else after the prom disaster.

This outfit is all he'd left lying around at Maria's. Still, his messy brown hair looks as though every tousled strand was meant to look that way. Like his careless look isn't careless at all, and dang, *he looks good.* Not to mention his tan sure makes him stand out in the crowd of pale Canadians who haven't seen the sun in months.

"Holy sweet mother of goodness."

*Here we go.*

"Who's the hottie?" Allie whispers, covering her mouth, and although, I appreciate the effort, we all hear her loud and clear.

"I'm Haze. Nice to meet you," he chuckles and steps forward, holding out his hand to her. She shakes it clumsily.

"Allison. Nice to watch yo… I mean, meet you."

I snort. *Nice save.*

"So, Winter, I didn't know Florida handed out Calvin Klein models as goodbye gifts." She fans herself with her right hand, and I laugh.

That's Allison Gardner for you. She's always been a bit boy-obsessed. You know that phase most girls go through as kids when we think boys are just yucky monsters who eat their boogers? Well, Allie never had that phase. With a mother who's been divorced five times, she's always had trouble with deep feelings, practically seeing someone new every week. She says she has the rest of her life for serious. Not texting back and ghosting guys she's gone out with is her thing. She says when she finds the one, she'll know it. But that day hasn't come yet.

"Allison, meet Haze, my boyfriend. Haze, meet Allison."

"Excuse me? A boyfriend? Since when? Winter, I'm so happy for you!"

I notice Caleb isn't paying attention anymore, his eyes glued to his phone.

"Haze, do you have a brother, by any chance?" Allie asks him, and Haze and I exchange sideways glances.

Trust me, Al, you do *not* want to know his brother.

"Sorry, it's just me." Haze shrugs, and my heart aches for him. He's right. It *is* just him. The night of the reception at his parents' house cut all remaining ties between Haze and his family.

"How'd you know I was coming back today?" My gaze drifts to Caleb.

He proceeds to explain that Allie was the one to send him a text saying to get his ass to the airport early this morning. I texted her a week ago, but she said she couldn't make it. Never once did the thought that she'd come to surprise me cross my mind.

"Hey, my mom told me to tell you you should come over for dinner sometime this week." Caleb says.

"I'd love that." I always liked Sophie.

"Then maybe we could go out for drinks, you and I." He stares at Haze as he speaks, testing the water, checking to see if he's the possessive type. Haze doesn't object, but the frown covering his face should be enough answer for him.

"What about me?" Allie pouts. "Can I go out for drinks, too?"

Caleb wrinkles his nose. "Nah, you're already too thirsty as it is, Al."

Allie rolls her eyes, and Caleb pulls her into a hug, tousling her hair as she wrestles him.

"What were you guys doing just now? Do you have a ride?" Caleb asks, freeing Allie, who elbows him in the stomach. He eyes my luggage on the floor, probably wondering why Haze doesn't have any.

"No, actually, we were going to get a cab."

"What? Nonsense, Winter. I have my car. We thought we were picking you up. We should do something to celebrate your return."

"A cab is fine," Haze cuts in, dropping a somewhat awkward pause in the middle of the conversation.

Okay. He *really* doesn't like him.

"You think we're just letting you date Winter without a best-friend interview? I don't think so. You've got some answering to do, mister." Allie attempts to sooth the tension weighting on us to no avail. I can read how Haze feels about this in his eyes.

*No*, his gaze says.

*Please*, mine replies.

Haze sighs. Just like that, I know that I've won, but I can also hear his *"Goddamn it, you're lucky I love you"* from a mile away.

"Fine. But only if you're paying," I say, and my friends laugh.

"Come on." Caleb leads the way to the exit.

"FOR CRYING OUT LOUD, IT SHOULDN'T be legal to be *that* attractive." Allie's voice cuts through the deafeningly loud music filling every inch of space in the overcrowded bar. Analyzing the stage planted on the other side of the room, I watch the band create magic and absently tap my fingers on the wooden table. The massive golden sign stuck to the wall above the stage draws my eye. *Dolores's.* They renovated the pub. God knows it didn't use to be this nice.

When my friends said they wanted to celebrate my return, there wasn't a doubt in my mind that we'd end up here. We spent the day driving around town, gave Haze a frankly poor tour after we stopped at my parents' house to drop my luggage, went out to eat for lunch and here we are, at 10:30 p.m., sitting in an orange leather booth with two empty beer jugs on the table.

Caleb, Allie, and I used to hang out here all the time back when we were sixteen-year-old fetuses. To our defense, we didn't come here to drink—okay, fine, maybe we did once or twice—we came for the bands, pool tables, jukebox, and their out-of-this-world nachos. I glance up at the handwritten menus on a chalkboard above the bar. They changed it. That's a shame.

The owner's a friend of Caleb's dad, which is how we managed to get in then and how we got in now. To think that in just a few months, I'll be nineteen—the legal drinking age here—and able to get in everywhere. Surprisingly, I don't dread my birthday this year. Maybe because I have Haze now. Part of me knows, whatever happens and no matter where we are four months from now, I won't be spending my birthday alone.

"Earth to Winter?" Allie waves in front of my eyes.

"Mm?" I bring my attention back to her.

"I'm telling you this guy is too good to be true. He's either cheating, trying to sell you into human trafficking, or gay. I don't make the rules." She sticks her hands up.

"Duly noted." I grin. She doesn't know that I've already seen the worst of the worst. Throw a psycho brother, tragically murdered little sister, and coldhearted parents into the mix and you've got yourself a spectacularly damaged guy. But I don't mind the damage. There's no disaster, no tragedy, no baggage in the world bad enough to make me run.

Not when it comes to Haze.

My gaze lifts to him. To his tall, broad-shouldered frame leaning against the bar. To his obviously sculpted biceps accentuated by the cut of his shirt. He's still wearing his stupid sweatpants and white T-shirt, and yet he manages to look like *that.* He's waiting for the beer jug we ordered way too long ago, so beautifully unaware of the girls gawking at him it's almost laughable. The busty blonde bartender has been making eyes at him for fifteen minutes. She should be drooling in her margarita mix anytime now.

"You need to tell me everything and I mean *everything.* You can't just show up with a drop-dead boyfriend and not give me an explanation," Allie slurs, all the drinks she's had beginning to set in. I'm starting to feel it, too.

"It's a long story. I'll tell you everything, I promise. But not here." I do want to tell her, just not now. Maybe during a sleepover when it's just the two of us and I know for a fact the boys won't come back midstory. Caleb left twenty minutes ago to take a phone call. I'd rather not have any of them show up while I'm squealing to Allie about my first time with Haze.

The bartender finally decides to do her job and comes around with our order. She makes "fuck me" eyes at Haze while bending forward to place the beer jug on the counter in front of him. Since she's rather short, her breast comes flush with the bar, pushing her *assets* up and giving Haze a plunging view. A raw edge of jealousy burns through my chest.

*I mean, come on.*

Unbothered, Haze reaches for his wallet. The face she makes when he doesn't acknowledge her show is priceless. Haze uses his card to pay, and the waitress responds by grabbing his bill right out of the machine, writing something down on it—obviously her number—and sliding it over to him. Haze looks at it, looks up at her, and throws the piece of paper in a nearby trash can as he walks away.

*Ouch.*

Our eyes meet as he's trailing back to the table, and he smiles. He has no idea I just saw that.

"Finally, we were growing old here." Allie claps her hands

when Haze braces the jug down on the table. I scoot over and he glides in the booth next to me, stretching before he circles my shoulders with his arm.

"Maybe if the staff actually worked instead of flirting with the customers," I mutter to myself.

"You saw that?" Haze puts the pieces together.

"All of it."

"How'd I do?" he teases, and I slouch against his muscular body, my mouth finding his ear.

"Keep being this perfect and I might just have to take you up on that bathroom sex offer." I refer to the joke he made on the plane. I meant for it to be funny, but as soon as I say it, the tension between us shifts.

A smirk spreads across his face, and his hand drops to my thigh. "Is that so?"

"I said I might. I might need a bit more convincing, Adams."

"I'll convince you all right." My breath hitches in my throat when he leans forward until our lips are almost touching.

"Hey! Still here!" Allie shrieks. I lift my hands to Haze's chest with a laugh and push him away. "Is this what it's going to be like with you two? I mean, holy fuck, way to make me feel single."

"We'll behave, promise." I cross my heart.

"Maybe," Haze adds, and I smile, resting my head on his shoulder.

"So, Haze, let's get to know you, shall we?" Allie says.

"Sure." Haze shifts uncomfortably. We all know how much he loves answering personal questions. Allie slaps her serious face on, glaring at him as though she wishes to intimidate him, which only makes me chuckle. He gives her surface answers at best, telling her as little as possible and keeping all the juicy details to himself. Not that I'm surprised. He used to do the same with me.

"Sorry, it took longer than I thought." Caleb comes up to our booth, his phone in his hand. As soon as he reveals himself to us, Haze stops laughing.

So… safe to say their relationship isn't off to a great start?

## *Haze*

Slamming down the empty shot on the table, I watch Allie and Winter gag. I know Winter's had enough from her tendency to laugh for no reason. My baby's getting tipsy, but I love seeing her so happy. It's been a while since she was this carefree.

Allie, Winter's friend, seems nice, genuinely interested in others—an overall decent friend. I like her so far. But the dipshit who's been making eyes at Winter since the second I met him? *Not so much.*

"Remember when you forced me to come to your Tinder date at McDonald's and crash it?" Winter reminisces.

Allie throws her head back with a laugh. "Wait. What was my excuse again?"

"Are you serious? You don't remember? You made me get up in panic and say I started my period," Winter fake-scolds her.

"Poor dude. Was he really that bad?" Caleb asks.

No, but you are.

"Don't even try, Cale. You're worse. Remember the time you made me pretend I was your girlfriend to scare away a cougar who was flirting with you at work?"

"Of course I do."

*Yeah, of course you do. Dating Winter Kingston is at the top of your Christmas list, jackass.*

"Didn't even work, by the way. She didn't stop harassing me. I get it though. We never kissed. She probably just thought you were a friend."

Oh for fuck's sake, how can she not see how into her he is? I bet my ass he thought that, when she came back from Florida, he'd get a go at it. Didn't expect her to show up with me, that's for sure.

"Thanks to you, Martha the cougar had to be banned from Walmart." He chugs his beer.

Downing another shot, I watch Winter laugh. Her eyes travel to mine, and she flashes me one of her earth-shattering smiles. I can't fucking stand this Caleb guy, but I get it. Who wouldn't fall in love with her?

"Hey, Winter." Caleb sits up straight. "Can I talk to you for a minute?"

I fight the urge to bark *Fuck no.*

"Huh, sure." She nods, a bit uneasy. I don't flinch, my arm still tightly wrapped around her shoulder.

"Alone," Caleb adds.

"Oh, okay." She turns to me. "I'll be right back." She smacks a kiss to my cheek and wiggles out of my hold.

"What's that about?" I follow them with my eyes until they're out the front door.

"Don't know." Allie shrugs. "I'm sure they're just catching up."

I nod as an answer, but part of me wants to go out there and find out for myself. Something felt off at the airport. Winter seemed in disbelief to see him there. Why would she be *that* surprised that her so-called best friend would keep his promise to pick her up? It doesn't quite add up.

"So… how'd you all meet?" I ask. Maybe I can find out what Caleb's deal is. Allie tells me she and Winter met at school. She goes on about their epic friendship for a minute or so, and although I do like hearing about Winter's life, I grow irritated at the absence of Caleb's name in the conversation.

"And Caleb? How long have they known each other?" I finally get a word in.

"Oh, man. They go way back. They met before Winter and I did. They were neighbors."

"They were pretty close, then?"

Allie plays with her now-empty shot glass, her gaze fleeing mine.

"Yeah, they were," she says with her head hanging low.

"Were?"

"They kind of drifted apart a few months before she left."

I frown. "Why? Did something happen?"

"No, not that I know of. They just… stopped talking. But people drift apart all the time, you know? I'm just glad they're talking again."

Everything about what she just said rubs me the wrong way. Did they get into a fight? Is that why Winter didn't really know what to call him when she introduced us? I'm about to ask Allie another one of the handful of questions ravaging my mind when Winter turns the corner with Caleb.

"We're back. Did you miss me?" She sends me a flirty look.

"Terribly." I scoot over and open my arms for her. She snuggles up to me with a giggle. Caleb seems pissed. What happened back there?

No, what happened *back then*?

I have no idea.

But I sure as hell am going to find out.

"I TOLD YOU. I'M NOT SHRUNK," Winter slurs, tumbling out of the cab before I can even pay the driver. I practically have to throw a fifty at the poor fella and run out of the cab just so I can catch up to her before she falls and breaks a leg. I love this girl, but fuck, she can't hold her liquor.

After the fifth round of tequila shots Allie and Caleb got to celebrate Winter's return, I knew my baby was wasted. We ended up splitting a cab as everybody was fucked-up, except for me. I was just starting to get a buzz. I used to spend my nights getting blacked out with the West side. My tolerance is way up there.

"You're right. You're not drunk. You're hammered." I circle her wrist with my hand, pulling her back to me before she trips.

"A hammer? What do we need a hammer for? Are we building a house?"

I scoff. "Not hammer. *Hammered*, as in you're wasted."

"Wasted? I don't want to waste anything. I'm earth-friendly."

I crack a smile but don't bother answering her nonsense.

"So this is where you grew up?" I help her walk.

She nods.

The streetlamps allow me to assess the regular-sized brick house in front of me. I briefly saw it earlier when we stopped by and Winter ran inside to drop her stuff, but I didn't really get a good look. A reasonably large driveway, bright red picket fence, a garage. It's a pretty nice house. Just doesn't belong to a very nice lady, from what Winter told me.

A faint light can be seen inside, but the driveway's empty. I assume her folks forgot to turn off the lights before they left. I remember Winter telling me her family is coming back to town tomorrow morning. I guess that means Winter's mom will have to see me walk into her kitchen. Way to meet your girlfriend's family for the first time. This can either go decently right or terribly wrong. Winter told me her mother is overly strict and hates having guests over. Never once let Allie spend the night. I already hate the woman, and I've never even met her.

We stop at her front door.

"Give me your keys." I hold out my hand.

"I already did."

"No, you didn't?"

"Yes, I did. I gave you the key to my heart."

I bite back a grin. *Wow.*

"Man, are you going to hate waking up tomorrow."

"I won't. Because you'll be there." She gives me a lazy smirk, gets on her tiptoes, and smashes her lips to mine. I can taste the alcohol on her breath. It starts out as a harmless kiss until her wandering hands drop a little too low, and her tongue slips past my teeth. She's kissing me like she wants us to get down and dirty right here on her porch.

I pull away. "Baby, I can't believe I'm about to say this, but not now."

"Why not? We're home alone." She wiggles her eyebrows and kisses me again, sucking my bottom lip into her mouth and tracing the curves of my chest through my shirt. I always forget how straightforward she gets when she drinks. I groan and slap her hand away from my pants. As much as I'd like to throw her over my shoulder and strip her down in her childhood bedroom, she's drunk. She needs to get inside, have at least seven glasses of water, and pass out.

"Keys please?" I insist.

Rolling her eyes, she stuffs her hand down her purse and hands me her sunglasses, then her wallet—pretty much everything except what I asked for—until, finally, on try number three, she gets it right. I insert the key into the lock. As I turn it, the door opens by itself. What the fuck? Why isn't it locked?

"Are you sure your parents aren't home?"

"A thousand percent," she slurs.

My mind runs a million miles. This is weird. Either they forgot to lock up or… someone's inside. We *just* got to Canada. It hasn't even been a whole day yet.

No, I can't believe someone would be psycho enough to follow us all the way back to beaver land. My brother? The West side? So many less than desirable options clash in my brain.

"Stay back," I tell Winter, instinctively pushing her behind me. I open the door slowly. My fingers seek and find the closest light switch. The lights come on, and Winter jumps back a step.

*No fucking way.*

# THREE
## *Surprises*

*Winter*

"About damn time! We've been waiting here for hours."

Overwhelmed, I hold on to the nearest piece of furniture I can find, trying to take back my sobriety from the killer tequila shots in my veins.

"Dumbass. You jinxed it. We were supposed to scream *Surprise!*"

This isn't possible.

"Shit. You're right. *Surprise!*"

I blink once.

*Still here.*

I blink twice.

*Still here.*

I can't believe it.

Will and Kendrick are sitting in my kitchen.

"What the fuck are you guys doing here?" Haze asks. I bring a hand to my racing heart and relive the memory of leaving them in Maria's kitchen less than twenty-four hours ago. I cried for these idiots. But now they're here. In my house. In Canada.

"Ask Kendrick. It was his idea." Will motions to my cousin, who's shamelessly sitting with one of his legs on the table, with his chin.

Kendrick gets up. "A little bit after you left, I realized I had no plan for the summer. School's over, I'm getting real fucking tired of all these attacks on us, and what happened to you yesterday, it just… it made me think, you know? I've had enough. I'm free for the first time in forever. Not to mention my mom talked to yours today, and Lauren told us we could come visit anytime. So, long story short, I've decided to spend the summer with my lovely family in their covered-in-snow country." He gives me a wide smile. "By the way, key under the welcome mat, not the best hiding spot—you should tell your mom."

This is all so unexpected that it takes both me and Haze a solid second to understand what's just been said. So, basically, my cousin, whose family I visited for a few months, is now visiting my family for the summer.

*To think I was worried I'd miss him.*

"And you?" I turn to Will. I know wherever Kendrick goes, Will usually follows, but I didn't think that rule went as far as changing countries.

"I…" Will starts, but his words trail off. I've never, in the whole time I've known him, seen this guy speechless—except for when he saw Kass in her prom dress. He eventually shrugs and says, "I needed to get away."

I nod, but I'm not convinced. He looks like hell. Dark circles rim his empty, almost ghostly eyes, and his smile is so forced it must hurt his face. He doesn't look like… well, *Will.*

Something's definitely up. Trouble in paradise, perhaps? Last I heard, Kass was getting sick of him refusing to tell Kendrick about their relationship. But then again, I saw Will pull Kass into a room at prom. They never returned, and I assumed it meant they'd made up. Did they break up? Did Will finally tell Kendrick? No, I doubt they'd be here together, on a summer trip, if he had. Finding out that your best friend has been sleeping with your little sister behind your back can't be good on a friendship.

"I was very disappointed that there's no snow, by the way," Will says.

"Oh, for God's sake, it's the summer. Does the entire world think we have snow all year long?"

"Well, yeah, duh." Will cracks a faint laugh, but I can tell his heart's not in it.

"Where's Alex? He didn't come with?" I glance around the room.

"Nah. He couldn't make it. He had some things to do this summer, but don't worry, he'll happily annoy you from afar. He promised to call," Kendrick says.

"He had some things to do," Will scoffs. "More like *someone*. Does he really think we don't know he's met a girl?"

I frown. "You mean he's cheating on Mia?"

"Oh, right, you don't know. They broke up," Kendrick says.

"What? Why? I thought things were going great." I think back to the few times I talked to Mia. I liked her.

"Not sure, really. Alex just said she wasn't who he thought she was." Kendrick exchanges furtive glances with Will. The atmosphere feels so heavy I'm positive I'm missing something here.

"And where are you two idiots going to stay?" Haze asks.

"Right here. Think of it as Lauren repaying my mom."

"Does my mom even know you're here right now?"

"Yep. We talked on the phone a few hours ago."

So, Kendrick gets a phone call but not me. *Thanks, Mom.*

"And Maria's okay with this?" I ask.

"I won't be getting in trouble or making a mess in the house. Trust me, she's never been happier." Kendrick snorts.

Kendrick may be laughing, but Haze is not. Barely a few hours ago he was telling me how much he *wouldn't* miss having them around. Funny how life works. Sure, he and Kendrick made peace after our prom disaster, but there's a difference between tolerating and liking each other.

Kendrick smirks. "Which one's my room, cuz?"

I slur something about the guest rooms upstairs at the end of the hall, and next thing I know, the boys have disappeared up the stairs with their luggage.

I glance at Haze over my shoulder. *Shit, the room's spinning.*

"One day. We couldn't even get one fucking day," he huffs,

and I laugh, grabbing his hand and leading him up the stairs. I almost trip over my own feet five times—Will and Kendrick's surprise visit might have slightly sobered up my brain but not my body, apparently. As I push the door to my old bedroom open, I can't help but think that, although I'll never admit it to Haze. Maybe, just maybe…

I'm happy the guys are here.

I WAKE UP TO THE SOUND of a woman screaming. Opening my eyes a crack, I wince at the bright sunlight coming in through my window and listen. "What on earth were you thinking?" I hear the woman say, and it doesn't take long for the mystery voice to find an owner. That woman is not just any woman.

That woman is my mother.

The smell of burnt food sneaks in through the gap under my door, and a smile stretches my lips. I don't even need to go down to understand what happened.

*Kendrick and Will happened.*

The guys tried to cook, didn't they?

I roll over to my side, only to see Haze sleeping safe and sound on his stomach. He doesn't seem bothered that my mother is shouting at the top of her lungs or that it smells like someone set the house on fire. I swear this guy could sleep through anything.

"I didn't sign up for this. You better clean this up!"

Lauren Kingston has never been a morning person. Her default mode is moody and cold, and I can't even imagine how two guys making a mess in her kitchen—which she can't stand as the neat freak she is—will enhance her already unpleasant personality. Here's to hoping she won't lose it when she sees Haze walk down the stairs. With my luck, she'll get mad that someone stayed the night without her permission and kick him out.

The fire alarm going off finally seems to be enough to pull Haze out of slumber. Opening and closing his eyes a few times, he groans.

"What the hell is going on?"

"Oh, you know, the guys almost burnt the house down. The usual." I slip out of bed, walking to the large windows and drawing the hideous pink curtains I've had since I was nine. "And my mother's in a mood."

"Awesome." Haze flips on his back, blocking the sun with his hand.

"Get up. It's past ten." I pull on the blanket, almost drooling when the sunrays illuminate his perfectly defined torso. My eyes trace every curve, every highlighted muscle on his body, and I'm suddenly tempted to jump right back into bed with him.

"She's literally going to bite my head off when she finds out a stranger stayed the night." I roam my bedroom anxiously. "Hey, Mom, what's up? Meet the boyfriend you didn't even know I had."

"Wait, you didn't tell them about me?" He rubs his eyes, still out of it.

Guilt is evident on my face.

He pouts.

"Hey, don't give me that look. I wanted to, okay? I just didn't get the chance." I climb into bed, straddling his bare chest and bending forward to cover his lips with "forgive me" kisses. A smile eventually crosses his tired features, and he hooks a hand behind my neck to kiss me back.

You know the moment I was talking about? The moment where it sinks in and I realize that the guy I love more than my own damn self followed me to another country?

Well, that moment is now.

I'm so happy I feel like my body can't possibly contain all this joy and it's going to come bursting out of me at any moment. Haze's fingers get lost in my hair as he kisses me. I can feel his morning wood strain against my silk shorts, and I know if I don't get away from him, we might not get out of bed anytime soon. He rejected me yesterday, and with good reason, but it doesn't change the fact that I'm horny as f—

"What are you thinking about?" Haze looks at me curiously, his fingers smoothing over my right thigh.

"Just… *stuff*," I stutter and pick myself off his body.

I kneel down to unzip my suitcase, on the hunt for a decent outfit, and a few minutes later, I'm dressed, much to Haze's disappointment.

"Time to go get yelled at."

Haze's eyes carefully follow me around my bedroom as he sits up straight and runs a hand through his messy hair.

"What if we don't tell her?"

I stop. His eyes land on my window, and he grins. *I know that grin.*

"No, no way. You're not sneaking out the window."

"Why not? Wouldn't be the first time."

"Because they'll see you."

"No, they won't. Then, all I have to do is knock on your door, pretend that I got here today because I realized I couldn't live without my amazing girlfriend, and introduce myself. Everyone wins." Haze gets out of bed and makes his way to my window to check out his escape route. "Piece of cake."

I sway from one foot to the other, chewing on my lip.

"Listen, from what you've told me, she's going to hate me either way but not nearly as much as she will if she finds out I came into her house without her approval."

*Shit.* He kind of has a point.

"Fine." I can't help but check him out. He's standing there in his boxers, looking so effortlessly perfect and putting my morning hair to shame. I think he notices because he grins. I shake my head in an attempt to gather myself. "You should… hm… get dressed and wait a few minutes. I'll go downstairs. Text me when you're coming down. I want to be the one to open the door."

Haze nods and picks his shirt and sweatpants up from my floor. We *really* need to go buy him new clothes while we wait for his to get here. And he needs to make arrangements to sell his old apartment's furniture as soon as possible. He said he knows a guy who helped his family out in the past—the guy who emptied their first house in less than a week before its demolition and after what happened to Desiree. He'll clear out whatever Haze can't get shipped.

Grabbing my phone on the nightstand, I peck him on the lips, walk out, and glide down the stairs.

First mission of the day: stop my mother from murdering Kendrick and Will.

The living room is empty, exactly the same as it was the day I dragged my suitcase down the stairs and left for Florida. I assess the perfectly clean house. No sign of Jaden playing video games, no sign of Maika breaking every single doll my parents buy for her—I don't know what she does with them, but I feel bad for the headless Barbies she carries around—and especially no sign of my mother.

A laugh falls out of my mouth when I step into the kitchen and see Kendrick and Will on their knees, scraping the kitchen tiles. I take in the scene of the crime. Opened pancake mix lies on the counter next to dirty pans. The guys' faces are covered in flour. My guess is they tried to make pancakes, somehow ended up throwing flour at each other like the two-year-olds they are, and burnt their food.

"What on earth happened here?"

"It's his fault," Kendrick grumbles.

"Not true," Will says.

"Where's everyone?" I glance around the silent house.

"Your dad went to drive your brother to a friend's house. Maika's with him," Kendrick explains.

"And my mom?"

"She's downstairs, looking for something to get *that* out." Will points up. I follow his motion and gasp at the sight of what I assume to be pancake mix on the ceiling.

"How did you even… No, you know what? I don't want to know." I walk to the fridge to pour myself a glass of juice.

"Hey, Canada, where's your boyfriend?" Will asks.

Kendrick glances around, looking for Haze. "Yeah, I was kind of looking forward to Aunt Lauren freaking out."

"We've decided to pretend he just arrived today. He's going to come knocking on the door in a little while. If I hear a word from either of you, you're dead, got it?"

"Why all the trouble?" Will questions. "Would it really be so bad if your mom found out he stayed the night?"

Kendrick and I make eye contact and both say the exact same thing at the same time. "You don't know her."

He has no idea who he's dealing with. My mother never, not once, let my friends spend the night here. She crushed Allie's and my sleepover dreams all throughout my high school years.

I can already hear her speech: *This is my house! I decide who comes into it. As long as you are living under my roof, you will follow my rules.*

I watch the boys struggle until the basement door slams in the distance. My mom's on her way back from the laundry room. For some reason, my heart beats faster at the thought of seeing her again—and not in a good way. I suck in a breath when her tall frame turns the corner. She looks great, per usual. Her brown hair is pulled into a neat bun, and she's wearing a white blouse with black pants. She holds a mop and bucket full of cleaning products in her hand. Her inability to smile may knock some points off her score, but nevertheless, my mother's always been beautiful.

"Winter," she says when she notices me.

"Hi." I muster a weak smile.

I wait for her to say something else, to display some sort of emotion, but she doesn't. If we had a regular mother-daughter relationship, I'd be in her arms by now—after all, we haven't seen each other in months—but she's never been the hugging type.

"You're here." She states the obvious, her eyes raking over my body as she analyzes my outfit. I can hear her mentally judging me. I'm wearing blue jeans and a sleeveless black shirt. It's nothing to write home about, but I like it. I thought it was cute. Clearly, she disagrees. My mother's one of those people who have the ability to make you question every single decision you ever made with one look. "When did you come back?"

"Last night. Caleb and Allie took me out to celebrate." I

nervously tug at my shirt.

"Oh." She nods. "Well, welcome back."

"Thanks."

She walks around me, letting me know that our reunion is over, and tells the boys to get out of her way so she can clean up their mess. My mother and I have never been what one would call close. Our relationship has been on the rocks since… well, *since I was born*? If a lifetime of trying to impress and satisfy her has taught me one thing, it's that I will most likely never get it right with her. I killed myself trying to be the perfect daughter for years: I studied hard, got good grades, did laundry, said please, but nothing I ever did seemed good enough.

Over the years, people started to notice how distant she was. Some said, "I'm sure it's not personal. It's probably just who she is as a person." I found some comfort in that story. Until Maika came along. That's when I found out that she could, in fact, be loving and warm to her children. That she isn't cold to everyone. Just me.

Must be why she called me Winter.

*First bad pun of the day? Check.*

But I have Harry, and he's enough. He married my mom when I was so young, I can't seem to recall my life before him. He taught me to ride a bike, covered my scraped knees with Hello Kitty Band-Aids, tried to give me the talk. He's my dad, biological or not.

I'm ripped away from my mommy issues when the front

door swings open and a familiar voice erupts behind me.

"Pumpkin!"

My heart swells with happiness.

"Dad!" I jolt toward him and practically throw myself into his arms.

"Where's my little girl? What have you done to her?"

"It's only been a few of months," I chuckle.

"I know, but yesterday, you were this big." He feeds me the universal dad line.

"Winter!" someone blurts out.

I pull away from my father's warm embrace and spot Maika, my baby sister, on the porch. Fidgeting with her floral red dress, she smiles widely. Curly blonde hair flows down her face, covering her hazel eyes and stopping at her shoulders.

"Hey, princess." I bend down to her level and open my arms for her. She jumps in excitement and runs to me.

"I missed you." She wraps her tiny arms around my neck.

"I missed you, too, Mai."

Soon enough, she breaks away from me, making it clear that she has more important matters to attend to, and runs to the living room where her toys await her.

"When's Jay coming back?" I glance at my dad.

"Tonight. He was excited to see you, but his friend just got a new game. You know how it goes."

"I get it. Priorities and all," I mock although I'm not surprised. I'm pretty confident there isn't a single person in this world Jaden loves more than his video games.

"Tell me everything. How was it? How was Florida?" Dad asks, removing his coat. "I'm assuming things went well since these guys loved you so much they followed you home," he motions to Will and Kendrick.

Will scoffs, and I glare at him. I know what he's thinking. I'm not sure almost dying a few times qualifies as *well.*

"Come here, son." My dad motions to my cousin.

"Hey, Uncle Harry." Kendrick walks to him for one of those man hugs they always give each other.

That's when my phone vibrates in my pocket, and I realize that I'm an idiot. I completely forgot about Haze. I haven't been paying attention to my phone, so wrapped up in my family moment I didn't think to check if he texted me that he was coming down. I grab my phone in my back pocket, read Haze's text, and begin to type a quick "Okay," but I can't press Send. Because I'm interrupted by a scream.

A high-pitched, little-girl, panicked scream.

Maika comes running into the room the next second, a look of horror on her face.

"Sweetie, what's wrong?" Worry fills my mother's voice.

"There's a…" She stops, out of breath. "There's someone. I… out of the window."

It hits me.

*Holy fucking shit.*

You can see my bedroom window from the living room's.

Not only can you see it, but it's at a perfect angle. How could I be so stupid?

"What? You saw someone going out the window?" my dad asks, on alert, and Maika nods, still in shock. Events unravel so fast I can barely keep up. Maika tells my dad the intruder's in the backyard, and my dad tells my mom to call the police. I can't bring myself to speak, chasing my father as he runs around the house, looking for his first-choice weapon—a baseball bat.

"No, Dad, wait!" I try, but he's so pumped on adrenaline, he doesn't look my way.

"If this scumbag thinks he can break into our house and steal from us!"

"Dad, stop, he's not stealing!"

"Why else would he be escaping out the window? He's clearly robbing us."

"Dad, listen to me!" I beg, but he's already out of the house. Will, Kendrick, and I rush outside, trailing after my infuriated father.

*Shit. Shit. Shit. Shit.*

I see him in the distance. He spots us and freezes in place. His jaw falls at the sight of my father dashing toward him at full speed with a baseball bat.

*What? Not how you expected to meet my parents, babe?*

"Dad!" I shout again, but he keeps on running, paying me no mind. Only a few steps separate us now. Haze gives me a look, and I know exactly what it stands for. He's going to defend himself if he has to. I call it the "*I love you, but I'm not getting beat up by a baseball bat.*"

"You think you can break into my house? You're going to jail." My dad takes a swing, aiming at Haze.

The loudest, most piercing "*Stop*!" I've ever heard in my entire life rings out in our backyard. A second is required for me to realize that it came from my own mouth. My father halts himself right before impact, and, with my heart beating so fast it hurts, I stride to Haze, stepping in front of him and acting as a human shield.

"What are you doing? Step away! Why are you protecting the thief?" my dad yells.

Kendrick and Will are barely holding back laughter in the background, their faces scarlet.

Did I say I was happy that they're here? *I take it back.*

"He's not a thief," I pant.

We hear the front door slam and my mom comes running toward us with Maika in one arm and the phone pressed to her ear. She's calling the police. She stops next to my dad, confused as to why we're all standing there instead of apprehending the intruder. Anticipating the shitstorm that will come pouring down on me the second I say the words, I inhale a sharp breath.

"Mom, Dad. Meet Haze."

*Someone kill me now.*

"My boyfriend."

# FOUR

## Deadlines

My parents are petrified. Not a move. Not even a blink. My words echo through the most dreadful of silences, and I pray that someone will say *something.* My father looks like he's just seen Medusa. As for my mother, she's mad, furious even. She hangs up the phone, and her eyes travel back and forth between Haze and me.

"Your what?" my mom blurts.

"You heard me," I say with a faltering voice.

"A… A boyfriend? When did this happen?" Dad struggles to say the word as though it's impossible for him to wrap his head around the possibility.

"W-When I was in Florida." I grab Haze's hand. The cat is out of the bag, but my stomach remains clenched into a tight knot. I don't care much for my mother's opinion, but if there is one person I don't want to disappoint, it's my dad.

"What is this imbecile doing sneaking out your window? No, what was he doing in our house to begin with?" my mother spits. Unable to hold back anymore, Kendrick flinches and snickers.

"Is something funny?" My mom glares at him.

Kendrick clears his throat, fighting to keep a straight face. "No. Of course not. Will just told me a joke, Aunt Lauren."

*Your existence is a joke.*

My mother's attention comes back to us. "Answers, now!"

I sigh. "Haze left Florida to move here with me. Yesterday, he slept over after Allie and Caleb took us out to celebrate my return. It was extremely late. I… I couldn't possibly leave him to sleep outside. I'm sorry I didn't tell you. I knew you'd be upset. We just need a place to stay until we find an apartment." I'm hoping I can convince her not to kick us out and force us to live off vending machines and dirty motels. I know Haze would probably try and pay for a luxurious hotel room if that were to happen, but I'm not going to let him waste his money because of my evil mother.

"So, you decided to, what, pretend he hadn't spent the night?" My mother crosses her arms over her chest.

"Yeah," I admit, shame thick in my voice.

"Then what? He was going to come knocking on our door like nothing happened?"

"I just wanted him to make a good first impression, and I thought if he just walked into the kitchen in the morning, you would—"

"Whose idea was this?" My mom cuts me off, raising an accusatory finger at Haze. He opens his mouth to speak, but I squeeze his hand so tightly he smacks his mouth shut. If he admits to being the mastermind behind this disaster, we're done. And I mean *done*. She'll never, ever let us stay here until we find a place.

"It was mine," I lie.

"So… he had nothing to do with it?" She arches an eyebrow, doubtful. "It wasn't his influence on you?"

"No, of course not. He's always been a good influence on me."

Will snorts. "Was that before or after he kidnapped you?"

*I'm going to kill him.*

Kendrick elbows Will in the stomach so hard, he knocks the breath out of him. I know he's talking about the time Haze showed up at the penthouse, knocked out Kendrick, and threw me over his shoulder to take me to his hometown so he could protect me in his own messed-up way.

"What did you just say?" my father asks Will.

Thank God they didn't catch that.

"Nothing," Will coughs.

Kendrick runs to Will's rescue. "He was just… talking to himself, Uncle Harry. He's weird."

"Yes, I'm weird," Will agrees, and my mother rolls her eyes. It hasn't even been one full day yet and she already hates having them around. *Twenty bucks says she's going to change her mind and ship them back to Maria.*

Still as furious as can be, she drags a long and deep sigh, probably considering taking that baseball bat from her husband's hands and finishing the job herself. My father, on the contrary, seems a bit… amused? No one speaks for the longest time. Until my dad offers Haze a grin.

"How's that for a first impression?"

I let out a breath of relief, the fear in my stomach disintegrating. He's not mad. That's a start.

"I'm sorry I almost hit you with a baseball bat—Haze, is it?"

"Yeah. And no worries." Haze gives him a small smile.

There is *no way* the first real sentence my father ever said to my boyfriend turned out to be this one.

"Are you mad?" I ask my parents, hopeful.

"No."

"Yes."

Both answers come out at the exact time.

My father said no.

And my mother said yes.

They exchange glances.

*Awkward.*

"Can we stay?" I plead.

"Your mother and I need to have a discussion, pumpkin."

"There has to be a punishment for what you did," my mother jumps in. "We didn't raise you to be a liar."

I bite my tongue so hard not to tell her, You *didn't raise me. Harry did.*

"We'll be right back," my dad says, and my mom puts Maika down. We watch them distance themselves from us to get some privacy. I know my dad. He never holds a grudge. And if it were up to him, we'd stay. I have a good idea of what their argument looks like right now: my father is trying to convince my mom to let us stay until we find an apartment while . scoff

him to kick us out.

"Winter's got a Prince Charming?" Maika my spinning thoughts. I glance down at my lit see her staring at Haze with sparkly eyes. "Are ) -g to get married?" she says, in awe of him.

Kendrick and Will burst out laughing simultaneously. I can hear them thinking, *Haze Adams? Married?*

"I-I don't know, Mai. Maybe one day." I huff out a nervous laugh. Haze and I never really talked about this before. He once joked about me being his future wife, but that's all.

"Why not now? Don't you love her?" she addresses Haze.

"I do. Very much," Haze says, and I internally squeal. "But we're still young. We've got time."

Maika nods, satisfied with his answer. "He's so handsome," she tells me, battling her eyelashes at Haze.

"Well, thank you. How old are you, cutie?" Haze smiles, kneeling down to her level. She blushes at the nickname.

"I'm five." She lifts four tiny fingers to show him, and he chuckles, not bothering to correct her. "Do you want to play dolls with me when Mommy and Daddy are not mad anymore?"

"You don't have to," Kendrick says.

"No, I don't mind. I'll play with you if they let me stay."

Excited beyond belief, Maika bounces up and down and jolts around, running toward the toys she left out in the backyard.

"You have no idea what you just got yourself into," Kendrick

"There is one thing that kid never gets tired of, and it's ...aying dolls."

Haze glances at me, his eyes asking me to confirm or deny Kendrick's statement.

"I'm sure she won't remember it tomorrow," I reassure him.

"You wish. She still bugs me about last Christmas when I told her I'd play. You're screwed, man," Kendrick mocks, and Haze half-smiles. I'm still not used to them being somewhat civil toward each other, but I like this evolution.

My breath leaves me when my parents make their way back to us.

"So?" I ask as soon as they reach us.

"You can stay as long as you want," my dad says.

Relief is all I can feel. "Thanks, Da—"

"But he can't." My mother motions to Haze with her chin.

*Shit.*

"He has a week to find a place. Then, he's gone. Understood? And meanwhile, he sleeps on the couch in the basement—nonnegotiable." A smile tugs at the corner of her lips.

"A week? That's nothing. Do you have any idea how hard it is to find a decent and available apartment on such short notice? We'll need more time."

"Maybe you should've thought about that before lying to us, Winter." My mother seems to be enjoying this moment so much, it makes my blood boil.

"Plus, if he doesn't find a place, you can still stay at home, pumpkin. You don't need to move out. Only he has to go," my father says to ease his guilty conscience. I can tell this decision isn't his. It's hers. It's a wonder he convinced her to let *me* stay.

"It's fine. If he goes, I go," I sigh. Haze did not just leave his entire life behind for me to live alone in an unknown city.

"As for you two—" My mother's eyes travel to Will and my cousin. "—Maria asked me to take in Kendrick for the summer. Nothing was said about his reckless friend who makes a mess in my house. Kendrick, you can stay, but he has to go." She points to Will. "I'm sure Florida will be glad to have him back."

Kendrick stiffens up. "But… he can't go back."

"If he can't afford a plane ticket, I'm sure there are cheaper alternatives," she suggests.

"It's not that." Kendrick's eyes drop.

"What? Did you two make a blood oath to leave Florida together or something?" I tease, but neither Will or Kendrick reply, seemingly uncomfortable. Why are they being so weird?

I'm about to press them for an answer when my mother adds, "Well, in that case, I hope you'll have enough space in that new apartment of yours for one more, Winter."

*Wait… did I just get forced into hosting Will for the summer?*

"And if I were you, I'd start looking now. Like you said, it's pretty hard to find a decent available apartment this time of year." She turns on her heels, pulls Maika with her, and heads for the house.

"I'm so sorry, sweetheart," my dad says and follows her.

The moment they are out of sight, Haze speaks.

"What a lovely woman."

Against all expectations, I crack up.

"I told you." I wrap my arms around his neck and lean forward for a kiss. He circles my waist with his tattooed arm, pulling me into him. For one fleeting moment, I forget that everything went to shit. To my disbelief, I'm not worried. If I've got him—if I've got *this*, I'll be fine.

Yes, the situation sucks. But things could be worse. Getting an apartment was always the plan even if, for some unbelievable reason, my mother had allowed us both to live at home until we got a place. We just didn't expect to be on a deadline.

Kendrick clears his throat, and I pull away from Haze, sending my cousin a look over my shoulder.

"You know when your mom said she hoped you'd have room in your apartment for one more?"

"Yeah?"

Please don't tell me he's going to ask me to…

"Make that two."

*Yep. I just got forced into hosting Will* and *Kendrick for the summer.*

"Listen, we'll pay for our shit and split the rent. But if he can't stay here, neither can I."

You have got to be kidding me.

It only takes one second.

Haze looks at me. I look at him. He knows I don't have a choice. They're family. No matter what.

"Fine," I give in.

Here I am, on a deadline to find a decent and affordable apartment to live in with the most annoying guys this world has ever known and my boyfriend, who happens to have a short temper. I mean… What could go wrong?

Seriously, Winter?

What could go wrong?

Everything.

Everything could go wrong.

# FIVE

## New Place

"This the place?" Kendrick asks, craning his neck to get a glimpse of the large apartment complex through the car window. Haze turns into the visitor spot and kills the engine. Snatching my phone, I pull up the ad and triple-check the address.

"This is it." I assess the five-story building cautiously and bring my eyes back to the screen. Three bedrooms, a balcony, an elevator, and a door buzzer. The rent costs an arm *and* a leg, and if it were up to me, we wouldn't even be here right now. Sure, I have savings from my old job, and my father put some money aside to help me through school, but there is no way I can afford a full year of this lifestyle. Haze fell in love with it and insisted that we give it a shot, but I'm positive that we're wasting our time here.

Shortly after my mother gave us a deadline, all four of us got our phones out and began scouring the internet for a place to call home. Six hours later, we were lucky enough to have landed three visits. The first landlord never showed, and we just came back from the second visit. Two words: false advertising. The place looked nothing like it did in the pictures. The wallpaper was coming off the walls, you could hear the neighbor's baby throw a fit as if you were in the same room, and the tenant was smoking inside. The boys were pretty vocal about the smell the second we passed the threshold. The handyman giving us a tour admitted the pictures were taken years ago when the building was brand-new and, apparently, back when the apartment was inhabited by someone with taste. The low price should've been a red flag.

"What time did they say to be here again?" Haze asks.

"They said to be here in…" I check the time on my phone. "Now. We're late. Come on."

We hurry out of my dad's car—thank God he was nice enough to let us borrow it—and make our way to the entrance. A woman with a bright smile is waiting on the inside. She unlocks the door for us.

"Hi, Winter, right?"

"Yes, nice to meet you." I return her smile.

She tells us her husband is the owner and she's in charge of the visits as she leads us into the elevator and selects the fourth floor. We come to find out that the apartment is available right now due to the last tenant being evicted for missed payments. Considering the rent, I can't say that I'm surprised.

The apartment is everything I could ever want it to be. *Of course it is.* Large windows light up the spacious living room, and new hardwood floors spread across all common areas. There's a freaking fireplace, and don't even get me started on the view. It's close to everything—my school, the supermarket, pharmacies, restaurants, the mall—and it might actually be big enough to forget Will and Kendrick live with us. Something tells me that's why Haze likes it so much. The kitchen is slightly smaller than I thought it would be, but the marble counters and white cabinets make up for it. In other words, it's perfect. But with perfection comes a price—a very high one.

Haze says we can afford it.

Translation: he can afford it.

I know Haze's parents have kept his bank account full over the years—probably to make up for their lack of love and parenting skills—but I didn't know just how *full* we were talking. Until now. From what he's told me, he's got nothing to worry about even if his parents cut him off after the reception from hell. As for me, I'm not sure how I'll afford to eat something other than air.

We ask the kind lady to give us a second, and she nods, stepping on the balcony to take a call.

Haze's blue eyes find mine. "What do you think?"

"It's perfect," I painfully admit.

He smiles. "So, we're all set?"

"Babe, this… It's way too expensive. I can't afford it."

"But I can."

Uneasy, I pace around my dream living room. I can't stop a bunch of worst-case scenarios from spinning in my head. What if we break up? I couldn't afford one month of this rent on my own. *Winter, stop, you couldn't be further away from a breakup.*

For the first time in forever, no one is after us. No psycho brother, no vengeful fighter. Even with my mother being the real-life version of Cruella, Haze and I are finally in a good place. A perfect place. Nothing is standing in our way anymore.

No secrets.

No games.

Just love.

But I have to be smart about this. I can't ignore the risks.

"You don't get it. I don't even think I can pay my half in full." I admit, a feeling of embarrassment sinking into my skin.

"Who cares? I got it."

I arch an eyebrow. "Wow, you really don't know me at all, do you?"

He begins to reply but stops himself, glancing at the guys. "Can I have a moment alone with my girlfriend?"

Will and Kendrick huff and puff but drag their feet out of the apartment. Haze waits for their footsteps to fade down the hall before continuing.

"You can give me as much as your budget allows, then. We'll figure something out."

"But they're only staying for the summer. We don't actually need that much room. We can get a two-bedroom and put these two in the same room, you know?"

"Are you kidding? I'm not putting them in the same room. If I do, their fat asses will always end up on my couch, and it's bad enough that they're living with us for two months." He does have a point. The boys need their own space.

"You're not letting this go, are you?"

"Nope." He grins.

"Why are you so stubborn, Adams?"

"Why are *you* so stubborn, Kingston?" He steps forward.

"I get it, trust me. It's amazing. But we could find something a bit less amazing that doesn't cost an organ."

Without another word, he sighs, takes my hand, and leads me to the master bedroom at the end of the hall. My eyes travel around the four walls as he closes the door.

"See this room?" He motions to the empty space.

I nod.

"It's isolated. Away from the others. Perfect for what I have in mind."

I frown. "And what is that?"

He smiles as though he finds my question adorable and fills the remaining space between us with one step. His hands start at my shoulders, skitter down my arms, and stop on my waist. My breath catches in my lungs when he grips my hips and jerks my body to his. I blink at him, taken aback, and he leans forward until his mouth hovers near my ear.

"You know… a bit of you screaming my name, a lot of me stripping you down. That sort of thing."

My eyes widen.

"Oh." I can feel my tinted cheeks burn. *I like the sound of that.* He pulls away. "I'm not fucking moving into an apartment where I can't have you whenever I want. I don't care if they're here."

I clear my throat, too affected for my liking. "Even if I agree to getting the place, you think I'm going to say yes to all those things?"

"I know you'll say yes." He flashes a cocky grin, his gaze dropping to my mouth as he leans in. "Actually, you'll say it over." He leans in a bit more. "And over." Then so close our lips are almost touching. "And over again."

*Oh, for God's sake. Calm down, ovaries.*

Eager, I surrender to the need and go in for the kiss he's been dangling in front of my face, but he stops me, pressing a finger to my lips. It feels like invisible strings are drawing us together, and the longer he denies me, the more my body aches for him.

"I need to hear you say it."

"What?"

"You know what."

"But… what if we break up?" My words instantly upset him. Annoyance twists his features.

"Don't think like that. That's not going to happen."

"But—"

"Winter, we're never breaking up. Deal with it."

My heart swells in my chest. How on earth am I supposed to say no to him now?

"Okay," I exhale.

"Okay as in we're getting the apartment?" His face lights up.

"Okay as in you're goddamn stubborn, and we're getting the apartment." I smile. Joy colors his features, and that sight alone is enough to set my heart on fire. He pulls me into his arms, picking me up and spinning me around as I laugh into his shoulder. He kisses me as soon as my feet hit the ground. His lips feel like a breath of fresh air to my lungs. That's what this guy does to me—the one thing that will never change. He holds my heart in the palm of his hand and could easily crush it. If only he cared to try.

My phone vibrating with a new text message breaks us away from each other.

It's from Kendrick.

> Are you guys going to make out all day or are you going to tell us if you're getting the place? *shaking my head from afar*

I find myself laughing. It's official. We're that couple. We're *that* predictable. Haze reads Kendrick's message over my shoulder and scoffs.

"Come on, let's go tell them." He grabs my hand, and I follow him out of our soon-to-be bedroom. When he turns back to smile at me once more, my doubts vanish into thin air. I don't need to worry. It's Haze. I know him. Better than anyone. Nothing can tear us apart.

And, if he's ready to take that step with me?

I'm ready to take that step with him.

*Haze*

"This one's my room," Will shouts from down the hall, his voice echoing in the empty apartment.

"Like hell it is. I'm calling dibs," Kendrick chimes in, following Will into the master bedroom.

"What? You can't do that. I just called dibs two seconds ago."

"Well, I'm calling dibs on top of your dibs—deal with it."

"Should we tell them the room is ours?" Winter chuckles, leaning into me as I extend my arm around her shoulders.

"Nah. Let them fight." I kiss her forehead.

The lady left to go get the papers. Once we sign them, they'll run a background and credit check on us. She said it shouldn't take too long, and we'll know if we're approved in a few days.

"The amount of Canadian chicks I'm going to bring back here, man," we hear Kendrick whisper to Will.

"Bring a girl over and you're dead," I call out. "I swear if one of them has sex on my new furniture, I'm throwing them out the fucking window."

"The furniture or the guys?" Winter asks.

"Both." I tuck a piece of hair behind her ear, and she laughs. "So, when are your summer classes starting?" I bite my tongue not to tell her I don't think she should be burdening herself with journalism classes this early—she has the whole summer to worry about this shit—but, as much as I hate it, her absence is going to suit my… needs.

"Next week. I know that's not much time to settle in, but I only have three classes a week, so I'll still be home pretty often."

"Does that mean I'll be stuck here with dumb and dumber all summer?" I wince.

"I'm afraid it does."

"Damn it, Kingston. What I wouldn't do for you."

A soft giggle spills out of her, and my phone goes off in my pocket. I take a look at the caller ID.

Private Caller.

*Fuck. Not now.*

"Is everything okay?" Winter asks, stretching her neck to see my screen.

"Yeah, yeah, everything's fine," I speak quickly. "It's probably the landlord. His wife said he'd call. I'll be right back."

She nods as I walk to the double sliding glass doors and step onto the balcony. A frosty wind ripples my clothes as I lean against the railing and glance back inside the apartment over my shoulder. Winter's out of sight.

"What the fuck, Ricky? I told you not to call me during the day."

A deep laugh lingers down the line.

"How else were you going to tell me you moved to Canada?"

My breath catches in my lungs.

"Nice of you to join us, by the way."

"How do you know about that?" Questions I can't answer wreck my brain. "And what do you mean join us? You're here?"

"Of course we are. We go where the scumbags go, man. They sent me over as soon as they got suspicious. Plus, we got a few more guys we think might be hiding out here."

The dots connect themselves. He was probably already in Canada when he called me at the airport.

"So, you're *all* here?"

"Nah, it's just a few of us for now. Trust me, my bosses got way better things to do."

"Where are you?" I tap my fingers against the metal barrier, terrified that someone is going to come bursting out of the apartment any second and hear me.

"Manitoba. You?"

I curse under my breath. We just couldn't be in the same place. That would've been too easy. How the fuck am I going to justify going out of town to follow a lead?

"Toronto."

He scoffs. "Maybe you should tell that pretty little girlfriend of yours her city choice isn't helping your revenge."

Every single muscle in my body tenses up.

"What the fuck did you just say?"

"Oh, yeah, we know about her, too."

I clench my fists so tightly I can feel the blood drain from my hands.

"How?" I say through gritted teeth.

"Same way we knew you moved here. Come on, man, we're chasing wanted criminals. You really thought we wouldn't check up on our clients? You know a lot about us. We're partners, but we don't like loose ends. Just making sure you're not one."

I fight the urge to belt out that he's wrong and I don't actually know shit about them. When Tanner hooked me up with these shady-ass guys for tips, he told me the strict minimum. The organization is what he called it. Apparently, they owed him big-time, which is why they agreed to pay back a debt and help me out. He said they get *every* job done—I don't even want to think about what that means—find the guys you want found, and sometimes, if you're lucky like I am, they hate the guy you hate just as much as you do and put the bounty on him on top of the pile.

Marcus slipped through the cop's fingers for years. They had nothing—no suspects, not even one fucking lead—on the robberies in the rich neighborhoods near my hometown and my sister's murder. But these guys, who knows how many of them there are, they don't follow rules, or the law. As much as I hate relying on an illegal organization, without them, I wouldn't even know where to start. Or what the bastard looks like, or should I say *looked* like. Since I never saw his face during the attack, they showed me pictures of him when he was much younger. It's all they had. Brown hair, wicked smile, crooked nose: regular-looking fella. He looked around my age.

Crazy to think he's a coldhearted murderer.

They couldn't even give me his full name. He'd made up a bunch of fake aliases back then. They said twenty-year-old Marcus owed them a lot, and I mean a *lot* of money, and ran away overnight. They've been searching for him ever since. Only heaven knows what he looks like now. It's been years. They're not doing much better than the cops, but they're my only shot.

"I've got to be honest with you, I didn't think you had it in you. You know, the whole moving to another country thing? I thought he wouldn't be enough reason and you'd give up. But then…"

A heavy silence falls down the line.

"Then I met your reason."

Anxiety slams against my rib cage.

"Well, not like met-met. More like saw. She's a solid ten, by the way. Tight ass, nice tits. Good choice."

Anger blinds me. If I could reach through the phone and choke him, I would.

"Leave her out of it," I growl, beating myself up for losing my temper when she's this close.

"Relax, we just want to be certain you've got your head in the game and nothing…" He pauses. "*No one*," he rephrases, "is going to fuck this up."

"What's that supposed to mean?" I lower my voice, but inside I'm screaming.

"Nothing. As long as she's clueless, you'll be fine. But one word, kid. Just one and bad things might start to happen. Not to mention you can kiss your precious tips goodbye. Got it? We might owe your bro, but we don't owe you."

My guilty conscience tests the rage inside me. They collide in my chest, fighting each other until the weak link shatters and my conscience loses. The weak link—*my* weak link—is her.

"I won't say anything," I grumble.

"Good boy."

"So, you got anything for me?" I glance inside the apartment. Winter, Kendrick, and Will are gathered in the kitchen. Will and Kendrick are seated on the counter, and Winter is laughing at what I'm sure is the dumbest joke known to mankind.

"We're not sure we're in the right place. We think he's on the move."

"That's it? That's all you've got?" I grow impatient.

"We'll tell you the rest in person. I'll send a guy to meet you."

"I can't right now." I make eye contact with Winter. She offers me a bright smile that I return.

"Then when?"

"Give me a week." In seven days, we'll be done moving and Winter's summer classes will take up a lot of her time. *Perfect.*

"A week. No more," Ricky spits, each word coming off as a threat. "We'll call you tomorrow to tell you the time and place."

He hangs up. Tense, I erase my caller history, my self-hatred escalating. I know it's wrong. I know if she finds out, I might lose her. For good. But I can't break my promise to Des.

I won't.

# SIX

## Sooner Or Later

### *Winter*

Sometimes in life, certain places remind you of a certain song. Certain songs remind you of a certain feeling, and certain feelings remind you of a certain person. As we drive in silence toward my mother's house, I listen to the song raging on the radio: "Highway To Hell."

*Oh, the irony.*

Grabbing my phone, I read the conversation between me and Allie. I've kept her updated all throughout our apartment hunting.

FOUND A PLACE!

NO WAY? ALREADY? YOU KNOW WHAT THIS MEANS, RIGHT? HOUSE-WARMING PARTYYYY ;)

YES. But we might need some furniture first.

Good point. Furniture shopping tomorrow?

You know it.

Text you when I leave
my house. CAN'T WAIT!

I smile and lean back into the passenger seat.

Allie and I had planned on moving together as soon as I came back from Florida. We were going to go furniture shopping together, argue for hours, only to end up opting for our first choice; we had it all mapped out. It goes without saying that my showing up with a boyfriend shattered our hopes and dreams.

To make up for ditching her, I promised I'd ask for her opinion on *everything* regarding my apartment, which is why I'm taking her shopping with Haze and me tomorrow. On the bright side, my backing out of our agreement actually worked out in her favor since she's a bit tight on money. She's going to stay at her mom's and save up until her apartment is available in July, because, yes, contrary to me, her mother is *not* a mix of every single villain ever created.

A distracted and thoughtful Haze pulls up to the driveway of my parents' house. He's been like this since the phone call with our landlord. Is he having second thoughts about us moving in together? I sure hope not.

We just dropped Kendrick and Will at a rent-a-car place. Truth be told, we were more than happy to get a break as our brains were close to imploding from listening to them laugh at their own jokes all day. Will faked most of it, I could tell—he still has this haunting sadness in his eyes—but Kendrick took his job as his own biggest fan very seriously. They said they wanted to explore the city, but we all know they just weren't keen on driving around in my dad's van all summer. I know Haze wants to get a car, but until then, we'll proudly own up to our titles of coolest caravan-driving kids in town.

I notice my mother's car isn't in the driveway and frown. It's past six. My family should be home eating dinner by now. My stomach screams at the thought. I'm starving. We haven't eaten since breakfast.

Still trapped in this heavy silence, we make our way to the front door. The kitchen is empty and so perfectly clean you'd never know it was the victim of a pancake attack just this morning. A crumbled piece of paper lies on the table.

Went out to eat, be back later. Love you,

- Dad

"Please let there be food." I drop the note where I found it, walk to the fridge, and open the door only to find it empty. *Great.* My family went out of town for the weekend, which means my parents didn't do their usual Sunday grocery shopping. "Well, I hope you like pickles, because it's literally all we have."

I jump when Haze's arm curls around my waist from behind. He doesn't say anything, pushing the door to the fridge closed with his palm and pressing his torso to my back.

I shiver, overly sensitive to his touch, but in my defense, he's been teasing me ever since we got here. We haven't gotten around to really *celebrating* our news yet. You'd think him moving to another country for me and us getting a place together would earn me at least one hot night of passion.

"Are we alone?" he asks.

"Yep. It's just us… and the pickles," I laugh nervously. *Really? A pickle joke?*

He doesn't speak again for a short moment.

"Why?"

"Nothing. I just don't want your parents to walk in while I'm taking you on their kitchen table."

My jaw drops.

Before I can reply, he's dipped his hands under my shirt and positioned his mouth to the soft spot of skin behind my ear. He kisses my neck slowly but firmly, and I can't move away, completely and undeniably at his mercy. He takes my earlobe between his teeth, and I emit a short yet embarrassingly loud moan. *Shit.*

"My… my parents could come home any second," I whisper.

"I know."

"They could see us."

"I know," he repeats, still without a single fuck given.

"I…"

"Something wrong, baby?" His breath bounces off my skin. I can't focus on anything other than the sensation of his mouth working my neck.

"Haze." His name slips out of my mouth, and the sound sets him off. It's like a switch, a click. He grips my waist, spins me around, and plasters my back to the closed fridge with a force I didn't expect. At first, I think he's going kiss me, but the cockiness gleaming in his gaze tells me he's not done playing with me just yet. He leans in, stopping right where he shouldn't, only inches away from my mouth. He smirks.

*Asshole.*

I pout. And his smirk evolves into a smile.

In a heartbeat, he lowers his lips to mine. The kiss is unbearably slow, gentle. He wants me to beg for it. *Let's be real, I already am.* I grip the collar of his shirt, yearning for more. His left hand trails down my side, and he cups my a…

"I think I just threw up in my mouth."

I push Haze off me so fast you'd think your girl developed superpowers.

There, leaning against the kitchen doorway, is a girl-making-out-with-boyfriend-in-her-parents'-house nightmare.

The fourteen-year-old brother.

"Jay?" I bring a palm to my rising chest. "You're… You're home," I state, but it comes out as a question.

"Looks like it, doesn't it?" My brother grins, his eyes swinging between Haze and me for long seconds. "Dad said you were back. I wanted to see you."

*Idiot, you knew he was coming home tonight.* I can't believe I thought he went to the restaurant with them. I should've known.

You'd have to pay this kid to get out of the house. I bet he only went on a trip with them last weekend because he bribed my dad into buying him a game he wanted.

I take in his appearance. He hasn't changed one bit, wearing his go-to overwashed Iron Man T-shirt and cargo pants. His long, dirty, brown hair—I'm not talking color, it's literally dirty—falls in front of his eyes and stops a bit under his shoulders, making me wonder how he's not considered legally blind by society. We've been trying—and failing—to convince him to get a haircut for the past three years now. He says he looks better like this. I say his future self will have a good laugh one day. Oh, and showering is also an unknown concept to the kid. We're hoping that changes once he gets a girlfriend.

"How long have you been standing there?" I ask, horrified.

"Just walked in," he says, and relief rises within me.

Jaden and I have always been close. I was his role model growing up—weird, I know. As a kid, he'd constantly follow me around, desperate to hang out with me and my friends. I remember finding that so annoying. Typical sibling problems. I'm sure he would've preferred having a big brother, but he got me: crazy Winter, who dared him to fit ninety marshmallows into his mouth before our mother came back from the bathroom. Then puberty showed its face, and he started groaning at anyone who dared talk to him. I consider myself to be lucky. He says actual words to me sometimes.

"Are you going to introduce me to the guy shoving his

tongue down your throat, sis?"

I almost choke on air.

"Jay! You can't say things like that." I sound so ridiculous I cringe at my own words. Trying to discipline him is a complete waste of time. This is Jaden. He once walked up to an overweight lady and asked her when her due date was in the middle of Taco Bell.

"Yes, I can. I just did?" He arches an eyebrow.

I clear my throat. "Jaden, this is Haze. Haze, this is Jaden."

Jay scoffs. "Haze, huh? Weird name. Your parents hated you or something?"

I glance back at Haze, who doesn't seem a tiny bit fazed by my brother's complete lack of manners.

"Yeah, they did, actually."

Jay's mouth opens. Caught off guard, he searches for a good comeback but fails, pressing his lips into a line. He walked right into that one.

"In my defense, they hate the entire human race," Haze adds, and I bite back a laugh. "How old are you?"

"None of your business," Jay spits out. Man, he's mastered his rude teenager lines down to a T.

"He's fourteen." I direct my attention back to my brother. "Don't be rude!"

"Since when do you have a boyfriend?" he deflects.

"A few months ago," I say and watch him head for the fridge. He finds out, just as I did, that it's empty and groans, settling for a glass of water. He walks by us, heading back to the living room. But then he turns around and our eyes lock. He gives me a look I don't want to see. I know that look.

I hate that look.

"So… How does Caleb feel about this?"

It's a simple question, short and straight to the point, but somehow it holds so much meaning. Haze frowns, lifting his eyes to me. Jaden smiles victoriously and walks off. I'm sure he's just being an asshole because A, he's threatened by the new guy in the house, and B, he's in his "I'm mean for no reason" phase, but I could strangle him right now. He probably guessed I didn't tell Haze about what happened.

I can feel Haze's confused gaze on me. He opens his mouth to ask, but the front door swinging open keeps him from it. My mother, father, and sister walk in, radiating happiness and carrying takeout bags.

"Hey, pumpkin." My dad smiles at the sight of me. "You two hungry? We got leftovers."

"Yes, please. I'm starving." I jump at the opportunity. "Want some?" I ask Haze. He forces a smile, nodding as I take the food my Dad is offering us. We sit around the table, and I hope to hell the questions my father bombards Haze with will wash away the memories of what just happened. But I know better than to think it won't come back up. And I might've avoided this talk for now… but I won't avoid it forever.

# SEVEN

## *Laundry*

Silence. It's all I can hear. Lying in bed with my eyes open, I contemplate how the average human will spend the majority of his life sleeping. Funny that, right now, sleep is avoiding me like some deadly disease. *Ha. Just as every boy I flirted with during my freshman year of high school.*

Tossing and turning, I reach for my phone on the nightstand. It's 3:00 a.m. I can't stop thinking about Haze alone in the basement. My mom wasn't kidding about us sleeping apart. We even had a curfew. She sent Haze to "bed"—the crappy pull-out couch in the corner of our laundry room—at 10:00.

After my parents came back from the restaurant, we couldn't dream of getting one moment alone—luckily for me. I'm sure if we had, Haze would've asked me about my brother's comment, and I really didn't want to discuss this in a house full of people.

What happened between me and Caleb is in the past. We agreed to forget about it when he pulled me aside at the pub, but I don't plan on hanging out with him any more than I have to. We may be on good—well, *better*—terms now, but it doesn't make his presence any less uncomfortable for me. I feel guilty every second that I'm around him, and I can't stand it. It doesn't exactly help that there's a good chance I'll have to see him again since he's still very close friends with Allie, and I could never bring myself to tell her about that night.

Unplugging my phone, I let my fingers sail the empty space where Haze should be. I've gotten so used to the warmth of his body next to mine, to his arms around my waist, even to the sound of his breathing, that trying to sleep without him feels… unnatural. I'm on a goddamn Haze Adams withdrawal.

I consider texting him for five minutes, talk myself out of it for four, and eventually give in.

Can't sleep without you. Look what you did to me, Adams.

A few minutes go by. Radio silence. He must be sleeping. I'm about to put my phone down when three dots pop up on my screen.

I haven't done anything to you.

Yet.

My lips pull into a smile.

Idiot. Did I wake you?

Nah. I can't sleep. Your basement's full of spiders.

I literally have to laugh into my pillow as memories of the day he took me to the abandoned high school rooftop and confessed his fear of spiders fuel my laughter.

Aw. Do you want me to come and protect you, princess?

The dots pop up again.

I mean, I'm definitely okay with the first part of your sentence.

I frown in confusion and reread my text. Do you want me to co…

*Oh.*

Jerk.

Prude.

Perv.

Thanks.

No, but seriously, I can't sleep.

Too busy picturing me naked?

Ironically, that's my brain's cue. Images intoxicate every inch of available space in my mind. I see his half-naked body spread out across the uncomfortable couch in the barely lit basement, his bulging muscles as he stretches and pushes the blanket off his… *Okay, chill.*

HAHAHAHAHAHAHA

Maybe.

Come downstairs and I'll show you more than a picture.

Feeling all hot and bothered, I stop answering to think of a good reply. The dots show up almost right away.

???

Enjoying his desperation, I wait a bit more.

You still there?

Still here.

Are you coming down??

Not sure.

I see what you're doing. I could just take care of myself and do without the teasing, you know ;)

I laugh at his text and consider my next move for a few seconds. Finally, I peel my oversized T-shirt up and open my phone's camera. I'm only wearing panties since I tossed my bra—I could never sleep with a bra on; I will not submit myself to such torture. I make sure the camera doesn't catch my face, because I may trust Haze with all of my being, which is the only reason I'm willing to do this, but who knows where this could end up in a worst-case scenario. The room is dark, but light enough that you can discern the curves of my bare body as I cover my nipples with my forearm and snap a pic. My fingers are shaking, both with excitement and nerves when I type a reply and attach the picture.

I can take care of myself, too.

*Winter Kingston sent a picture.*

It doesn't even take a second.

Get your cute little ass downstairs NOW.

A chuckle leaves my lips. Giddy with anticipation, I tug my shirt back into place and slide a pair of white shorts up my legs. Sneaking out into the hall and tiptoeing down the stairs like a criminal, I hold my breath as I pass my parents' room. I see the basement door in the distance.

Three more steps.

Two steps.

One.

I lay a shaky hand on the handle. The door opens with a loud creak, and I wince, the possibility of getting caught just as thrilling as it is terrifying. I wait and wait for something to happen. For someone to walk in and bust me. I wait for a moment that never comes.

The basement is engulfed in darkness. I can't see anything past the first step, and the thought of sleeping down there alone sends shivers, and I don't mean the good kind, down my spine. No wonder Haze can't sleep.

*Come on, Winter. Don't be a pussy.*

I suck in a breath, a rush of adrenaline roaring in me, and close the door as I go down, careful not to be too loud. The old steps screech under me, and I know there's no way Haze won't hear me coming. I sigh in relief when my toes meet the ceramic floor, but I don't have time to fully appreciate that I made it down in one piece. Because I'm immediately pushed up against the brick wall behind me.

My heart lurches forward when a strong body traps me into a corner and large hands cage my hips.

"What took you so fucking long?" a voice rasps in the dark.

His voice.

I don't reply—too focused on trying to breathe—but he doesn't seem to want me to, holding me in place like he's afraid I'll slip away if he lets go. I'm about to speak when I feel his length digging into my stomach. I can't help but smirk.

"Nice to see my picture had the wanted effect."

He growls in annoyance. "I should punish you for being such a fucking tease, you know that?" His hands curve behind me and inside my shorts to squeeze my ass cheeks.

*Two can play this game, Hazie.*

My fingers fall to the hard bulge straining against his underwear, and I palm him through the fabric, causing his breath to hitch.

I lean in and whisper, "Do your worst."

His reaction is instant. He takes a fistful of my hair and pulls my chin forward. He grazes the corner of my lips with his slowly to tease me, to give me a taste of what's coming. His mouth latches onto my neck, kissing, licking, biting until my head falls back and I'm losing what's left of my sanity.

"Haze, please." I drop the act. *Please don't make me wait any longer. Please kiss me and put me out of my misery.*

He stops for a second, like he's considering whether or not I deserve his mercy.

Then he crashes his lips against mine.

I can feel my whole body drop with relief when our tongues collide. *Finally.* I kiss him back, the freezing wall behind me clashing with my hot skin. I still can't see a thing, but I don't need to. I just need to feel more. Way more. More of him. Of this. Of us.

Wrapping his hands behind my thighs, he picks me up into his arms, and I hook my legs around his waist, letting him carry me to his bed. I gasp in surprise when my butt connects with the coldest of surfaces. Wait. He didn't take me to the couch. He dropped me on the washing machine. The cold as *shit* washing machine.

"What are you doing?" I screech, and a deep laugh reaches my ears. He doesn't reply, tugging at my shorts and pulling them down my legs in one swift move. Then he says it:

"*Laundry.*"

His mouth crashes back on mine before another protest can break free. He kisses me hungrily, and I'm so eager for him I don't even care that I'm freezing my butt off.

"Spread your legs."

With a thundering heart, I do as I'm told, propping myself on my elbows and lifting my knees up as I brace my feet on top of the machine. Gripping my waist and pulling me forward until my ass hangs off the edge, he reaches for my shirt and grabs the bottom to lift it over my head. The cold air hits my nipples, and shivers flare down my spine. Haze stands back, admiring as much as he can see of me in the dark. I'm sitting there in my panties, legs spread and breasts out, but somehow, I've never felt more at ease. My eyes have adapted to the dark, allowing me to see his face: the fire in his gaze, his lip trapped between his teeth. And heaven help me, the look in his eyes makes me want to melt into a puddle at his feet.

His mouth finds its way back to mine, and he flicks my painfully ready nipples with his thumbs, sending jolts of electricity to my stomach. When his hand find my panties and he starts to strokes me, running his fingers up and down without ever *really* touching me, I lose it.

"Stop teasing me," I whimper, wriggling around, and he immediately halts his motion, arching an eyebrow like he's asking me if I know what I'm asking for.

Then he nods.

"Okay."

I almost cry out when he pushes my underwear to the side and buries two fingers inside of me.

"*Haze!*" I bite down on his shoulder. He kisses me to muffle my moans, pumping in and out so fast that I clench around his fingers. I expected this to hurt, for the sudden thrust to feel uncomfortable, but I've never been more turned on and it shows. His thumb rubs rough circles in exactly the right place, his way of reminding me that I'm his, and his only. He keeps it up for as long as it takes, never once slowing down until my legs are shaking and he's got me exactly where he wants me. His reckless pace becomes too much, and my back arches on its own.

"Haze, I think I'm…" My words fail me, but he reads me loud and clear.

"Fuck, yeah." He picks up the pace and strength of his circles, until my self-control depletes from my body and I come undone on his fingers. He mutes the sound of my unraveling with hot kisses, only pulling away once I stop shaking.

Oh.

My.

God.

"So fucking hot," he grunts against my mouth. I can't describe the state of euphoria I'm in, and when he pulls on the waistband of his underwear, tossing them to his feet, I know it's about to get even better. Curling his arms around my thighs, he pulls my body flush to his and slowly slides his length up and down my center, relentlessly rubbing an already sensitive spot. He's not done with me. Not even close. I came down from cloud nine, but I'm not so far away from it that I won't pay it another visit soon if he keeps this up.

He keeps drawing quick and strong circles on my clit, and just when I think I'm about to fall apart again, he stops. No warning, not a word, he just stops. He turns around and walks away. Baffled, my eyes follow his silhouette until I lose him to the darkness. I hear him going through some stuff. What stuff, you ask? I don't know, but it better be a question of life or death. After what feels like an eternity, he comes back with a condom, and I smirk. *That's my boy. He knows I never go bareback.*

"Sex in a house full of people? I thought you didn't want to risk it." I throw the conversation we had earlier in his face.

He stretches the condom down his length and looks me dead in the eyes before lowering himself to my entrance.

"You're the risk I'll always take."

Then he pushes forward and takes me completely.

*Holy sh…*

The intense sensation takes my breath away. We both groan when he withdraws entirely and fills me again with an even more powerful shove. We're both too engulfed in the moment to speak, but the connection, this feeling, the way our eyes lock as he holds my legs open and moves inside me—it speaks for itself.

"It feels like it's been five fucking years," he groans.

"I know." I quiver, well aware that we won't last long.

I'm surprised when he pulls out sooner than I would've liked and circles my wrist with his hand to guide me down the washer. My feet hit the ground, and my still-wobbly legs almost give out from under me, but Haze catches me, spinning me around and bending me over the cold steel. He holds my leg up on the machine. My nipples press against the top, and goose bumps creep all over my skin. I mentally laugh at the fact that my mother constantly tells me I should learn to love doing chores, such as laundry.

*Well, Mom, I sure like it now.*

I bite down on my own hand not to cry out again when he enters me, this time from behind.

"You have no idea how much I wish I could see you better right now," he says, continuing his fast thrusting and gripping my ass so tightly I'm sure it'll earn me a souvenir hand print, but I wouldn't want it any other way. He starts to tremble, his movements frantic. "Shit. Not yet," I hear him curse. Defeated, he loses the battle. Twisting my hair around his fist, he pumps so fast my eyes roll back. Then he empties into the latex, jerking a few times.

We remain quiet for a while, high on each other and this feeling. Silence fills the dark basement, the only recurring sound our heavy breathing. I can't believe this just happened. I just had sex on the washing machine I used to hate using, at 3:00 a.m. in my parents' basement. *What is life?*

Soon, he pulls out of me, picking my spent body off the machine and into his arms. He carries me to the old couch where we both collapse, sweaty and exhausted. Pressed up against his chest, I nuzzle his neck with my nose and seek the calming sound of his heartbeat.

"I love you so fucking much, Winter," he says in a whisper, and my heart tightens.

"I love you more." An enormous smile spreads across my face, and let's just say that...

In that moment,

I'm pretty damn happy I couldn't sleep.

HOURS. IT'S BEEN HOURS. NEVER-ENDING hours of movers knocking on our door to deliver furniture so expensive I could cry, hours of unpacking and arguing with Haze on where to put things, hours of telling Will and Kendrick "Don't touch that" when they open boxes of my stuff and wanting to bash my head against a wall. Four days ago, I thought finding an apartment would be hard. Now I know it was the easy part.

Today marked our fifth day in Toronto. We got the keys to our apartment two days ago but could only get our furniture shipped today. I was convinced I'd be beyond happy to move out of my mother's house, but turns out, if moving is stressful, moving on a deadline is a one-way ticket to burnout.

Standing in the middle of my apartment and admiring the now decently filled rooms, I entertain the idea of calling my housewarming party off.

It all sounded great when Allie suggested it a few days ago. But now? All I want to do is crawl into bed and sleep for the next seventeen years.

Things this whole moving fiasco taught me: furnishing an entire apartment on a budget is *not* easy. Even used, extremely low-quality furniture is expensive, and if it wasn't for Haze insisting on buying a brand-new bed, I'd probably be sleeping on the floor tonight. To my greatest disappointment, Haze had to do most of the heavy lifting—cough, *paying*, cough—while I moped around, resenting my broke college-student status. I promised to pay him back my half of the furniture as soon as I got a job, and, in typical Haze behavior, he asked me, "What half?"

"Food's on its way." Kendrick enters the room and hangs up the phone. Will comes trailing behind him, empty eyes straying to the floor. He's somewhere else. Has been since he got here. I still haven't gotten around to asking him what on earth happened back in Florida. He's not just moody—that's full-on heartbreak right there.

"I'm guessing that means it's too late to cancel?" I throw myself right next to Haze on the couch and pick my phone out of my pocket. Allie sent me a text thirty minutes ago.

BE THERE SOON. JUST
NEED TO GET THE BOOZE.
GET READY BISHH!

I heave a chuckle and notice Haze reading over my shoulder.

"Definitely too late to cancel," he says with a grin.

As soon as I told her I was moving out, Allie insisted that we order our weight in food, drink our worries away, and watch a bunch of horror movies to celebrate me getting my own place. I slap a smile on my face to trick my mind into positive thinking. I've read somewhere that smiling, even if it's forced, convinces your brain of genuine happiness. *Fake it 'til you make it.*

"What are we watching?" Kendrick asks, joining Haze and me on the couch while Will sits at the kitchen table by himself. Kendrick doesn't seem to notice how miserable his best friend is, staring at his phone like a sad puppy dog, and it breaks my heart in five. Turning the TV on, Kendrick begins scrolling through Netflix.

There's a quadruple knock on the door the next second.

"I got it." I smack a kiss to Haze's cheek and get up. "Kendrick, get your dirty-ass shoes off the couch or I'll rip off your balls and make you swallow them," I say as I pass him.

Kendrick's eyes grow and he pulls his feet down, quickly kicking his shoes off. Haze scoffs, earning a death stare from my cousin.

"Coming!" I call, reaching for the handle and opening the door with a smil…

There goes my smile.

Crap. Why did she bring *him*?

"I've got the goods," Allie squeals, a bottle of champagne in one hand and a bottle of tequila in the other. She comes in for a hug that I welcome, but all I can think about is Caleb's persistent gaze piercing into the side of my head

Al, I love you, but why?

*Why wouldn't she invite him, Winter? She doesn't know.*

I've been ignoring his texts since we went out to celebrate my return. It's one thing to say things are back to normal and another to actually act like it. He says he's fine and ready to put it all behind us, but part of me doesn't believe him. I thought keeping my distance was for the best.

But now, he's here, on my doorstep, staring at me.

*Yay, awkward moments!*

"Welcome to my crib." I crack a nervous laugh and step aside. Allie walks in, gaping at the apartment and commenting on everything she sees. I know I can't ignore him for much longer. He's right there.

"Hey." He smiles, but it's unsure, hesitant. He feels the

tension. How could he not?

"Hey, Caleb." I avoid his gaze, but that doesn't stop him from yanking me into a hug that I struggle to return. I glance over Caleb's shoulder, only to see a clenched-jaw Haze glaring at us. Allie is already halfway to the bedrooms by the time I break the hug, leaving me with the guy I thought would never talk to me again.

One thing's for sure: this is going to be one hell of a night.

Emphasis on *hell.*

# EIGHT

## Never Have I Ever

Have you ever noticed how the people closest to you often put you in the worst situations? Like when you had a crush in high school and your best friend made it her pleasure to ruin your life every time he passed you in the halls by saying something like "Hey, here's your husband" or pushing you in his way and screaming "Get some"?

Allison Gardner is that friend. Always has been. And when she brings her champagne glass to her red lips, chuckles, and slurs, "Let's play Never Have I Ever," I find myself wishing I could be anywhere else but here.

Haze's been making dagger eyes at Caleb since he walked in. He hates him and isn't bothering to hide it. Not that my brother's comment helped in the matter. The tension is crushing me like a pile of bricks. I keep waiting for the ball to drop, for Caleb to tell Haze what I couldn't and ruin the night.

Empty glasses of champagne are scattered across the living room table. We've been drinking for over two hours. Safe to say we're a bit tipsy. I thought alcohol would take the edge off. I was wrong. Now I'm paranoid *and* dizzy.

"What are we, twelve?" Will mocks.

Kendrick shoots him a look. "Some of us are."

Allie laughs obnoxiously.

*Never mind, she's way past tipsy.*

Will doesn't acknowledge the slander, sipping on a beer and fidgeting with his jeans. He'd usually jump at the chance to bicker, but he's been taking Kendrick's snarky comments like a champ recently. He bites his tongue, sits back, and pretends nothing happened. I can practically hear him think, "All right, I deserved that."

"We're too old for that crap," I say.

"Come on, it'll be fun," Allie insists.

Leaning back into Haze's frame, I look up at him, my face screaming, "Help me out here." He doesn't nod or agree with me. Far from it.

"Yeah, why not? It'll help me get to know Caleb."

*What the hell, Haze?*

He stares at Caleb without flinching. He just full-on death stares until Caleb shifts in his seat, searching for my gaze. I deny him eye contact for the billionth time tonight. I thought I was imagining it all until I caught Will frowning. He didn't even need to speak. I know he noticed, too.

"Great. Where's the vodka?" Allie's eyes wander around the messy room. Unopened boxes are piled up on the kitchen table and spread across the floor. We unpacked the essentials today, but we're far from done. Spotting the glass bottle on the kitchen counter, Allie gets up and brings it over.

"How about we spice it up?" She sits back on the couch. "If you did the thing, you take a shot, but you have to give us a backstory if someone asks or you take two."

"Is that really necessary?" Will complains.

"What's wrong? Have something to hide, Will?" Kendrick accuses.

There he goes again, poking at Will. This is weird. Maybe I was wrong. Maybe Kendrick did find out about him and Kass? Whatever it is, he's punishing Will for something.

"Just wondering what the point is." Will shrugs.

"The point is to make the game interesting. Now quit whining." Allie reaches for the bag at her feet and gets six shot glasses out. She sure came prepared.

"Isn't your version a cheap knockoff of truth or dare?" Kendrick asks.

"Trust me, my game's way more fun," she smirks, bending forward to line up the shot glasses on the coffee table. I catch Kendrick's eyes lingering on her for a second too long, and Allie flushes. Still, she holds his gaze, never backing down.

*Wait…*

*Am I sensing sexual tension?*

I blink at my cousin, who doesn't notice my disapproval, too busy undressing Allie in his head. Nope, not happening. He can have anyone. Literally anyone *but* Allie. He's been all over the place since Nicole broke up with him again. He straight up changed country on a whim. He's acting on impulse right now, and I will not let my best friend be his rebound.

"Who wants to start?" I can't believe I'm the one pressing for this nightmare to begin, but I can't watch them eye-fuck each other for a second longer.

Allie snaps back to reality. "Right, I'll start. Never have I ever…" She stops to think for a moment. "Had my heart broken."

We all drink, even Will.

So, Kass broke his heart? I was right. Something did happen.

"Who broke your heart, Will?" The question falls out on its own. Color quickly drains from Will's face while Kendrick glances away in disgust.

That's when it hits me.

*Oh my God. He knows.*

But then why are they here together acting like nothing happened? Why are they still friends? I thought Kendrick would've cut his dick off by now.

Will doesn't say a word, throws a shot back so he doesn't have to answer, and sends me a killer look. The questions get dumber and dumber as the minutes pass. The shots keep coming. So do the giggle sessions. And, for a second there, I even catch myself having some fun.

Then Caleb's turn comes.

"Never have I ever…" He pauses, his eyes set on me. Part of me wants him to spit it out, to get it over with already, but the other dreads what he's going to say. He clears his throat, sits straight, and drops the bomb. "Lied to my partner about my past with someone."

No one drinks.

Not a single soul.

I don't have the guts to turn around to witness Haze's reaction, but I know from the way his hold around me grows firmer that it can't be a good one. The others have no idea how awkward this is. To them, this is just another Never Have I Ever, but Haze's already suspicious of something and the suggestion in Caleb's tone was unmissable.

I glare at my ex-best friend. What kind a sick game is he playing? Why is the guy who picked me up at the airport claiming to have been over it trying to put me on the spot?

"Next." I clear my throat. "Who wants to go?"

"I'll go," Will says, and the look he gives me says it all.

*Oh, it's payback time.*

He takes the luckiest of guesses, probably because he noticed how Caleb was staring at me, and proceeds to ruin my life, "Never have I ever kissed someone in this room."

Allie offers Haze and me what I like to call an Allie wink, meaning that she closes both eyes at the same time—yeah, that's her thing; she could never wink—convinced that this one is for us. Man do I wish it was.

Haze drinks.

I drink.

And finally… Caleb drinks.

That's how I know I'm screwed.

Haze immediately tenses up, staring at Allie. He's probably waiting for her to say, "Oh, right, I remember that one time," since Caleb sure as hell didn't make out with Will, but I know she won't tell him what he wants to hear.

Because she never kissed him.

I did.

"What are you talking about?" Allie frowns. "We never…" She pauses, realization punching her in the face. She looks at me with widened eyes. "What? When?"

"What the fuck?" Haze gets up from the couch before I can blink.

*Shit.*

He frowns. "Were you two together or something?"

I rise up. "We… I…" *Winter, English, damn it.*

Caleb jumps up, too. "You didn't tell him? Seriously?"

"Caleb, shut the hell up," Allie snaps.

Haze's face collapses as he turns to me. "Wait, did you… Did you sleep with him?"

The hurt in his voice daggers me straight in the heart.

I can't speak.

I should've told him sooner. I never intended to keep it from him. But I also never thought I'd have to see Caleb often after we went out to celebrate, so why bother telling Haze about the time I ruined my longest friendship on one of the worst nights of my life? He didn't tell me about all the girls he slept with.

I see the pieces of the puzzle connecting in his eyes. "He's… He's your first time, isn't he? He's the guy that sucked."

Caleb makes a face. "Okay, *ouch.*"

If awkwardness could kill you, I'd be six feet under by now.

"That's why you were acting so weird," Haze says, more to himself than me.

"I wasn't hiding it from you, I swear."

"Why do you think she didn't tell you, bro? We have history. She just met you," Caleb cuts in, taking a threatening step forward. Haze tilts his head, warning him.

"Guys, stop," I say, panic taking over me. This is getting out of control. Caleb's anger lessens when our eyes meet.

"I… I'm sorry." Caleb shakes his head. "I think I had too much to drink. I'm going to go home." He hurries to the door.

"Would you look at that, he says smart things sometimes."

"Haze!" I scold him.

"What did you just say to me?" Caleb's face twitches in anger, and he strides back to us. God he has no idea who he's dealing with. Haze could destroy him with his eyes closed.

*Goodbye, Caleb. It was nice knowing you.*

"You heard me." Haze's arrogant expression could set off the calmest person on earth. Caleb attempts another step, but my hands fly to his chest.

"Cale, stop! Go home, please."

Haze scoffs. "Yeah, go home, Caleb. Go dream about my girlfriend because that's the only way you'll ever have her in your bed again."

We all gasp.

*Holy shit.*

It seems to happen in slow motion, yet too quickly for me to keep up. Caleb shoves me out of the way and puts up a fist, launching it at Haze, who easily dodges the incoming hit. Haze captures Caleb's fist midair and bends him down, twisting his arm behind his back. We hear a cracking sound the human body definitely shouldn't make, and Caleb whimpers in pain.

"Are you fucking insane?" Kendrick yells at Haze, stepping into the action and barely tearing them away from each other. Caleb winces as he holds his arm, while Haze stands there, blinded by rage, chest rising and falling with heavy breaths. He glances around the room, takes in every scared eye set on him, every shocked face. But the one that seems to hurt him the most… is mine.

A mix of emotions collide in his blue eyes. Regret, pain, anger. I know him by heart. I know exactly what he's thinking when he gives Caleb and me one last look and turns around.

"Haze, wai—"

Then he's out the door.

# NINE

## *Mistakes*

THEN

I'd never sat on my bathroom floor.

I'd never noticed how high the ceiling was or how uncomfortable the tiles were. But I'd also never locked myself in a room with a bottle of rum to ugly cry on my birthday either. So, I guess tonight was a night of firsts.

Throwing my head back with a sigh, I watched the room spin and clumsily wiped the tears burning my eyes. The party was still raging downstairs. Twenty-One Pilots boomed out of the living room speakers, making the walls shake and barely drowning out the sound of glass breaking in the distance.

I hoped it was my mom's crystal vase.

I hoped it was something she loved.

*Oh, right, sorry. She doesn't have a heart.*

I'd decided that being abandoned on my birthday earned me a few hours of bitterness. I sure hoped Mommy dearie wouldn't mind that I invited the football team over to spend those hours with me.

I didn't know why I'd expected this year to be different. The note on the fridge was the same. So was the empty house. The previous year, her excuse to avoid pretending that she was happy about my existence had been work—at least she'd left me with my siblings that time. But since she'd just lost her job, she'd had to be imaginative.

She'd really thought this whole thing through, even found something she couldn't invite me to in case my dad asked why she took off on my birthday. She knew damn well Jaden and Maika's grandmother didn't want a relationship with me. She'd made it clear that I was in no way blood related to her son Harry, therefore not a part of their family.

Lauren was probably going to blame it on Harry's mother's heart condition, say that Claire was getting old and the kids needed to spend as much time with her as possible, and my sweetheart of a dad would buy it. *Of course he would.*

He'd had to go out of town for work this weekend and promised to celebrate with me when he returned, which I knew he would, but waking up to an empty house and finding that note had ruined my day before it could even start. You know how they say you only remember the bad comments?

My mom's the bad comment I will never forget.

I played the note over in my head.

*Went to visit your dad's parents. You're an adult now. I trust you to be responsible while we're gone.*

I tipped the bottle back, letting the alcohol course down my throat. I winced at the taste, squeezing my eyes shut so tight a tear fell out. I'd never been much of a drinker, but, hey, like she said, I was an adult now. Well, technically, I'd be an adult at midnight, but who cares? She sure didn't.

There was a knock on the door.

"Someone's sick in here," I shouted.

The person strangled a curse and walked off.

Technically, it wasn't a lie.

I *was* sick. Sick of school, sick of being denied by my own mother, sick of never feeling good enough. Maybe spending the last few months of my senior year in Florida wouldn't be such a bad idea after all. When my mom told me I had to move there for a bit, I wasn't keen on the idea, but now?

Anywhere was better than here.

Another knock, this time louder, made me jump. He really couldn't take a hint.

"I said someone's sick!"

"Winter?" a familiar voice asked.

Ah. Shit.

"Nope. Sorry. No Winter here." I took a sip and muttered under my breath. "What kind of whack name is that anyway?" I always did wonder what my mom was thinking. She could've chosen something more common like Sarah or Jennifer, but nope, she'd given birth to me in Canada, a place where it snowed almost all year long, and called me Winter—freaking *Winter*.

"How fucked-up are you?" He tried to turn the knob. "Open the door."

"Go away, Caleb."

"You told Allie you were going to the bathroom two hours ago. We were worried."

"I'm fine. Go back to the party."

There was a beat of silence.

"I can just get the key your mom keeps in the kitchen drawer, you know?"

Downside of being friends with someone since you were three: they know *everything*, even the stuff you don't want them to.

I considered my next move for a few seconds and groaned in defeat, pulling myself up to unlock the door. The knob twisted open, and I drooped back down, leaning against the tub and cradling my knees to my body.

Caleb stood with one foot in the doorway, not completely inside but not out into the hallway either. He took in my breakdown, zeroing in on my mascara-tinted cheeks, red eyes, and finally, the glass bottle at my feet.

"Hiding from your own party, huh?"

I scoffed. "I highly doubt they miss me."

"What happened?"

"What do you mean?"

"All this. You throwing a last-minute party. The drinking. This… This isn't you, Winter."

*And you think I don't know that?*

When I didn't reply, he walked in, closed the door, and sat down on the floor next to me. "What's wrong?"

I still didn't utter a word, bringing the bottle to my lips. His disapproving eyes stung but not nearly as much as the ache in my chest did. So, I kept drinking.

"I'm not going to stop bugging you. Might as well spit it out."

I sighed. When I'd called Allie that morning to tell her my mom and siblings were going out of town and I wanted a party, she was so excited she hadn't bothered to ask why. Not that I would've told her if she'd questioned my change of heart. I'd pushed my feelings down, eaten breakfast alone, and pulled myself together the best I could. But right now, all I wanted to do was tell someone. Anyone.

Maybe just so I could get some sleep that night.

"It's my family. They… hm… They didn't leave tonight."

"What?"

"They left this morning. When I was still sleeping. My mom took my siblings on a trip. I—"

"Wait." He paused. "She left you?"

I nodded, terrified to meet his eyes.

"Did you… spend the whole day alone?"

The pity lacing his voice cut right through me.

"Yeah, but it's okay. I had homework anyway."

He didn't know what to say, which was understandable.

"Twenty bucks say she won't even come and pick me up at the airport when I get back from Florida," I cackled.

"I'll do it."

I frowned, assessing my best friend.

"I'll come and pick you up, no matter what, I promise."

His kindness felt foreign to me, unprecedented.

That's when the waterworks hit.

My heart betrayed me. It shattered the walls I built around myself, the lies I'd tried *so hard* to believe. The drizzle turned into a storm, and I started to sob.

"I'm sorry." I covered my face in embarrassment, "God, I'm such a baby."

"No, you're not."

"Yes, I am. It's not a big deal. So what if my mom hates me? Some people don't even have a family, and I'm over here crying like an idiot. I—"

"Hey!" His hand flew up to my jaw, and he lifted my chin up. "I don't care if somebody else has it worse. You can't tell the guy with a cut that his blood isn't real because someone's hemorrhaging next to him. If you're feeling it, it matters. End of story."

His words comforted me but also validated my pain, which only made me cry harder. Caleb wrapped one arm around my shoulder, and I released my knees, leaning into my best friend's chest. I cried and I cried into his cardigan, and he let me.

"Sometimes, I think I hate her," I sobbed. "But then I realize I hate me more."

The alcohol spoke for me, but it understood my pain better than I did. I'd never talked about my feelings toward my mother before—*really* talked. I'd mentioned it to my friends a few times, of course, but I'd never dived deep, tear-my-wounds-wide-open-and-pour-salt-into-them kind of deep. "I don't know how to explain it. It's like you want to blame your parent, but you can't because… deep down, you're so desperate for their affection, so you blame yourself instead. You blame your mere existence. And you wonder how anyone could ever love you if…" I sniffled. "If the one person in the whole world who's supposed to doesn't."

Speechless, he looked at me for long seconds.

"You're wrong."

I stared at him through the tears.

"It's easy."

"What?"

"Loving you."

I'd had Caleb tell me he loved me many times over the years, but in a playful way—one of those *you know I love you* when he annoyed me type of thing—but somehow, combined with the way he was looking at me, this one felt different.

Overwhelmed, I mumbled, "What?"

He hesitated for a second and grabbed the rum bottle right off the floor to chug what was left of it as if to give himself courage.

He sucked in a breath. "It's true. You're funny, beautiful, you're kind. Winter, you… You're amazing."

Words failed me. But his didn't. He said the three words—the ones that have the power to destroy any friendship in minus two seconds.

"I love you, Winter. I've loved you since we were kids. I… I was scared to tell you, but you don't deserve this. Your mom is awful. It's not your fault. It was never your fault." He wiped one of my tears away with his index.

In that moment, my hazy thoughts blurred everything: my actions, my feelings, the lines. The alcohol in my veins stole what was left of my common sense. I leaned forward and kissed him. He kissed me back. *Stop, this is wrong. So wrong.*

When we ended up naked on my bed, in the dark room where we once played hide-and-seek as kids, an alarm went off on his phone. He stretched his arm and pulled it out of his jeans pocket on the floor. He turned the screen over to me.

Midnight.

"Happy Birthday, Winter." He smiled, but all I wanted to do was cry. Crawl into a ball and sob until I couldn't breathe. Cry until the sting between my legs disappeared. My head was spinning, pounding along to the beat downstairs. I couldn't believe I'd just done this, crumbled under the pressure of wanting to get my first time out of the way. I would've chased any high to get me out of this low, to feel wanted even for a second. "Are you okay?" he asked, worried. I nodded, but the tears rolling down my face didn't lie. He was an amazing guy. The right guy.

Just not *my* right guy.

I realized the expectations weren't true—life is rarely perfect, firsts aren't always made of fairy tales, and the guy I'd known forever? The guy I'd cried to when my fourth-grade crush George Bay had gotten a girlfriend? The guy I'd never, ever thought I'd kiss? Well, I'd slept with him and I didn't know myself anymore.

But I did know one thing: I didn't sleep with him for the right reasons.

It wasn't because I loved him.

It was because I loved that he loved me.

## NOW

Lying in bed, I adjust my pillow with a heart so heavy I'm surprised my body hasn't sunk into the mattress yet. The apartment is quiet. Allie and Caleb went home, Haze is long gone, and Kendrick and Will passed out shortly after the Never Have I Ever disaster. Allie's been blowing up my phone, asking me why I never told her about that night. I was honest with her: I was ashamed, plain and simple. A lapse of judgment, a drunk mistake. That's all it took to completely wreck a lifetime of friendship.

The clock reads 2:00 a.m., and as exhausted as I am, I can't close my eyes. Not when he's somewhere out there, doing God knows what alone in the middle of the night. I stare at the one-sided conversation on my screen.

Where are you?

Please come home.

Haze, please. I'm worried sick.

Nothing.

I don't even think he opened them.

There's so much he doesn't know. I can understand why he might feel betrayed that I kept a secret from him, especially one that he had to find out this way, but I never intended to lie to him. I just thought I'd spare both of us the heartache, because, to me, it was nothing but a bad memory: The night where I lost both my virginity and my closest friend, all in a span of hours. Definitely not my brightest moment.

When I think I hear the front door open, I hold my breath, begging, *praying*, that I didn't imagine it. That he's really here. Home. Safe.

A sharp sound.

Then a low curse.

"Fuck." He ran into something. Probably the empty boxes we left by the door.

*Yep. That's Haze.*

My heart jolts as I climb out of bed, swing open the bedroom door, and hurry down the hall. There he is. Standing in the dark kitchen. Relief overwhelms me. We didn't hang curtains to conceal the city lights yet, which allows me to see his tired features and the twinge of pain glimmering in his eyes. He's wearing the black T-shirt he left in. It wasn't a warm night. He must've been cold as heck. None of us say a word.

"Where were you?" I'm the first to speak.

"Nowhere." He shrugs and tumbles down the hall. I mirror his every step.

"That's not an answer."

"I needed some air."

"Until 2:00 a.m.? I was worried out of my mind, Haze. I swear to God—"

"Relax, this is Canada," he snorts. "You can sleep with the keys in the door here."

I roll my eyes so hard they enter a new dimension. He walks into the bathroom, flicks the light switch on, and lowers the light's intensity to its minimum. The faint orange lights above the tub come on, illuminating the room as he twists the tap and waits for the water to cool. That's when I see his hand. His knuckles are scraped. It doesn't look too deep, more like a surface wound, but it's enough to send me spiraling.

"What the hell happened?" I gasp and close the door.

"I'm not sure." He places his hand under the freezing water and smirks. "I think there was a wall behind my punch."

"What? You punched a wall? Are you insane?" I scold him. "Can you move your fingers?" He does but not without a slight wince. "Does it hurt?"

"Nah. It's all right. I found something to numb it." He gives me a lazy grin. He's been drinking, that much is clear. He's not wasted, but he definitely had a few more drinks after he left.

"We really need to talk about what happened."

His cocky smile fades away, leaving a stern face behind.

"No, we don't. So, you had a past before me. Big fucking deal." He continues to watch as the water drowns his hand.

"You say that, but you're mad. I know you are."

He doesn't reply at first. Just sighs.

"I spent the whole night trying not to be," he admits.

"Why did you do that?" I flinch at his bruised hand. "You could've broken your hand. You could've gotten really hurt."

He shuts the water off and shakes his head, as if to expel memories out of his mind. "It's just… the way you looked at me earlier. The fear in your eyes. I…"

"I promise I wasn't afraid of you." I step closer. "If anything, I was afraid for Caleb. I knew what you could do to him, and he needs his legs. He's a soccer player."

He releases a weak laugh and glances down at his feet.

"I'm sorry I freaked out. I get it. It was before me. You were best friends, and you had a thing for him. It happens. I just—"

"No, I didn't. I didn't have a thing for him. That's exactly the problem." I step forward. "God, there's so much you don't know."

He cocks an eyebrow. "Then tell me."

I oblige and tell him everything. From beginning to end. I tell him I burst out crying after Caleb and I slept together. That

I panicked and shut down, telling him to get out and destroying what was left of our friendship in the process. I explain that the next day, Caleb came over begging for us to talk, and I told him the truth: that I didn't feel that way about him. I confessed to being a sad mess and doing this for all the wrong reasons. He didn't take it well, as one can understand, and left. We never spoke again after that. Not once during the months leading up to my departure for Florida. This is how Jaden knew we had a fight; he never found out exactly what happened but told me he'd always suspected Caleb had feelings for me.

Haze is at a loss for words, his eyes boring into mine.

"And you're right. It *was* before you. Before I met you, and I fell in love with your stupid jokes, perfect smiles and—"

He cuts me off. "I love you."

Relief pours over me.

"I love you so much, Winter, too much, and it scares the shit out of me because I'm going to fuck it up somehow. I know I am. I'm going to ruin it by being…" He exhales. "*Me.*"

"You won't ruin it."

He scoffs. "In case you couldn't tell, I'm a fucking mess."

I press my forehead to his.

"In case you couldn't tell, I am, too."

We laugh quietly, forehead to forehead, for a short moment I wish could last forever.

"You're not going to ruin us," I repeat.

"Yes, I am." A hint of annoyance drips from his voice. The

way he says it—like it's inevitable and there's absolutely *no doubt* in his mind—throws me off. "Eventually," he retracts himself. "Trust me, I've spent my entire life fucking up everything that matters."

"So what? You can change that. What you do next is up to you. You're not your past."

"How can you be so sure?" he argues.

"Because past you didn't have me."

He chews on his bottom lip as an answer. I cup his face with both hands so that our eyes lock. "I'm going to be there to keep you from going off the rails every step of the way. Every time you get too close, I'll bring you back. I'm always going to be there, Haze. If you just let me."

Silence ensues. He holds my gaze for a few seconds. Then he says it.

"I'm going to marry you."

My heart stops.

I drop my hands to my side. "W-What?"

The look on my face must be something because he laughs the next second.

"Relax, Winter, this isn't a proposal. I'm just telling you. Someday, I'm going to marry you."

"Oh… okay," I say awkwardly.

*Oh, okay? Did I just "Oh, okay" a future marriage proposal?*

"Why?" He frowns. "Would it really be so crazy if I decided I wanted to spend the rest of my life with you tomorrow?"

"I mean… a little, yes," I admit. "We're still so young. We haven't even lived together for a whole year yet. What if you hate living with me? What if I'm messy? What if I snore so loud you want to throw me out the window? You'd be stuck with me forever, and you'd regret doing something so important on a whim."

He shakes his head and pulls me into him. "Yes, it's a big step, but it wouldn't be on a whim. Nothing about loving you is on a whim, Winter. You're a no-brainer. Always have been."

His words crawl back inside my head. *Would it be so crazy if I decided I wanted to spend the rest of my life with you tomorrow?*

Images of us growing old together fill my mind, and I'm forced to admit that… no, it's not crazy. Or nuts. Or insane. Every nerve in my body tells me it's right. Just not now.

"Tell you what." I wrap my arm around his neck and rest the tip of my nose atop his. "From now on, we tell each other everything. Even the dumb things we don't think matter. Even the small details. Let's promise to never keep a secret from each other again, okay?" I smile. "Then hopefully we can get to *someday*."

A sharp pain flashes in his gaze, the kind that flees as quickly as it came but leaves a trace long after it's gone. I can't shake the feeling that he doesn't believe it—that he can change. That his future can be better than his past, if he just tries.

He leans in, taking his warm lips to mine, only pulling away to whisper a faint "I promise."

# TEN

## Blackmail

*Haze*

The smell of coffee and food wakes me up. Scratch that—the smell of coffee, pancakes, *and* the incessant bickering of Will and Kendrick wake me up. With my eyes sealed shut, I groan and seek Winter's body next to mine. Nothing.

Why is she up so early?

Ah. That's right. Her summer classes start today.

I sit up, assessing my bruised hand. It's looking a lot better already. I don't know what the fuck drunk me was thinking. No, I *wasn't* thinking. All I could see was the look on her face, the panic, the fear. For a second there, I was back to being the covered-in-blood kid sitting in a police station. For one fleeting moment, I was the town's freak again. The boy people loved to watch destroy himself from afar.

A phone rings.

It's Winter's. I roll over to her side of the bed and pick it off her nightstand.

*Caleb is calling.*

He's been blowing up her phone, trying to apologize since

the party two days ago. A text pops up on her locked screen.

> I'm sorry. I really want things to go back to normal between us.

I scoff, but my stomach lurches with irritation. If this guy thinks he's going to be allowed anywhere near Winter ever again, he's got another thing coming.

I slip out of bed, throw on a T-shirt and pants, and eye the boxes sitting on the floor at the foot of our bed. We're almost done unpacking, and to say it's about goddamn time would be an understatement. I'll never fathom how Winter can have so many clothes. Or want so many pillows. She's been saying she needs to make our living room "Pinterest-worthy" for days. I still have no idea what that means.

I turn into the kitchen, and a big silly grin broadens on my face when I see her in her pajamas, pouring smoking-hot coffee into a mug.

"Look who's up," she teases. "I was starting to think I wouldn't see you before I left." She draws the kitchen cabinet open and gets another mug out for me. I pour myself a coffee.

"Right. Your summer classes start today," I casually say like I haven't been full-on obsessing over that day for a week. I'm meeting a guy for tips today. They say they have something for me, something good.

It better be.

One step closer to finding him, my head says.

One step closer to losing her, my heart counters.

*Woah, that was some sentimental shit, Haze.*

I brush off the guilt eating me alive and put my coffee down on the kitchen island. I tug her body closer, and lean in for a kiss she denies. She feeds me a line about brushing her teeth first. She knows I don't give a fuck about that, but that's just Winter being Winter. She overthinks silly things, but that's my baby. God knows I wouldn't change a thing about her.

"I'm sorry, you desperately need me to kiss you? Well, if you insist." I reel her back in, pressing my lips to hers. She doesn't fight back, immediately surrendering to my touch. As crazy as this girl can drive me with her decoration obsession, I've never felt more at home than with her. Living with Winter is everything I hoped it would be—minus the East side holding my couch hostage and eating the entire contents of my fridge.

Our new life mainly consists of burning a lot of food, showering together to "save the planet," and making sure there's no hot water left for the guys by the time we're done f… *Finding diverse ways to show our love.*

"What time are your classes starting?" I hook my arm around her waist from behind while she flips over the pancakes that surprisingly seem edible.

"Twelve thirty. I'll be back at around six tonight." She wiggles out of my hold to get plates out of the cabinet on her right.

"Let me guess, I'm babysitting the guys?" I peek at Kendrick and Will inhaling breakfast at the kitchen table—and by breakfast I mean the leftover pizza from last night.

"Promise I'll pay you for your services when I come back," she hints, and I read between the lines, kissing her again when she hands me my breakfast. I didn't even ask her to cook for me, but she did it anyway, which officially makes me the luckiest bastard on earth.

"What did I do to deserve you?" I say and notice she didn't get a plate for herself. "Aren't you eating with me?"

"I already ate," she explains, her eyes jumping to the time on the stove. "Crap. I really have to shower."

"Want company?" *Can't blame a guy for trying.*

"Not today. You know how long our showers take." She traps her bottom lip between her teeth, reminiscing. Damn, she's not helping me let her go alone. I follow her as she rushes down the hall. She begins closing the door, but I stick my foot in the threshold.

"We'll make it quick." My dick jerks just thinking about it. She considers my offer for a second but quickly shakes her head, coming back to her senses.

"*Out.*" She gives my chest a small push.

"That's not what you were saying last night."

"For the love of God, we're eating," Kendrick whines.

"Hey, you're the one who wanted to live with us," Winter fires back and pecks my mouth. "Love you." She closes the door, and I walk back to the kitchen island to eat.

A loud ringtone sounds. It's not my phone. It's Will's. The life drains from his face when he picks it up.

"Who's that?" Kendrick is quick to ask.

Will sits silent for a little while, obviously not knowing what to do with that call.

Or himself.

"I said who's that?" Kendrick insists.

"It's not her. Chill," Will spits defensively. "I have to take it." He gets up, sprints down the hall, and locks himself in his room. Kendrick gives out a quiet sigh and finishes eating. A few minutes later, he walks to the sink to wash his plate and turns to me.

"Hey, so… I need you to get Winter out of the apartment tonight."

I frown. "Why?"

"None of your business."

I take my attention off him, finishing my pancakes.

"Okay? And why would I do that?"

"I don't know. Maybe because you don't want me to tell her to watch out for the weird phone calls you've been taking lately."

I stop chewing, moving, *breathing* all at once.

It takes me longer than I'd like to regain my composure.

"What the fuck are you talking about?" I barely manage to swallow my last bite.

"Hey, I'm not judging." He puts his hands up. "I know the

street fight shit. I was knee-deep in it, remember? I'm familiar with the shady calls late at night. I get it, man. You've got to have your lot of unfinished business from leaving your whole life behind, but I'm sure Winter doesn't need to be concerned about it, does she?"

I think back to the call I got a few days ago. They wanted to let me know the time and place of our meeting. I sneaked out of bed when Winter was asleep and stepped out onto the balcony. I thought I saw motion in the apartment through the glass doors.

It was Kendrick. Had to be.

"Let me get this straight." I raise an eyebrow. "You're blackmailing me. In my own apartment."

He stops to think before he says, "Yes, I am."

*Shitbag.*

"Who's the girl?"

"What girl?"

"The one you want to shag. She better be worth it."

He doesn't reply, but his eyes read *Busted.*

"You've got to give me something here." I insist.

Finally, he flinches.

"Allie."

I scoff. "Winter's best friend? Really? *That's* your go-to?"

He can't hold my gaze.

"She's going to kill you when she finds out."

"Who says she has to find out?" Kendrick shrugs.

"Didn't you learn anything from my friends-with-benefits

nightmare? Don't do that shit. It never ends well."

"We just started texting. I don't even know if that's what she wants. We're just spending time together is all," he explains.

"Just spending time together my ass."

"Would you rather I tell Winter?" he threatens.

"Tell me what?"

Fuck.

We both jolt around. She's standing in the doorway, drying her wet hair with a towel and assessing us curiously. She's wearing an oversized white hoodie with I'D RATHER BE SLEEPING written on it in black letters, black leggings, and barely any makeup. She looks like a fucking dream, per usual. How long has she been standing there? Obviously not long enough or she'd be going off on Kendrick for the Allie thing.

"That Haze's taking you out for dinner tonight," Kendrick says. She frowns, glancing at me for answers.

"Yeah, it was a surprise, but I guess it's ruined now," I fake laugh, and her frown progresses into a smile.

"Really? What's the occasion?"

"Everything. Us moving in together, you starting school. It's something to celebrate." I lie my ass off.

"Where are we going?" Excitement replaces her doubt.

"You'll see tonight. Now, come on, you're going to be late."

Will walks back into the room before she can answer, his phone in his hand. His face is pale—blank.

"Will, come on. You're driving me," Winter affirms. "Haze's

got a lot planning to do for our date tonight." I know she's been wanting to talk to Will alone for a while now. Probably saw an opportunity to find out what's up with him and took it. Will doesn't even put up a semblance of a fight, nodding and pulling the keys to his rental car out of his pocket. Dude looks like he just found out someone died.

"Oh, and Haze, did you call to make the hotel reservation yet?" Kendrick adds.

Man, do I regret letting him beat me that night at the Downside instead of whooping his ass right now.

"What hotel reservation? We're going to a hotel? You didn't have to do that, babe." Winter's face lights up, and she strolls to me, arms wide open.

"I know. I wanted to." I wrap her into a hug and glare at Kendrick over her shoulder.

"Isn't he the best?" Kendrick squeals.

*Shitbag, part two.*

"Okay. I really have to go now. Text you when I get there." She kisses me, grabs her bag, and drags Will out of the apartment. Their footsteps fade down the halls. I don't waste another second on Kendrick, rushing to our bedroom and kicking the door shut. I have two hours to plan a believable date and make a hotel reservation. Then I'm meeting some guy that'll hopefully tell me how to find my sister's murderer.

Just another regular day.

HAVE YOU EVER WONDERED HOW MANY times you've walked by someone who has done horrible things without knowing it? Maybe you ran into a murderer at the mall. At the library. At the restaurant. Maybe you passed them on the sidewalk. *Haze, for all we know, the stranger next to you could be a monster.* This is what my brother used to say. He believed you can never truly know who you're dealing with.

Ironic that, in the end, he was the monster.

Why am I thinking about my backstabbing bro right now? I'm guessing it has something to do with the pit in my stomach, the guilt twisting my gut. I feel like a monster. *I feel like him.*

Speed walking toward the set meeting place, I play with my keys and curse my nerves. This is stupid. I have nothing to worry about. I'm practically going to a meeting with myself. They called to let me know no one would meet me an hour back. Just said they left something for me there, whatever the hell that means.

Pulling my hood on, I glance around the sketchy alley. The sound of my footsteps and my heart pumping blood echo in my skull. Is this what criminals feel like? Do they enjoy the stress, the constant possibility of getting caught? Or do they become completely paranoid, too, crippled by what-ifs and maybes? I keep thinking that Winter is going to appear at every street corner, put the pieces together, and leave me forever.

I'm haunted by someone I've never lost.

Already missing a love that's still mine.

My source made it clear. She has to stay in the dark, no matter what, but it's still killing me. Chewing at my insides every time I see that heart-wrenching smile of hers. My phone lights up with an email confirmation. *Thank you. Your room has been booked.* I got a suite in a five-star hotel—my baby deserves the best, last minute or not.

Following the instructions given to me, I dive deeper into an isolated area, distancing myself from the crowded streets with each step. I know Florida like the back of my hand, but this place? Might as well ask people on the street for directions to the creepy drug alley.

I jump at the sound of an incoming text.

It's Winter.

*For fuck's sake, Haze, calm down.*

I've done plenty of dangerous things before, so why? Why is this time different? Why can't I fucking breathe?

I read Winter's name and it hits me.

She's why.

For the first time in my pathetic, miserable life, I actually have something to lose. Something to fight for.

Someone.

> This class is killing me. Teacher keeps spitting. Poor guy in the front is drowning and I'm soaking wet in the third row. SEND HELP!

I laugh at that. Yes, laugh. I'm in the shadiest place on the planet, on the verge of possibly ruining the only source of happiness in my life, and I'm laughing. That's what this girl does to me.

Did you just use the words soaking wet in a sentence about your teacher?

Instant reply.

Ew. Ew. Ew. Why did you have to say that?

You're literally ASKING me to be dirty minded, Kingston.

How's it going at home? Did you get into a fight with the guys yet?

Nope. But I don't trust myself to stay with them all day. Went out to get some air.

That's probably wise. Gotta get back to it. I'm so excited for our date tonight. I love youuuuu

I love you too. Now tell that teacher of yours no one can make you soaking wet but me.

STOP REMINDING ME.

I smile, walking until I stumble upon the darkest alley I've seen so far. I check the GPS on my phone. This is it. I venture into the darkness, beginning my search for whatever it is that they left for me. Ricky was in a rush and hung up barely five seconds into the call. The idiot couldn't just tell me "We left such thing in such place." Nah, that would've been too easy.

I curse, scanning my surroundings thoroughly. A brick in the wall captures my attention. It's lighter than the rest, older. It quickly becomes apparent that it wasn't there originally. I narrow my eyes and step closer for a better look. Unsure, I tug on the brick with both hands. The complete absence of resistance surprises me. It easily comes off the wall, weighing on my palms. I focus on the hole in front of me. I bet drug dealers are very fond of this place.

I activate the flashlight on my phone. A bag of weed lies inside, untouched. I scoff. *I knew it.* Looks like someone didn't come to get their stuff yet. When, at first sight, I don't find anything else, I think that while this may be a transaction spot for many, it isn't mine.

That's when I see the tiny piece of paper rolled up into the corner. I'm careful not to tear it as I unfold the crumbled mess.

*H*, it reads on the back.

I turn it over. An address.

*32 Holland Avenue.*

I trap the piece of paper inside my fist, push the brick back into place, and hurry out of this bad area. As soon as I get inside Winter's dad car—he's been nice enough to let us keep it until I get a new one in two days—I type the address into Google. The results shock me.

A two-star motel.

But that's not what freaks me out the most.

*Thirty-five minutes away from you.*

I begin to boil on the inside, disbelief and victory fighting for a spot in my chest. I can't believe that there's a chance he was this close. So damn close. He could've been anywhere in Canada, any-fucking-where, but this motel is here.

It's a sign.

I start the engine and drive off, intending to go back to the apartment so I can pick Winter up from school in an hour. I'm mad, yet relieved, because, finally, for the first time in fucking forever, there's hope for my sister.

And I'm getting closer to my revenge.

## *Winter*

"Are you kidding me?" I stalk inside the hotel room Haze unexpectedly booked for us. "It's official. You're crazy."

He opens his mouth, but I cut him off.

"And don't say crazy for you. That's way too cheesy."

He squeezes his mouth shut. *Ah, do I know him or what?* He walks in after me, the door barely shutting before he swoops me into his arms and carries me straight to the large bed. I didn't even get a chance to scour the room, but I can't find it in myself to care when Haze drops on top of me, covering my cheek with hot kisses. Truth is, I've been waiting for this moment all day.

"Does that mean you like the room?" he asks.

"Meh. It's okay," I shrug but I can't stop smiling. This is, by a long shot, the nicest room I've ever stayed in, and he knows it.

"Glad you approve." His mouth finds mine for a heated kiss. I think back to the moment he pulled up to my school in my dad's car, rolled down the window, and threw me his best Colgate smile. The snobby girl I'd just met in class was waiting for her ride as well and hit me with a confused "That's your boyfriend?" Poor girl was conflicted. Hot as heck young guy driving a minivan? She was almost as amazed as she was weirded out.

Walking out of the building to see Haze waiting for me completely turned my mood around. He took the crappiest of days and made it bearable. Just one smile and I could barely remember why I was upset to begin with.

I thought journalism was my calling, *thought* being the key word here. I'm not so sure anymore. Between one of my teachers being a human tsunami and another saying most of us would not make it to graduation, I didn't exactly have a blast.

Mr. Spit invited a full-time journalist to come present herself as well as her job to the class. Come to find out the woman was mostly writing about run-over dogs and liquor store holdups. She said she's been working for the same company for years and still struggles to write about something she cares about.

I kick the unpleasant thoughts aside and sneak out from under Haze's strong body, eager to explore our room. I expected many things from this perfect date. Walking into a gigantic suite to find numerous roses creating a path to the bed was not one of those things. I know Haze promised me a hotel room and a romantic dinner, but this is something else.

You see, I have this theory that Haze Adams secretly wants my heart to explode.

I twist the knob to the bathroom and gasp.

"There's a hot tub?" I squeal, my eyes drifting to Haze over my shoulder. He's lying on the bed, arms under his head. "That's the part you tell me you're kidding and take me to the regular room you booked for us."

"You might be waiting a while." He makes his way over to me. A huge basket filled with more rose petals, champagne, lube, and condoms sits on the bathroom counter.

"Well, *someone's* got a plan for tonight." I pick up the five linked condoms.

He snorts. "This is the romance suite, Kingston. What did you expect? Puzzles?"

I laugh and he picks the hanging condoms from my hands, wrinkling his nose. "This won't do."

"Why not?"

"We're going to need way more than that," he smirks, so unbelievably sure of himself.

"Haze, you're doing that thing again." I lean against his chest, my lips teasingly hovering over his.

"What thing?"

I get on the tip of my toes, leaning so close he shuts his eyes in anticipation of a kiss. "That thing where you confuse your dreams with reality."

Without another word, I leave him stranded with his eyes closed. I can't stop laughing at the look on his face when he comes running after me. Next thing I know, he's thrown me over his shoulder.

"Put me down," I scream in between laughter.

"What's a guy got to do to get some gratitude around here?" He smacks my ass. "I take you on a romantic date and this is what you do to me?" He throws me on the bed again, his blue eyes meeting mine as my heartbeat increases considerably. I laugh louder when he starts tickling me. *Just a heads up: I am not responsible for breaking any part of your body if you tickle me.*

"Say you're sorry."

"You're sorry."

"Say it." He tickles me until I'm laughing so hard my stomach aches and I can't take it any longer.

"Okay, okay!" I relent, out of breath, and stick my hands up. "I'm sorry."

"There. Wasn't so hard, was it?" He pats the top of my head, and I swat his arm repeatedly. Annoyed, he pins my wrists on both sides of my head. Our gazes tangle. We're putting on a show, but we're both holding back smiles. God, he makes me so happy I don't know what to do with myself.

"I love you," I exhale.

"I know."

Pretending to be offended, I attempt to wriggle out from under him, but he stops me, keeping my arms in place.

"I'm kidding, I'm kidding," he laughs, and I struggle to bury my grin. I can't even pretend to be mad. "I love you, too. You know I do."

"Then prove it."

He takes his sweet time, leaning forward and back, twisting a strand of my hair around his index finger, until I'm desperate for him.

"Kiss me," I urge. He leans in some more, his lips brushing mine, and stops.

"We have to be at the restaurant in ten minutes. Go get changed." That's all he says before getting off me. I watch him head for the door with my mouth agape.

"Seriously?"

"It's called payback. Look it up." A taunting smile warps his lips as he motions to the bathroom door. "Come on, we're going to be late."

Silly me. Guess I should've known.

Haze Adams is big on revenge.

"YOUR MOM NEVER TOLD YOU NOT to strip in front of people?" This might just be the last thing I expected Haze—well, *anyone*, really—to tell me tonight. When I send my heels flying across the room and wince in pain, I'm reminded of why I never wear heels—as in ever. I love them, but I love my feet more.

I finish tugging my tight dress down my legs, aware of Haze's eyes tracking my every move. He's right. I walked in, closed the door, and pretty much started stripping without a warning. That's how comfortable I am around him. I dig into my tiny luggage and slide an oversized T-shirt over my head with a sigh of relief. *Way better.*

"My mother didn't tell me much. That would require communication," I state, jumping onto the bed. It's close to midnight. Dinner was amazing. The food was great, the company even better, but we were both eager to return to the hotel to pass out. Haze joins me on the bed, only taking off his jacket.

"Yeah, well, your mother's awful, so there's that." He shrugs. I roll over to cuddle him.

"I don't know what I ever did for her to hate me so much."

"She hates everyone," he says to make me feel better. I

remember him saying that exact line to me about his own parents once. Crazy how two people with different backgrounds can relate to each other so deeply.

"Yeah. But she hates me more."

"Was it always like this?" he asks.

I nod. "As far as I can remember."

"Even when you were a kid?"

"Worse when I was a kid. She used to throw these monster parties in our one-bedroom when I was five. I swear, sometimes I'd be up until 3:00 a.m. playing in the sandbox out back. I hated the loud music."

Haze's jaw hardens like he can't stand the thought. "And no one did anything about it?"

"Well, the cops showed up once. A neighbor saw me outside, and this lady came to talk to me at school the next day. I never knew what she wanted, but she asked me a bunch of questions about my mom. I didn't think twice about it, but now… I think maybe social services tried to take me away."

The gravity of the situation tugs at my heartstrings. I haven't looked back upon this moment in years. I never saw the lady again, and my child brain tossed the memory so deep into the trash, it faded to the point of oblivion. But now that I think about it, there's so much that didn't add up.

"Then what happened?"

"My mom got with Harry a few days later. Before I knew it, they were getting married and we were moving into the house they have now." The remnants of a smile color my face. Harry isn't technically my dad. But he gave me a childhood—a home.

"Talk about good timing," he points out.

"I know, right? Almost too good." I've often wondered if it was all some sort of arrangement for my mother. My life changed in the blink of an eye. Barely a week after the lady came by, the twenty-one-year-old partying every night was trying on wedding dresses and getting a job.

"I'm so sorry, Winter." He grabs hold of my hand.

"It's not your fault. Hey, look on the bright side, there's no one she hates more than my dad." A sharp edge of pain crawls up my throat.

"Harry?"

"No. My real dad. You know, the one who left."

I tell myself that crying won't change a thing, that a tear shed over someone who doesn't care is a monumental waste. Still, my feelings spill down my cheeks one by one.

*Go away, tears. Nobody invited you.*

"Baby, don't cry." He holds me tighter. "He's an idiot. He missed out on knowing the best person in the whole world." He plants a kiss on my forehead. "And you have Harry. He loves you to the moon and back. You do have a dad, Winter. Biological or not."

The tears lessen until they stop altogether. He's right. I have a dad, and the best one by far.

Silent, I draw small circles over his shirt.

"What would you do?"

I look up at him.

"If you met your biological father, what would you do?"

The question rings out in my head.

"I'd ask him why," I whisper. "Why we weren't worth it. I get that he was young, and he probably didn't plan on knocking someone up, but still, he could've tried. I just want to know why he didn't try."

"Would you want him in your life if he showed up?"

"I don't know." I admit.

My resentment wants me to say no, but in all honesty, I have no clue what I would do if I were to see him in real life. If he were standing in front of me, begging me for a second chance, I'm not sure I could blow him off the way I convinced myself I would.

"You know what my mother used to say to me? Before…" Haze pauses. "Before Desiree died."

My heart aches.

"When life denies you what you want, it just means you deserved better."

We don't speak again after that. We don't feel the need to. We just lie there, in each other's arms. I listen to his heartbeat, he plays with my hair: It's the perfect escape.

I think about what he said. That I deserve better. People used to say that about him all the time. They said "better" wasn't Haze and it would never be. Because they all know so much about being a good person.

I think being good isn't always doing the right thing without a second thought. It's not having the right choices, the right words, the right moves on speed dial. In some cases, it's being tempted by the darkness, lured in and completely immersed. It's getting hurt over and over until finally, the darkness spits you back out and leaves you to make a choice. Fight or fall. It's having lived through the worst of the worst and surviving it. And after you survive it? After you've had your soul picked apart piece by piece? It's lifting yourself up and choosing the light. Again. One last time. *That's* being good. Haze taught me that doing the right thing doesn't come easy. It might just be the hardest thing you'll ever have to do in your whole damn life, but that's how you know it's worth it…

That it's real.

When his breathing becomes regular, I reach for his jacket, that he's using as a mini blanket, and walk to the beige couch in the corner of the suite. Haze didn't pay this much money to sleep on top of the covers. I'll have to wake him. I drop his jacket on the sofa and frown when a piece of paper slips out of his pocket, floating all the way down to the floor. It's small, crumbled. For all I know, it could just be an old bill, but my curiosity gets the best of me. I pick it up, glance back at Haze, who's still sleeping like a baby, and unwrap my discovery.

An address.

*32 Holland Avenue.*

# ELEVEN

## *Busted*

Sitting on the edge of the hotel bed, I fiddle with the wrinkled piece of paper in my hands. Haze is still asleep. He looks so peaceful, worriless—basically everything that I'm not right now. I spent the entire night tossing and turning, haunted by questions I couldn't answer, the main one being why on earth is there a motel address in my boyfriend's pocket?

No words can explain the dread I felt when I typed the address into the internet search bar and landed on the creepiest motel I've ever seen. *Holland Motel*, named after the street it was built on—because that's original.

The old exterior is something, but the inside could give a grown man nightmares. Everything about the place felt off. I wager this is a first-choice spot for all sorts of shady business: drug deals, money laundering… scandalous sex?

*Stop, Haze would never do that*, I try to convince myself.

*Then what the hell is he doing with the address*? the devil on my shoulder laughs.

I wince at the thought of him kissing some other girl in there. Undressing her. Holding her. Making her…

*Snap out of it!*

"Morning, gorgeous."

I jump.

He laughs quietly. "Sorry, didn't mean to scare you."

I don't move a muscle. I can't even look at him, infuriating images still holding my mind hostage.

*Winter, you're literally making yourself mad with scenarios you made up in your head.*

"Baby?" he says in a husky voice.

I take a breath, debating myself on whether or not I should confront him. Collecting my courage, I get up and swivel to face him. He's lying in bed, hair an adorable mess and blue eyes small from just waking up. He smiles at me, in all of his I-just-woke-up-but-I'm-still-annoyingly-perfect glory, and I wish I could go through this entire conversation without looking at him. *It's his eyes, I swear. They make it hard to think.*

"What is this?" I say quietly, holding the piece of paper up.

The smile on his face disappears in a matter of seconds.

"It fell out of your jacket last night," I explain.

He sits up straight and opens his mouth to speak. Except no sound comes out. Not on the first try. Not on the second. I wait for the rational explanation I pray is on its way, and a ton of scenarios pop in my head. What is he going to say?

*"It only happened once. She didn't mean anything. I… I got caught up in the moment."*

I shake my head, chills of horror running throughout my entire body, and erase this option from my head. Nah, he's not going to say that. Maybe something like "I'm selling drugs?"

*Nope. Not going to say that either.*

I focus on him. He finally speaks.

"I wanted it to be a surprise."

I frown. "What?"

"Come here." He pats the bed. When I don't move, he arches an eyebrow. "Please."

Half-heartedly, I grant his wish, climbing next to him.

"Remember when I said I wanted to step out of my father's shadow?" He takes my hand.

I nod.

"I've been thinking about starting my own business for a while, and I thought I could look around deadbeat places to hopefully buy and sell the lots. I just… The location is great. The only reason it's not doing well is because of the way it looks."

No matter how doubtful I am in this instant, I feel like the weight of the world has been lifted off my shoulders.

"Please don't hate me. I didn't want to tell you because nothing is official. That's just one of the places I found. Wrote it down so I wouldn't forget." He avoids looking into my eyes, and I can't tell if he's doing it out of shame or because he's not telling me the whole story. My stomach twists.

"Haze, if… if you're lying to me," is all I say.

He doesn't reassure me the way I expect him to. An awfully long silence crushes me. I'm being ridiculous. I know him. It's Haze. I would know if my own boyfriend was lying to me, right?

*Right?*

I cup his face, forcing him to meet my eyes. "You wouldn't lie to me, would you?"

"Of course not." He intertwines our fingers, leaning forward and kissing my knuckles. Conflicted, I steal my hand back. Worry creases his forehead. "You believe me, don't you?"

I hate myself for saying this, but…

*No, I don't. I don't believe him.*

I think back to the moment we shared two days ago. We said we'd tell each other everything. He promised. I have to give him the benefit of the doubt.

"I believe you. I know you'd never do anything to hurt me, and I trust you." His eyes light up with something. It's dark, raw, *real.* He opens his mouth to spea—

There's a loud knock on the door.

"It's probably room service. It comes with the suite," Haze says, glancing at the clock on the nightstand. "Right on time." I watch him walk to the door. As predicted, a fancy breakfast is waiting on the other side. After he's brought the food in, he says he needs a shower and locks himself in the bathroom. He didn't ask me to join him. *Something is definitely bothering him.* Unable to ignore the bad feeling burning within me, I eat breakfast alone and hope the rest of my day goes better than the way it started.

THE DRIVE BACK TO THE APARTMENT is awkward. Yep, awkward. The sort of awkward I've never known with Haze before. Something has shifted between us—a bad something. Worst part is, it's not for my lack of trying. I keep on cracking jokes, asking him questions he barely answers. He's somewhere else. Somewhere too far for me to follow.

I didn't dare bring up his motel investment story after he got out of the shower. I'm afraid he'll get offended and think that I don't trust him. I do trust him.

Or at least… I really, really, *really* want to.

He lowers his right hand to my thigh while driving and squeezes. The gesture, as small as it may be, brings me comfort. When he rolls into our parking spot and kills the engine, I'm tempted to ask him what's on his mind, but the sight of my best friend exiting my apartment building stops me.

What is Allie doing here so early?

She speed walks to her car parked in the visitor spot, and my gaze walks with her. She seems… emotional, distressed even. Before I know it, her car is nothing but a memory speeding down the street. I turn to Haze, who witnessed the whole thing.

"That's weird," I say and get out of the car, hurrying to the entrance. The elevator takes forever to get down, which only irritates me. Why would Allie be there when I'm not? Guess I'll just ask the boys. Haze trails behind me, the same torn expression he's had since this morning darkening his features. When we reach our front door, he grabs my wrist.

"Winter, wait, I know why Al—"

The front door opens from the inside.

In the doorway is Will.

Let me rephrase, Will and his luggage.

"Will?" I analyze the scene. "Are you leaving?"

*No, he packed his entire life for fun, Winter.*

"Yeah, I am." He wraps me into an unexpected hug. "Thanks for letting me stay here, Canada."

"But… why?" I ask, a bit emotional, even though the conversation we had when he gave me a ride to school yesterday sure gives me a hint. I catch a glimpse of Kendrick sitting on the couch over Will's shoulder. His eyes are glued to the floor, his jaw hard as a rock. This isn't good. They definitely had a fight.

"I just…" He breaks away from me, quickly glancing at Kendrick with pained eyes. "I really have to go home. My flight's in a few hours. Take care, okay?"

"I… I will." I'm going to miss this idiot.

Will turns to Haze. "Don't fuck this up. You never know how much time you have with someone."

Haze nods. By the time I've grasped what just happened, Will is long gone.

"Did we miss something? Why did he leave so suddenly?" I walk in and question Kendrick, who looks guilty of every single crime ever committed, sitting by himself with his head hanging low.

"You heard him. He had to go home." He makes his way to the fridge to get himself a beer.

"Are you really drinking at…" I pause, checking my phone, "10:00 a.m.?"

"Today's been a shitty day." He opens and tips the bottle back.

I frown. "But the day just started."

"Exactly my point."

With all this, I almost forgot about Allie.

"Hey, what was Allie doing here? We saw her leaving." I drop the bag of clothes I packed yesterday on the kitchen table.

Silence.

"Who?" Kendrick shrugs.

"Oh, fuck off," Haze spits.

I frown. What's that about?

"She forgot something here, that's all," Kendrick says.

Haze scoffs. "Was that something your dick?"

Kendrick's jaw falls.

"Excuse me?" I blurt.

"I don't know what he's talking about." Kendrick rubs the back of his neck, the way he always does when he's lying. Does this guy never learn? Something snaps inside of me. I'm sick of feeling like the whole world's lying. Kendrick's just rested his phone down. If he's keeping something to himself, I'll most likely find it in there. I act on autopilot, walking over and scooping his phone off the marble counter so fast it takes him a solid second to realize.

"Hey," he yells.

I have just enough time to lock myself in the bathroom.

He pounds on the door. "What the hell are you doing? Give

it back."

I unlock his phone. "No password, huh? We like living dangerously, I see."

"Winter, I'm not fucking kidding!"

"Where should I start? Camera roll? Text messages?"

He pounds louder.

"Yeah, you're right. Text messages."

He's got a conversation with his mom, one with Alex and… wait, *Allie*? I click. There aren't many messages. Something tells me he deleted the rest like the sneaky bastard he is.

Are you okay? You just ran out.

Yeah.

Is there something wrong? I thought last night was great…

What the…

Me too. But I don't think it should happen again.

Why not?

??

Looks like he got *Allied*—that's my way of saying blown off because that's practically the girl's brand.

"Winter, stop!" It sounds like he's trying to beat the door down. If he thinks *he's* angry, he hasn't seen anything yet. I slam the door open with all my strength, and he jumps back a step.

"You slept with my best friend?" I shout.

I'll spare you the part where I chase Kendrick around with a frying pan. Along with the part where Haze has to play moderator so we don't wreck the entire apartment.

"Look, I didn't plan it. She came over, we hit it off, and it just happened. Why are you so upset?" Kendrick argues.

*This coming from the guy who can't stand to see his best friend with a family member.*

"Plus, she rejected my ass. She doesn't like me," he says, his bruised ego showing.

I remember how upset she was when she ran out. The look on her face, I've never seen it before.

*Shit.*

He's wrong.

She does.

I don't waste another breath on him, grab my coat, and head for the door.

Haze chases after me. "Where are you going?"

"To see Allie. I'll be back tonight." I smack a kiss on his cheek. "I love you."

"I love you, too," he says two seconds before I'm out the door.

ALLIE'S HOUSE HAS ALWAYS BEEN SOME sort of sanctuary for me. While my mother forbade sleepovers, Allie's mother encouraged them. While my mom refused to buy me makeup, Allie's mother had boxes and boxes of it from her job as a makeup artist. It was always one of my favorite places to hang out at, but now that I'm standing on her porch, uninvited, I wonder if I should go home. Maybe she needs to be alone.

I texted her before I left my apartment, and although she didn't see my messages, her gray car is the only one in the driveway. After arguing with myself for a minute, I decide I didn't come all this way for nothing. I knock. Once. Twice. Three times.

I hear footsteps.

The door opens.

Allie blinks at me in surprise. Today's her day off from work. She changed into her pajamas, her hair is up in a ponytail, and she looks done with… well, *everything.*

"Winter? What are you doing here?" She glances around.

"I know what happened last night." I cut to the chase.

Her reaction is instant.

"Oh my God. I'm… I'm so sorry. I swear I didn't plan for it to happen. I was going to tell you today. I thought it couldn't hurt if we just hung out and then… things got out of control and… Ugh," she groans, covering her face with her hands.

I stop her. "Al, it's fine. I'm not mad."

*I'm not Kendrick. I don't think I own the right to tell people who they can be with.*

"Really?" She peeks at me through her fingers.

"I just wanted to make sure you were okay. I saw you leaving when I came home. You looked upset. You still do."

She steps aside to let me in and closes the door. I open my arms for her. She walks into my embrace.

"So you like him, huh?" I say mid hug.

"What? No, I-I don't." She trips over her lies.

I cock an eyebrow. "Let's try that again. With less babbling this time. Then maybe I'll believe you."

We pull away.

"I swear, I don't know what it is about him," she gives in. "After we…" She pauses. "*You know*, I felt different. I didn't want to leave or sneak out when he was sleeping. I didn't even want to block him on everything and change my name. So when he asked if I wanted breakfast, I… I ran for the hills."

"Let me get this straight. You ran for the hills *because* you wanted to stay?"

She stops to think for a second and nods. "Yep."

I laugh and walk to her kitchen. Same ol' Allie.

"Where's your mom's not-so-secret wine stash? We're going to need it."

## *Haze*

*Don't do it, Haze.*

*Don't fucking do it.*

Sitting in my car and staring at the creepiest of buildings, I battle my inner voice. I shouldn't be here. I should be home, watching Kendrick mope around and waiting for Winter to come back from Allie's. I also shouldn't go in this motel—but fuck, do I want to. My phone goes off in my pocket.

It's a text from Winter.

Hey babe. How's your night going? I made amends with Allie but am currently reconsidering it.

Why?

She ordered pineapples on her pizza. Can you order Holy Water?

I laugh quietly, text back that I miss her, and ask when she's coming home. I need to be there when she does. She's already suspicious because of this morning. *Investing in a shitty motel? Really, Haze?* I cringe just thinking about it. I panicked and a bunch of BS burst out of my mouth. She didn't believe me at first—of course she didn't. Nothing can describe the fear I felt when she pulled away from me, took her hand back like she wasn't mine. I told her I was going to take a shower, locked myself in the bathroom, and sat on the floor with my head in my hands for five minutes straight. I tried to think of a way not to lose her. Because I can't lose her.

No fucking way I'll survive losing Winter Kingston.

I'm stuck. I can't tell her the truth—the organization made that clear—but now? I'm not sure I even want to. If this morning is anything to go by, she most likely wouldn't take it well. She'd think I only came for Marcus. That I used her. She'd be wrong. Dead wrong. Why can't I just let it go, be happy with my girlfriend, unsee Desiree's blood on my hands? Forget her cold, tiny fingers wrapped around mine?

It would all be so much easier.

Dragging myself out of my car, I walk to the entrance of the hellhole. Maybe it'll look less creepy on the inside.

The door opens with a creak and a bell goes off.

*Nope, definitely just as creepy on the inside.*

The red carpet looks like it hasn't seen a vacuum in years, the wallpaper is coming off the walls, and don't even get me started on the smell… Shit, weed, cigarette, cheap perfume. The combination makes my eyes water, and I wonder how long I can hold my breath without dying.

A counter with the words "Check in" on a folded piece of paper stands a couple of steps away from me. *A piece of paper.* Could they at least pretend to give a fuck?

Behind it is a woman loudly chewing gum and checking out her nails. She appears to be in her fifties. Artificial tan covers her wrinkled face, making her look like a human orange. An uneven smile twists her lips when she sees me. She assesses me from head to toe, bending forward and leaning against the counter. I whisk my eyes away from her breast, which she obviously wants me to focus on.

"What can I do for you, sweet thing?"

*Gag reflex.*

"I'd like to talk to the owner."

"You're looking at her," she says as though she's actually proud to own this place.

"I need information." I find myself wondering how I'm casually going to ask her if a murderer stayed at her motel. I didn't think this thing through.

"Ask away."

"Are you familiar with a man named Marcus? He's been traced back to this place."

I think I see her eyes flash with *something* for a second there, but she gathers herself so quickly I'm not sure if I imagined it.

"Who's asking?"

"Someone who needs answers."

"And why would I help you? Time is money, sweetheart. I have a business to run." She pauses. "I mean, unless you're willing to work something out… I can always be convinced." Her tone tells me everything I need to know.

Gag reflex, *the return.*

"What do you say, handsome? You help me. I help you." She pops the second button of her shirt—which is frankly useless as I already see way more than I want to from her plunging V-neck. I dismiss her proposal, digging into my pocket and slapping two fifties on the counter. She eyes the money without a word and takes it, stuffing it inside her bra.

"What does this Marcus look like?"

I curse myself for not having a picture of him. All I have is the memories of the pictures I saw forever ago.

"Brown hair, crooked nose, around forty years old."

"I'm going to need more than that, kid."

"Strange man. Maybe a bit jumpy? He's been on the run for a while."

She narrows her eyes, as if to show me she's racking her brain for answers. After a while, she shrugs. "There was this one guy a while back. He looked like shit. Smelled like it, too. He stayed in room twenty-nine and registered under a ridiculous name. We assumed it was a fake one, but we didn't bother to look into it. Happens all the time here."

"Did he match the description?"

"How the hell should I know? It's not like I remember every face."

I've never gotten another fifty-dollar bill out so fast.

She glances around the room and picks it up, shoving it inside her bra again. I mean, damn, does she keep missing children in there?

"Now that I think about it, he did."

I know there's a very good chance she's wasting my money and my time, but she's all I have.

"Do you have surveillance tapes I could watch?"

She frowns. "What are you? A cop?"

Nope. But I'm doing the job they couldn't.

"Not exactly."

"Well, unless you're a cop, that's not happening. I can give you a call if he comes back, but that's it. Or did you need help with other things?" She offers me a wink.

"I'm good," I say, cold as ice, and rush out of the dusty-ass motel before she can blink. Well, this was a complete waste. One hundred and fifty for this shit. I get inside my car, take a deep breath to get my anger under control, and drive off. I'm right back to square one. With nothing but a name.

But I'm not giving up.

* * *

The woman watched the young guy climb back inside his car through the window. She didn't move, didn't breathe. She stood still and listened, waiting for a specific sound: his tires screeching down the road. The van took off at full speed, and she ran to the phone behind her, frantically dialing a number she knew all too well. It rang a total of five times, until finally, someone picked up.

Not a word was uttered down the line.

"You were right about the transaction. They tracked it," she spoke quickly. "But there's something else."

# TWELVE

## Before The Storm

*Winter*

FOUR MONTHS LATER

"Haze, wait, don't go." My footsteps echo in the empty apartment we used to call home. Everywhere I look is a reminder of how bad we screwed this up. A reminder that, in the end, our best shot still wasn't good enough.

"I can't. I… We're a lost cause, Winter. It's best if I just go." His hand lies on the doorknob.

"But why? What happened? What changed?" I can barely see him through the tears. "We were so happy."

He stops, his back facing me. He stands still for a quarter of a second, until, finally, he ushers himself back to me. "Were we?" He cups my face and wipes a rolling tear off my cheek with his thumb. "Or were you?"

What?

"Deep down, you know something's wrong, don't you? You've known for a while now."

"No, I haven't. I don't… I—"

"Yes, you do. You just refuse to see it."

"See what?"

"The truth."

"What truth?" I hold on to him for dear life. In every way that I can—his clothes, his arms, nothing is off-limits. He reaches for the handle again. I'm sobbing at this point. "Haze, please."

"I have to go." He opens the door.

"Why?" Desperation eats me whole.

This time, he's the one reaching out for me. He grabs my shoulders and shakes them, hard, as if to knock some sense into me.

"Winter, wake up!"

MY EYES JOLT OPEN. I CAN'T breathe. I can't think. Where am I? Doesn't matter. *I have to find Haze. I have to understand.*

"I said wake up, you lazy head," a high-pitched voice says, and I slowly come back to my senses. Maika's face is the first thing I see. I sit up straight, rubbing my eyes and taking in my surroundings. I'm on the couch. In my parents' living room.

Relief pours over me.

It was a dream.

Just a stupid, meaningless dream.

Why am I here again? Shit, that's right. I'm babysitting. Or at least, I was. I'm assuming falling asleep on the job terminated my shift.

"And they say I'm the one who needs to nap." Maika teases.

"How long have I been asleep? Did you—"

"She didn't set the house on fire if that's what you're wondering." I recognize Jaden's voice. My eyes dart across the room to my brother. He's looking at me with a mocking grin, sitting in my dad's leather armchair. "You're lucky I showed up when you fell asleep."

"Thank God." I exhale. I would've felt awful if I'd left Maika unattended. I study the couch, which is covered in opened notebooks, and beat myself up. I had one job. One job and I couldn't do it properly. School's been so demanding recently, I thought I could catch up on some of my assignments while Mai watched a movie. I must've closed my eyes for a few seconds, if that, and I was gone.

There's a knock on the front door.

"Hazie's here," Mai squeals like an overexcited fangirl, and I rejoice in energy at the sound of Haze's name, or should I say, *Hazie*. She heard me call him Hazie once, and from that moment forward, everything was lost. Haze shall be called Hazie for the rest of his life whether he likes it or not.

An unpleasant feeling throbs in my chest, the dream I just had leaving a bad taste in my mouth. What was that all about?

"Come in," I call, and the door opens. Haze walks into the room with that breathtaking smile of his a few seconds later. He frowns at the sight of me.

"Did you just wake up?"

"No." I try fixing my messed-up hair.

Jaden snorts. "Did you want fries with that lie?"

Haze grins. "Sleeping on the job, huh? I thought the kid was supposed to nap."

"Hey! I just said that," Maika giggles, running into Haze's arms—the way she's been doing every Wednesday night for close to four months now.

"No way. Fist bump!" Haze picks her up, and my sister obliges, more than happy to partake in the cutest fist bump I've seen in my life. He gives her a spin that turns up her laughter and puts her down. Seeing this guy interact with kids will never, and I mean never, stop being the most adorable thing in the world to me.

When Haze's eyes land on me, I know it's my turn.

"Hey, babe." I walk over to him and peck his mouth. Annoyed, he doesn't say a word, pulling my chin forward for more. His lips brush against mine, awakening butterflies I didn't even know resided in my stomach.

"*Eww.*" Maika covers her eyes but still ends up watching through her fingers. I laugh. She's curious, I get it. I remember being little and wondering what it would be like.

Jaden gets up to greet Haze. "What are you doing here? Winter said you were working tonight."

"Hey, man." Haze and Jaden bro hug like they've known each other their whole lives. "Yeah, they let me off early."

That awkward moment when your brother loves your boyfriend more than he loves you.

Haze and Jaden's relationship sure changed during the past four months. Especially considering the way it started. Jay didn't like Haze—he made that very clear when he brought up my fight with Caleb within five minutes of meeting him.

God, it all seems so far away now.

After much consideration, I decided to see this journalism thing through. I'm in my second semester now, and even if I'm not one hundred percent sure I can see myself in this field in the long run, I'm giving it another chance. I have four classes a week and spend the majority of my off days wondering how the students who have more classes than me find time to breathe. I picked up an online job as an English tutor. It doesn't pay much, but at least I'm making something.

Kendrick decided to extend his vacation and stay in Canada. Even though his mother was born here, he didn't get the dual citizenship at birth—doesn't work like that. He's our "kind of official but not really" roommate now. Since Kendrick and Haze got into the country as visitors, they will both have to go back to the US after six months, which means, two months from now, we'll be saying goodbye. Just for a short while, but still. There's a small chance they'll be denied entrance to Canada at the border when trying to get back in, which sucks, but we should've known leaving their entire lives behind on a whim would come with consequences.

Kendrick's decision to stay didn't come as a surprise to me. Or to anyone. He didn't tell us much, just that he didn't miss the drama back home and loved his new life here. We all know what he really means is: he loves Allison Gardner. Plain and simple.

I had my doubts about these two at first, but after one insufferable summer of them denying their feelings and chasing each other, they finally made it official. Kendrick spent the summer living on the rather large sum of money he had left from the fights, but he drained all of his savings paying his half of our ridiculous rent. When he got into school, Maria sent him the money she saved up for his studies. He also got himself a construction job that pays in cash—it's a bit shady but it's something—since he can't get a regular one as he's American. Long gone are the street fights days, and I believe this move to be the best thing that's ever happened to him—except for Allie, of course.

As for Haze, he's still living on his "my rich parents didn't know how to give me love, so they gave me dollar bills" money, but he got a side job to keep himself occupied since I'm rarely home due to my hectic schedule. I came to find out that Bea, Haze's best friend's girlfriend, got Canadian citizenship and, more recently, a scholarship to the University of Toronto. It motivated her to move away from Colton Gate. Vic agreed to come with her and get a student visa to enroll in school. Since a bit of Bea's family lives here, they know people, which allowed Vic to get himself and Haze hired at some auto-repair shop.

Same as Kendrick, these two are not allowed to work in Canada, which is why they're paid in cash.

Haze still has to get his residency to stay in Toronto long-term. He's not aiming to become a citizen for now, just a permanent resident. Heaven knows the process can take forever, especially for Haze, who, thanks to his bank account, falls under the entrepreneur category. A lot of money means a lot of questions: Do you plan on investing here? What are you going to do with that money? It goes on and on. Immigrating to Canada is a killer headache, that's for sure.

We haven't heard from Will much since the day he packed his bags and left. We know he's still alive from Alex, who's now seeing Morgan, Kass's best friend, I think. Speaking of Kass, last I heard she was kicking butts in law school. We still text, just not as much as we used to. I miss her, but she seems to be doing well. She told me she moved out of Maria's house and into a dorm with her friend Ethan.

Sometimes, I wonder what happened between her and Will. Did they get back together? Did Will go home to her that day he left? All I know is Will and Kendrick don't talk anymore. It's sad. These two used to be like brothers.

"You got time for one game?" Jaden asks Haze, throwing himself on the couch and turning the TV on.

*Oh hell no.*

"Nope. Not losing him for another five hours," I cut in.

"You heard her." Haze circles my waist with one arm and

pulls me to his side. Last time they played "one game," I had such a hard time getting Haze to leave, I asked myself if I still had a boyfriend. Almost signed up to Tinder for a second there.

I had no idea when I agreed to babysit Maika every Wednesday when my parents go on a date that Haze would tag along almost every time. He first started playing video games with my brother, then it was basketball in the backyard, and, just like that, the Haze and Jaden bromance was born. I think we all know the day Haze beat Jay at video games is the day my moody little brother started respecting him.

Haze pretty much has my entire family wrapped around his finger at this point. All except my mom, of course. She's still a monster in human form, but my dad likes him, and that's a big deal. Keep in mind we're talking about the man who once asked my fourteen-year-old date, "Do you have any intention of touching my daughter tonight?" then gave us a ride to the theater and watched the movie *with us.*

"Just one game," Jay begs.

"Not tonight. Mom and Dad will be here soon. It's 8:00."

"Mom said they're coming back at 8:30," he says.

"If mom says 8:30, she means 8:15, you know that."

Jay sighs and starts a game by himself. I watch Maika lose interest in our conversation and stroll off to play with yet another headless Barbie. One day, I'll find out what she does with them, I swear it on my life.

Haze yawns his jaw off next to me. I have no idea what

they've got him doing at the shop, but he always comes home physically and emotionally drained. He's also never there when I wake up, and some nights, he only shows up when I'm already asleep.

"Long day?" I reach for his hand.

"You have no idea," he groans. I plop down on the couch next to Jay, and Haze follows. He hooks his left arm around my neck and kisses my temple. Maika's eyes widen from across the room, and she makes her way to us.

"What's that?"

"What's what?" Haze asks.

"That." Maika points at something. The sleeve of tattoos on Haze's arm.

He smiles. "These are tattoos."

"What's a tattoo?"

Haze gives her a quick summary.

"Did it hurt?" She blinks at him.

"Yeah, at first."

"Did you cry?" She climbs on top of Jaden without a care in the world. *Where most people see a teenager, my sister sees a seat.*

Jay protests for a second but quickly gives up, tilting his head to the left to see the screen as he plays.

"Nah, I put my big-boy pants on," Haze grins.

Her beady eyes grow even bigger as if she can't imagine getting one of those without crying a river.

"Do you have one?" She turns to me.

"Me?" I laugh. "No, I'm too much of a chicken. Plus, Mom would probably never speak to me again."

"Does that mean you want one?" Haze asks.

"Yeah. I've always wanted one. I just never had the guts. Maybe one day."

"Why not now?" Maika urges.

"I don't know. I guess I'm waiting for the right moment."

Jay blesses us with his feedback. "Not to mention that you're poor."

I swat his arm. "Shut up."

The front door opening stops our bickering. My parents are home. I glance at my phone. *8:15 sharp.* I get up from the couch and hold out my hand to Haze, who doesn't react. He whines when I pull on his arm, forcing him to get his ass off the couch. We're both exhausted. As we head for the kitchen, Maika pushes past us, her energy uncontainable. Putting her to bed is going to be fun.

"Hey, guys," my dad greets us. "How was the studying, pumpkin?" My mom doesn't spare us a look, walking past us and straight into the kitchen. *Well, hello to you, too, sunshine.*

"Dad, I dressed up as a pumpkin for Halloween once. *Once.* You need to let it go." I'll never admit it, but I got used to the nickname. Wouldn't trade it for the world.

"Sorry, you're going to be my pumpkin for the rest of your life. Deal with it."

I chuckle.

"I'm still waiting to see those pictures, by the way," Haze reminds him.

"Come on over anytime you'd like, son." My dad pats him on the back. Images of Haze and my dad bonding over pictures of me on the potty flash in my mind.

"You will never see these pictures as long as I'm alive, thank you very much," I snap, and Haze laughs.

"Okay. Fine. What about high school pictures?"

"In your dreams, Adams."

Jay walks into the room. "Wait, has he never seen you with braces? What a shame."

"Wait, you had braces?" Haze asks.

"Okay. That's enough. We're leaving now." I drag Haze to the door.

"No, stay! We have pictures of Winter wearing the same princess costume for ten days in a row," Jay mocks.

"I was five. Give me a break."

"Mom, Mom! Can I get a tattoo?" Maika chimes in.

My mother's mouth falls open.

She glares at Haze. "Now, who put that idea inside your head?"

A smile tugs at the corner of his lips. "It's probably me, I'm sorry."

"You know what? Maybe bringing your boyfriend on Wednesdays isn't such a good idea after all," she says, picking Maika up into her arms and storming out. Thankfully, we're so used to her unpleasant behavior, it barely affects us.

"She doesn't mean that. You know you're always welcome here." My dad apologizes on her behalf, per usual. Haze nods, and I hug my Dad again, then my very uncomfortable-with-human-touch little brother. We say our goodbyes and depart from my parents' driveway a minute later. Haze turns up the radio, resting a hand on my thigh.

"How was your day?" I intertwine our fingers.

He shifts in his seat and offers me a small smile. "It was fine." That's what he always says. No details, no anecdotes on his job—he stops at *fine.* "How was yours?" He brings our linked hands to his lips, pressing a kiss to my fingers.

"Oh, you know. Same old. Went to school, babysat, fell asleep on the job, and somehow convinced my five-year-old sister to get a tattoo."

He laughs. "Your mom is never going to forgive me for that one, is she?"

"I wouldn't get my hopes up. She still hasn't forgiven me for being born."

We laugh. Then Haze stops.

"Shit. Do you realize how dark that was?"

"Wow, you're right."

A few seconds of silence.

We start laughing again.

Ten minutes into the drive home, I ask him, "So, have you thought about it?'" I make my best puppy eyes at him. Key word: *puppy.*

A smile stretches his mouth. "Stop looking at me like that. We're not getting a dog."

"But… But… why?" I pout. "It'd be so cute. And the landlord's fine with it. Plus, it gets lonely at home when you work late. Kendrick's always at Allie's. Please, please, please."

"No." He shakes his head. "It's too much work. You have to walk it at least once a day. Then there's the barking. We're not getting a dog, Winter. Let it go."

"Then how about a cat? You don't have to walk it. It's relatively low-maintenance. *Please.*"

"You know what's not low-maintenance?" He shoots me a look at a stop sign.

"What?"

"You."

"Ouch." I bring a hand to my heart and dramatically wipe away nonexistent tears from my eyes. Haze scoffs. "Please, I'll do anything," I say as he pulls up into our apartment parking spot. He kills the engine, but we don't get out right away.

"Anything?"

"Anything." I smack my palms together and beg.

He doesn't move, chewing on his lip as though he's actually considering it.

"Nah."

*Oh my God.*

"I hate you." I climb out of the car and rush to the entrance.

Haze catches up to me, leaning in to kiss my cheek. I try to dodge his lips, fake-mad at him, but he gets me anyway. We walk inside, teasing each other, wrestling in the elevator, and finally making out against our front door for five minutes.

The last four months have been a dream. The transition from dating him to living with him was surprisingly easy. Dangerously easy. He practically became an extension of my arm. Sure, we annoy each other. We get into silly arguments like this one—arguments that usually end in intense makeup sex—but overall, it's been perfect. We've been happy: no fights, no problems, no street fighters or crazy brother, just genuine happiness.

Still, it feels like I'm waiting for hell to come pouring down on us. For something to go wrong and blow my heart into a billion pieces. And that dream? The one where I cried my eyes out and begged him to stay? It's not helping my nerves.

I love him. More than I thought possible.

And that's exactly what scares me.

Because when the sun's been shining for too long, a storm is waiting around the corner.

"HOLY SHIT. GUYS, WAKE UP. YOU need to see this!"

You know how in the morning you have that moment of complete oblivion? That very short instance of peace. That little while when you don't remember a thing? Then, progressively, the memories wash over you, and piece by piece, your problems come crawling back into your brain. That's what happening to me right now. And my problem is…

I still live with my pain in the ass of a cousin.

"Guys, you need to see this! Come on," Kendrick calls from the living room, and his footsteps rush down the hall. A loud knock on our bedroom door makes me jump. I open my eyes with a wince and reach for my phone on the nightstand.

*8:05 a.m.*

*Really? He has nothing better to do at 8:05?*

"Get your ass in here." Kendrick hurries back to the kitchen. I glance at Haze, whose head is buried under not one but two pillows to muffle Kendrick's voice. His hard, defined back is all I can see from this angle. And his arms. *God, he's hot.* Eagerness slices through me. Our schedules didn't align last week. He came home when I was sleeping almost every night. It must've been a week and a half since we've had some action.

His exposed muscles call out my name, and I'm happy to answer. Sadly, I'm reminded that I didn't wake up at 8:05 to check out my boyfriend when Kendrick yells, "*Guys! Come on!*"

Haze rolls onto his back, his eyes still semi closed, and says in a raspy voice, "Dear Winter, I'm sorry I killed your cousin. It's not my fault he was the most annoying person in the world."

A chuckle leaves me.

"*Guysssss*!"

"Oh, for fuck's sake," Haze hisses, then raises his voice. "We're coming." We painfully drag ourselves out of bed, sharing each other's frustration. I'm off today, and Haze only works this afternoon. We had plans to sleep in. As soon as we open the door, the sun pulverizes our eyesight. We both wince, blocking the light out with our hands as we march down the hall and into the living room. That's when I see it.

The first snow.

Slowly falling on the other side of our window, a soft snow covers the city, not giving a damn that it's not even November yet. I laugh at Kendrick's hanging jaw.

*Seeing snow for the first time will do that you.*

Every year, I can't wait for the snow to melt. But then, every year, I also get excited for the first snow to come. It's a never-ending cycle. Approaching the window until his nose is merely inches away from the glass, Haze joins Kendrick in his staring session.

"It's beautiful," Kendrick states. "I don't know why you guys complain all the time."

"Ah. Just wait until you step outside. Shovel for three hours straight to get into your car, and then maybe we can talk. Canada, come for the culture. *Stay because your car won't start.*"

Haze and Kendrick snicker, unable to take their eyes off Mother's Nature show.

"Don't get too excited. The first snow never stays. Most of it will be gone by the end of the day," I point out and Haze's smile transitions into a frown at my statement.

"Aw, don't worry. Soon, it'll be here to stay, then you'll realize what a huge mistake you made and run back to Florida."

"Don't hold your breath." He opens his arm for me, and I move toward his bare chest. He didn't bother to put on a shirt yet. His skin is burning hot—no surprise there—but I still find myself sighing in relief at the sensation.

Once the guys are done fangirling, we all eat breakfast. Haze is more than happy that, once we've brushed our teeth, I'm willing to kiss him.

"What do you want to do before work?" I stalk to him in the kitchen. I'm hoping I can convince him to visit an animal shelter. He pulls me into his arms and cups my ass through my pajamas.

"I have some ideas." He leans forward.

Kendrick gags next to us.

Haze and Kendrick exchange glances, and I can tell from the way Kendrick rolls his eyes that they did it again. Recently, all they have to do is look at each other to communicate. Don't ask me how—I don't get it either. Usually, their eye conversations concern Kendrick going out for a little while so we can have some alone time.

I'll probably never get used to how close these two got during the past few months. Haze might call Kendrick annoying, but we all know they kind of like each other now.

"Nope. Not happening. I wasn't home last night. You should've done it then. Gee." Kendrick throws himself on the couch.

Haze doesn't budge.

"I said no. I'm staying. Deal with it, you filthy animals."

"I'll give you twenty bucks," Haze says.

Kendrick arches an eyebrow. "Forty."

"Done."

My cousin keeps trying. "Fifty?"

"Don't push it."

"Forty-five?"

"Forty. Final offer," Haze says.

Kendrick caves. "How long?"

Haze grips my hips, turning his full attention over to me. "I'll text you."

"Can you hurry up? I have shit to do today," Kendrick hisses.

"No promises." Haze jerks my body forward, not giving a single fuck that we have an audience, and my breath jumps. The way he's looking at me… like he's imagining exactly what he's going to do me and how… *Jesus, I need a minute.*

"Use protection, kids" is the last thing Kendrick says before he shuts the front door. A smile lifts the corner of Haze's lips, and he swirls me up into his arms. He carries me to the bedroom, kicks the already halfway door open, and lays me down on the mattress, no questions asked.

His body sinks into mine and demands for more of me. I give it to him, parting my legs until his knees find the sweet spot between my thighs. I'm wearing a T-shirt, silk shorts, no underwear, and this mind-spinning lust like a bodysuit. Everywhere he touches me, my skin cries out with shivers. He pushes my head forward, takes my lips prisoner, and I want him so bad I let myself have him. I grab the already solid budge in his sweats, and he groans inside my mouth. I trace him, tease him, squeeze him. But only for a second.

Because a stroke of genius hits me the next.

I free him, lifting my hands to his chest and pushing him back. His breathing is clogged with need when his eyes sway across my face.

"Can we get a dog?"

Horny, shocked, confused, he's many things, but the main one is irritated.

He frowns. "What?"

"Can we get a dog?"

"Are you… seriously doing this right now?"

I tug at the waistband of his sweatpants, a painful reminder of what I was just doing to him, and he sucks in a breath. "Just say yes and it's back to fireworks."

"I can't believe it. You're using sex to blackmail me into getting a dog?" He's scandalized.

I give him a big wide smile.

"That I am." I push him off me.

His lips part.

"What are you saying? No sex until we get a dog?"

*The look on his face.*

"No sex. No kissing. Nothing." I stride out of the room. Haze's footsteps closely match mine.

"Please tell me this is a joke." He pins me against the

bathroom door before I can open it. Slamming both his hands on each side of my head, he keeps me drilled into place. He's still hard as a rock, aching for my touch.

"Do I look like I'm kidding?" I slip from his reach through the void under his arm. I've never, in my entire life, walked into the bathroom and locked the door so fast.

"Fucking hell, Winter. I hate you so much right now." He tries the knob a few times and pounds on the door.

"I love you, too." I start the shower.

"Don't play this game with me. I promise you're going to lose, and defeat is going to hurt," he warns.

"How about this? First one to touch the other loses. If it's you, we get a dog. If it's me, you'll never have to hear the word dog again. Now if you'll excuse me. I have a shower to take."

"Just open the door. I swear to God—"

"What was that? I can't hear you." I slide my shorts to my feet and enter the shower's hot steam. He doesn't answer for a while. Then, finally, just before he walks off, he says words even hotter than my shower.

"Game on."

# THIRTEEN

## Closer

*Haze*

What would you do if life gave you a second chance?

Would you take it?

Or tell yourself that everything happens for a reason?

If someone came up to you with a time machine and asked, "Do you want to go back?"

*Would you?*

I'm guessing many would, and part of me would, too.

But the other part…

The other part knows that what happened to Desiree led me to Winter. My obsession with Marcus, the urge to learn to fight so that I would never be weak again, all of it carved the path that took me straight to her.

To the only girl I've ever loved.

Would I give up love for family? Would I lose Winter to save Desiree? I think that's a question I'll never be able to answer. My head is down, my throat sore and my breathing sharp. It's become a goddamn habit of mine. Whenever I'm meeting up with Ricky, I'm also meeting up with my fears. The anxiety never leaves me.

*But Winter will.*

Shut up, inner Haze.

You would think four months of dead ends would make this easier—it doesn't. I clench my fists as I recall the ridiculous leads that I've been following since June. After we tracked him to the creepy-ass motel, it all stopped. The transactions, the clues, *everything*. Almost like someone wanted me to find the place. It was too easy. I haven't been able to stop wondering if it was a test. A way to see who would come looking. A means to an end.

On a slightly brighter note, I'm starting to know the area's poorly frequented spots like the back of my hands. From abandoned warehouses to sketchy bars, I've seen enough dumps for a lifetime. I met up with the shadiest people on earth, but none of them told me any valuable information. Some say they've seen a guy who matches the description, but seeing the guy and knowing where he is are two very different things. Not to mention there's no way to know if they're being truthful or taking advantage of a desperate kid. The last dirtbag said he heard of a Marcus: a guy on the run, a drunk, a drug addict, a waste of oxygen.

But I don't think putting my trust in the hands of someone whose only friend is the bottom of a bottle is a good idea.

I just dropped Winter off at Allie's house for the day. She said she didn't want to stay home alone during my "shift" at the auto-repair shop.

*I fucking hate myself.*

She would hate me, too, if she knew where I was really going. Where I've been going every night since we moved in together. I had to come up with an excuse so she wouldn't get suspicious whenever I went to meet Ricky.

During the drive to Allie's, I didn't reach for her hand, didn't kiss her goodbye before she got out of the car, didn't even comment on how great her ass looked in her jeans. Now that I can't touch her, it's all I'm thinking about. She's good—really good. She "accidentally" dropped her phone right in front of me, and "randomly" chose to wear the tightest jeans she owns today. I'm already fucking dying from not feeling her for a whole week. *Shit, I'm totally going to lose, aren't I?*

Walking alone, I tuck my hands in my pockets. It's getting colder out. Soon we'll be buried in snow. Winter was right—the first snow melted before it even touched the ground. I'm starting to think I won't be happy once it's here to stay.

I grab my phone and dial Vic's number.

Two rings.

He picks up.

"Hey, man." His voice is faint, barely there.

"Hey… Is everything okay?" He sounds like crap.

"Yeah. I'm fine."

"Vic, what's wrong?" I've known him since we were kids. He's lying through his teeth.

A long silence sits between us.

"It's Bea. She's cheating on me."

I wince. They've been together for years. He loved her so much he moved to another fucking country for her.

*He did what you couldn't*, my conscience taunts me.

"I'm so sorry. How long?"

"Since we got to Toronto. But I don't want to talk about it."

"Are you… going to stay here?" I really hope he doesn't run back to Colton Gate. He's already studying here. Might as well stay.

"I don't know. I can't think about that right now. I'm going out with some guys from school tonight and finding myself a rebound pussy. You coming?"

"Rain check. I still got a shit ton to prepare for Winter's birthday this Saturday." I feel awful for not being there to cheer him up.

"No worries."

A noise.

"Hold on." I swivel so quickly I scare off a bird on the ground.

What the…

*Footsteps?*

No one.

I'm alone in the alley.

I bring the phone back to my ear. "Sorry. I'm fucking paranoid. I could've sworn I heard something."

He scoffs. "Yeah, well, lying to your girl for months will do that to you. Hey, did you need something? I got to get to work, then I have to go drink until I don't remember Bea's name."

With a bad feeling, I glance around the alley once more. "Yeah. I just need you to cover for me if she calls."

"Another shift, huh?" His tone gives away how disappointed he is in me.

*Believe me, Vic. No one's more disappointed than I am.*

He's never approved of my obsession with finding Marcus. Although I've never said a word to him about the organization providing with me tips to keep him safe, he's the only one who knows apart from Tanner that I'm actively looking for Des's killer, and he gives me shit about it every chance he gets.

"How long are you going to pretend to work at the shop? She's not an idiot. She'll figure it out eventually, and trust me, if it's not from you, you're screwed. It's over."

I continue to walk, watching my back every two seconds. I don't feel alone.

*Haze, relax. It's just your guilty conscience fucking with you.*

"You don't get it… I can't. And even if I could, what the hell would I say? 'Hey, babe. You know how I moved to another country with you and said it was because I love you? Well, I lied. The real reason I came with you is because I found out that my sister's killer might be here. Yes, I've been looking for him. For years, actually, and I never told you. But we're fine right? You're not mad? Cool. Thanks for understanding. Let's get married.'"

A beat of silence.

"But you do love her, right?"

I almost laugh. That is the dumbest question I've heard in a while.

"Are you serious? Of course I do. More than anything. I would've followed her as soon as I got rid of the bastard."

"Then take it from someone who just found out the person they trusted the most on the planet has been lying to them. You can't keep this up, man. You have to tell her. Soon. Or if you can't for some fucked-up reason, you have to let her go. I'm covering for you at the shop again, but she deserves better than that." He pauses. "I got to go. I'll hold you to that rain check."

He hangs up.

*Let her go. Like it's that fucking easy.*

I brush off the bad vides in the air when I arrive to the meeting spot. My foot squelches in something wet, sticky, and I curse when I notice I've stepped in something that, at first sight, looks like mud. Or is it dog shit?

Getting abandoned with a massive boner this morning and stepping in possible dog shit now? This day just keeps on getting better and better.

I scan the area, waiting for Ricky to show his emotionless, psychopath face, and spot a silhouette down the alley. He's got his cap on, his hands in his pocket. He's on time. For once. What's he going to give me today? More dead ends? More threats about keeping this to myself?

I send the dumpster behind me a glare and try to forget the noise, the footsteps. But I can't. Vic's speech comes back to me.

Not only does it come back, it also hits me where it hurts. *She deserves better than that.* I know what he really meant to say is *She deserves better than* you. He's right. I don't care about the consequences. She might leave me. I might lose her forever. But I'm going to do it.

Just after her birthday,

I'm going to tell her.

## *Winter*

"It smelled like death. I'm telling you. Don't use whipped cream during foreplay. It smelled so bad Kendrick and I almost puked when we woke up."

Listening to Allie go on and on about her bedroom disasters has always been entertaining for me. Until now. Turns out being related to the guy she rambles on about makes it… weird.

I try to tame my brain.

*Stop, brain.*

*Don't picture your cousin with whipped cream on his nipples, brain.*

Let me tell you: it is hard.

"You two are unbelievable." I slouch into the couch.

She laughs. "Says the girl who's literally paying people so she can sleep with her boyfriend."

"Wait, you know about that?"

"Yeah, Kendrick texted me."

*Of course he did.* Nothing goes on in the apartment without Allie knowing anymore.

"Well, Haze's going to want his money back because I told him I'm not touching him until he agrees to get a dog. First one to flinch and touch the other loses."

"No way? How'd he take it?"

"Almost beat down the bathroom door when I left him with a hard-on, so, not well?"

What? Girls conversations aren't always classy. *Known facts.*

"Who do you think's going to win?"

I pause for a second, thinking back to the tension filling up the car when Haze dropped me off.

"I was pretty confident this morning, but now, I'm not so sure," I admit.

"That good, huh?"

"You have no idea." I bite on the inside of my cheek.

Maybe I made a mistake taking on a challenge I can't win. *No, Winter. Do it for your dog. Do it for Waze*—yes, I might have already named the dog by combining our names. Sue me.

Allie's eyes widen when she sees the time on her phone. "Is it really five already? I thought Haze was picking you at four thirty." Anxiety flares in her voice.

"Uh, yeah, I'm sure he's just stuck in traffic. Why? Are you expecting someone?" I joke, unsuspecting that I am right on.

"Actually…"

A knock on Allie's door cuts me off.

"See, he's here." I get up and glide down the hall.

"Winter, wait." She follows me. "It's not—"

I open the door and instantly regret it.

"Haze," she finishes.

Caleb.

I haven't talked to him once since the night of my housewarming party. He's been trying, to the point of insanity, to get me to talk to him: texting, calling, even sending letters to my apartment—you name it, he's done it. I've been giving him the cold shoulder, certain that we can never be as close as we once were again. I destroyed our relationship beyond repair, and I have to learn to live with that.

His eyes grow at the sight of me. "Winter, hey. I didn't know you were here."

Allie's eyes apologize profusely.

"Just a second," she tells Caleb and practically shuts the door in his face. "I'm so sorry. You weren't supposed to run into each other. I thought you'd be gone by the time he showed up. I told him to come at fi—"

"Al, it's okay." I gather a reassuring smile. "You're allowed to still be friends with him. I think we can manage a few minutes together."

"I'm sorry," she says again and opens the door. "Come on in." Caleb obliges, but barely two steps inside, Allie shrieks, "Hey, shoes off!" She takes in the poor appearance of his muddy shoes. *Gee, where'd he go?* "Who do you think I am? Cinderella?"

Caleb gives out a faint laugh and kicks his shoes off. "Sorry, Mom."

Because my life is unfamiliar with the concept of good timing, I hear a car door closing outside. I draw the curtain off the closest window with the back of my hand.

Haze. Crossing the street.

Soon after, he rings the doorbell. I swing the door open, dreading the possibility of a messy boyfriend versus ex-best friend confrontation. Haze's eyes lock on Caleb the second he comes into view, but Caleb doesn't flinch, drilling holes into Haze's head from inside. Haze frowns but abstains from commenting.

"Hey, babe." I almost hug him but stop myself at the last second, letting my arm droop back down awkwardly.

"Hey. You ready?" He doesn't seem to know what to do with his hands either, sliding them inside his pockets as he shifts from side to side. *Stupid, stupid game.*

"Haze, do me a favor—" Allie sticks her head into the doorway. "—just get her a damn puppy already."

"She's going to have to win for that." Haze grins. "Allie, you still coming to Winter's dinner party Saturday?"

"Wouldn't miss it for the world," she assures him.

I hug Allie goodbye and get off her porch with Haze.

"Still not touching me?" he asks as we cross the street.

"Still refusing to get a dog?"

"Looks like it."

"Then I'm still not touching you," I confirm.

With the weight of mutual attraction crushing us, we climb

inside the car and buckle up. Haze doesn't ignite the engine right away, his nails digging into his legs. If this morning's tension was heavy, this one is near suffocating. I want to straddle him already. Just let my desires run wild right there on his lap. His white-knuckled hands squeeze the steering wheel, a sign that I'm not the only one struggling to harbor my urges.

"Screw it," he snaps. "We're getting this over with tonight. You want a game?" He turns the key, pushes the gear into drive, and accelerates down the road. "I'll show you a game."

WHEN HAZE UNLOCKED THE DOOR TO our empty apartment and ordered me to sit on the couch, I found myself wishing I could go back in time and put out the fire that started this. Just so I wouldn't have to find out what sick revenge game he had in store for me. But now, as we sit in silence, close, but not nearly enough to touch, I'm dying from suspense.

"What are we doing?" I speak first.

"*We* are not doing anything. At least, not at the same time."

I frown. "What?"

He pulls his phone out and sets a five-minute timer. Without pressing Start, he throws his phone between us on the couch. "We both have five minutes."

"To do what?"

"Whatever the fuck we want. For five minutes, you're mine. You don't get to say no. Or touch me. If you do, you lose. Then, if you manage not to break the rules, it'll be your turn."

Heat pulses between my legs.

I worry my lower lip. "And if none of us flinch?"

"Not gonna happen." He shrugs off my concerns.

Realization creeps up my spine. "Even if I wanted to, Kendri—"

"Is not coming home." Haze slumps back into the couch. "I texted him."

"And he just agreed to stay out all day?"

"He needed a bit more convincing, but yeah."

I snort. "You mean he needed more cash."

He doesn't deny nor entertain my claim. "So, you want to play?"

That's when I understand that I've got it all wrong.

I might've started the fire.

But he's the one keeping it alive.

"Only if I can begin." I'm surprised by my own guts.

He's a bit surprised himself. "Okay. Then start."

*Oh, Hazie, you won't have to ask me twice.*

Nodding, I get myself off the couch and stand tall in front of him. He's still seated, the perfect picture of nonchalance and cockiness. I bend forward, dropping the phone next to him and starting the timer. I never take my eyes off him. Not when I tug my shirt over my head, not when I pull on the waistband of my leggings, slide them off and kick them to the side. I strip without a care in the world, and his mouth full-on drops.

*Not so cocky anymore, are we?*

He stares me up and down, his eyes flashing with a carnal need that melts my insides. I'm still wearing my underwear, for now, and drop to my knees in front of him. Eager, I seek him through his jeans, running my palm up and down the fabric. The friction instantly makes him grow, but his pants block his size. I don't waste another second, unbuckle his belt, and get his pants off. I drop them on the couch next to him. I can't help a grin at the now massive bulge tempting me. Still, the rest of his clothes stand in my way.

"Lose the shirt."

Disbelief flickers in his gaze.

He looks like he's thinking, *You're joking, right?*

"Underwear, too."

The seriousness of my request finally dawns on him.

"Fuck, Winter. You can't ask me that," he pleads.

I arch an eyebrow. "I'm sorry. Did you just say no?"

Annoyed, he gives in, tugging his shirt over his head. His underwear is next. Sliding his boxers down to his knees, he frees himself. My stomach flips with desire. He's beyond ready—ready and desperate. He sucks in a breath, tight fists lying alongside his body, when I lower my mouth to his...

"Winter, don't you dar—"

*Oops. Too late.*

I grab him at the base and suck. Hard. He immediately presses his mouth shut, agony and pleasure mixing on his face. His head falls back. Still he doesn't budge, keeping his hands to himself and his eyes on the ceiling. It's as though he *knows* that looking at me would stand for immediate defeat.

"Look at me," I tell him.

His eyes widen and he jerks with spasms. He's not used to this. He's usually the one luring me over to the dark side. Like it requires every inch of self-control in his body, he does what he's told, meeting my eyes.

He watches as I take him deeper and lets out a strangled threat. "Holy sh… I'm going to make you regret that."

I peek at the timer from the corner of my eye. What? I'm down to two minutes already? *This isn't working. I need a new tactic.*

Releasing him, I push to my feet and toward the couch. I straddle his now completely naked body and let my hands explore his defined torso, rocking my hips against his. He's thick and hard under me. An unplanned moan slips free from my mouth, and he exhales an irritated grunt. I may be playing him, but the sensation of him sliding up and down my slit against the thin fabric of my underwear is still very real.

I shamelessly use him, angling my hips forward until he hits exactly the right spots. I'm tempted to destroy the last barrier behind us and take my underwear off, to *really* feel him, but I'm enjoying the tortured look on his face way too much. I snake one arm behind his neck and the other in his hair. My breasts comes flush with his chest and, for a second there, as I grind against him, I almost forget about the sick origins of this moment. I don't even care that he's not touching me. I could get off just doing this.

"Haze." His name falls out without my consent.

"Fuck, baby." He clenches his teeth.

The memory of why I'm doing this hits me almost as hard as the overwhelming buildup in my stomach. *Eyes on the prize, Winter.* I lean in and my mouth hits his ear. "I'd love to. But you're not giving in."

Finally, he touches me. Scratch that, he starts to. He lifts his arm and I shiver, every nerve ending in my body anticipating his touch the way a drug addict awaits his fix.

But my fix never comes. Because he stops. Why did he stop?

Only then do I hear it.

The timer.

*Shit, shit, shit.*

Victory creeps into his eyes.

"No, no, no! That doesn't count—you were just about to touch me!" My speech thunders out of me quickly, giving my speeding heart some serious competition.

He smirks. "But I didn't, did I?"

"Haze, please. You know I won that. This isn't fair," I insist, and he picks his phone off the couch to kill the timer.

"Life isn't fair, Kingston." He cups my cheek and slowly traces along my lower lip with his thumb, as if to wipe the pout off my mouth. "My turn."

He gets something out of his jeans on the couch next to him. A condom wrapper. It doesn't take a genius to figure out his intention when he tears it open and stretches the latex down his size. Tingles eat at me, but I make it a priority to remind myself of what losing this game implies. *I want my dog.* I open my mouth, with every intent to argue my way out of this, but he cuts me off with just the touch of a finger. He starts the timer again.

Then he slides my panties to the side, grips my waist with both hands, and buries himself deep inside me.

I gasp so loud I have to cover my own mouth.

"No more teasing," he grunts, shifting under me and guiding me down onto him harder. It feels better than the best, and usually I'd brace my hands on his chest, give myself a few pushes, but I can't touch him and it's driving me mad.

"Take off your bra," he orders.

So, I do. Correction: *I try.* But apparently not quickly enough for him because he almost immediately reaches over and does it for me. My breasts break free, bouncing at his rapid thrusting. I wait for him to touch me, but he never does.

"Touch yourself."

"What?" I stifle a moan when he pulls out completely and fills me again. *Oh. My. God.*

"You heard me. Touch yourself."

It's not that Haze and I have never tackled on this topic before. I'm not embarrassed with the idea of taking care of myself, but we're usually so infatuated with each other in bed that the opportunity never comes along.

"I-I don't know."

"I'm sorry, are you arguing with me?" He twists the hair on the back of my head around his fist and pulls back until I have a clear shot of the ceiling. Then he leans in and bites my neck. It's not gentle. Or sweet. It's rough and hungry for blood.

"God, I hate this game." I taste my lie for a few seconds and surrender, cupping each of my breasts and teasing my nipples until he grunts. The fact that I can't see myself helps tune out the self-conscious voice in my head.

"I fucking love this game." He keeps me bouncing up and down his length so fast that the sensation knocks the English vocabulary out of my brain. Between each of my frivolous heartbeats, he leaves my body and claims me again. When he rips my hands from my chest and tells me, "That's enough. I want you to come on your fingers," heat rushes to my cheek. He's so raw, unapologetic. My hand travels downward, but I'm cautious to keep my eyes where he can't see them. "Look at me." He shoots me an arrow made of my own words.

I obey yet another one of his commands, staring him dead in the eyes while I rub myself, slowly at first, then so fast my faded, uncompleted climax from earlier is given a second chance.

"Shit, I can't watch you. Come here." He roughly smashes his lips to mine, his tongue sweeping inside my mouth as he continues to pound into me. The last of my restraint flies right out the window, and I cup his face with one hand to deepen the kiss. He doesn't comment on me touching him. I'm not sure he even notices it at this point. A hurricane of pleasure sucks me in, and I clench around him. Haze's thrusting, as well as his lips against mine, grow a bit sloppy—frantic. The timer goes off next to us. But we both know the game ended a long time ago.

Fireworks detonate within my stomach as I finish myself off. Still kissing me, he gives one last powerful pump and empties into the condom. Breathless, we stop moving, still high on a game with unbroken rules. I never thought bowing to someone's every demand could feel this good. I never thought losing control could be this freeing.

And when he pulls me into his arms, I'm glad I didn't break his rules after all.

# FOURTEEN

## *Forever*

There are multiple ways to wake up on your birthday. To say most females don't usually expect their significant other to try and organize something special for them would be a big fat lie. Maybe he'll go for a cute and yummy breakfast in bed. Maybe he'll play with your hair until you wake up. Or maybe he'll open the door, jump on top of you like a maniac—all the while making sure to bury you under his entire body weight—and scream, "Happy Birthday!"

I should've known Haze Adams would choose option number three.

"What part of let me sleep got lost in translation?" I groan and rub my eyes. I told him not to wake me up early on my birthday, which also happens to be my day off this week. Yesterday, he nodded. But did he have any intention of listening? *Of course not.*

"Sorry, I thought you said 'please wake me up early so we can do the things my amazing boyfriend has planned for me,'" he says in a ridiculous high-pitched voice.

"I don't sound like that." I push him off me.

"I don't sound like that," he says, still in his incessant voice, and I chuckle.

"The dinner party is like…" I pause and reach for my phone on the nightstand. "Ten hours away. I have a whole day before what you planned. Good night." I lift the blanket over my head.

He quickly pulls it off me and swats my cheek with kisses. "You're adorable." *Kiss.* "You actually think…" *Kiss.* "I didn't plan…" *Kiss.* "Anything else."

I glance at him with a raised eyebrow.

"You didn't?"

"Oh, I did."

"What?" I'm a tad more nervous to hear the answer than I should be. If he says bungee-jumping, I'm throwing up on the spot.

"Come on. Get up. Breakfast's waiting." He kisses my cheek as a parting gift and carries himself off our bed.

"Wait, you made breakfast?" My stomach grumbles at the mere mention of food. Haze rarely cooks. I know he's much better at it than me from the number of times he saved me from burning down the apartment, but for some reason, he hates doing it. I smelled food as soon as I woke up but didn't suspect that he could be behind it. "I thought it was Kendrick."

"He spent the night at Allie's. He's only coming home for your party." He says before he walks out.

I've never run out of my bedroom quicker.

A feast is waiting on the perfectly set kitchen table.

"Do I smell bacon?" I shriek, and he smiles.

*Man, our love story is almost as beautiful as my story with food.*

"You did all this?"

He nods. "You like it?"

"Do I like it?" I fling my arms around his neck. "Are you serious? This is amazing. I thought you didn't cook."

"I do today." He pecks my lips. "For you." I could cry when he motions to sit down and serves me. "Now, eat. We have a long day."

"NOPE. NO WAY. YOU ARE NOT blindfolding me." I run around the kitchen, and Haze chases after me. "That sounds like the beginning of a bad porno." After we devoured what I can confidently say was the best breakfast I've had in a while, he told me to get dressed. He didn't tell me where we were going, just said to keep it casual and comfortable.

"I promise it'll be worth it." He catches up to me and corners me against the front door.

"Why do you need me blindfolded?"

"I can't have you seeing where we're going. It's a surprise. *Please.*"

I sigh. He seems to have put a lot of effort into this. Might as well play along.

"Fine."

Satisfied, Haze wraps the bright red scarf he found in my stuff around my head and ties it into a tight knot.

"I'll help you to the car." He captures my hand into his and opens the front door.

"Wait. Why couldn't you just wait until we got into the car to blindfold me?" I say as Haze leads me to the elevator.

He scoffs. "Where's the fun in that?"

I roll my eyes. "Jerk."

"Prude."

Haze saves me from certain death—and by certain death I mean tripping over flat surfaces multiples times on the way out of the building—and guides me into the passenger seat of his car. He even buckles up my seat belt while poorly muffling his laughter.

"I can hear you mocking me, you know."

"Congrats. You have ears."

He shuts my car door. A few seconds later, the driver-side's door opens, and I hear him get in. We take off in a loud purr.

"Are you ever going to tell me where we're going?"

"Nope."

"Can you at least give me a hint?"

He pauses, debating. "It's something you've always wanted to do."

A million options gnaw at me, but I've told this guy about so many of my hopes and dreams in the past that I can't seem to decide which one is more likely. Hopeless, I force patience upon myself. After a few minutes of silence, Haze scoffs.

"What? What's so funny?"

"You should've seen that lady's face. Pretty sure she thinks I'm kidnapping you."

I chuckle, imagining a blindfolded girl randomly sitting in the car next to you in traffic.

"We're here."

"Can I take it off?" I urge.

"Not yet." He parks the car. I'm so excited I shift in my seat and not so patiently wait for him to come and get me. As soon as he does, I word-vomit all the questions raging in my brain, only to get a "You'll see." Walking toward the unknown, I hold on to him for dear life.

"Careful, there's a step," he warns.

I raise my foot. Nothing. I can't find anything that even resembles a step.

"Higher."

Still nothing.

"There's no step!"

"I know. I just wanted to see you struggle."

*Why am I dating him again?*

"I hate you," I whine, and he laughs, smacking a kiss to my temple.

"There's a step," he says again.

Annoyed, I'm careful to ignore him, but my feet hit concrete and I almost trip. Strong arms catch me at the last minute.

"What are you doing? I told you there was a step." He laughs louder.

"Haze, I swear to God, if I didn't need your guidance so much, I'd punch you in the face right now."

"You're so hot when you're mad."

"I'm not with a blindfold on?" I mock.

"Winter, you could wear a potato sack and still turn me on."

Before I can answer, a door opens and a bell chimes above our heads. I'm assuming we're in some sort of store. But which store? I'm nowhere near figuring that out.

"Hold still." He unlatches my hand from his arm, and I feel him untie my blindfold. Bright light hits my eyes.

I blink a few times.

"Can I help you?" A woman's voice emerges on my right.

My eyes jump to her. The woman behind a large counter.

"Yeah. I have an appointment at 12:30," Haze says.

The woman says something else and walks off. I didn't hear a single word. No, I didn't *listen* to a single word. I'm way too busy shitting my pants. I'm in a bright red room. Designs and drawings cover every available wall. A bright neon sign hangs above the now deserted counter. *Tattoo shop.*

"Surprise." Haze throws his hands up, his voice heavy with doubt.

"You… You can't be serious right now." I step back, as if I'm about to sprint out the door. "I… I can't do this."

"Yes, you can."

"No, I can't." I shake my head.

"Why not?" He reaches for my hand and laces our fingers together.

"Because I haven't thought this through. It's a big decision,

Haze. A tattoo's for the rest of your life."

"So? They have a bunch of books to show you. I'm sure you'll find something."

"And if I don't?"

"Then we'll just come back some other time. It's your birthday gift. Your choice."

"But… What's my mom going to think?" I only realize the absurdity of what I've just said when I catch Haze's frown. He knocks some sense into me without speaking. I can't believe that, after all this time, I still have it in me to worry about this woman's opinion. After she abandoned me on my birthday too many times to count, after she denied me love and affection during my entire childhood, part of me still wishes, deep down, that she'll change her mind one day. That she'll wake up and love me. The way a parent should.

Because even after every fucked-up thing Lauren Kingston has done… she's still my mom.

"Hey, listen to me." He moves toward me. "You spend too much time worrying about other people. This is for you. No one else. You said you've always wanted a tattoo. Well, now's the time."

He's right. There are so many things I never did because I wanted my mother's approval. Getting a tattoo was just one item on the list. I also didn't get my hair dyed. My ears pierced. All because she spent my teenage years calling Allie's wrist tattoo self-harm and saying colored hair was for attention seekers.

"Isn't it going to be expensive?" I wince.

"That's not for you to worry about."

"But—"

"Winter, stop. I know you want this. Let me give it to you."

His reassuring smile soothes me. I inhale a breath and walk straight into his arms. No warning. He's surprised but grants me the hug I need, resting his chin on the top of my head.

"Thank you," I whisper, and he holds me for as long as I want. This is one of the things I've always loved about him. Some people merely hug you *back*. Haze just hugs you.

"Why don't I get you one of their books?" He grins when I break free from him. I lose myself in his clear eyes, and the answer comes to me, or rather, it *appears* to me, because it was always there, hiding in a tiny, isolated corner of my heart—just waiting to reveal itself.

"I don't need to look at the books."

His eyes bore into mine.

"I know exactly what to get."

"JUST BREATHE, OKAY? YOU'RE DOING GREAT," Haze says, and I make a mental list of all the reasons why I'm an idiot. Getting a tattoo is already a pretty painful experience as it is, but my dumb ass had to go and get one on the left side of my rib cage which ranks pretty high on the *don't get a tattoo here* scale. Before we started, I asked Haze what getting his sleeve had felt like. He said it was like getting scratched by a cat a few times.

He was right on.

Except that the cat is a tiger.

And a few times is forty-five years.

"How much longer?" I blink back tears.

"Almost done," Jeff, the person who will possibly be responsible for botching my tattoo and ruining my life, says.

"Why won't you tell me what you're getting?" Haze stresses. I told him it concerned us, but insisted on meeting with the tattoo artist alone to share what I had in mind. I also insisted that Haze keeps his distance. I want him to see it when it's done.

Yes, I've been crying like a baby for a few hours, but the good somehow outweighs the bad. I feel free, happy. In a way, I'm rebelling against my mother's expectations. Finally letting go of my need for her approval.

"Winter, I swear if you're getting my name tattooed…" Haze warns.

"What kind of idiot do you take me for, Adams?" I turn to Jeff. "Is that even a thing? Do people still do that? Getting someone's name tattooed?"

The tattoo artist smiles. "Sadly, they do."

A few more minutes of never-ending pain pass me by before Jeff washes away some of the excess ink on my skin and tells me he's done. He tells me all about my tattoo aftercare and asks me if he can post the tattoo to his social media. I accept. He puts a filter on the picture in front of me, presses Post, and sends me the final result. Swaying from side to side, Haze can barely contain himself. Then comes the time for the big reveal.

When he sees the ink under my left breast, he exhales a shallow breath, swallowing feelings that escaped his grasp. Somehow, he's not as flattered as I thought he would be. He seems… rather upset, actually. I tell myself that it's just a lot to live up to. If he were to dump me, he'd have to live with the fact that I have a constant reminder of him on my body, but it's my decision, and I stand by it.

He speaks after a while. "You shouldn't have done that."

"I wanted to." I glance down at the picture the tattoo artist sent me in awe. It's everything I wanted it to be. A single meteor surrounded by stars as it free-falls. A wink to the meteor shower Haze and I saw on the night of our first kiss. Actually, the meteor shower we *missed* because we were making out, but let's not get technical.

That night on the beach is the moment that fucked it all up for us. The moment we knew we were screwed. Or at least, I did. Because that's when I realized that I was falling for the one guy I shouldn't.

*Hard.*

Some moments are so precious, some memories so important, that you want them to be more than a part of your story. You want them to be a part of you.

Forever.

And that's what Haze is.

Just like the ink on my skin…

We're forever.

Even if I lost him, even if we fell so far from each other that we couldn't fall back, I'd always have a piece of our story. A story nothing, not even time, could wipe away. He hooks his hand around the back of my neck and crashes his mouth to mine, but somehow, this kiss feels like a promise. Like our lips made a deal. They say birthdays represent moving forward, growing up and welcoming the future.

Mine's different.

Mine's a trip down memory lane.

And it's the most beautiful trip I've ever taken.

WHEN I CHECK THE TIME ON MY phone, I realize that, while I've waited a long time for my birthday, time sure didn't wait for me. It's already past five and we're mere hours away from the dinner party Haze organized.

I decided to have two birthday parties this year: one with my friends, and one with my dad and siblings tomorrow. My mom will most likely come up with some last-minute event she can't get out of. Allie texted me that she and Kendrick will be at the apartment at eight, which means we should probably be heading home soon, but I don't want this day to end.

After I made a life-lasting decision in a matter of minutes and got a tattoo, Haze took me to one of my favorite restaurants for lunch. We inhaled our body weight in food, talked and laughed for a few hours, and I even got free cake. Then we decided to go for a walk around town. So far, this day has been perfect.

The kind of perfect you usually don't enjoy while it's here and miss once it's gone.

The sky is darkening by the second, here to remind us that, as much as we'd like to, we can't escape the cold anymore. Soon, we'll wake up to a pitch-black city, have barely a few hours of sun a day, then go back to complete darkness by 4:00 p.m.

"Is it six already?" Haze's eyes widen. "We have to go."

"Back home?"

"Not yet."

"Then where?" Don't tell me after all this, he has *another* surprise for me. My heart can't handle any more of this cuteness.

"We have one last stop on the list." He speed walks through the streets, dragging me with him. He knows where he's going, that much is certain. I did wonder why he insisted on walking in this specific area.

"What? No blindfold this time?" I tease.

"What's the point? We already can't see shit. *Thanks, Canada.*"

Sniggering, I try to keep up with him. Ten minutes of walking lead us to a park my dad and I used to visit often when I was a kid. A water fountain lit up by yellow lights is bordered by a broad concrete path. Surrounded by tall skyscrapers and businesses, the park adds much-needed green space to the working area.

"Cute walk in the park, huh? And you say you're not

romantic." I rest my head on his shoulder, tangling my arm with his.

"What? No, we're going to the fishing store close by," he says, and my mouth drops for a second. Until he laughs.

"Shut up." I bite back a grin.

The stars are nearly impossible to see, due to all the city lights, but once in a while, I'm lucky enough to catch a glimmer. Haze says they're planes, but I like to believe they're shooting stars, passing in my life to remind me that I have nothing to wish for anymore. Haze brings our intertwined hands to his lips and places a kiss upon my knuckles. I look at him and I know…

My wish came true.

*I'm so cheesy I think I might puke.*

When we get to the fountain, Haze stops.

"Right here," he says to himself.

"Why here?" I ask.

"Because it's perfect."

"Perfect for what?"

He takes a breath. "For this."

He gets down on one knee.

My heart stops.

"Haze Christopher Adams, what the hell are you doing?" My hand flies to my mouth. He doesn't speak for a while, leaving me to fend for myself against my last two brain cells.

Then he smiles and takes my hand.

"You know I suck at things like this… but I have to try.

Because you deserve it. You deserve someone who tries." He clears his throat. "My whole life, I thought I was alone. And I was. But… not because people kept on leaving me. Because I kept on convincing myself that they would." He stops to collect his thoughts. "Before you, I was an asshole. Still am, to be honest."

I laugh through the tears. *Shit, when did I start crying?*

"But back then, I was an asshole with a mission. To keep everyone away. No connections, no real feelings. I thought it made life easier. I lived on this fucked-up belief that we come into this world alone, we live alone, and die alone. When Desiree was murdered…" He pauses, needing a second. "I became terrified of loving anyone else. Because I knew how it felt to lose them. To have that void in your chest, eating at you, begging for something that'll never come back. To have to live with it every day. I thought I couldn't survive another void. But then… you happened. You just walked straight into my life and called me out on my shit. You challenged me. Made me question everything. And when you kicked down my walls without blinking, I realized that while I'd spent my entire life trying to keep people's hearts at bay, I should've spent more time protecting my own."

The tears are blinding me.

"I love you. And I want to keep waking up next to you. I want to watch you burn our pancakes, and I want the movie marathon, even the chick flicks where I constantly fall asleep. I want it all. And I want you. Forever. So I'm asking you…" He pauses. "Winter Kingston, will you do me the honor…"

I swear, in that moment, it feels like every never-ending math and history class I've ever had teamed up to make this wait unbearable.

His blue eyes collide with mine.

Time stops.

Then he says it.

"Of accepting this dog?"

*Wait, what?*

I'm so shocked when the words escape his lips that I almost lose my balance, tumbling a few steps until the backs of my knees hit the stone of the fountain behind me.

That's when I hear a dog's barking.

I turn around and see Vic, Haze's friend, standing a few feet away from us. In his arms is a puppy. A Shiba Inu. Exactly the dog I wanted. Speechless, I blink at Haze in disbelief. Since I ended up touching him at the last minute during our dumb game, he told me that I lost and had to kiss my dog goodbye. I was so mad at myself. Was he planning this all along?

He rises from the ground and pulls me closer with one move. "I heard you when you said that we're too young. And I respect your wishes, so I'll wait. For as long as it takes. Until you agree to marry me someday. But when you're ready. And on your own terms. Consider this puppy the first step toward the rest of our lives. My promise to you." He rests his forehead against mine.

I finally bring myself to speak. "Let me get this straight. You just did this entire speech… to give me a promise dog?"

He stops to think for a second.

"Pretty much."

*God, I love this idiot.*

That's my cue. I start sobbing, and I mean *full-blown* sobbing. Without giving the waterworks on my face a single thought, Haze slams his lips to mine, his fingers banding around the back of my head. I kiss him back but can barely breathe, trying not to choke on my own mucus. We break away for air.

"You're crazy," I say between sniffles.

"Can I say it?"

I immediately know what he means. I usually limit his cheesy lines. But not anymore. Not right now.

"Knock yourself out."

"I'm crazy *for you.*"

Laughing, I throw myself into his arms, but I don't stay there for long. I'm way too excited to meet the new love of my life. Haze motions to come closer, and Vic makes his way to us. My heart threatens to burst out of my chest when he hands me the bundle of energy that is now my baby. The overexcited puppy wiggles around and gives my cheek a long lick.

That's it. I'm in love.

"Hi, Waze," I whisper and pet him behind his ears. His wagging tail hits me repeatedly.

"Waze?" Haze mocks.

"Yeah, it's our ship name."

"Isn't that like an app?" Vic mocks.

"Not anymore it's not." I shrug, and the guys laugh.

A shiver brushes my finger, and I look down to see a tiny snowflake melting on my hand. Joy floods my chest. It's snowing—really snowing. It's not melting this time.

It's here to stay.

This is the first time Haze's ever really been in the snow. As any first-timer would, he stares up at the sky and unfolds his hand to catch a bit of magic. A collection of snowflakes trickles down onto his palm. Waze barks as if to remind us of who's the real star here.

"Waze, meet Haze." I march toward my boyfriend, who also gets a lick from the agitated pup. Haze laughs and traps my hand into his before saying, "Happy Birthday, Kingston."

# FIFTEEN

## Broken

"What's taking so long? They'll be here soon." Haze knocks on the door. As soon as we got home, I ran into our bedroom in the hope of finding a decent dinner party outfit. I'm guessing I should make an effort at least once a year and that "once a year" should probably be my birthday.

"I have nothing to wear." My eyes wander around the floor, where the majority of my closet now lies. Haze swings the door open, crosses his buff arms over his chest, and leans against the doorway.

"What's wrong with that?" I catch his perverted smile.

I grin and turn to Waze, who's sitting on our bed with his tongue out. After he ran around his new home for a good half hour, he found happiness in our bedroom, which is where he'll be sleeping from now on since I'm never parting from this dog again.

Haze told me on the way home that he decided to get me Waze weeks ago. He pretended he didn't want a pet and agreed to play my stupid game entirely so I wouldn't suspect his gift. As for the rather hot game he came up with? He just said a guy knows an opportunity when he sees one. Is anyone surprised? *Didn't think so.*

I was a bit worried about the barking when we came home, but Haze said he'd already talked to the tenant downstairs. Turns out our neighbor is a lovely seventy-year-old half-deaf woman who didn't even know people had moved in upstairs.

"What do you say, buddy?" I say to Waze as I hold up a black dress under my chin.

He tilts his head to the side.

"Good point. Too dark."

Haze snorts. "You're talking to the dog now? How many conversations am I going to get left out of?"

"Only the ones in which you're not helping." I pick up my second choice: a pale blue dress. "How about this one?"

Waze barks.

"Yeah, that's the one. Thanks."

Haze laughs as I change out of my clothes and slip into the dress. We hear the front door close.

"We got the stuff you wanted from the store," Kendrick calls from the kitchen. "For God's sake, are we feeding a country?" I scoff at his exaggeration. We asked them to get some bread and a bottle of wine—*big deal.*

"Just Winter," Haze teases. "So, yeah, we are."

I punch him in the arm on my way to the kitchen. The new addition to our family doesn't miss a beat and follows us.

"There's my new favorite roommate!" Kendrick braces his grocery bags on the counter and drops to his knees. Waze enthusiastically runs to him, not giving a single thought to the fact that Kendrick is basically a stranger. Waze is more than a friendly dog. Waze is that dog who chills with the robbers and shows them the best things to steal around the house.

"Wait. You knew?"

Was I the only one completely clueless here?

"Of course I knew. He told me weeks ago. This one can't keep a secret to save his life." Kendrick mocks Haze, whose only reaction is to smile awkwardly and turn away.

Kendrick gets back up and pulls me into a quick embrace. "Come here, you. Happy Birthday."

"Thanks." I smile. "Hey, where's Allie?"

"She had to take a call. She'll be right up," Kendrick explains. "Smells good in here. What's for dinner? You still haven't told us what Haze's cooking."

We stashed some of the food we ordered into the fridge while we waited for them to get here. I could hardly see myself leaving all that expensive food out on the table for an hour.

"Why does it have to be Haze? Is it so hard to believe that I cooked?"

Kendrick raises an eyebrow. "Well, yeah. Considering there isn't any sign of a fire."

Haze muffles a laugh, and I elbow him.

"None of us cooked. We were out all day. We ordered in," I say. Kendrick doesn't have a chance to reply, cut off by a loud, insistent knock on the door.

At first, I find it weird that Allie would knock.

Then I understand. My instincts were right.

*She* wouldn't knock.

And the person hounding my door isn't Allie at all.

"Stop. You need to go home. Now!" is the last thing I hear before the door bursts open and someone tumbles into my apartment.

Caleb.

Correction: a very drunk Caleb.

Squeezing a liquor bottle, he can barely stand. Allie comes in seconds after him, out of breath and panicked.

"Cale, you need to go. I'm serious." She turns to us. "I'm so sorry. I couldn't stop him."

He must've been the one she was talking to on the phone.

"A tattoo?" Caleb shouts so loud I jump back a step. "You let her get a fucking tattoo?"

We all follow his hateful glare to Haze. So many questions emerge in my head. How does he even know about that?

I glance over at Allie, who shamefully stares at her feet. *He found out from her.* Only logical explanation. I texted her a picture of my tattoo as soon as we left the shop. Told her all about its meaning.

"Since when do you have a dog?" Caleb spits at the sight of Waze.

"Today. Haze got it for my birthday," I reply.

Caleb's eyes burn with fury. "Are you fucking serious right now? A dog *and* a tattoo? How far are you going to take this?"

What's his problem with Haze?

"Cale, please, it's her birthday. Don't do this," Allie begs.

"You think I don't know that? I know it's her fucking birthday." He turns to me. "We used to spend all of them together, remember? Or did your perfect boyfriend make you forget that, too?"

Guilt twists my stomach.

"How long are you going to keep this up, huh?" Caleb shouts at Haze again. I expect for Haze to be unaffected, careless. What I sure as hell don't expect… is the look in his eyes.

He's scared.

No, he's *terrified.*

"How many more ways are there for you to lie to her?" He rushes forward and pushes Haze, who barely loses his balance.

What the fuck?

*It's probably just drunk blabber. Don't panic.*

I frown. "Lie to me? What is he talking about?"

"Tell her!" Caleb pushes him again. This time, Haze pushes him right back without batting an eye. Caleb almost falls backward, gripping the closest piece of furniture.

"Tell me what?" It's my turn to yell.

Haze can't even look at me.

"What is he talking about?" I repeat.

"Tell her or I fucking will," Caleb barks. When no answer comes from Haze, Caleb continues. "He's lying to you, Winter. The bastard's been lying to you for months."

I shake my head. "What? No. He wouldn't do that."

Haze's gaze finally meets mine. His eyes are red, his jaw clenched. He doesn't speak. But his eyes do.

They're filled with anger, pain… shame?

"I followed him. A few days ago, when you were at Allie's. I followed him to his so-called *job*." He makes air quotes with his fingers. "And you want to know what I found out?"

"That's enough." Haze threatens Caleb with a step, but Caleb walks out of his reach.

"He never ever went to the auto shop. He probably doesn't even work there."

"Caleb, stop!" Haze growls, but I can hear the desperation in his tone. He's *begging* him. Unfortunately for Haze, there's no compassion, no second chances to be found in Caleb's eyes. Nothing but pure anger.

"Tell her. Tell her why you really came to Canada. Tell her the truth for once in your goddamn life."

I keep waiting to wake up from this nightmare. For Haze to give me a rational explanation or deny Caleb's accusations, but he never does.

Instead, he reaches for my hand. "Baby, please, just… come with me. I'll explain everything. Just let me take you somewhere else."

"No, tell me here." I move away from his grasp, growing terrified.

Caleb pulls his phone out before I can blink.

That's when I hear it.

The voice.

*"Yeah. I just need you to cover for me if she calls."*

Haze's voice.

Caleb flips his screen over to us.

It's a recording.

Color instantly spills out from Haze's face.

*"You don't get it… I can't. And even if I could, what the hell would I say? 'Hey, babe. You know how I moved to another country with you and said it was because I love you? Well, I lied.'"*

I stop breathing.

*"The real reason I came with you is because I found out my sister's killer might be here. Yes, I've been looking for him. For years, actually, and I never told you."*

Anything he says after that is a blur.

Tears fill my eyes, and my throat starts to hurt so bad I'd rip out my own vocal cords if I could.

I take my lower lip between my teeth in a miserable attempt to stop the tears from pouring down my face. Needless to say, I fail. They say each heart breaks differently. One's heart might break due to infidelity. Another's might break when confronted with death. There are a thousand reasons why a heart shatters into a million pieces. But for me…

One recording, a few seconds, one button.

That's what did the trick.

"He didn't come for you. He never did. Not so fucking

perfect now, *is he*?" Caleb's bitter words echo in my brain. It feels like the oxygen in my lungs has been replaced with acid. Like I'm breathing something toxic.

Each breath feels like death.

It's like I'm breathing *heartbreak*.

The pieces of the puzzle assemble themselves in my head. His weird behavior, the shady motel address in his pocket, the random phone call at the airport. How he suddenly changed his mind on a whim. I was a mess, begging him to come with me. To fight for us. When he ran up to me, whisked me into his arms, granted my wish, I thought I was dreaming…

*God, I'm such a fucking idiot.*

It was a lie.

All of it.

All along.

"Winter, wait, please. Just listen to me…" He tries to grab my hand again, but I yank it away. "I never meant to keep it from you. I wanted… I wanted to tell you so many times, I swear."

"You lied to me for months?" My voice breaks. It's so weak, so tiny, almost nonexistent. Exactly the way he made me feel.

When he doesn't deny it, it becomes real.

It dawns on me. *It's true.*

He made me believe that he was giving up his entire life for me. That he loved me so much he was willing to leave his home. I straight up asked him if he was lying to me, and he looked me dead in the eyes and lied some more. He let me make that bullshit promise about being honest with each other while he knew…

*I think I'm going to be sick.*

I back away without realizing, and Haze matches my every step. I need to get out of here.

"Winter, you don't understand. I was trying to protect you. I…" he says with teary eyes.

I can't find it in myself to listen to a single word he says. Anticipating my every move, he walks slowly like he's afraid he might scare me off. Like he's afraid if he so much as blinks, I'll disappear forever. I glance around the room. At Kendrick, Allie, Caleb. *Waze.* The pity in everybody's gaze crucifies me.

I lose it.

For the second time today, I start to cry. But the difference is, these tears aren't tears of joy. Acting on impulse, I run to the bedroom and throw the suitcase I keep in the closest on my bed. I start filling it up with the first clothes I can find—dirty clothes, clean clothes, I don't even care to check.

"Winter, please." Agony laces his tone. "Don't do this. I'm begging you."

The second his hand approaches me, I snap. "Don't touch me."

I can barely see him through the tears.

"There's so much you don't know. Let me explain." He tries to grab my wrist again, but my hands fly up to his chest and push him away. I'm packing so fast it's hard for him to keep up. Hell, it's hard for *me* to keep up. I must have like three decent outfits in there, but it'll have to do. I get my toothbrush in the bathroom and dash down the hall while he chases after me. Caleb is gone. Looks like he did what he came here to do, destroyed what he needed to destroy, and took off.

"What can I say to make this right? Tell me. Tell me what to do, please," he begs.

"Don't you get it? Nothing!" I swivel around to face him. "There's nothing you can do. We're done. It's over, Haze. We're over."

He doesn't speak for a few seconds.

Then he shakes his head.

"You… You don't mean that."

"Yes, I do."

It seems to hit him like a hundred trucks.

His mouth drops open.

A tear slowly escapes his eye.

Then two.

Then three.

Until he's full-on crying in silence.

*Fuck, I can't watch this.*

"But…" He stops and whispers a faint "I love you."

My heart splinters right in the middle. I shake my head. *Don't you dare fall for it, Winter.*

"Stop lying." I wipe the tears off my cheeks.

He won't go down without a fight. "I'm not! Winter, I love you. I love you so fucking much. You have to know that. Please tell me you know that."

"We're leaving. Come on." Allie steps in, grabbing my arm.

He doesn't miss a beat, following us. "Yes, I lied. Yes, I'm the biggest piece of shit on earth, but I never lied about the way I feel about you. I didn't make this up. I didn't make us up. I love you." His voice is weak, fragile—like cracked glass threatening to break. "Winter, please, I… I can't lose you."

In one last desperate attempt, he successfully snatches my hand into his. I don't have the strength to reject him. Our eyes meet for a second—the longest, deadliest, most unbearable of seconds. His teary eyes flicker with hope. Hope that I destroy in one move.

I take my hand back.

"Waze, come on," I call over my shoulder, and the pup runs to me. I pick him up into my arms. Kendrick grabs my suitcase without me asking. Then Allie, Kendrick, and I walk out of the apartment together.

*One step.*

*Two steps.*

*Three steps.*

*Four steps.*

Counting the steps leading to a heartbreaking moment might seem like a bit of a stretch, but for some reason, I'm doing it. Right now. I'm counting my steps.

*Five steps.*

*Six steps.*

As if it'll somehow get easier as the distance between us grows. It doesn't. But you know what does grow?

The pain.

When the sting of my fresh tattoo makes me wince, I'm reminded of the pretty words I fed myself a few hours ago.

*Just like the ink on my skin,*

*We're forever.*

Well, I guess…

Forever ends now.

# SIXTEEN

## *Regrets*

As heavy snow falls on the other side of my frozen window, I cradle my knees against my chest and search for the answer to a question that may very well end me: Can you die from a broken heart?

The internet says no.

The ache in my rib cage says *we'll see.*

Tightly wrapped in a blanket on the couch with a not-so-hot chocolate in my left hand, I pet Waze, who's snuggled up next to me, and glance at the fireplace I've literally never used until today. The fire will be dead soon, but keeping it alive would require my nonexistent energy and motivation. I'm surprised I'm even keeping *myself* alive at this point.

The night of my birthday was arguably the worst night of my entire life, after the ones where I got taken and slept in a basement, of course—ah, *fun times.* I must've gotten ten whole minutes of sleep, if that. I woke up every hour with my eyes sealed shut from dried tears, wiped them open, then cried some more.

Haze showed up at Allie's the next day. They didn't let him in, but he told Kendrick he was moving out of the apartment so that I could stay there. Said the least he could do was spare me having to move back in with my wicked mother. I do appreciate the gesture. It'll give me some time to search for a new place, and I don't think I would've survived Maika and Jaden's questions. I could hear their pestering from miles away. *Where's Haze? What happened to Haze? Are you still together? When's Haze coming over?* I went so far as to cancel my family birthday party so I wouldn't have to be reminded of how head over heels the whole world is over the boy who broke my heart.

Coming home to an empty apartment and walking into our bedroom to see half of Haze's clothes gone fucked me up in a way I didn't think possible. He left some of his stuff, but he had very few items to begin with.

I guess it hadn't fully dawned on me until then.

*Haze and I are over. Done. The end.*

I still can't believe it.

It's been four days.

Four days of torture.

Four days of asking myself questions with no answers. Well, technically, I could get answers. I'm just not emotionally ready for them. The familiar buzzing of my phone interrupts the racing thoughts in my head.

*Haze Adams is calling.*

I press Decline. How many missed calls do I have? Thirty? Forty? I've lost count. Don't even get me started on the unopened texts. I know him. He's not going to stop until I hear him out.

But I can't.

I can't answer him. I can't see his face, his smile. I can't hear his voice. I'm terrified if I do, I'll want to keep hearing it. If I do, I'll start crying again, and I just got myself to stop.

Allie's been staying with me and Kendrick since Haze moved out. Proud member of team Waze, she keeps on telling me that I'm being too hard on him. She says it's clear he didn't *only* come for his revenge and that the one thing he did wrong doesn't erase all the things he did right.

Problem is, the thing he did wrong was the foundation of all the things he did right.

And, in the end… we built a house on a land made of lies.

"God, it smells like sadness in here," Allie says when she walks inside the apartment and shuts the door. She's been out for a few hours. She had classes today. I've been getting some assignments from one of the girls from school, but I haven't been able to bring myself to go. I've been considering dropping out, if I'm being completely honest. I wasn't a hundred percent sold on journalism even before any of this happened.

Waze jumps off the couch, barking and running toward Allie. She pets him with a smile. He's starting to like her more than me. Understandable as she's the one who's been walking him for the past few days.

"I got Chinese. I'm not letting you starve over a boy." She takes off her coat and kicks her boots off. It's been snowing for three days straight.

"Where's Kendrick?" I ask.

"He went to run some errands. He'll be back soon. Hey, hm… Caleb called me again. He told me to tell you he's sorry."

I shrug as a response, and Allie knows better than to insist. I can't technically be mad at him for exposing Haze. Yes, he was the biggest asshole I've ever met, but in the end, he was the only one to be honest with me.

What hurt the most is how satisfied he was when he told me. How much he seemed to enjoy driving a stake through my heart. And did he really have to do it on my birthday? In front of everybody to top it all off?

"Seriously? You haven't moved at all since I left? You're going to merge with the couch, Winter. What's next? A wedding?" Allie rests takeout boxes in front of me and drops down on the couch. I bend forward and pick my food off the coffee table.

"You know what? Maybe I should. At least the couch won't lie to me."

She laughs. "Winter Kingston, now dating furniture after giving up on men."

My phone lights up again.

*Haze Adams is calling.*

I press Decline and hope she didn't see it. I don't want her to talk about hi—

"He's persistent, I give him that."

Shit.

"You still won't talk to him?"

I don't reply.

"Listen, I know I don't get to tell you what to do, but you should pick up. At least give him a chance to explain."

"Why? For him to lie to me again? Roberto and I are good, thanks." I pat the couch, and she chuckles.

"Now she's naming the couch. That's it. Get up." She plucks the takeout box from my hand before I can take a bite.

"Hey!" My empty stomach screams at me. I haven't eaten once today, and it's past 1:00 p.m.

"Later. Did you shower today?" She arches an eyebrow. I shake my head. I probably look like Shrek. I've been doing my best to avoid mirrors. I already have a broken heart; I don't need nightmares, too. "You, my dear, are in desperate need of an Allievention."

"Allievention?" I frown.

"Allie intervention, duh. Get your ass off the couch," She pulls me to my feet. I groan. "Hop in the shower. We're having a girls' day."

## *Haze*

I curse under my breath as my call goes straight to voicemail for the billionth time today. I want to throw my phone against the wall, take a baseball bat to the screen until shattered pieces spread across the floor. I want to break it, wreck it. But I know

I'll just end up running to the store to get a new one so I can keep calling her—sorry, getting *ignored* by her.

She's been dodging my calls for the past four days, and I'm losing my goddamn mind. It's gotten to the point of thinking I hear her voice everywhere I go, almost having a heart attack whenever my phone lights up. Every time, I hope it's a message from her, and every time… it's not.

I can't stop thinking about her alone at home. I wonder what's stopping me from driving over there and begging her to listen to me. She won't have a choice but to forgive me.

I know she needs time and I shouldn't come back until she's ready to talk to me, but fuck, it's hard. Crashing at Vic's is already pissing me off. He's going through heartbreak, too. And while I'm a fucking mess, I'm nothing compared to him. You see, I'm a mess with hope—*he* has none. He's sloppy, rude, getting drunk at every hour of the day, and he's bringing random girls home every night. He goes out, finds someone to fuck, brings her home, and kicks her out. Then he goes back out the next day and does it all over again.

*It's over, Haze.*

Her words rip me open.

No, it's not.

It's not over.

Not for me.

I miss her. So bad. I even miss Waze, which is ridiculous considering I've barely lived with him for a couple of hours.

*Waze*. I wince. Our ship name. I hope it's not gone forever.

"Dude, we going out tonight. You coming?" Vic pounds on the guest room's door.

The same question.

"Pass."

The same answer.

I hear him sigh. He's been hanging out with the shittiest people lately, a bunch of frat boys that drag him deeper into depression. He's desperate to get me to be his wingman, but I don't give a single shit about picking up girls at the club.

I have a girlfriend, I told him.

She dumped your ass, he replied.

And he isn't wrong.

I know I fucked up. I always knew if she found out, she'd think I only came to avenge my sister. I have to prove myself to her. She has to know that I wasn't just using her to get to Marcus. She has to know that all I did, I did for her.

*One word, kid. Just one and bad things might start to happen.*

Ricky's words claw at me. There's so much she doesn't know. So much she doesn't want to hear. All I can do is pray they don't know that she found out. Sure, Caleb didn't know or tell her shit about the organization, but I doubt they'd see it the same way.

Fuck, how can I keep her safe when she won't even see me? I need to do something. But what?

"Have you seen my earring?" some girl Vic brought home squeaks in the living room. From what I heard last night, she's a screamer.

Her sentence slaps me right in the face.

It all becomes clear.

I know what I have to do.

## *Winter*

When I step out of the shower and hear laughter, I wonder if Allie is watching reruns of *Friends* or laughing at her own thoughts—which wouldn't surprise me. Maybe Kendrick came home? Whatever it is, I doubt she invited people over. I didn't exactly make tons of friends since moving back.

I dry off my hair with a towel and throw on the black dress Allie picked out for me. She said my pajamas aren't good enough for what she's planned. *Agree to disagree, but okay.*

When my eyes come in contact with my reflection in the mirror, nostalgia rolls over me. This is the black dress Ryder bought for me when Haze and I were playing runaway in Colton Gate. This seems like forever ago. Allie had no idea about the history of this dress when she randomly picked it out of my closet. Haze wasn't big on me wearing it at first. I find myself smiling at the thought. Then my smile fades completely.

*Well, he can't stop me anymore.*

I step out of the bathroom, my slightly wet hair falling down my back. I'm all dressed up, looking a lot better on the outside than I feel on the inside. I even put on a little bit of makeup. Not that I really had a choice. I'd rather not make any children cry today.

"There she is," Allie cheers when I turn the corner. Sitting on the couch with Kendrick, she smiles at me.

I narrow my eyes. "You two made all that noise by yourself?"

She grins. "Not exactly."

I let out a yelp when three people jump up from behind the couch and scream a loud "Surprise!"

I blink a few times.

Kass, Alex, and Will.

All standing in my living room.

"Missed us?"

# SEVENTEEN

## *Unexpected*

"Guys? W-What are you doing here?" I ask, overwhelmed with emotions. I haven't seen them in so long. Especially Kass and Alex, whom I haven't seen in person since I left Maria's house at the beginning of the summer. Kass and I have been texting here and there, but she's been busy with law school. As for Alex, I only kept in touch with him through Kendrick.

"I heard from a little birdie that my girl's going through a rough time." Kass opens her arms for me, and I walk right into her embrace, already a mess.

"I can't believe you're all here. How did you…" I'm at a loss for words.

"It was her idea." Kendrick nudges Allie.

"No way? You set this all up?"

"Well, you kept on saying how much you missed your family, and I thought it was about time I met my boyfriend's friends. I reached out a few weeks ago, and they were all free around the same time, so I convinced them to come and, well, here we are."

"Al, you're insane." I hug her, and she laughs.

Will's eyes widen. "Wait. Did she just say boyfriend?" His gaze sways between Allie and Kendrick. "As in you two?"

Kendrick nods. "You missed a lot, man."

Words fail to describe how happy I feel when Kendrick and Will bro hug the way they used to.

I'm so glad they made peace.

Last I heard, they hadn't talked all summer. I have no idea what happened for them to reunite but…

*Wait, Kass is here.*

Isn't that weird for them? Unless they're together again and Kendrick finally got over himself? They sure as hell don't seem together standing as far away from each other as humanly possible.

"So… You just happened to invite them exactly when I'm having a mental breakdown?" I ask.

"Oh Lord, what's the idiot done this time?" Will pulls me into a hug. Alex is next in line.

"Are you familiar with this?" Allie chuckles. "I can barely keep up with those two."

"Familiar?" Alex scoffs.

"Please, we've seen this a million times," Will laughs. "Here's how it goes: Haze does something stupid, Winter leaves his ass, he realizes what he's done, tries to win her back, and she makes it hard on him until she eventually gives in and comes crawling back into his arms."

"Gee, thanks, guys." I roll my eyes, and they laugh.

"Let's just say we know better than to bet against Haze and Winter by now." Kass loops our arms together and rests her head on my shoulder. I missed her. I missed all of them.

Will spots my untouched Chinese food. "Hey, whose food is that?"

"Winter's," Allie says.

"Are you going to eat that?" he asks, but before I can reply, the box is in his hands and his mouth is full.

"Actually, I haven't eaten in two days and I'm starving, but help yourself, you pig."

"I'll leave you some." He smirks. "Maybe."

*Charming.*

"Answers, please. Why did you break up?" Will insists.

Anxiety rushes through me at the mere thought of reliving my birthday party all over again. Allie catches on immediately.

"Nope!" She sticks her finger in the air. "Today, we don't talk about him. We don't mention his name. Haze Adams doesn't exist. No, you know what, let's spice it up. For every time Winter talks about Haze in any way, she'll have to take a shot tonight when we go out, how about that?"

They all agree, happily taking part in my future misery. I wish I could say that they're wrong. Confidently state that I can resist talking about him for the rest of the day, but that would be a big, fat lie.

After all, breaking the rules is what got me in this mess in the first place…

"DON'T YOU ALL JUST LOVE SHOPPING?" Allie

smiles, bags upon bags of new clothes dangling off her arms.

"I fell asleep three times during that sentence," Kendrick says, making Will and Alex laugh. After my unexpected guests settled in, Allie decided we weren't staying inside the entire day and dragged us out to the mall. We've been here for two hours tops, and the girls have already spent around two hundred dollars each.

Kendrick and Allie said they'd sleep at Allie's place to leave the two guest rooms to Kass and the guys. Will still had to take the couch, but I'm sure he'll manage. They're not staying for long. A few days at most.

I wonder what Haze is doing.

If he's as miserable as I am.

Man, if I had to take a shot every time I *think* about him, I'd be throwing up in the water fountain by now. As for talking about him, I'm already at three shots. I tried. I really did. But I can't help it. Everything I see reminds me of him.

"I can actually hear you thinking about him." Allie elbows me jokingly. "Is this guy really all you can think about?"

*Yes.*

"No. Of course not."

"Why did we agree to come to Canada again?" Will whines.

"Because you love me." I shoot him a smile.

Will gasps. "Oh my God."

I frown. "What?"

"She smiles."

I give out a quiet laugh. He's right. I've had a scowl stuck to my face since this morning. But their visit really turned my mood around. When we pass a video game store, the guys say their goodbyes and enter the only store in the entire mall they're actually interested in. I seize the opportunity when we lose them into the crowd.

I turn to Kass. "Okay, mind telling me what the hell happened between you and Will?"

"What do you mean?" She plays dumb.

"Please, I barely know you guys, and even I feel the sexual tension," Allie remarks.

"What happened when he went back to you after he left that first week? Did you ever get back togeth—"

"Wait." She cuts me off. "He left the first week?"

"Well, yeah. He was a mess the whole time. Then he just packed his things one morning and took off."

Color spills from her features. "I… You mean to tell me he was back in Florida all summer?"

Crap. Maybe I should've kept my mouth shut.

"I mean, I'm not sure. He just said he had to go back home. He and Kendrick got into a huge fight. He didn't go back to you?"

She traps her lip between her teeth, pain flashing in her gaze. "No, he didn't. Today's the first time I've seen him since he left with Kendrick four months ago."

What the hell?

"But he was such a wreck over you. I could've sworn—"

"It doesn't matter. It's over." She shuts me out. "I don't want to talk about it."

I'm about to fight her on this, to try and piece back their relationship together, but composure depletes from my body when I stare ahead of me.

My heart breaks all over again.

Haze.

He just walked out of a jewelry store, holding a small see-through bag. In a perfect world, he'd walk in the opposite direction, turn away, and never notice me. But in this one?

He heads right toward us.

One second is enough. He gives us a quick, careless glance. Then his eyes widen as if the information just registered.

Right away, he does a double take.

My gaze collides with the iciest blue eyes I've ever known, and the feelings I've been repressing infiltrate my cracked heart.

"Shit, is that Haze?" Kass comes in late to the party.

Both Kass and Allie grab my arm and begin dragging me in the opposite direction. But I know it's pointless. That's Haze we're talking about. He saw me. He isn't about to just let me run off. As predicted, he sprints over to me in record time. Dark circles rim his eyes. He looks exhausted. I flinch under his gaze and stare at my feet.

"Hey," he says, almost in a whisper.

"Hey? That's all you have to say. Hey?" Allie gets all up in his face like an overprotective watchdog.

"Five minutes, that's all I want," he begs, and I pray that Allie won't fall for it. I know that she likes him. If it were up to her, we'd be together forever and have a thousand babies.

Allie's eyes ask if I'm okay with talking to him. *Am I?* I don't know. Part of me wants to run to him, hide into his arms, forget any of this happened. But the other… the other is crumbling when he stands this close to me.

Succumbing to the pressure, I nod.

"You have one minute," Allie says before dragging Kass two steps away to listen.

Silence.

My eyes remain fixated on the ground.

"Winter, look at me."

I draw a sharp breath and oblige. Looking into his eyes makes it all that much worse. Pain slices through my beating heart like butter. Like it was meant to be there. Like it was meant to destroy me.

"I've been calling," he starts.

"I know."

"Texting, too."

"I know."

"Winter, please…" He steps forward, which results in me stepping back so fast you'd think I was trained. I'm acting like a hurt puppy. Untrusting, terrified to suffer again.

"Don't," I warn. The closer he gets, the harder it is for me to keep it together.

"I'm so, so sorry. If you would just let me explain… I miss you. So much. I'm losing my fucking mind here. Please let me come home so we can talk about this."

I snap. "Talk about what? The fact that you've been lying to me for months? The fact that you made me believe you loved me so much you'd leave your entire life behind for me, when, all this time… You were just… choosing your revenge over me?"

"I didn't choose my revenge over you. I know that's what it looks like, but—"

"It doesn't just look like it. That's what happened."

"I didn't choose. I could never choose." He steps forward, and this time, I let him. "I guess I just thought I could have both. And I know it sounds fucked-up. I know I'm a fucking disaster, but I'm a disaster who loves you. Don't ever doubt that."

I can feel the tears amass in my eyes. *Not now.* I was fine barely a second ago, but seeing him in front of me, hearing his voice, getting wrapped up in his scent, it leaves me defenseless. *This* is exactly why I didn't want to see him.

"I should've told you why I couldn't go with you the first time. I should've told you that the second I found him I'd be on the first plane back to you."

"No, it's okay. I hope you find him, I really do. I want him to pay for what he did. I hope you get justice for your sister."

He stares at me, dreading what's coming.

"But?"

"I just hope he's worth it."

Pain ripples through him, but I don't let myself watch a second longer, terrified that every second near him is a second closer to my undoing. I tear my eyes away, turn on my heels, and walk back to the girls.

TWELVE. TWELVE TIMES. I'VE BROKEN THE "no Haze" rule twelve times in less than five hours. Even after the random encounter with him at the mall, I told myself I'd keep the Haze talk to a minimum. Did it stop me from bawling like an actual baby and telling the girls all about him the second we came home? Nope. Luckily for me, the guys stayed at the mall longer than we did, which earned my liver a chance in hell at surviving tonight.

Sitting on my bed, I wait patiently for Kass to finish straightening my hair while Allie hypes me up. I know she means well, but I can recognize a pity compliment when I see one. The boys are playing video games in the living room. I'm sure Kass was glad to get away from Will—even if it's just one room away. Being in Will's presence seems to soak up every drop of happiness from her body. I think she still has feelings for him, although she'd rather die than admit it.

I smile at Waze, who's sleeping peacefully at the end of the bed. In the past few days, he's made me so happy, yet so unbelievably sad. I feel awful about it. It's not his fault. He's perfect, but everything about him reminds me of Haze. I mean, his name literally represents our entire relationship for God's sake.

Bringing the glass of wine in my hands to my lips, I stare blankly at the wall.

I hate red wine.

But it tastes better than my tears.

*Wow, that was really dark.*

"What do you think was in the bag?" Kass works the last piece of my hair.

"I don't know. An engagement ring maybe?" Allie suggests.

"He wouldn't dare propose just to get her back, would he?" Kass asks.

"I don't know. Not that it would work if he did. Hey, Winter, I'm sorry I lied to you for months, but would you marry me? For real this time?" Allie scoffs. "I mean, the guy's not that stupid, is he?"

"I beg to differ."

My eyes jump to Kendrick standing in the doorway. We didn't hear him come in.

Allie smiles at him. "Hey, you."

"Are you guys ready yet?"

"Five minutes," Allie promises.

Forty-five minutes later, we're ready.

Stepping into a cab, we find ourselves heading for the trendiest club in town. I'm not a club kind of girl. Never have been, never will be. But tonight, I'm willing to give it a try.

I assess the overcrowded nightclub in front of me. You can practically feel the bass vibrating from outside. Girls wearing short dresses parade in and out of the building, and I look down at my outfit. Allie and Kass got me all dressed up, but I'm wearing a big-ass coat and a scarf on top of my outfit. I don't care that we're clubbing. I'm not catching pneumonia tonight.

I hear the guys discuss the legal drinking age being nineteen here instead of twenty-one.

They're thinking numbers.

I am, too.

The final number is fourteen.

Fourteen chances to forget him.

# EIGHTEEN

## Drunk Call

With deafening music busting my ears, I slam the empty shot glass on the counter and sink my teeth into the lemon wedge with a gag. I'm not a hundred percent sure how many shots is too much. But I do know I passed my limit a long time ago.

"That was awful." I quiver in disgust while Alex, Kendrick, and Will cheer me on. Gathered around the bar, we stare at the countless tequila shots displayed in a line.

"What number was that?" It's got to be over ten, at least.

"Six," Will says, and I grimace. We've been at the club for a few hours now, and although the guys were nice enough to space out the shots, they weren't kidding about me drinking the memory of Haze away.

"Okay, enough! She's not actually drinking fourteen—she'll throw up for hours," Kass slurs and splits the eight shots amongst the guys. Allie, Kass, and I are already gone, thanks to our embarrassingly low tolerance, but the guys could keep going all night, and I don't doubt for a second that they will if given the chance.

"I got to take a leak," Kendrick says.

"Me too." Allie gets off her stool.

"I'll come with." Kass follows.

As soon as they squeeze their way through the crowd, Alex's phone rings. A smile spreads on his face at the caller ID.

"Who's that? Your girl?" I tease. I find Morgan and Alex to be a surprisingly perfect match. I absolutely loved Morgan during the time I spent in Florida. I'm glad they found each other.

He nods, his smile widening. "I'll be right back."

He walks off, leaving me alone with Will for once in a blue moon. I've been dying to talk to him since he got here. Just because my love life is a disaster doesn't mean his and Kass's should be, too.

I remember how Will's hands rolled into fists when some guy showed up at the bar and shamelessly hit on Kass earlier, the way he stared down the bottom of his beer bottle as though he was trying to drown in it. There's still something there.

And it's worth fighting for.

"Okay. What the hell happened with Kass?" I swap stools to sit next to him.

He scoffs. "Straightforward when we're drunk, aren't we?"

"I'm serious. Either you found out you're gay or you're really, really stupid, because you blew it, Will. Bad. You told me you loved her in your car that day and then—"

"Winter, can we not do this now?" he hisses and downs his tequila shot in seconds.

"Is it because of Kendrick?" I insist. "Because you're scared of what he'll say? He already found out, and you're obviously still friends. Who cares at this point?" Apparently, six tequila shots make me persistent—more like *annoying*, but whatever.

"No, it's not that…" He pauses. "You wouldn't get it, okay?"

He tilts his beer back to take a sip.

"Do you want her with someone else?"

He stops moving.

Finally, he puts the glass bottle down and meets my eyes.

"Do you want her to move on from you? Is that what you want, Will?"

His eyes drop to the bar.

"It's clear she still has feelings for you *for now*, but it won't last forever. Sooner or later, you'll lose her. For good. Some other dude will realize how great she is. She'll meet some nice lawyer guy at college, fall deeply in love with him, and forget all about you. I don't know why you left that day, or why you didn't go back to Kass, but keep this up and you might just have to live the rest of your life wishing you'd had the balls to get the girl."

I anticipate the rising of his walls but get the complete opposite. His barriers unravel before my eyes, falling to oblivion and leaving him unguarded.

"Okay, fine," he gives in. "I'm going completely insane, but what the fuck am I supposed to do? I left. She probably hates me."

"Did you try talking to her? Explaining?"

He nibbles on his lip. "I figured she'd moved on. She's been icing the hell out of me. You really think she still cares?"

*Boys are so stupid.*

"I think you won't know unless you try."

He gets up, doesn't say a word, and begins to walk away.

"Go get her, tiger!" I cheer, and he turns his head one second before the crowd sucks him in.

"Winter?"

"Yeah?"

"Thanks for being a stubborn pain in the ass."

"No problem." My smile wavers. "Wait, what?"

He's already gone.

"HOW MUCH DID YOU HAVE TO drink?" Allie leans forward and screams through the EBM music. The dance floor is packed, the kind of packed that would usually suffocate me, but I'm way too drunk to care.

"Just one drink." I lift my glass to her eyes. "That I filled up multiple times."

Allie breaks into laughter, circling my shoulders with her arm as we dance. It's been an hour since I talked Will up. No sign of either him or Kass since then. Allie and I have been dancing by ourselves for a good thirty minutes while the guys took part in a chugging contest with strangers. When Kendrick and Alex push their way to us on the dance floor, Allie flings her arms around her boyfriend's neck. They kiss, grope—the whole package—and for the first time since they got together, I have to look away.

I focus on the blinking lights, the dizzying bass, everything but the happy couple next to me. I keep dancing, finishing my drink in one gulp, and by the time I turn around…

Everybody's gone.

How long have I been dancing alone?

I get off the dance floor, stumbling my way toward the entrance of the pub for much-needed fresh air. My phone rings, and I pull it out, expecting it to be Allie calling to ask where I am. It's not.

*Haze Adams is calling.*

My heart sinks.

I don't answer, and a new voicemail pops up on my screen.

A couple of seconds pass. He calls again.

*Does this boy have absolutely no clue as to when he should give up?*

I watch the incoming call for a while. Then I do something I'll probably regret tomorrow.

"You do know one voicemail is just as effective as thirty-four?" I blurt.

He doesn't speak right away,

"Winter?" He sounds in disbelief that I picked up.

"Who else?"

"Are you… okay?"

Now that I finally took his call, he's not sure what to say.

"No, I'm not okay. I fell for a fucking moron! You keep lying to me. Why are you always lying to me? Is there a sign on my forehead that says *I'm a dumbass, please lie to me*?"

"Are you drunk?" His tone shifts from shocked to worried.

"I would've done everything for you, but you keep fucking with my heart and… You know what? I want my heart back. You don't know how to take care of it. I'll be expecting a refund in five business days." I snort at my own joke until I'm hit by the urge to start sobbing. *Drunk-girl problems.*

"You're completely wasted," he states.

"Well, thanks, Captain Obvious."

"What have you been drinking?"

I scoff. "You mean what I have *not* been drinking."

"Winter," he warns.

"Chill, Mom. Just tequila."

"Where the hell are you?"

"In the closet, looking for Narnia."

*I don't know this girl.*

"Answer the question," he insists.

I tell him the club name. Why am I still talking to him?

I want to go back inside the second I walk outside. It's cold as heck, and I left my coat at the coat check.

"Are you alone?"

"Of course not. I came here with Allie, Kass, and the guys, but everybody left me to go make out. Turns out some boyfriends aren't lying pieces of shit." I almost trip over my own feet.

He completely dismisses my insults. "I'll be there in ten."

The line goes dead.

Only then do I realize what I've done.

*Well, shit.*

## *Haze*

Parking my car in the no-parking zone in front of the building without a care, I scan the large fluorescent sign reading the club's name in capital letters. I can't think straight, blinded by anger. Why did she do this to herself? A million scenarios, each worse than the last, clash in my head. She's wasted and vulnerable in a place filled with perverts preying on drunk girls. Guilt stabs me.

*She's in there getting drunk because of you.*

Pushing people out of my way, I sneak into the nightclub while the bouncer is checking out the tits of a blonde in line. I scan the crowd, searching for her face. I spot her at the bar, talking to some asshole. I immediately recognize her dress. She looks so fucking good, and I hate that I'm not the only one noticing.

My feet lead the way. Next thing I know, I'm standing tall next to them. She fake-laughs at something he said. I know Winter's laugh, and this one? *Complete bullshit.* Still, it still ignites a spark of jealousy within me.

"What's a babe like you doing here alone?"

My fists clench. He's going to need a face transplant if he calls her that one more time.

"She's not alone," I cut in, and she jumps at the sight of me.

"Haze? I told you not to come," she scolds, almost falling

off her stool. I've never seen her this drunk.

"Do I look like I care? We're leaving." I reach for her arm, but she flings it away from my grasp, her fingers adverting to her drink for another sip. "Give me that." I swipe the glass from her hand and throw its contents over my shoulder without bothering to check behind me.

A girl shrieks and glances around for someone to blame.

*Oops.*

"Hey!" Winter's angry face should probably be threatening, but it only enhances how adorable she is.

The guy interrupts us. "Do you have a problem, man?"

"Yeah, you," I say blatantly.

"What did you just say?" He gets up from his seat.

"Kyle, don't." She steps in between us.

"My name's Kevin," the guys says, offended, and I can't stop a mocking laugh from spilling out of me. She doesn't spare him a single look.

"I'll go with you. No need to freak out, Hazie."

Leading the way to the exit, she squeezes through the crowd, almost tripping over thin air multiple times. By instinct, I wrap my arms around her waist to help her stand. She stiffens up at my touch but doesn't reject it. Far from it. She leans back into me for support, her shoulders deflating with relief.

Does she miss me as much as I miss her?

If she was sober, she'd have kicked my ass about four times by now. I get her coat at the front, and we walk out of the club.

I help her get into the passenger seat of my car, then speed down the frozen roads in complete silence. A soft snow covers my windshield.

"Why did you do this to yourself?" I ask after a while.

"What, you mean have fun? Sorry, didn't know it was a crime," she grumbles.

"You don't have to get wasted to have fun, Winter."

"Maybe, but I have to get wasted to stop thinking about you."

My lungs miss a breath.

She said that so casually. Like it wouldn't wreck the fuck out of me. We come to a red light, and I look her way. I can't help zooming in on her pouty red lips. Her lipstick makes her mouth look like fucking candy to me.

"Well, here's a problem. I don't want you to stop thinking about me."

She severs the eye contact. "Sucks to be you, then."

Let me tell you: it sucks to be me all right.

When I pull into the apartment parking spot, I hurry out of the car in fear that she'll run to the door and go right back to ignoring me.

"Do you need a hand with getting inside?" I help her out of my car.

"No." She trips two steps in, and I catch her.

"Come on." I motion to the door with my chin.

"I said I don't need help."

"I don't care." I lace her arm around my shoulder with one hand on her waist, and she doesn't fight me further. I unlock the door for her. We enter the elevator, and I select our floor. Just as we're about to step into the hall, she wiggles out of my reach and presses every single button on the elevator panel.

"What the hell are you doing?" I rush her out before the doors close.

"I always wanted to do that," she snickers, proud of herself.

I can't help my grin as we march down the hall. I unlock the door for her and flip the light switch while she sends her shoes flying. Waze comes running down the hall with a waving tail. Excited beyond belief, he jumps on Winter, then on me.

"Hi, baby." Winter kneels down to pet him, and I wince at the scene. He was supposed to be ours. I wonder if she changed his name. Rising back up, she struggles to remove her coat. I tug on her sleeves to make it easier.

"What happened to you?" I frown at the sight of a huge stain on her dress. It smells and looks sticky as fuck. Makes sense that I didn't notice in the darkness of the club. "Is that booze?"

"No, it's piss." She rolls her eyes. "Yeah, it's booze, *duh*."

"We've got to get you changed."

"I just want to sleep." She pets Waze some more and rushes to the bedroom. I follow, but I can't stop her from jumping on our bed—sorry, *her* bed—in a starfish position.

"Sober Winter would commit murder if she saw you right now," I mock. Winter is kind of a clean freak; she got that from her mom. I usually have to take my shoes off the second I walk in. So, jumping on our bed with a dirty, sticky dress? She'd lose it. "Promise you'll get changed once I leave."

"Or what?"

"Or you'll sleep in your disgusting dress and regret it tomorrow."

She arches an eyebrow, propping herself on her elbows as she analyzes me intently. Then she gets off the bed and walks over to me.

"There are a lot of things I could do and regret tomorrow."

I can practically hear myself gulp at her words.

"Just promise you'll take it off and I'll lea—"

My eyes want to pop out of their sockets when she tugs her dress straps down her shoulders and strips right in front of me. The fabric falls to her feet, exposing her white lace underwear and perfectly curved body.

*Fuck.*

Feeling like I'm violating her, I tear my eyes away.

"Winter." I scold.

"What? You don't like the view?" She moves forward, so close her breasts mash against my chest.

"You need to sleep." I keep my eyes firmly on the wall, every fiber of my being begging me to take just one look.

It's fine. I can do this. I can control myself… *I think?*

"I should go." I clear my throat and begin to turn away, but she stops me.

"Don't. Stay." Her face is barely an inch from mine.

"You don't mean that. You're just dru—"

I'm cut off by her mouth colliding with mine.

Sirens and warning bells blare out in my head. Still, I kiss her back. I jerk her body closer and cave to her familiar and eager lips. Tequila lingers on her tongue, but she tastes like fucking relief to me.

Relief, happiness…

Misery.

The misery I'll feel when she comes to her senses and leaves me again.

I take her lip between my teeth, and a moan emanates from somewhere deep within her throat. I'm already so fucking hard you'd think we were doing way more than kissing.

*Stop, this isn't right.*

My body won't comply to my brain. I missed this. Her skin, her lips, every inch of her. I thought I'd never get to feel her this way again. Every touch feels like running out of time. I want more. I *need* more. But more may never come, so I can't let go while it's here.

I lift her up into my arms, and she closes her legs around my waist the way she's done so many times before.

Winter.

My Winter.

I collapse on top of her on our bed, and she grinds against me with clear intent. She's this close to being completely naked, and I know if she—

She unhooks her bra in one move and lobs it to the floor.

Just like that, I'm a goner.

My instincts take over, and I slide my hand up her ribs to grab a handful of her tits. I nibble at her neck, suck on the soft skin under her ear. Her breathing grows hollow, and when I twirl my tongue around her nipple, biting the tip lightly, she cries out. She captures my face and slams our mouths together again, seeking my belt to unbuckle it.

"I think someone's awake," she smirks and curves her hand inside my jeans.

*Haze, what the fuck are you doing?*

"Stop!" I snap back to reality. "We can't."

I'm off her body and back to my feet in seconds. I could punch myself. Talk about poor self-control.

"What? Why?" she questions.

"Because you're not yourself right now."

She's about to say something, but she clamps her mouth shut, suddenly very aware of her nakedness. She covers her nipples with her arms. Silent, I walk to the closet and throw her one of the T-shirts I left here. One, because I couldn't possibly pack everything all at once, and, second, because I needed an excuse to come back.

"I'm not sleeping with you knowing that you'll regret it tomorrow. I respect you too much."

"I won't. I won't regret it. Haze, I'll never regret you." The glimmer in her eyes kills me. The worst part is, I know, right now, in her drunk, non-Winter state, she genuinely believes that.

"Yes, you will," I protest.

*You already have.*

She pulls my shirt over her head. I love seeing her wear something that's mine. If it's the only way part of me will ever be close to her again, I'll give her my whole goddamn closet.

*I'm such a whipped little bitch.*

"I really should go." I shake my head, inwardly cursing my lack of judgment, and walk to the door.

"Don't," she yelps.

I stop.

"Please, stay. Please." she begs.

*Just the alcohol talking, Haze. Not really how she feels.*

I glance at her over my shoulder. "You're going to wake up tomorrow and want me to leave."

"No, I won't." She shakes her head. "I promise, I won't. Just stay, please. I don't want to spend another night without you. Not again. Not ever."

How I wish she could wake up sober and still mean that.

"You hate me," I remind her.

With sad eyes, she says, "Almost as much as I love you."

Her words rip me open.

Then piece me back together.

Then tear me apart once more.

I didn't know how bad I needed that confirmation until now.

To hear her say that she still loves me. That there's still hope. I get my coat off, walk over to the bed, and slip under the blanket. She snuggles up to me, resting her head on my chest and nuzzling her nose in my neck. This feels so different. So fragile. I extend my arm around her and stroke her shoulder.

"Good night, Haze," she murmurs.

And in that moment,

For a brief instant, the tiniest, fleetest of seconds,

It feels like we're okay and I'll see her smiling at me in the morning.

# NINETEEN
## *Risks*

"What the actual fuck?"

A voice wakes me up. A female voice, to be exact. Forcing my eyes open, I grimace at the light of day. Allie is standing in the doorway with her arms crossed over her chest. Not going to lie, she looks like hell. Her hair is all over the place, and her makeup is smudged down her cheeks. Winter isn't the only one who got hammered last night.

Winter.

My eyes drift to her. To her body next to mine. She's still sleeping.

"Good morning," I say coarsely.

"What are you doing here?" she asks, quietly this time.

I rub my eyes. "I called Winter last night. She was blackout drunk and all alone. I picked her up and brought her home."

"Tell me you didn't sleep with her when she was drunk, Haze?" She zeroes in on my bare chest. I tossed my shirt sometime during the night.

"What? Of course not."

The irony isn't lost on me.

"I hope you know this doesn't change anything," Allie says.

"I know." *Boy, do I know it.* "She just didn't want to be alone last night."

"You should go before she wakes up," Allie advises.

"Yeah, you're probably right," I agree half-heartedly. "Can you please make sure she gets this?" I sneak out of bed and tiptoe around the room. Picking my coat off the floor, I pluck the black box I got for her out of my pocket and hold it out to Allie.

She takes the box hesitantly. "Haze, if it's what I think it is…"

"It's not an engagement ring if that's what you're wondering. Just give it to her, okay?"

She gives in, nodding and closing the door as quietly as she can. I throw my T-shirt on, pick up my coat, and walk to the nightstand to open its drawer. I reach for the painkiller bottle I keep in there, spread out a few pills on the nightstand for Winter to see when she wakes up, and give her one last look…

Before I leave the only person who feels like home.

## *Winter*

I wake up with a sledgehammer rattling my skull—at least that's what it feels like. Wincing, I peel my eyes open, only to squeeze them shut right away. The pain is slightly more bearable with my eyes closed, but the pounding in my head doesn't lie: six tequila shot was *definitely* over my limit.

The memories of the previous night burst through my mind uninvited, and my eyes fly open, headache be damned.

Haze is gone.

He left.

A handful of confusing emotions seep into me: relief, regret… disappointment? I wish I could say I don't remember the previous night, but I do.

I remember everything.

Haze calling. Me picking up in a moment of weakness. Him rushing into the club and getting into an argument with some dude at the bar. I remember him trying to change me out of my yucky dress. The way I practically threw myself at him. His teeth on my nipple, his tongue on my neck, my moans…

*How fucking pathetic can I be?*

I even asked him to stay. So much for being mad at him. I face palm myself and glance sideways. Painkillers are laid out on the night table. I reach over and capture the pills into the palm of my hand with a small smile. I know he left them for me. After all this, after I flat out told him he was a moron last night, he still couldn't help himself.

I grab my phone, secretly hoping to see a text from him. There isn't one. I do, however, have a message from Caleb. He's been blowing up my phone, too.

I didn't tell you everything.
There's more.

I delete the text with a swipe of my thumb. I'm not letting him hurt me anymore. I glance down at the oversized T-shirt swallowing my body whole. Pain radiates off the fabric, digging into my skin and reminding me of who the shirt belongs to.

When I step into the kitchen, I'm greeted by an excited puppy, Allie swallowing pills, Will and Alex eating cereal, and Kass cooking eggs. I hear the shower in the distance and assume that's where Kendrick is.

"Damn, Winter. You didn't tell us you got cast in *The Walking Dead*," Will grins at the sight of me, and I roll my eyes.

Kass turns at the sound of my name. "Hey, what happened to you last night? We couldn't find you anywhere."

She and Will exchange a not-so-subtle look.

*The look.*

"Not that we were really looking," Will mutters, so quietly I almost don't hear him, and keeps eating.

A smirk creeps onto my lips as I pick up Waze and kiss him like a maniac. I'd pay to know what happened after I talked Will up last night. Did he finally grow some balls? Did he win her back?

"I was…" I'm hesitant to tell them. "I was wasted, and Haze picked me up."

"You called him?" Kass fails to hide her surprise.

"Technically, he called me." I put Waze down, walk to the fridge, and grab a water bottle for the painkillers.

"So, *that's* why I saw him sneak out this morning." Will's

insinuations are as clear as day.

"Nothing happened." I bring his dirty thoughts to a stop. *But you wanted it to*, a voice in my head taunts.

I can't help but be disappointed that he took off without a word. He could've at least left a note or something. Not that I blame him. He probably thought that I'd kick him out anyway.

"Speaking of." Allie's head snaps up. "I came to check up on you this morning. I told Haze to leave."

Realization finds me. "Oh."

*She's* the reason he left?

Ah. Shit. I hate that I'm mad. I can't feel this way.

"He asked me to give this to you." She dives her hand into her pocket and hands me a box. No doubt in my mind that this is what he bought when we saw him at the mall. "And no, it's not an engagement ring. Or so he said," she assures me.

I stare at the black box between my fingers and walk back to my bedroom for some privacy with Waze on my tail. I crash on my bed with a speeding heart. Waze lays his head on my lap.

I open the box with trembling fingers. Its contents steals my breath away. It's a golden bracelet. Very plain, simple. It's gorgeous. Exactly the type I would wear. Haze knows I've never been into tacky, big jewelry.

In the box is a folded note. I pick it up. The five handwritten words inside make my heart swell.

In case you ever forget.

I pick the bracelet up, and my composure dissolves at the

tiny yet easy to read quote carved on the inside.

*You are the risk I will always take.*

Tears come up to my eyes, building up and fighting the heck out of me until I lose and allow one to fall. I remember the moment he said that to me so clearly. It was our second night in town when my mom forced him to sleep down in our creepy basement. I sneaked out and joined him when everyone was sleeping. In the middle of mind-blowing sex, I asked him why he was willing to risk getting caught for me.

I was completely oblivious back then.

Maybe, just maybe, this quote is Haze's way of telling me that the perfect moments we shared before I found out about his lies… weren't lies, too.

I wipe the tears off my face and reach a point of no return.

I call it the "*Fuck this shit.*"

I grab my phone and dial a number I know by heart. I can't believe I'm calling him. But I have to know.

It rings twice.

A familiar voice comes down the line.

"Winter?"

I consider hanging up but decide I've come too far to back down now.

"Hey, we need to talk. Can you meet me?"

PULLING UP INTO THE PARKING LOT of the small coffee shop near my place, I overthink my decision and consider driving back home. I recall our conversation. He was beyond thankful that I agreed to see him even if I had all the reasons in the world not to. I told Alex, Will, Allie, and Kass that I had to run some errands. Allie and Kass seemed suspicious but let me go without questions.

I push the door open and scan the warm and welcoming coffee shop. The walls are a pale shade of blue, and white Christmas lights hang all around the room. He's nowhere in sight. I order a cappuccino and sit at a table near the large stone fireplace, waiting for him to arrive.

As soon as he walks in, he gazes around the crowded shop until he sees me. He waves on his way to my table.

"Hey, I'm so glad you called," he says and sits before me. Hope and expectation shine in his eyes.

"Caleb, I… I don't want you getting the wrong idea."

His smile fades.

"I called you because you said there was more to the story, and I need to know."

"And you couldn't ask Haze?" he hisses.

"We're not talking at the moment, but I'm sure you knew that." My tone is colder than intended.

"Let me guess, you're hoping there's more to the story so you can convince yourself the bastard is worth forgiving and run back into his arms?"

"Caleb, please," I sigh. "I'm so sorry about what happened between us. I ruined our friendship. I've said it before, and I'll say it a hundred times if you want me to, but… right now, I need you to try and put our differences aside."

With a clenched jaw, he stares blankly at the table.

"You don't get it, do you? I was happy that you ruined the friendship, Winter. What sucks is you weren't."

Regret climbs up my spine. I can't even blame him. He has feelings for me. Seeing me show up with a boyfriend after I rejected him so harshly couldn't have been easy. I grew up alongside him. He's a good guy, I know he is, but he was hurt. And he acted out.

"You're right. This isn't fair of me to ask. I'm sorry." I reprimand myself and rise off my chair.

His hand flies to my wrist. "Winter, wait."

I look down at him.

"I didn't say I wasn't going to help."

Unsure, I sit back down.

"I have to warn you. If you're expecting to feel better, you're in for a big disappointment."

I wait for him to continue.

"The day I followed him… he met up with some shady guy who gave him a few names, addresses. I didn't stay through the whole thing, but I heard them talking about…" He doesn't complete his sentence, eyeing me cautiously as if to decide on whether or not I'm ready. "There's no easy way to say this. Are you sure you want to hear it?"

Fear grips me.

"Tell me."

"Haze's idea of justice is not to put this guy behind bars. He wants to kill him. Said he's going to pay with his life."

My heart drops.

"No, he wouldn't." I shake my head. "Haze would never kill anyone."

"I heard him say it, Winter."

Of course.

Of course Haze would be planning to kill Marcus.

How could I be so stupid to think he'd be satisfied with putting him in jail? Fourteen-year-old Haze had to watch his baby sister die. Watched her bleed out, held her in his arms while she gasped for air, watched her eyes close. That's why he started working out and learned to fight. He said it was to learn to defend himself and protect the people he loved.

But it was to kill Marcus.

All along.

"Winter, goddamn it. Do you even realize what I just said? Your precious boyfriend wants to kill someone. I just… I don't understand how, after all of this, you still love him. I'd never treat you like that. I'd never lie to you the way he does. Can't you see—"

With glossy, empty eyes, I jolt up and grab my coffee. "I have to go."

"What?" he blurts.

"Thank you for coming." I'm barely aware of my footsteps

tearing through the crowd and out of the establishment. Caleb calls my name once. Twice. I don't turn around.

Caleb's wrong. This isn't the Haze I know. He's not a murderer. Haze's a good person. Just a really, *really* damaged person.

Getting into Kendrick's car—I had to get here somehow since I don't have a car—I open the numerous unopened messages Haze sent me. My eyes glaze over every word as I scroll up to find what I need.

> I'm staying with Vic. Please answer your phone.

He's at Vic's.

I'm done running from the truth. I'm done running from him. He's been begging me to let him explain for days.

I'm going to do just that.

THE SOUND OF MY TIRES SCREECHING against the silent roads is all I've been hearing for the past ten minutes. Vic's area is beyond confusing. Everything looks the same, every building a sad shade of gray. It's like they copied and pasted the whole neighborhood. I narrow my eyes in a desperate attempt to remember the one and only time Haze and I visited Victor. When my gaze finally lands on the building that seems most familiar to me, I park my car in the guest spot. What can I expect? I don't have the slightest idea.

Glad that the front door isn't locked, I barge in and go right up the stairs leading to Vic's floor. I walk for a while, then come to an abrupt stop in front of door 234.

Am I even in the right building?

I knock with an uncertainty I have never felt before. Time passes. No answer.

This is my cue.

I'm about to walk away when the door opens in a creak.

In front of me stands a very lightly dressed brunette who seems to be in her early twenties. Chewing on gum mannerlessly, she looks me up and down. Her red eyes and the smell of weed spilling into the hall leave very little to my imagination.

"Can I help you?" She arches an eyebrow. The ink on her collarbone reads the name *Steve* in italic letters. Around it are two poorly done hearts. Was the tattoo artist blind? I cringe. Getting the name of your boyfriend tattooed. Never a good idea.

*Says the dumbass who immortalized her first kiss with her ex.*

"Uh… Yeah. Is Haze here?" Why am I even bothering? I'm clearly in the wrong place.

"Who's asking?"

I open my mouth to speak, but someone beats me to it.

"Winter?"

I crane my neck to peek over the drunk girl's shoulder.

He's right there.

In the hall.

With wet hair and nothing but black sweatpants on. It's clear that he just got out of the shower. My eyes drop to his abs for a second too long. He looks drained, tormented, yet so overwhelmingly handsome it's irritating

Yep, he's still perfect.

I wish he looked as awful as the way he made me feel.

"Let her in," he snaps at the girl. I have no idea who she is or why she's here, but she doesn't seem like the type of girls to be friends with Beatrice, Vic's girlfriend.

Twirling a piece of her hair around her finger, tattoo girl steps aside. I walk in.

"Where's Vic?" Haze asks her.

"Passed out in his room. He's going to need that rest, trust me," she smirks, leaving me and Haze equally disgusted.

Wait, Vic's not with Bea anymore?

"Is this her? The reason you've been a fucking soap opera?" Tattoo girl analyzes me some more. "She ain't all that."

"Shut up, Kelly," Haze snarls.

She gives me the nastiest look she can muster and disappears down the hall.

Apologetic eyes drift to me. "Ignore her. She destroyed the few brain cells she had left today."

I nod faintly. Expecting me to say something, he buries his hands into his sweatpants pockets and sways from left to right. He gives me the puppy eyes, and I don't even think it's intentional.

I miss him.

*He broke you. Did you forget that part?*

I shut the door with one hand. Only then do I become aware of my surroundings. The neat apartment I once visited is now a complete and utter mess. Cigarette butts and holders are scattered across the living room. The couch is covered in bongs, empty glass bottles, empty takeout boxes.

This is where he's been living?

"It's not as bad as it seems," he says like he's reading my mind. He knows me so well it's annoying. "So… you read my texts." His smile is sincere. Hopeful.

"Yeah, I needed to know where you were staying."

The *maybes* in his eyes take a blow.

"Did you get my gift?" He gives hope one last try.

"I did. It was very thoughtful. Thank you." My tone is hard, but my heart is liquifying. I don't know what he wished would happen after he gave me the bracelet, but the look on his face displays that this wasn't it.

"What can I do for you?" He runs a quick hand through his wet hair, and my gaze clings to the drops of water rolling down his pecs. *Eyes up here!*

"Can we go somewhere private?" I clear my throat.

He nods, walks toward what I remember to be the guest room, and pushes the door open. A sliver of guilt throbs in me. He's sleeping on an old pull-out couch that seems so uncomfortable my back aches just looking at it. He shouldn't be here. He should be home.

With me.

He breaks the silence. "Winter, if you came to tell me that you never want to see me again… Please don't."

*Heart squeeze.*

"I didn't," I reassure him, and he sighs in relief. "I came because I want to know."

My sentence catches him off guard.

"Everything. You said you could explain. Well, now I want you to. I need you to." I hang on to what Caleb told me earlier. I have to see if he's going to admit it to me. Or lie. *Again.*

Haze nods and beckons me to sit. We both do, the awkward silence in the air so thick it's hard to breathe.

"Shit, where do I even start?" He drags out a sigh. "It all started at the airport. I got a call saying that Marcus was in Canada, and I swear, before my source told me, he was the only thing, and I mean *the only thing* keeping me from getting on that plane with you. The second I would've found him, I would've been on my way back to you." He goes in for my hand, and I don't have the strength to oppose.

"I know you think you weren't enough. That I never came for you. But you're so fucking wrong, you have no idea. I thought I was protecting you. I thought I'd let you go home where you'd be safe, keep you out of harm's way while I sorted my shit out. I thought I could get this over with before I started over in a new life with you. I'm so sorry."

I suck in a sharp breath. "Then what? What did you expect

to happen when you found him? What were you going to do to him?"

Please, Haze. I'm begging you. Don't lie.

*Don't make me give up on you.*

Strangely enough, he seems to know how important this answer is because he chooses his words carefully.

"Send him to jail."

It hurts like hell.

He lied.

"Or at least, that's what I told myself." He adds.

My eyes snap up to his.

"I… I want him to die, Winter. I know it's wrong. I know that I shouldn't, but… Fuck, sending him to jail isn't enough. He doesn't deserve to grow old. He…" His eyes are red, but not from tears—from pure rage. "Des won't get to. Why the fuck should he? She won't get to have children, start a family, laugh so hard she cries, kiss the wrong boy and ask me to kick his ass. She won't get to make mistakes and learn from them. She won't get to fall so madly in love that she doesn't know what to do with herself." He gazes at me so intently I can't shake the feeling that he's talking about me. "Tell me, how the hell am I supposed to move on knowing that he's out there, living his life as a free man when he stole hers?"

I blink back tears. That's all I know how to do recently.

"And I know you have every right to hate me. You have every right to never want to see me again, but you have to believe me… I didn't *only* come for him."

"How many times did you lie to me? I want to know when you lied, what you lied about. All of it."

He rubs the back of his neck. "I really don't think that's a good idea."

"It's the only chance we've got," I press him.

Under my pleading stare, he caves. He goes on to tell me he lied about his job, which I already knew, about the address in his pocket, which I also suspected. He tells me he lied about many phone calls. I take it all the best I can.

He lets out a bitter scoff. "Look at me. Running around like a fucking idiot not to lose you, only to lose you anyway."

I can't help myself.

"But that's the point, Haze. You *didn't* lose me."

His lips part.

I rise to my feet and pace around the room. "And I hate myself because I still want you. I still…" I stop before I say too much.

He doesn't speak, nor does he acknowledge my embarrassing declaration. He just gets off his nightmare of a bed and steps forward. I don't move away, but I refuse him eye contact. Not having it, he lifts my chin up with his index.

I shiver at his touch and lift my arm up to cup his cheek. He relaxes at the contact, closing his eyes for a half second. My long sleeve ripples down my arm, revealing the shimmery bracelet on my wrist. He sees it. His features light up.

"You're wearing it," he points out.

"Well, it… it looked expensive. I felt bad." I almost choke on my excuse. He's smiling now. He begins to lean in, with every intent to finish what we started the night before. Except that this time is different.

This time, I can't blame it on the alcohol.

This time, it's all me.

He brushes my lips with his ever so slightly, but just before we can cross the line, he backs away.

"Wait," he says in realization. "There's another reason why I couldn't tell you."

I frown. "What?"

My phone rings.

Annoyed, I pull it out of my pocket, about to send the call straight to voicemail, but the number on my screen stops me.

My brother.

"I'm sorry, I have to take this." I flip the screen over to him, and he nods. I pick up. "Jay?" I expect this to be a butt-dial since Jaden never, as in *ever*, calls me.

"Winter?" I immediately know something's wrong by his tone.

I hear distant voices in the background. He's in a crowded room. Sniffles? Is he crying?

"Winter, you have to get here. Mom isn't anywhere. I don't… I don't know where she is. They said they called her. Please hurry."

"Where are you? What's going on?"

"I'm at the hospital." His voice is shaky.

At the hospital.

*Hospital.*

I replay the word in my head a million times.

"What? Why are you at the hospital?"

Muffled cries fill my ears. He's barely holding it together.

"It's Dad."

My stomach flips.

"He got into a car accident. They don't know if he's going to make it."

# TWENTY

## Explanation

"What the hell is going on? Winter, talk to me!" Haze follows closely as I rush to the exit of Vic's hellhole. So many questions without an answer. How did Jay end up at the hospital? Why isn't my mother with her kid? How did the accident occur? Why do the worst things happen to the best people?

"Winter, stop!" Haze has to smack his palm to the closed door to stop me from opening it. "What did he say to you?"

"It's my dad. He's been in an accident. It's bad. Really bad." The tears keep spilling down my cheeks uncontrollably. I'm in shock, empty, the shell of a heart—cold and broken. "Jay's alone in the waiting room. I have no idea how he got there, but my mom is a no-show. Maika's at a birthday party today. She has no idea. I just… I'm sorry. I have to go."

"I'm coming with you." He runs back to his room and comes out with a shirt on, his coat hanging off his arms, and his keys. "I'll drive you."

I don't oppose. No time for that. I just dash out of the building with Haze on my heels. Plus, I am *not* okay to drive right now. I'll run every red light and hit every old lady crossing the street if I do.

Not knowing. It's maddening. The traffic isn't too bad, but the drive still feels so excruciatingly long it makes me want to scream out in rage. Haze and I don't exchange a single word on the way there, both asking ourselves the same question: Is he going to make it?

Haze drops me at the entrance, telling me to go in while he finds a parking spot. My breathing is unsteady, my palms sweaty, my heart beating out of my chest as I push through the motion on the way to the emergency room. I feel like I'm going to collapse when I see Jaden sitting alone with tears spilling down his face. I run to him, and as soon as he sees me, his eyes flash with relief. It doesn't even take a second. He launches himself into my arms. I hold him tighter than ever before.

"It's okay. I'm here," I whisper, and he sobs harder. "What happened? How did you get here?"

"I was in the car with him."

"Oh my God, are you okay?" I examine him like a crazy person, and he nudges my hands away.

"I'm fine. I was in the back seat. I have no idea what happened. The car… it just came so fast, and I was texting. God, I don't know." He hyperventilates. "He just hit Dad's side out of nowhere. They pulled me out in minutes. I was lucky, but…" He pauses. "Dad wasn't." I can't even begin to imagine the horrific events he's witnessed tonight. "They said they called Mom. But she's not here. She should be here."

"And the other driver?"

"I don't know. It was a hit-and-run."

"What?" I blurt.

"The police wouldn't tell me anything after they interrogated me. Just kept on asking me if someone would have a reason to hurt Dad. I told them they were crazy."

"But… who would do that?" Tears well in my eyes. I have to get a grip before I start spiraling. This is the police's job. Not mine. "Forget it. How was he? How was Dad? What did he look like at the scene?"

"I barely had time to see him. They took him away in an ambulance, drove me here, and said to wait for mom. Then they told me they were taking him into surgery."

This isn't happening.

This isn't real.

My dad is not in surgery. He's home cooking dinner and reading the paper. He'll call me pumpkin when I walk through the door and annoy me about how fast I've grown.

My father is fine.

He's not in critical condition.

*He's not dying.*

"Maybe Mom's picking up Maika," I say to convince myself.

"Bullshit. She'd be here by now. She knows about the accident. They called her. She doesn't care, Winter."

I always thought that Jaden not being related to my mother in any way played an important part in how close they were. He was so young when my mom and Harry got together, he eventually started to call her Mom since his actual mother passed away. And even if she's a lot nicer to him than she is to me, she's still never really shown him the love she shows Maika.

"What about your grandparents? Do they know?"

"They tried calling them, but they weren't home. I wasn't able to reach them either."

"We need to try them again. Give me your phone."

I snatch it from his hand, since I don't have their number, and press Call. Claire, Harry's mother, answers after a few rings. I inform her of the situation and ask her to go pick up Maika at her friend's birthday party. She says that they'll take care of it and be on their way to the hospital, but I can't wrap my head around what they'll say to my sister. How do you tell a five-year-old who still believes in happy endings and fairy tales that the worst thing that could've possibly happened… *did*?

## *Haze*

I've never understood how a mother could hate her own kid. How a parent, the one person a kid should always be able to turn to, could despise her own flesh and blood is beyond me. Lauren hates Winter—she made that clear. But I never thought she was heartless to the point of leaving her goddamn kid alone while her husband is fighting for his life.

It's been several hours. Kendrick and Allie have been waiting with us for a while. Will, Kass, and Alex went to check Winter's house in case Lauren showed her face. She never did.

Winter and Jay fell asleep with tears dangling off their eyes and their hearts on their sleeves. No sign of Lauren anywhere. We called her new job—nothing. I have no idea what she's doing, but she better have the best excuse on the planet. I'll only accept two reasons: she died or…

She died.

Yep, that summarizes it.

Winter had to deal with Jaden and Maika's annoying-as-fuck grandparents, and it took everything in me not to punch their dentures out of their mouths. They don't consider Winter to be family as Harry's blood doesn't flow through her veins. They wouldn't even look at her, only paying attention to Jaden and Maika—like Winter isn't about to lose her father, too.

Harry's the only parent who deserves one hair on her head.

They took Maika home at around nine. They said they'd be taking care of her until we can get a hold of Lauren. No news from Harry either. He's been in surgery for God knows how long, and I'm not sure if no news means good news or *We don't know how to tell you* news. If Harry dies, Winter will lose it. And, chances are, she won't even let me be there for her.

I jump out of my seat at the sight of the doctor heading our way. It's up to me. Winter and Jay are asleep, and Allie and Kendrick went to get coffee. If he's coming to tell me my girlfriend's dad is dead—sorry, *ex*-girlfriend—I want to be the first to know so I can tell Winter. I don't want her finding out that her only parent died from a stranger.

"Who's here for Harry Gale?"

I stride to him.

"Family?" He arches an eyebrow.

"I'm his daughter's husband," I lie. I won't have him tell me I'm not "family enough."

"Okay." He blows out a breath. "Overall, the surgery went well. Your father-in-law is stable. He's a very lucky man. I've seen people go for a lot less."

My shoulders shrink with relief.

"But… he's in a coma."

*Fucking shit.*

He goes on to tell me about a bunch of medical conditions I don't understand. Something about his leg, a concussion and broken ribs.

"We're doing everything we can for him right now, but the rest is up to him. He might wake up tomorrow like he might wake up in a year." His eyes apologize profusely.

"What are his chances?"

"The simple fact that he made it through is a miracle, so at this point, anything could happen. I'd say his chances are pretty good, but we make no promises."

"Thank you."

"Get them home." He motions to Winter and Jay sleeping. "Get some sleep and come back tomorrow for visiting hours. You'll be able to see him. I assume the police will also want to talk to you first thing in the morning, so you kids need to rest."

He begins to walk away.

"I'm sorry. I have one more question. What happened to the other driver? I know it was a hit-and-run, but maybe someone who fit the profile was admitted later tonight?"

"Not that that I know of, I'm sorry, but I'm sure the police will know more about this than I do."

I thank him again and return to the waiting room.

I squeeze Winter's shoulder. "Hey, wake up."

She slowly comes back to her senses. "What time is it?" She rubs her eyes and sits up straight with a stretch. Even with her hair a mess from sleeping on a waiting room seat, she's the most beautiful girl I've ever seen.

"Three thirty," I reply and sit alongside her. "You've been out for a while."

"Any news?"

Here we go.

"Yes. He's stable."

She seems as relieved as I am, if not more.

"But…"

I know this is going to break her heart.

"He's in a coma."

She breaks apart right in front of me. Tears pool in her eyes and fall freely.

"What?" Her voice cracks.

"The doctor said his chances of waking up are pretty good,

but we can only wait and see. The police are on the hit-and-run right now. They'll want to talk to you tomorrow. We all need to go home and rest. Doctor's orders."

She pulls herself together and nods. "I'll wake up Jay. He's coming to sleep at our place tonight, okay?"

My mind is a whirlwind.

Did she just say *our* place?

As in I'm supposed to sleep there tonight, too?

I don't dare question it in fear that she'll realize what she just said and change her mind.

"Of course."

"Kendrick and Allie can drive us. Jay doesn't have any clothes. Would you mind stopping by my house, picking some up, and meeting us at home after? I don't know how long he's going to be living with us."

"No problem," I say. "Listen, I hate to bring this up, but… you know this might mean that something happened to Lauren, right?"

She sighs. "I know. If she doesn't show up tomorrow, we'll have to file a missing person's report."

She hands me her house key and wakes up Jaden to explain it all to him. He's just as emotional as she is but fights to keep a straight face. Soon enough, Kendrick's parked out front of the hospital with Allie. I watch Winter get into the vehicle with Jay, and we exchange small smiles. They're "*We're not okay yet but we might still stand a chance*" smiles.

I stride to my car and start the engine in a jerk. The drive to Winter's house goes by quicker than expected. All I can do is smile like a complete fool, desperately clinging to the tiniest of chances that I may not be sleeping at Vic's tonight.

I turn into Winter's driveway and hit the brakes so fast my tires holler at me.

There's a car.

Lauren's.

It's taking up half the driveway, carelessly parked sideways with the lights still on. I park in the street, kill the engine, and make my way to Winter's house. I unlock the door and step insi…

*What the fuck?*

I lift my foot in the air.

Broken glass lies beneath my shoe. Two broken liquor bottles mark a path all the way down to the kitchen. Frowning, I follow the trail. I have a good idea of what I'm going to see when I enter the room, but it doesn't make it any less disturbing.

Sitting around the kitchen table with her head hanging low is Lauren. A half-empty whiskey bottle sits next to her. She hasn't noticed me yet. It's when she brings the booze to her lips that she sees me and jumps. The glass bottle goes flying out of her hands and crashes to the floor.

"Haze?" Her eyes widen. She probably sees double by now. "You… You weren't supposed to see that."

Part of me wants to go upstairs, grab Jaden's clothes, and get the hell out of here already. But the other is imploring me to throw Lauren off a building. Not an easy dilemma.

"Do you have any idea how many people waited for you tonight? How fucking miserable your kids were?" I spit. It doesn't take a goddamn degree to figure out this is the reason she wasn't at the hospital. How could she be so cruel? Her husband is in a coma, and she's here getting wasted.

She pretends to wipe away tears. "Haze, you have to understand. I couldn't go. It's too hard. I love him so much and—"

"Drop the act," I growl. It's 3:00 a.m. I don't have time for her shit.

She's shocked, at first. Then she curses and throws her hands up. "All right. Had to try."

I don't waste another second on her and head for the stairs. This woman is nothing but a reminder that some people shouldn't be allowed to have kids. I go through Jay's mess of a room and throw every piece of clothing I can find into his backpack. By the time I'm done and charging down the stairs, Lauren's opened a new whiskey bottle. The one she dropped remains shattered on the floor. So much for being a neat freak.

I send her a look full of hatred as I pass through the kitchen. One second before I walk out, she croaks, "She looks like him, you know?"

I stop dead in my path but don't turn around, waiting to see if her speech is worth staying for.

"Winter. She's a spitting image of her father," she elaborates.

Still with my back facing her, I shove my hand into my pocket and grab my phone.

"I was sixteen. Just turned sixteen the month before. You should've seen him. He was so charming. Some would say irresistible."

I swivel around.

"Mysterious, reckless, gorgeous. The kind of guy who could get anyone he wanted without blinking. Girls would have killed for his attention, but he only wanted me. Or so he said." She gets up, miserably holding on to the table to maintain her balance. "I really thought he loved me, and God, did I love him. They all told me to stay away, but I didn't. Because I thought I had found the love of my life." She scoffs in a self-deprecating manner. "I was as stupid as Winter is right now. She really is my daughter after all. As soon as I found out I was pregnant, he changed. There was no forever, no I love you. You know all the bullshit promises you made my daughter? Well, he used to make them to me. My parents wanted nothing to do with me the second they found out. I was a shame. The family's disgrace. They wanted me to get rid of her. And when I didn't listen, they tried to put her into the system. Said I wasn't keeping her for the right reasons. I was so naive. I thought he'd change his mind and come back to me if I kept the kid. I was sixteen for fuck's sake."

That's why Winter was treated like a piece of furniture since she was a baby. Because Lauren got dumped.

"Maria, on the other hand, was so perfect. She got perfect grades, led the student councils, had her entire future mapped out. She was going to become a doctor, marry this American guy she'd met, move to Florida with him, have kids. Then there was me, the troubled daughter who got knocked up before she could pass her driver's license test." She steps forward. "Every time I look at her, I wish I had gotten an abortion."

My fists clench on their own.

"That's your daughter you're talking about."

"You think I don't know that?" she cackles. "That's precisely the problem. Some great fucking idea it was to keep the baby. I've tried… I've tried to look at her the way I look at Maika, but I can't. I'm guilty." She pauses, as if to savor the moment. "I don't love her. There. I've said it. I don't love her, and I never will. Because every time I look at her, I see him." A wicked smile stretches across her face. "God, it feels so good to finally say it out loud. I've never let myself admit it. I don't love her. I can't stand to even look at her." She laughs in realization.

"Congrats. You're a piece of shit. If you can't see that your daughter is the most beautiful, amazing, and caring person on this goddamn planet, you're absolutely insane. She's the best thing that's ever happened to me."

She doesn't reply, eyeing me.

"I've got to give it to you, you put on a quite show. I'm sure you got her fooled into thinking you love her."

I scoff. "Aw, don't be jealous just because no one loved you enough to stay."

"You say you love her now, just wait until she gets knocked up. We'll see how fast you run back to Florida." She mutters under her breath, "I wish she'd run back to Florida, too."

I snap. "Are you seriously blaming your child for being born? It's not her fault you fell in love with the town's trash."

She snickers and makes air quotes with her fingers. "*The town's trash* didn't look so trashy, trust me. In fact, he was as gorgeous as you." She stalks toward me, careful not to step in glass. She braces a finger on my chest, tracing down my torso, and I move away in disgust. "Muscled body, chiseled face. You remind me of him a lot, Haze. You look like the guy who ruined me. Such a shame that he was also the best sex I ever had." She bites on her lower lip and rests her hand on my bicep to feel my muscles.

"What the fuck?" I shove her away from me.

"Come on, humor me. My husband's dying. I promise, I won't tell." She plucks the first button of her shirt open.

I need to sanitize my eyes.

"Do you even hear yourself? Your husband is fucking dying. How could you do this to him?"

"Give me a break. It's not like I ever loved him anyway." She walks back to the table, takes a long sip of whiskey, and wipes her mouth. "He was a respectable man. He had the job, the money. And I wanted the kids. Kids I could actually love. They said he has very little chances of making it anyway." Her eyes grow in realization. "When he dies, I'm going to lose the house—can you imagine? Be forced to move back into some shitty apartment because I can't afford this lifestyle. I'll even be stuck with his son." She crinkles her nose in disgust. "Can you blame me for needing a drink?"

"Harry is a great man and a great father." I grit my teeth. "I can't believe he married you."

"Oh, I assure you I was quite the view in my days. So was he. Too bad he lost it all. Maybe I wouldn't have had to bang the neighbor for years if he'd kept the abs."

At this point, nothing she says surprises me.

"I'm leaving now."

"Have it your way." She tumbles back to her seat. "Oh, and Haze? Be a dear and don't tell anyone about our conversation, will you? One word and I'll make sure Winter never sees her siblings again." She smiles widely.

This woman is a psychopath.

I shrug off her warning and hurry to the door. After everything she's just revealed to me, I'm very possibly the biggest threat to her perfect little life made of lies. So many thoughts are at war in my head. I climb inside my car, well aware that she's watching my every move through the window. I feel sick to my stomach.

*Winter…* My baby. She deserves so much more.

But I know I still have a chance. Lauren Kingston is going to lose everything—I'll make sure of it. She'll be the one begging to see Jaden and Maika by the time I'm done with her. I start the car and pull my phone out of my pocket.

Then I smile.

And stop recording.

# TWENTY-ONE

## *On Hold*

If someone had told me a few hours ago that I'd be dragging my feet walking into the elevator of our apartment complex, I would've laughed. Me? Dreading going back to the place I've been so desperate to live in again? *Good one.*

Fiddling with the phone in my pocket, I try my best to prepare for what's about to happen. I'm not ready. Not even close. I know once I walk through that door, I'll have to tell her.

Worse, I'll have to *show* her.

I don't want to think about what hearing that recording will do to her. I think she always knew Lauren was a heartless piece of garbage, but knowing it and hearing her mother point-blank say that she hates her daughter are two different things.

The door opens before I can get my keys out. Kendrick and Allie stand in the doorway, on their way out.

"Hey, man," Kendrick says at the sight of me. "You look like shit." I crack the ghost of a smile. I know that's his way of saying *"It's good to see you around here again."*

"Feel like it, too."

"She's letting you sleep here tonight. That's progress," he points out.

"Understandable after the day she's had. But you're not off the hook just yet," Allie teases.

"Trust me, I'm aware. You think you could put in a good word for me?"

She smirks. "I don't think I have to, since she's letting you sleep in her bed."

My eyes grow. "Wait, what?"

They laugh at my reaction.

"She's in her room." Kendrick pats me on the shoulder before they disappear down the hall.

The apartment is silent. I glance over the living room. As stupid as it may sound, when I see Jay sleeping on the couch like a baby, I'm relieved. They were right. No sign of a bed on the floor, and the guest rooms are all taken. I kick my rising hopes back down. Maybe she just ran out of blankets. After all, we have Alex, Kass, Will, and Jaden living with us right now.

I walk to our bedroom and push the door open quietly. She's lying on her side with her head propped on her bended arm. My eyes travel down her body against my will. She's wearing shorts, a tank top and… no bra. Most likely because she's going to bed soon. On a mission to fuck with me, my hormones decide now's a good time to picture her naked.

"Hey." Her voice startles me.

I must be beyond obvious because she sits up and cradles her knees to her body, covering her hard nipples in the process. She looks like she feels awful. I could make her feel better.

"Hey." I rip my eyes back to her face. "I've got the clothes."

She nods faintly. "Thanks."

"Did you want me to stay tonight or… ?"

I already know the answer, but I need to hear her say it.

Panicky, she blurts, "I mean, unless you don't want to. If you don't want to, you can go. It's fine, I—"

"Winter." I shut down her spiraling. "I want to."

"Oh." She flushes. "Good."

I sit on the edge of the bed.

"Where do you want me to sleep?"

Okay, this one is for my ego.

"I'd make you a bed on the floor, but we're all out of blankets so… with me? Is that okay?"

I almost laugh. Is that okay? *Is that okay?*

"It's fine."

"Thanks. I know it means a lot to Jay."

I frown. "Jay wanted me to stay?"

"Yeah. He doesn't know that we broke up yet and… He seemed so happy to see you at the hospital. I just… I couldn't tell him. And he could use the familiar face. He trusts you, you know?"

He trusts me.

But she doesn't.

"I'm sorry. I'll tell him that we broke up soon."

Her words sting the hell out of me. I'd rather think that she's the one who wanted me to stay, but I don't care. I'm here. That's all that matters.

"How are you feeling?" I remove my shirt, the way I always do before I go to bed, and toss it. I catch her gawking at me from the corner of my eye and smirk. *Still got it.* I decide to keep my pants on for now. Don't want her to be uncomfortable.

"Dead inside, but what's new?" She slides under the covers and buries her face in the pillow with a groan.

I laugh quietly and get in bed next to her. "He's going to be okay."

"You don't know that," she counters.

I stretch my arm out and turn off the lamp. Darkness fills the room. Her back is facing me, but the moonlight outlines her perfect silhouette, the curve of her ass.

*Hormones, shut the fuck up.*

"It's called hope," I whisper, and she rolls over to look at me. "Hey, listen, I thought maybe we could finish what we started at Vic's. I never got to tell you… you know, everything."

Her response is immediate. "I can't do this."

"But—"

"You don't get it. I physically can't. Not tonight, okay?" Her voice is faint, weak.

I nod. Guess I can forget about playing her the recording while I'm at it. Her eyes connect with mine, and something shifts in her gaze.

"Can you just hold me?" she croaks.

When tears start pouring down her face, I don't think, I just act. I ease my arms around her shoulders and let her cry. When she trembles against my chest, I want to believe that she needs me as much as I need her. She's been through hell today. There's a chance she'll never speak to her father again, and it's just starting to sink in.

"This doesn't change anything, okay?" She sniffles.

My heart twists.

I play with her hair. "Okay."

## *Winter*

WHEN I SNUCK MY WAY OUT of Haze's embrace at seven thirty this morning, it physically hurt to let go of him. We got a call from the police when we came home last night. I washed my face, put on some clothes, and waited for the police officer we were told would show up at eight this morning. A few days back, I thought I wouldn't survive losing Haze.

But if my father dies…

He might as well take me with him.

"We still don't know who did it," the police officer told us. My brother and I sat down in the living room and answered every single question they dropped on us for over two hours. So many questions to ask for so little answers to give.

They kept asking if someone might have a reason to want my father dead, a grudge of some sort. Wondered if we had noticed anything suspicious in the weeks prior to the accident, but thanks to my father being the nicest person on earth, each of our responses were useless. To make it better, they came up empty-handed when searching the scene of the accident.

I'm not sure why I asked Haze to stay last night. I pretended it was because of Jay, and in a way, it was, but in the end, I needed him more than Jay ever could. There's still so much we need to discuss, but I'm not in the headspace for forgiveness.

All I can think about right now is my dad. He still hasn't woken up, and every second he spends in a coma is a second I wish I could take his place.

"Morning." Haze's voice drifts through the quiet kitchen.

I bring the mug in my hands to my lips for a sip of smoking coffee. Alex, Will, and Kass are still sleeping, and Jay just got in the shower—we thought he needed a day off from school—which means I have no idea how long I'm going to be alone with my ex.

"Slept well?" I ask.

He stretches, lean muscles shifting under his white T-shirt. "A lot better than I did these past few days."

I know what he means is *a lot better than I did when I wasn't with you.*

*Same, Haze, same.*

"Did the police come?"

"Yeah."

"How'd it go?" He makes his way over to me, gets a mug out of the cabinet, and leans forward to pour himself a cup of coffee.

Goose bumps erupt all over my skin when his arm so much as brushes mine. I distance myself from him. God, I can't function when he's near me.

"It's not looking good. They still haven't found who did it, and they said a hit-and-run that isn't solved within the first few days has very low chances of resolution. They couldn't track the car from traffic cameras, and there were no admissions at the hospital, no one who fits the profile of the other driver. They said it's almost like someone planned it."

Something gleams in his blue eyes. He looks anxious.

"What is it?" I worry.

"Nothing."

"It doesn't look like nothing."

"I just can't believe someone would do that, that's all." He takes a sip of coffee.

I sigh. "Tell me about it."

A beat of silence.

"Winter, do you…" He stops himself, hesitant as to whether or not he should resume. "Do you want me to stay today?"

Yes.

So, so bad.

"No."

Disappointment fills his gaze.

"Yes."

He frowns.

"God, I don't know." I rest my coffee on the counter and

prop my face between my hands. He laughs. I hear him put down his coffee, too. Next thing I know, he's removed my hands from my eyes. His tall frame towers over me, so close my knees threaten to fail me.

"Haze, we're still broken up." The words come out in a whisper.

"I know. But we slept in the same bed last night, didn't we?"

"I told you, it doesn't change anything."

"Okay? Then, what is this? A pause?" He arches an eyebrow. "You're putting our breakup on hold whenever you feel like it?"

I snap. "You know what? You're damn right I am. I'm putting this on pause because I can't lose you and my dad at the same time. I just can't, okay?" I try and walk past him.

He reaches for my wrist, tugging me back to him. Our eyes collide.

"You never lost me."

Argh. *Too many emotions.*

"You know what I mean." I attempt to walk around him once more, but he steps in my way.

"So, let me get this straight, you're not ready to talk about us, but you still want me to stick around?"

Why is he pushing this?

"Yes. I can't be with you, and I can't be *without* you. I can't deal with you being here, and I can't deal with you being gone. You happy?"

His eyes light up as if everything's just become clear.

"We're allowed to put this on pause, then?"

"Absolutely," I declare.

"Great."

My heart loses its shit when he backs me up against the counter with one step and crashes his lips to mine.

His fingers slip through my hair, and I kiss him back so quickly I feel him smile in victory. He knows what he does to me. *Cheeky bastard.* He sweeps me into his arms effortlessly and plants me on the kitchen island. He positions himself between my legs, and I'm all over him within seconds. I hate how fast he's got my body begging for his touch.

"I love you," he rasps between kisses. "I don't care how long it takes. I'm not giving up on us."

I'm at a loss for words.

"You don't have to say it back. I just needed you to know."

With my heart beating a thousand miles per hour, I offer him a thankful smile. Truth is, I wouldn't have said it back. I couldn't have, and I don't know that I will anytime soon. He kisses me slow and hard again. My head is spinning in circles when he…

"Sorry to interrupt."

We jump.

Will.

He's smirking, leaning against the doorway with his arms crossed. I hustle down the kitchen island as fast as I possibly can and smooth down my wrinkled clothes.

"Will, hey." I awkwardly fix my hair. "Did we wake you?"

"Let me see." He brings a finger to his chin. "Did the sound of you groping each other like horny teenagers wake me up? Nah. All good."

Haze and I exchange glances. I fail to repress a smile.

"For fuck's sake, can't you two just get back together already and put us all out of our misery?" Will teases and walks to the fridge to get milk.

How I wish it were that easy.

"Are you guys going to see Harry today?" Will asks, pouring himself a bowl of cereal.

"Yeah. They said we should be able to see him. Oh, and you'll never believe the call I got this morning. My dad's parents finally got a hold of Lauren."

"They did?" Haze's eyebrows jerk up.

I summarize the ridiculous conversation I had a few minutes after waking up. Claire, my dad's mom, fed me some sob story about Lauren being so devastated over her husband's accident that she couldn't bring herself out of the house. Lauren told her she spent the evening trapped in crushing anxiety attacks and uncontrollable tears. She claimed her decision to stay away was for her kids' sake. We all know that's bullshit, but bullshit or not, she's Maika and Jay's legal guardian, and my hands are tied.

"Did you eat yet?" Haze asks me out of nowhere.

"Not yet. Why?"

"We're going out for breakfast."

"But… we have to go visit my dad."

"It won't take long. I promise. An hour tops. And visiting hours haven't even started yet."

I sway from side to side. "I don't know. What about Jay?"

"I think he can manage an hour alone. Come on, it's on me. There's something I want to talk to you about."

"Canada, just go out with the poor guy and release us from the sexual tension," Will whines.

"Fine," I relent.

Haze rejoices, treading back to the bedroom to get his phone. I don't know why my agreeing to go to breakfast seems so important to him. What does he want to tell me, and why does he need me out of the apartment to do so? Normally, I'd be worried, but I doubt anything he throws my way could faze me, even a little bit, at this point. Not after the past twenty-four hours. Anxious, Haze leads the way out of the apartment and into the elevator.

I ALWAYS FOUND IRONY IN THE word *ex*. So many terms flood my mind at the mere sound of it. Ex as in *excruciating*, *exhausting*, *extremely annoying*, *exterminate the bastard*. I never thought I'd refer to Haze as my ex. I still can't get used to the idea, and deep down, I have a hunch the term isn't meant to stick around our relationship.

The ride to the breakfast restaurant was silent. Haze looked tormented. What truly worried me was the fact that he didn't talk about the rather *hot* make-out session we shared in the kitchen this morning. I would've anticipated his life mission to become teasing me back into his arms. That's what I love about him. He always made me feel so alive, so free. The electricity between us could never find an equal.

We had breakfast as he wanted. When I asked why it was so important to him, he said that we needed to talk, so we did: we talked about the weather, how Waze is slowly learning to shake hands, anything and everything but what he wanted to talk to me about.

Question marks cross my gaze when Haze parks the car in our apartment spot but doesn't move a muscle. He fiddles with his phone lying flat on his lap.

"Are you ready?" I let out.

"For what?"

"To spit out the thing that's been eating at you all morning."

He lowers his eyes to his hands and drops a sigh. "There's something I didn't tell you yesterday. It just seemed like too much at the time, but I know the worst thing I could ever do is keep the truth from you again."

I appreciate his honesty. Yes, Haze made mistakes—monumental, near impossible to forgive mistakes—but he sees the error of his ways.

"When you asked me to go to your house yesterday… Lauren was there." He unlocks his phone with a swipe and pulls up his recordings. "She was wasted. She'd been drinking all night. That's where she was, Winter. She wasn't crying in bed.

She was getting hammered."

I'm not surprised, although I wish I was.

"She started rambling to me. I didn't know what to do, so I took a leaf out of Caleb's book and recorded her."

Part of me knows where he's going with this. No matter how much I wish I could excuse her absence, I know there are only so many *terrible parenting* passes I can give the woman.

"What did she say?"

"A bunch of BS. That's all that matters. Things that Harry should really know if he…" His voice leaves him.

"If he survives," I finish.

He doesn't reply, acquiescing.

"I want to hear it."

There are lots of words I've regretted saying in my life. Words such as "I want another slice of pizza" or "Sure, I can handle another shot," but these words, right here, right now, might just turn out to be the ones that haunt me for the rest of my life.

"You really don't need to listen to her nonsense, Winter."

"I want to," I insist. "How will I know what to say to my dad when he wakes if I don't?"

I'm aware my use of the word *when* instead of *if* is dangerous. Chances are, he's never going to wake up, but I'm not ready to accept, nor consider, that possibility. So, I won't. I'll hold on to every shred, ever splinter of hope that my dad's going to wake up. That he'll be around to walk me down the aisle, call me pumpkin, play with my kids and tell them stories.

I stretch my arm forward to press Play, but he yanks his phone out of my reach. "I said no. Drop it. I'll just tell you what's on there. Same fucking thing."

"Haze, *please*."

The conflicted expression on his face sneak peeks how bad the recording is. I knew it was bad, but this… this isn't bad. That's *horrible.* He winces when I pluck the phone from his hands and press Play in the same way you'd rip off a Band-Aid—quickly and with my eyes shut in anticipating of the burn.

"Winter, please don't do this."

His begging is muffled by a hoarse voice.

*"I was sixteen. Just turned sixteen the month before. You should've seen him. He was so charming. Some would say irresistible. Mysterious, reckless, gorgeous. The kind of guy who could get anyone he wanted without blinking. Girls would have killed for his attention, but he only wanted me. Or so he said. I really thought he loved me, and God, did I love him."*

This is the first time in my entire life I've ever heard my mother talk about my biological father. She always refused to answer my questions. She wouldn't even tell me his name. I hate that I'm hanging on to every hateful word.

*"They all told me to stay away, but I didn't. Because I thought I had found the love of my life. I was as stupid as Winter is right now. She really is my daughter after all."*

The more she speaks, the harder it is to breathe. She exposes bits and pieces of her rotten soul with each sentence, until finally, it's all out for the world to see.

*"Every time I look at her, I wish I had gotten an abortion."*

That's the first bullet.

*"That's your daughter you're talking about."* I recognize Haze's deep voice.

*"You think I don't know that? That's precisely the problem. Some great fucking idea it was to keep the baby."*

That's the second bullet. Then comes the third, fourth, fifth. It never ends. I sink my teeth into my bottom lip to keep from crying. I'm so sick of crying

*"I don't love her. There. I've said it. I don't love her, and I never will. Because every time I look at her, I see him."*

Her speech creates a never-ending roar in my head, a piercing, deafening scream of rage I can't quiet. I'm angry. So angry that, after everything she did to me, it still hurts like hell to hear her say out loud what I've always known. But I guess, now, at least I know why.

Haze speaks again. *"Congrats. You're a piece of shit. If you can't see that your daughter is the most beautiful, amazing, and caring person on this goddamn planet, you're absolutely insane. She's the best thing that's ever happened to me."*

My eyes find his. This is so sweet my heart can't take it.

When he sees the tears welling in my eyes, he tries to steal his phone back. "That's enough."

I hold the phone tightly against my chest to stop him. I need to hear the rest. Plus, there's no way it gets worse than this, right?

Wrong.

When she tries to force herself on Haze, my breakfast threatens to make an appearance. I'm glad he rejects her, but I don't even have time to properly enjoy how amazing Haze is, because she says that she's been cheating on my dad the next second.

Only then does Haze successfully snatch the phone away from me and end the recording. I don't fight him further. Truth be told, I don't know how much more I could've handled.

It just kept getting worse.

Next, she would've come out as a serial killer, I'm sure.

He shoves the phone back into his pocket as I stare vacantly ahead of me with dried tears marking my skin.

"I'm so sorry. Please say something." He unbuckles his seat belt. No word seems appropriate or strong enough for this moment.

"Thank you for showing it to me," I whisper and get out of the car. Haze mimics my actions. I walk to the driver's side to meet him. It's cold as shit outside.

"What do you want to do from here?" He lifts his arm and rubs a tear off my cheek with his thumb. When his piercing blue eyes capture mine, my priorities change. They cluster around what matters: him. Everything falls into place. There is one thing I can conclude from the recording. My mother is an asshole, plain and simple.

But you know who's not an asshole?

Haze.

He's the *least* asshole person around. He made mistakes. He fucked up time and time again. But at the end of the day, his heart's in the right place. His question ricochets through my brain.

*What do you want to do from here?*

The answer is clear.

"I want to kiss you."

So, I do.

I grab the collar of his coat, push to my tiptoes, and press my lips to his before he can get a word in. In disbelief, he kisses me back, hauling me closer to him until the cold tips of our noses touch. I can practically hear my heart reconstructing itself as we sway from side to side, back and forth. To say it requires self-control to stop kissing him would be an understatement, but when I do finally free his lips, he shakes his head in disapproval and pulls me back in for more.

After a couple of minutes, we're forced to let go. I press my forehead to his. Both our faces are freezing to the point of pain—Canada is fun—but I couldn't care less.

"If I'd known all I had to do was ask you what you wanted," he breathes out, and I laugh.

An alarm goes off on my phone.

It's time to go visit my dad.

"Crap." I stand back. "I have to go. Visiting hours with Jay."

"Do you need a ride?" he offers.

"No, Kendrick's driving us." I jolt around, but he circles my wrist.

"Wait."

I look at him.

"I thought maybe I would go pick up my clothes at Vic's and come back to the apartment… if that's okay with you."

I know he's asking me way more than if he can move back in. He's asking me if we're back together.

I offer him a timid smile. "I'd like that."

His smile grows ten sizes.

"I'll see you soon, Kingston." He gets back into his car and speeds out of the parking lot while I rush inside the building to meet Jay. We're not officially back together just yet, but I've made up my mind.

I'm done convincing myself that this guy hasn't been the best thing that's ever happened to me, too.

## *Haze*

When I unlock the door to Vic's apartment and push it open, I can honestly say I've never been happier to see the dump on the other side. Because I'm seeing it for the last time. I'm going *home*.

Passed out on the couch is one of Vic's new friends, Greg. He's one of the douchebag frat guys Vic's been hanging out with lately. I walk into the guest room, only to see Vic snoring in my bed. I try not to wake him while I pack my shit, but he's a light sleeper.

"Haze." He wipes his eyes and blinks repeatedly.

"Sorry. I'm just getting my things." I can't hide my gigantic smile.

"Wait, I know that smile. She took you back, didn't she?"

Damn right she did.

"She didn't say that exactly, but she's letting me move back." I shove my clothes into the black bag I brought with me. "Want to tell me why you're sleeping in here?"

He groans. "Kelly puked all over my bed."

I can't hold back a laugh.

"Fuck you." He throws a pillow at me, and I catch it, tossing it back to him.

"I told you friends with benefits are bad news."

He gives me the finger, half-smiling.

"I'll see you later, man," I say and exit the apartment complex. For the first time in a while, I don't feel like I have the weight of a building on my shoulders. Wow, this has been a decent day, so far. *Is this a glitch?*

I sprint back to my car, and my stomach drops to my asshole at the sight of a piece of paper on my windshield.

A ticket?

So much for this being a decent day, huh?

I come to a short stop next to my car and literally freeze—surprisingly not because of the cold weather—when I realize that this is everything but a parking ticket.

A note.

*You told. Good old dad paid the price.*

I turn it over.

*She's next.*

# TWENTY-TWO

## *One Last Fight*

*Winter*

Is there anything creepier than a hospital? Anything sadder than a place where misery bounces off the walls, sucking and crushing every ounce of happiness from your soul? One bed empties, another fills up. This one comes and this one goes, a reminder of the cycle we'll never escape. In the end, the majority of us end up here. Between beeping machines and nauseating white walls.

That's why you have to make sure the story you lived is better than the way it ends.

Spending so much time at the hospital during these past few days has made me reconsider what I want out of my years on this earth. I want to live, not just be *alive*. I want to seize the moment while it's here and look back upon my choices with no regrets.

When I get home… I'm going to tell Haze how much I love him. I'll tell him that I never stopped. I should've told him in the car earlier, but I chickened out, afraid that I was forgiving him too soon. I passed a devastated family on my way in, heard them cry over their lost kid, watched them fall apart for someone who ran out of time. I'm done wasting mine.

My gaze jolts up at the nurse entering the room. Jay's hand grows firm around mine. The forty-year-old woman beckons to come closer, which we do without so much as a second thought. We offer grateful looks to Will, Kass, Kendrick, and Alex. They're all here. Allie had to work, but she'll be joining us in a few hours. There's no way Kendrick and Kass will be allowed to visit him today, but they're okay with that. Harry might be their uncle, but Jay and I need our dad most of all.

My father's parents decided it was too much for Maika to handle at the moment. What good would seeing her father on the verge of death do? I don't even know if someone's had the "death" talk with her yet.

Heading toward the woman who holds my entire world in the palm of her hand, I combat my nerves.

"No improvement," the nurse says regretfully. "Still no sign of anyone who matches the hit-and-run description either. He's in the same state as he was a few days ago, but you can go see him."

Linking our arms together, we walk toward the room that's been assigned to our father and give the door a strong push. When I see him lying there, lifeless—*gone*—it's like every drop of courage and strength I worked so hard to gain is squeezed out of me all at once. My teary eyes overflow and I'm crying before I can make it to his side. I enclose his hand with mine. He's cold. Not *dead* cold, but colder than he's ever been before.

He's pale, too, almost ghostly, and the only sign that he's still alive is the recurrent beeping of the machine monitoring his heartbeat.

I wish I could say how much time we spent with him, talking about the most mundane of things, telling him how much we miss him, but it felt so unbearably long and disturbingly short at the same time. Jaden confessed to stealing Dad's favorite pen when he was a kid, and even in a moment as shitty as this one, we laughed—truly. We could only imagine what he would say if he were awake. He'd most likely make a joke out of it and hug us. He'd be the great dad he's always been.

"Time's up." A nurse pops her head into the doorway.

"Come back to us, Dad. We love you," Jay whispers before we're both escorted out. When we step back into the packed waiting room, I dare assume that I've been through the hardest part of my day. Apparently, the universe disagrees.

Lauren is awaiting us, sitting with her arms and legs crossed, designer bag by her side. She has no idea that Haze showed me the recording, that I know everything. This woman is not my mother. She's a monster. She forces a smile and lifts to her feet at the sight of us.

"My babies." She wraps her arms around us, and I cringe. Jaden, who hasn't a single clue as to what she said, hugs her back, although still angry about her disappearing act.

"What are you doing here?" I pull away.

"What do you mean? I'm here to see your father. Why else?"

"Why weren't you here yesterday?" Jay spits defensively.

"I thought your grandparents told you, honey. I was completely devastated. I… I needed some time," she lies, false pain twisting her features. "But I'm here now. I'm here to see your dad and take my baby boy home."

My teeth clench.

*Hell no.*

Jay eyes her with uncertainty.

"I don't think that's a good idea," I say.

Her fake smile is slapped off her face and replaced by a frown. Long gone is the nice caring mom when her true colors burst out to play.

"Is that so? Care to tell me why?"

It takes everything in me not to throw it all in her face. To spill about the recording, just to see her façade shatter before my eyes, but I bite my tongue to keep from slipping. We can use her ignorance to our advantage. This could be an asset one day.

"Well, you work a lot, and I only have school a few times a week," is the lame answer I settle for.

"So? He'll be in school while I'm working." She fails to conceal the bitterness stuffing her words. "Plus, he needs to be with his mother right now."

Jay gives me a pleading look, one that says, *"Please, don't let her take me."*

"Not to mention that I'm his legal guardian, but I'm sure I don't need to remind you." Her smile grows.

My hands roll into fists. I'm completely helpless against her. She's right. The law wants Jay with his parent, not his sister.

"I don't want to go back with you!" Jay snaps, taking both me and Lauren by surprise.

"E-Excuse me?" Shock is thick in her voice.

"You heard me. I don't want to go home with you. Winter's more my mother than you ever were. She's the one who showed up. You didn't give a shit about Dad. Or me!" His outburst draws unwanted attention to the scene.

Her face twists in fury. "Jaden! What did you just say to me? I'm your mother. They told me you were okay. If there was even the slightest chance that you had been hurt, I would've been there in a heartbeat."

That's when the fake tears come into play.

Guilt decreases Jaden's anger.

"After all that I've done for you. I raised you and y-you think that I'd be capable of—" She lets out the worst fake sob I've ever heard, covering her face with perfectly manicured hands.

"Mom, stop, it's okay. I'll go with you," Jay gives in, suddenly acutely aware of the unwanted audience. I must give it to her. She's good. The witch knew there's nothing a socially awkward fourteen-year-old moody boy hates more than being the center of attention.

"You… You will?" She sniffles.

"Yes. Just… stop crying, please." He grimaces.

"Great." Her sadness quickly vanishes. "I have to go see your father, then we'll be on our way home." A nurse walks into the waiting room the next second, beckoning for my mom to follow her. I watch the distance between us stretch with only one thought in mind…

I will bring that woman down if it is the last thing I do.

HAZE ADAMS HAS PUT ME IN in situations I'd never experienced before multiple times since I met him. He's been my first real crush, my first boyfriend, my first heartbreak. He's been a million things to me, but what he has never been… is *gone.*

Radio silent, vanished without a trace gone.

He was big on disappearing before we got together, but since we made it official? He's never ghosted me without so much as a phone call or a text. He's not a quitter. The thirty-something missed calls I got from him last week made that clear.

Lying in bed with Waze's head propped on my stomach, I wait for the guy I love to come bursting through the front door. He didn't come home last night. Nor did he answer any of my calls and messages. He said he was going to get his clothes at Vic's, then return to me.

So, I waited.

And waited.

And waited.

But he never came.

Alex, Will, and Kass hopped on a plane to Florida early this morning, so yesterday we had a "goodbye" dinner party after I got back from the hospital. It was a great night, one that managed to take my mind off the disaster that's currently my life. Allie and Kendrick even announced that they were thinking of moving in together, which means my cousin will be clearing out his room as soon as Haze officially moves back in.

*But that would require Haze still being alive.*

Paranoia steals what's left of my sanity. What if something happened to him? What if he's hurt? Should I call Vic? The cops? If he'd ended up crashing at Vic's when he went to get his clothes, he would've called.

*Screw this.* Pushing Waze off me gently, I grab my phone and sit up straight. It rings five times. He finally picks up.

"Hello?" Vic's voice emerges down the line.

"Hey, Vic. It's Winter. Have you seen Haze?" I skip straight to the point.

"Haze? No, I haven't seen Haze. Why would I have seen Haze?" He speaks so rapidly, doubt creeps into my mind.

I smell bullshit.

Then I hear something in the background.

*Him.*

I can't tell what he's saying, but I'd pick out his voice amongst millions. Vic's lying.

"Why are you lying to me?"

Thrown off, he says, "Listen, Winter, I know this might be hard for you to understand, but just… stay away from him, okay? Trust me, this is for the best."

I frown. "What the hell is that supposed to mean?"

"I'm sorry. I have to go."

"But—"

The fucker hangs up on me.

Maybe I should've listened, left it alone, agreed to sit this one out, but I found myself on my way to Vic's place before my voice of reason could catch up with my emotions.

Striding down the hall, I try and remember which door is Victor's. Rushed footsteps echo in the distance and pique my curiosity. A gorgeous ginger girl in heels passes me five seconds later. We make eye contact, and my gaze lingers on her hoop earring as she walks—yes, earring, *singular*. She's missing one. I can only imagine the insane story she'll tell her friends.

*Must've been one heck of a night.*

Who knows, she may even be leaving Vic. From what Haze's told me, Vic broke up with Bea and it's led him to meaningless hookups.

I come to a quick stop in front of Victor's door and knock four times. Motion rises on the other side. Footsteps, whispers, murmurs. Then nothing.

The door opens.

"Hey," I greet Vic.

Shifting from one foot to the another, he says, "Go home, Winter. He's not here."

"I heard his voice on the phone." I glimpse at the guest room door over his shoulder. "Sorry, no time for manners." I push past him, inside the apartment.

"Winter, wait!" He grips my wrist. "I'm trying to help you here. Just go home. Don't do this to yourself."

If I thought I was scared before, I'd obviously never felt like *this*. Something in his eyes rubs me the wrong way.

It's pity. He's pitying me.

*What the fuck?*

Intent on getting what I came for—who I came for—I snatch my wrist away and close my hand around the handle, glancing back at Vic one last time. Ashamed, he eyes the floor. Weirded out by his behavior, I turn the knob.

I don't put the pieces together at first.

Not when I see Haze sitting on the pull-out couch he calls his bed with his head in his hands.

Not even when I notice his luggage piled up in the corner of the room.

The first red flag is the guilt radiating off him.

The second is the condom foil on his floor.

But what truly ends me…

Is the hoop earring on his nightstand.

I'm shocked—the kind of shocked that knocks you on your ass, steals your breath away, leaves you for dead. His blue eyes snap up to me.

"Winter, I…" He pushes to his feet. "I'm so sorry. I can explain."

No, this isn't real.

The girl in the hall…

She wasn't leaving Vic.

*She was leaving Haze.*

"Tell me you didn't," I beg, my voice so weak it's barely audible.

"I'm so sorry." He walks toward me.

"That's it?" I blurt. "That's all you have to say?"

"I never meant for this to happen. It's just… This time apart made me realize that I don't feel the same way about you anymore." He can't even look me in the eyes, too much of a coward. "I didn't want to admit it to myself. I didn't want to accept that what we have is gone. Vic and I went out for a drink when I came to get my things yesterday, and she was there. We started flirting, she kissed me, one thing led to another and…"

"You slept with her?" My voice cracks on the last word.

"You deserve better than me, Winter. You always have. I was never good enough for you."

"No." I shake my head in denial. "I don't believe you. You're lying."

He sighs. "I'm not."

"Yes, you are." I step forward and push him with all my strength. He tumbles back a step. "You're lying. We were so close to getting back together. Just yesterday, you said…" *Here come the tears.* "You said you loved me."

He rubs his neck. "I know, and I really thought I did."

I can't fucking breathe.

"But I don't."

Merely hours ago, I thought we still stood a chance. Even after he lied to me, I was dumb enough to think we'd find our way back to each other. But after this? It's really over. He did the one thing I can never go back from.

*Let that sink in, Winter.*

*He had sex with someone else. He cheated on you.*

I offer him the last thread still holding my heart together. "I need to hear you say it."

"Please don't ask me that."

"Haze, if you really cheated on me… if you *really* just destroyed everything we had for one night, I need you to have the balls to look me in the eyes and fucking say it," I snap.

He hesitates for a minute. Then, still with his eyes glued to the floor, he exhales. "I slept with her."

"Look at me," I insist.

So, he does. Stares me dead in the eyes and says it.

"I slept with her."

My heart sinks.

"And everything you said? About how you'd never give up on us? How I was the risk you'd always take? It was all bullshit? Just some twisted game?" I'm bawling at this point.

"It wasn't." He steps forward, his eyes devoid of the promises I thought would always be there. "I do care for you. But I'm not *in love* with you anymore. Haven't been for a long time."

*Ding! You've reached your quota of heartbreak for the rest of your life. Congrats.*

"I'm so sorry it took me cheating on you to understand that, but… Maybe we can still be friends."

That's the last straw.

I can't think straight. I slap him. Hard. I don't feel bad. Not even in the slightest. *How dare he mention the word "friend"?*

He clenches his jaw. "I deserved that."

I carry myself to the door, footsteps heavy, eyes full of tears. With my back facing him, I choke on words I don't mean.

"I never want to see you again."

I have to mean these words. *I need to.* It's not registering. That he betrayed me in the worst possible way. That he went back to being the guy he was when we met that first day in the hall. His redemption is gone. Forever. I rush out of the room to see Vic sitting on the couch with a beer in hand. I know that he heard the whole thing from the wrenching pity displayed by his features. I'm out of their rat hole in a heartbeat. Deep down, I expect him to follow me. To tell me he didn't really sleep with that ginger girl. Simply because that's what he would've done before. That's what the Haze I thought I knew would've done.

But *this* Haze doesn't.

And, as I walk down the hall alone, I know he never will.

# TWENTY-THREE

## *One Last Lie*

I always loved to believe that there was some sort of limit to the amount of bullshit the universe could drop on a person. I liked to think someone up there was keeping scores and saying, *"Woah. Okay, guys. Ease up on the poor fella before he gives up on humanity."*

What happened to me in the past few weeks is proof that I was wrong. There is no such thing as a limit of bad luck per person, and for as long as you're alive, you shall get served.

Barely keeping myself awake through the most boring class of all time, I debate on getting up and walking out right in the middle of my professor's lecture. Barely twenty minutes in, I knew I'd made a mistake by going back to school. Journalism isn't for me. Truth is, I have no clue what *is* for me, and that's okay. The answers are out there, I'm sure of it.

But I won't find them here.

Haze's sudden transformation into a human trash can incited me to reconsider many of my decisions. It gave me a whole lot of alone time, time that I admittedly needed to come to terms with my existential crisis and understand that when something feels wrong, it usually is.

It's been around eleven days since Haze cheated on me. I think counting the days is part of my defense mechanisms, my uncanny way of coping. I give myself a pat in the back for every day I get through without crying. *God, I hate what heartbreak has turned me into.*

Haze will be staying at Vic's until I move out at the beginning of December. We only talked once, and by talked, I mean we texted, and by *we*, I mean he texted and I ignored. He said he'll be paying the rent in full this month. That I'm welcome to stay there until I move back into my childhood home with lovely Lauren.

*Bitch, after what you did to me, don't mind if I do.*

Kendrick will also be moving in with Allie soon. We had to pay a huge fine to the landlord for severing the lease. It cost us three months' rent up front, which, even split in three, dug a gigantic hole into my savings.

Allie and Kendrick were as surprised as me to find out Haze cheated. The whole world was, to be honest. You'd think a guy who chases a girl's forgiveness for days on end wouldn't drop her as soon as she gives it to him. It took both Allie and me to stop Kendrick from driving over to Vic's and beating up Haze to defend my honor. To think these two were finally starting to like each other. I'm guessing we'll never know what happened. What changed for him to stop loving me overnight.

Mr. Spit telling us to complete a forty-page paper for next week is my cue. *Nope. I'm out.* I gather my things in the middle of the assignment description, throw my coat on, and walk out of the classroom without a care in the world. My plan for today is simple: get coffee, go visit my dad at the hospital, and finally, try and come up with a good enough reason to give him if he ever wakes up. He'll want to know why I dropped out of school and… I doubt that *life sucks* will cut it.

WHEN I STEP INTO THE APARTMENT that won't be mine for much longer, I shake off the chills skittering down my coat and remove my boots. I've really got to get a full-time job and buy myself a car. Kendrick is practically always at work or at Allie's nowadays, which makes it hard to hitch a ride to the hospital. I had to get a cab today due to the long distance and crazy snowstorm. No changes in my dad's state, but we're still hopeful.

Hanging my coat, I frown at the absence of my overexcited pup. Waze is always—literally always—waiting for me by the door. A frown creases my forehead when unidentified noises erupt in the distance.

"Kendrick, you home?" I turn the corner and quickly understand why my baby wasn't waiting for me. He's already all over someone else—the last person I wanted to see.

Haze is standing in the living room, playing with Waze—I think I'll have no choice but to change his name. Dangling off his arm is a gym bag full of clothes. He probably came to get the last of his stuff. He usually comes when I'm in school. I know because I notice his belongings disappearing from the apartment bit by bit along with the smell of his cologne and every trace of our love.

When he notices me, I pray that he won't talk to me. Or even look at me. I don't want to have to be civil. I want him to disappear until I forget the sound of his voice.

Don't talk to me.

Don't talk to me.

Don't talk to—

"Hey."

*Dang it.*

"Hey."

"I just came by to get the rest of my stuff." He motions to his gym bag.

"I can see that."

His blue eyes are empty, vacant. It's clear that he hasn't been sleeping. Probably too busy juggling conquests. Nevertheless, it feels like he's gripping and squeezing my heart at full force just standing there looking this good.

"How have you been?" he tries.

*Oh, you know, I've been partying every night to celebrate getting cheated on. One less goal on my bucket list.*

"Fine."

He nods, silently standing there with his hands in his pockets. Why is he forcing this? I sure hope he's not waiting for me to return the question.

He lowers his gaze to his feet. "I should go."

I nod and he heads for the door.

"Haze?" I say.

He swivels around, and for a brief second, I think I see a gleam of hope light up his stare. I must be insane.

"Please text me in advance if you come by again. I dropped out of school, so I'll be home often until I get a full-time job. I'll make sure we don't run into each other."

His eyes widen. "Wait. You dropped out of school?"

*Like you care.*

"Yeah. Journalism isn't for me."

He begins to reply, but he's cut off by the front door swinging open. Snickering, Allie and Kendrick stumble into the apartment with Chinese takeout boxes in hand. Their smiles slip away at the sight of Haze.

"That's my cue." He flinches under Kendrick's loathing glare. "Good luck with everything."

I don't reply and watch him exit.

"What was that?" Kendrick says the second the door closes.

I shrug. "He just came by to get more of his stuff."

"Again?" Allie exclaims. "It's been like five times."

Kendrick snorts. "Yeah, the guy doesn't even own that many things. He's just looking for excuses to come back, I'm telling you."

I almost scoff. When they see I'm not going to fuel their nonsense, they hop onto another topic and begin the classy inhaling of their food. A few minutes later, Allie sits by my side on the couch and bats her eyelashes at me.

"So… there's a party this Friday."

Oh, Lord.

"And?"

"And you're coming with me. You too, babe." She smiles at Kendrick, who doesn't seem sold on the idea. "Come on, it'll be fun."

Kendrick quickly surrenders to his girlfriend's pout and puppy eyes. As for me, I consider fighting her but lack the necessary energy.

"Sure."

She frowns. "Wait, just like that?"

"Just like that." I laugh quietly.

Yes, I'd rather crawl under a rock and never come out, but meeting new people could be good for me—might take my mind off my horrendous breakup. Today was step one to getting my shit together. I need to make a change. No, I need to make *changes*. I can't be the same Winter anymore. A new life takes work, and I might not exactly know where this new life is going to take me, but I do know one thing: it'll be far, far away from Haze Adams.

"THERE YOU GO, GORGEOUS. ALL DONE."

There are many things a girl tends to do after a breakup: get drunk, cry, sleep with a random guy, eat pints of ice cream, feel guilty about it, cry some more and… change her hair. I might have skipped many of the abovementioned steps, but I didn't escape the latest option.

When the hairdresser spins my chair around and I catch a glimpse of myself in the mirror, I blink in shock. I've always been curious about darker hair. I've been a brunette my whole life, clinging to my birth-given color and dreading changes. But now that my once pale brown hair shifts toward black, I don't regret it. I have no idea what it is about getting new hair that makes some girls feel empowered. Maybe it's like letting go of the past and looking forward. Getting a fresh cut means getting a fresh start.

"My, my. Them boys are going to need help picking up the pieces of their broken hearts when you're done with them." The kind hairdresser hypes me up. Little does she know the only person who needs help with their broken heart is me.

I miss him. Terribly. But he doesn't miss me, and he cheated. I can't ever forgive him for that. I sure hope for his sake that she was more than just a fling. Or else he ruined *forever* for a few hours.

When I head back to the front of the store, I can't help but wonder what he's doing. It's been two long days since he came to pick up the last of his clothes. He hasn't been back since, and I doubt that he ever will be. I can't believe that night was potentially the last time I'll ever see him.

Once I've paid, I pull my phone out. Seven missed calls

from the hospital. Five messages from Kendrick.

*Shit, something's wrong.*

I select Kendrick's messages with my heart crawling up my throat and read them too fast for their contents to imprint onto my brain. The victory doesn't seem real at first, overshadowed by an endless parade of tragedies. Until, finally, it sinks in.

Maybe there is a guy keeping scores up there, after all.

He's awake.

"WHERE IS HE?" I BURST THROUGH the doors of the waiting room with one mission and one mission only: see my dad. Kendrick, Allie, and Jaden jump from their seats.

"We can't see him yet." Jay strides to me. I pull him into a hug. We've been texting since he went back to live with my mom. Our conversations mainly consist of him begging me to come pick him up, but I can't add custody battles to my *school dropout, heartbroken mess* plate right now.

"They'll tell us as soon as he's ready," Kendrick adds.

"How did you even know?" I question.

"Don't be mad…" Kendrick says uneasily. "They couldn't reach Lauren. Or you. So, they went for the second number they had for you."

It hits me.

"Haze," I deduce.

The first time we showed up, right after the accident, we had to give them as many numbers to reach us as possible. Haze was there and insisted that if, for whatever reason, I couldn't pick up, he would, no matter what.

"He called you?" I'm surprised.

Kendrick nods. "I'm assuming he thought you wouldn't pick up if he tried, so he let us know instead. We picked up Jay from school right away."

I don't let the gesture affect me for longer than a split second. He was just doing what any decent human being would. Although I do have to wonder what happened to that sweet, caring Haze who would suggest adding his own number to the records to make sure I'd never miss a call.

"Where's Lauren?" I ask.

"On her way here," Jay says. "Pray that she's stuck in traffic."

Allie smacks a hand to her mouth. "Oh my God. Your hair!"

Bringing awareness to my makeover, Allie's statement earns me a handful of compliments from all three of them. I do appreciate knowing it doesn't look awful.

"Your father is ready," the doctor in charge of my dad tells us with a smile half an hour later. Jaden and I trail toward the room my dad's been moved to, brimming with confounding emotions: relief, fear, joy, sadness.

He's lying in the hospital bed we were so terribly afraid he'd spend his last days in. Jay throws himself into his arms, and my dad winces in pain at first, causing Jay to apologize profusely. He warns us as to having broken ribs, a fractured leg and a mild concussion.

"I'm here, son. I'm not going anywhere."

Jay cries harder, nestling his forehead on my dad's shoulder instead. My father's eyes drift to me. "Hey, pumpkin."

The nickname ends me.

Tears of joy come pouring down my face, and I'm next in line for the weird head-to-shoulder hug. There are so many things I want to tell him. Things I *have* to tell him before Lauren gets here.

"We came to see you almost every day." Jay sniffles.

"I know." My dad reaches for both our hands, squeezing our fingers tightly between his. "I heard you. All of you. I heard Haze, I heard—"

"Wait. Haze?" I frown.

"Yes," he confirms.

"Haze came to see you alone?"

He nods.

"I also heard that *someone* stole my favorite pen." He glances at my brother, who cracks a laugh. I had no idea Haze came to see my father. Why would he do that? I know they grew pretty close when we were together, but I didn't think it was to the point of coming to see him after we broke up.

Jay and I catch him up on everything he's missed, and my dad, being my dad, listens to every bit of our stories with a smile and genuine interest on his face.

"When are they releasing you?" Jay asks.

"They want to keep me a bit longer, but they're hopeful. It shouldn't be too long," he reassures us.

Minutes later, when I see that Lauren still hasn't arrived, I know it's now or never. I ask Jay if we can have a minute alone, and he halfheartedly agrees. He doesn't need to hear this. I can't let my father go back home with Lauren unless he knows exactly who he lies in bed with at night.

"What's wrong, pumpkin?"

"Dad, there's… something you need to know."

I get my phone out of my pocket, collecting the necessary nerves to press Play to the recording that'll surely destroy the man who spent his entire life building me up. The only thing getting me through the guilt of making him suffer is the thought that sometimes, we need to destroy…

In order to rebuild something beautiful.

WHEN KENDRICK TOLD ME MY DAD was awake, it was clear in my head that any plans I had for the rest of the day were officially canceled. There is absolutely nothing I could've seen myself doing except be by my father's side, especially after telling him a piece of news like that.

Yet, here I am, in my bedroom, bobbing my head to Beyoncé while Allie curls my now dark hair. I should've known better than to think she would let me escape her frat party plan. It turns out the doctor didn't want anyone in their way tonight. Not to mention my father insisted on being alone to process what he'd heard.

He didn't make a sound. Just sat through the recording and listened to every word down to the last second. Then, as if he wasn't already the best goddamn man on earth, he looked at me, shed a tear, and said, "I'm so sorry you had to hear this, sweetheart."

I'll never fathom how he found it in himself to make this about *me*. He's the one being cheated on, the one with a wife who tried to sleep with her daughter's boyfriend. *He's* the one with a partner in love with his wallet. He didn't say much else. Anger is not who he is, but his eyes told a million stories.

Broken. That's what he was.

He thanked me for showing it to him. Promised he'd do what was right for the family and take Maika away from Lauren. The doctor assured both me and him that they wouldn't let Lauren see him as forced encounters may have nefarious effects on an already fragile patient's health.

I couldn't bring myself to tell him that Haze cheated on me when he made me promise to thank him for putting up with Lauren and recording her that night.

"All done," Allie shrieks at the final result.

She has to practically drag my ass into the cab waiting out front when the time comes. She says this party is everything I need. I say what I need is my bed.

I changed my mind. I don't want to meet new people. I want to shut off the rest of the world until I get a certain blue-eyed boy out of my system. As we pull up to the packed-with-drunk-people frat house, I can't shake the feeling that this is either going to be amazing…

Or the worst night of my life.

# TWENTY—FOUR

## *One More Truth*

Pushing through the sweaty crowd with Allie, I consider telling her that I don't feel well and sparing myself while I still can. The last time I drank, Haze had to come and get my wasted ass in a place similar to this one. Everything about this moment is a reminder that tonight, he's not here to do it. Even worse, he's the reason I need a night out.

"Let's get Jell-O shots." Allie drags me and Kendrick deeper into the clusters of people. She was right. This party was the students' topic of the week. Posters were hung everywhere in the halls when I went back to empty my locker.

"Come to mama." Allie stops near the bar and reaches for three of the remaining shots. I throw the cup back as quickly as I can, secretly hoping it'll make my presence here any less painful.

News flash: it doesn't.

But what really kills my already weak mood…

Is the sight of Haze sitting on the couch across the room.

Next to him are Vic, a few other guys, and… a blonde. She's tall, busty, gorgeous, and sitting on the armrest next to him. I can tell from the way she keeps on adjusting her shirt to draw attention to her cleavage that she has every intention of bringing Haze back to her dorm tonight.

*I will make her swallow her hair extensions, I swear.*

He looks bored out of his mind, shifting uncomfortably and pushing her off every time she attempts to slide on his lap. It's obvious he's not interested in her, but she can't seem to take a hint. When she leans in to whisper something in his ear, he looks up.

And sees me.

Shock flashes in his gaze.

I can't tell what he's thinking—or feeling. Is he happy? Surprised? Mad? I'm not asking for a lot. I just need him to feel *something.* Any trace of emotion will do at this point.

When he peels his eyes away from me and becomes invested in the conversation with Miss Perfect, it feels like my heart is being slowly carved out of my chest.

Indifference.

Cold, hard indifference.

I don't look away. What's the point? Watching him flirt with her might be exactly what I need—a dose of reality.

*He cheated on you. What's it going to take to get that through your head? Do you need to actually see him fuck her?*

Allie's voice erupts behind me. "Just say the word and I'll accidentally pour a drink over that girl."

I shrug. "He's single. He can do whatever he wants."

She rolls her eyes. "What? Cut the crap. Everybody knows

you were this close to getting back together. He was head over heels in love with you. This makes no sense. You need to call him out on his shit."

She has a point, I know she does. Does that mean I'm going to have a go at my cheater of an ex-boyfriend while sober? Absolutely not. Allie tells me she's going to go to the bathroom, and Kendrick follows, which tips me off about what he *really* intends to do in there. A few minutes slip away. Still no sign of them.

So not cool, cousin.

Haze is still on the couch, downing beer after beer, as I lean back against the wall with crossed arms and watch wasted people dance. Four girls, all bearing drinks, stop next to me, and I step sideways to give them room.

My eyebrows shoot to the ceiling.

Amongst them… is hoop earring girl.

The girl Haze cheated on me with.

She looks right through me. She doesn't recognize me. Why would she? She doesn't care that the guy she banged after a night out had someone in his life. She was out to have fun, and I can't even blame her. The one I should hate is Haze. And I will hate him… *In time.*

"Holy shit. Who's that?" The brunette alongside Hoop fans herself.

"Who?"' Hoop says.

"The hottie next to Vic." Her friend points at Haze.

*Of fucking course.*

"Oh, new guy," Hoop figures out.

"Damn," friend number two agrees. "Is he single?"

"Trust me, you're going to want to pass on this one."

"Why?" the brunette questions.

"I know he's smoking hot and all, but he's got issues." Hoop guzzles the contents of a red cup.

"Girl, send him my way. I can deal with his issues anytime." The brunette smirks, causing her friends to snicker.

"I'm telling you. He and Vic were at the pub the other day, and he came up to me, straight up asked me to go back to his place. I was like *Yes, please.*"

I wince. I can't listen to her talk about how she slept with Haze. I just can't. I give myself a slight push off the wall and start to walk away, but what Hoop says next keeps me in place.

"Then nothing."

"What do you mean *nothing*?" Her friend frowns.

"He literally paid me a hundred dollars to crash at his place and do nothing. Dude wouldn't even look at me. Like I had a fucking disease or something. Then, in the morning, he just kicked me out at a specific time. It was so sketch, and I lost my favorite earring."

My heart flips.

"I think he was trying to get some girl off his back. I remember seeing some chick in the hall, but I mean, goddamn, a hundred dollars for someone to take a hint. Just dump her and be done with it." She cackles.

It's a wonder my knees haven't given out when one of them suggests hitting the dance floor and they scatter away.

Baffled, I grip the nearest piece of furniture.

Haze didn't cheat on me.

*Haze didn't cheat on me.*

He paid that girl to be there.

But why? Why would he want me to think he cheated? Why would he bulldoze my heart like this… when we were *this* close to being together again?

I don't think twice and make my way over to the couch, barely squeezing through the crowd. Haze seems surprised when he sees me approaching. The blonde girl sees me too and, probably because I look like I'm about to murder someone, she has the good instinct to walk away.

I stop in front of him, hands on my hips, eyes dark as the night. Conversations are cut short as the other guys seated on the couch notice me.

"Hey, beautiful," some guy says. "Need help with something?"

Vic elbows him and offers me an apologetic smile. At least he's still decent unlike *someone.*

"What do you want, Winter?" Haze huffs.

Dark-haired dude tenses up. "Hold on a second. *That's* Winter?"

Haze glares at him in response.

So, he's told them about me.

"What do you want?" Haze repeats.

"We need to talk."

He avoids my eyes. "Why? The whole point of not being together anymore is that we don't have to talk."

*Ouch.*

The idiots next to him cheer him on—all but Vic—and I swallow hard. Without a word, I clasp my fingers around his tattooed arm and force his ass off the couch. Prying eyes follow our every move as I drag him to a quiet corner. I open my mouth to speak, but the surprise on his face stops me.

A small smile tugs at his lips.

"Your hair." He tucks a loose piece of hair behind my ear. "You changed it." I'm taken aback by the sweet gesture. For a second there, I recognize him: the Haze I loved. But as though he's just remembered that he's supposed to hate me, he clears his throat. "What do you want? I don't have all night."

"Oh my God, aren't you exhausted? Just drop the act already. You're not telling me everything. What the hell happened? What changed for your feelings to disappear overnight?"

He keeps his eyes fixated on the floor.

"Maybe I got tired of waiting for you to give me a chance, Winter."

"What?" *Is he serious?* "I needed time. Can you really blame me? You lied to me for months. Months. Was I supposed to just let that slide?"

"No, you weren't, and I understand why you didn't want to be with me anymore, but, I guess… after a while, I got tired of chasing a girl I couldn't have. I don't feel the way I once did. You're just going to have to let this go, okay?"

That bullshit again.

"I know you didn't cheat on me."

His jaw falls.

Panic stirs in his blue eyes, but he quickly pulls himself together, driving his emotions away with a deep sigh.

"Doesn't change anything."

I step forward. "Why would you do that? Why would you go out of your way to break my heart?"

He worries his bottom lip, eyes darting back to his shoes.

"Haze, please." I can't believe myself when I defy my last shred of dignity and place a gentle hand on his cheek. The gesture screams *come back to me.* He closes his eyes under my touch, like he missed it as much as I missed him. Then he shakes his head and steps out of my hold.

"I knew it was the only way you'd really let me go. What we had was too strong for you to just accept that I don't love you anymore. It was the only way to make sure you'd leave me alone."

"So, that's it? You did all this just to get rid of me?"

"Don't make this any harder than it needs to be." He doesn't flinch.

"Fine." My voice falters. "Don't worry. I'll never bother you again."

He opens his mouth, like he wants to say something, but decides against it.

"Now, if you'll excuse me, I have a party to enjoy. After all, I'm single." I walk off, elbows ramming into my rib cage on the way to… *I don't know where?* I'm going to find Allie and tell her I'm leaving, that's where.

I'm heading for the staircase when I bump into someone. I tumble back a step and mutter an apology.

"Winter?"

My eyes snap up.

"Caleb?" I say with a surprisingly real smile. Before the night I ruined it all, before he fell for me, before he told all me about Haze on my birthday, he was my best friend. The guy I could always turn to.

He notices my distraught expression. "Are you okay? You look like you could use a friend."

I dodge his question. "What are you doing here?"

"You are aware that I have other friends, right? Someone invited me." He laughs. "What about you?"

My gaze wanders to Haze, who found his way back to the couch. But you know who also found their way back to the couch? The blonde girl.

Except that now, she's sitting on his lap.

*Death in 3, 2, 1…*

"Huh, mind telling me what the hell your boyfriend is doing

with Laura?"

*Breathe, Winter.*

"So, that's her name," I say more to myself than to him. "He's not my boyfriend anymore. We're officially over."

"You decided you couldn't deal with the lies, huh?"

"No, it's actually not my doing," I painfully admit.

"Wait, you mean… he's the one who broke up with you?" He sounds astounded.

"Yep. Made it crystal clear. He doesn't love me anymore."

He frowns, not buying it.

"Want to put that to the test?" He hooks one arm around my waist so fast my breath hitches in my throat.

"Caleb," I warn.

"Just trust me," he says with a reassuring smile. I can tell from the way he's looking at me that he's trying to prove a point. His right hand lies flat on my back while his other smooths down the fabric of my dress. Then he kisses my cheek. It's harmless, but I still feel uncomfortable. Caleb tilts his head forward to whisper, "He's mentally murdering me right now."

Certain that he's wrong, I pull away and send a quick glance in Haze's direction. Our eyes instantly connect through the dimmed red-colored lights. He's staring straight at us, his eyes loaded with anger.

"Doesn't mean anything." I focus on Caleb.

"Trust me, he's jealous."

He's probably just drunk.

"He's still staring," Caleb says.

"Doesn't he have Laura to keep him occupied?"

"She's practically shoving her tits in his face. He doesn't give a shit. I'm telling you, he's not over you."

I wish I could believe him, but I'm done searching for the hidden meaning behind Haze Adams's actions. His words told me everything I needed to know. I heard them loud and clear.

"He said otherwise." I peek at Haze from the corner of my eye. Wow, he's got this whole murder look down. *Does he practice in front of the mirror?* "Maybe we should go."

"Good idea." Caleb grabs my hand and intertwines our fingers. I frown as he leads me to the staircase. I halt my footsteps, hesitant. He murmurs, "Just go with it."

Torn, I decide that I have nothing left to lose anyway. We disappear up the stairs together, and he turns around seconds before we reach the second floor. "Believe me, once I'm done, you'll thank me."

# TWENTY-FIVE

## *One Last Night*

"Come on." Caleb kicks the door to the bedroom shut and walks over to the mini fridge pushed up in the corner. It's filled with booze.

"Are we even allowed to be in here?" I question.

"This is my friend's room. We're good." Caleb grabs the one bottle of water in the whole fridge.

"Why here?" I sit on the edge of the bed.

"People don't go up those stairs to play board games, if you know what I mean. I bet he's losing his mind out there, wondering what we're doing." He joins me.

"Yeah, well, he dumped me. He can't be jealous."

*He lost that right when he tore my heart out of my chest and stepped on it.*

He shrugs. "You two will find your way back to each other. You always do."

I'm surprised. "Caleb, I hope you won't mind me asking, but a few days ago, you were… I mean, isn't this weird for you?"

"Because I caught feelings for you?" He laughs quietly. "Nah. When we met up at the coffee shop and I saw how miserable you were without him, I don't know, I guess I had a revelation. I want to be loved like that. I want to be loved the way that you love him." He briefly pauses. "I think I fell for you because you were the closest thing I had to a girlfriend, you know? Because we grew up together. But in the end… you belong with him. I have my Winter waiting for me somewhere, and I'll find her, one day." He smiles.

It feels like a huge weight's been lifted off my shoulders.

"I never got to tell you, but… I'm sorry. About everything. It was wrong of me to tell you the truth on your birthday. It wasn't my secret to tell. I hope you can forgive me."

After everything I put him through when he had feelings for me, the way I led him on that night, I owe it to him. We both made mistakes. We're both guilty.

"It's okay." I smile.

*Several drunk couples walking in and out when they see the room is occupied* later, we decide it might be time for us to head back out there. Seconds before we exit the bedroom, Caleb steps in my way and pops the first two buttons of his shirt.

"What are you doing?"

"You'll see." He grins.

"Caleb…" I'm not sure I like where this is going.

"You want him to stop lying to himself or not?"

We hurry down to the first floor, and I'm relieved, yet a bit disappointed, not to see Haze anywhere. We enter the kitchen to play beer pong, and I instantly spot him. Chugging down a vodka bottle. Not drinking—*chugging*. This isn't good.

No sign of Laura.

One of his douche friends notifies him of our presence with a nudge. He looks up and stares… hard. When he sees Caleb button up his shirt, I swear I can hear him mentally planning the murder. *What's his deal?*

Caleb asks if I want to play beer pong, and I accept. Twenty minutes later, we've completely destroyed the two girls we were playing with. Caleb pulls me into a hug in the midst of joy, and Haze scampers out of the room with a tight jaw. The front door is slammed, but I don't move a muscle. I pretend that I didn't see it, that I'm unbothered, but all I want to do is follow and ask him why…

Why his mouth says something but his actions say otherwise. Why he pushes me away but can't stand to see someone else pull me closer. Why he's possessive of something he doesn't want anymore.

Why the one who threw my heart on the ground can't stand to see someone else pick it up.

THE SOUND OF THE DOOR CLOSING invades my silent apartment, and I strip off my coat in a hurry. It's close to 3:00 a.m. I search for Waze for a while, only to find him sleeping in my room. After a few hours of playing beer pong with Caleb, I managed to get a hold of Allie and Kendrick. They—big surprise—were quite *busy* the majority of the night. Tipsy, smudged-lipsticked Allie apologized a million times for leaving me alone, but I didn't hold it against her. She's in love. I'm happy for her. Kendrick said he would be crashing at Allie's place tonight and coming home tomorrow.

Caleb offered to drive me back to the apartment, but he was wasted, so we ended up splitting a cab. I'd had a bit to drink myself, although not nearly as much as he did. Before I got out, he hit me with a *"You're welcome."* I'm not sure what he meant by that, but I'm way too exhausted to overthink it. I just want to get into a scorching shower and sleep it off.

When I step under the hot water, every muscle in my body unwinds. Ten minutes later, I'm reaching for the towel hanging off the corner of the bathtub and wrapping it around my body.

That's when I hear them.

The footsteps.

I jolt around, holding on to my towel for dear life. This is it. I'm going to die. There's an intruder in the apartment. They're going to murder me, and the police will find me dead and naked in my bathroom, which, by the way, has always been my worst fucking nightmare.

I reach for the closest weapon I can find which happens to be a steel candleholder. The bathroom door creaks open, and I let out a gigantic breath of relief.

In the doorway is a very drunk Haze.

He's barely maintaining his balance, leaning against the doorframe drunkenly. His eyes are bloodshot from all the alcohol, yet so mesmerizing I can't tolerate staring directly into them.

"Haze, you scared the shit out of me." My chest inflates with heavy breaths. "What are you doing here?"

"As far as I know, I live here, baby," he rasps.

He's completely gone. Lights off. *No one's home.*

"You don't live here anymore," I correct.

He's about to say something but stops. "Why are you holding a candleholder?"

"Oh, right." I put it down, embarrassed. "I thought I was going to have to fight an intruder naked."

"With a candleholder?" He bites back a grin.

"Shut up." I can't help a small smile.

His pale eyes travel up and down my body shamelessly. He watches the drops of water rolling down my chest, the extra-small towel unsuccessfully covering my whole cleavage. It's practically a miracle that my nipples aren't showing. I can't pull the towel up without exposing too much down *there.* Shit, I really should've checked the towel I picked.

"Why didn't you go to Vic's?" I ask.

He shrugs carelessly. "Because I don't want to. I want to be here." His lips quirk up into a grin. "With you."

The lust in his eyes speaks a language only I know.

"Did something happen?" he asks before I can tell him to get out.

I frown. "What do you mean?"

"With that son of a bitch. Did something happen?" He steps

closer, anger clouding his judgment.

It clicks in my head.

"Caleb?"

He doesn't reply, but I read between the lines.

"Why do you care?"

"That's not an answer," he growls.

Something takes over me. "What? It's true. You shouldn't care if he took me from behind right there in that bedroom, Haze. You can't care. You don't love me anymore, remember?" I'm surprised by my own guts. *Who is this girl?*

His features harden. He always hated even imagining someone touching me—at least, he did before. His expression keeps me gushing down a self-destructive path.

"What's wrong, Hazie? You don't like that? You don't like thinking of another guy making me come? You don't want to imagine him fucki—"

"Stop," he snaps.

His anger catches me off guard.

"Relax. I'm just playing. Isn't that your new thing? Playing people?" I taunt.

"So, nothing happened?" He sure is persistent.

I give a sigh. "No. Not that it should matter to you."

His gaze remains locked on me. "It does."

Certain I heard that wrong, I search his eyes.

"*It does matter.*"

Right. That's why you wanted nothing to do with me a few

hours ago.

"I don't have time for this. Please get out of my way so I can put some clothes on."

All my request does is earn me a full, slow body scan. *Sure, Winter. Remind him that you're naked when he's drunk and horny as hell. Good idea.*

He doesn't acknowledge what I just said or walk out like I expect him to. Instead, he ventures farther into the room and slams the door. But that's not the important part…

The important part is what he does next.

He locks the door.

*Gulp.*

"What are you doing?" Tingles hasten down my spine.

He probably thinks Kendrick will be coming home soon. He doesn't know he's staying at Allie's.

"I… I can't do this anymore." His voice roars with defeat—like dropping to your knees and surrendering once and for all.

"D-Do what?"

He takes a step forward, and I can feel my pulse throb uncontrollably in my neck. No, he can't be doing this. Not when he just told me to leave him alone. Not when he went as far as to pretend he cheated on me to get me off his back.

"Haze, you're just drunk and lonely. Go home." My voice is trembling with pain… but it's also quaking with desire. *God, I wish I didn't want you. Fucking Haze Adams.* "You need sleep."

He continues to close in on me. "I need you."

Holy shit, has it always been this hot in here?

He steps forward until my back merges with the freezing tiles of the bathroom wall.

"You don't," I disagree. "You don't need me. You made that clear." I brush off his lies before they dig their claws any deeper into my heart. Without a care given, he presses his broad and sculpted body to mine, leaving no room to escape—I'm not sure I would if I could—and I quickly realize his muscles aren't the only *hard* parts on his body.

"I thought I could do this… I thought I could force you to stay away, but I can't," he rambles on, running his thumb across my lower lip. I desperately try and convince myself that he doesn't affect me.

*It's fine. I'm good. I don't feel anything.*

"Not even for something so important. I tried. I really fucking tried, but I'm losing my goddamn mind." He buries his head into the hollow of my neck, standing still for a few unbearable seconds until he starts to feather hot kisses up and down my jawline.

Okay. Fuck. I felt *that*.

"I can't live without you, Winter." He sounds so desperate I almost let myself believe him. Almost.

My throat closes up.

"Then why did you break my heart?"

I hate how vulnerable I sound, how fragile I feel when he stands this close to me. My walls are made of glass. And I'm terrified if he just looked closer, he'd notice. If he just blew on them, they'd shatter.

He gently cups my cheek, the lust in his gaze shifting into regret. "I never wanted to. I would never hurt you."

What on earth does that mean?

I'm about to ask him a thousand questions, but his touch shuts me up. The way his hands explore my body… it's precise, determined—like he designed every curve himself. His fingers dig into my hip bone, my tiny towel the only thing keeping him from my soaked skin. When he leans forward, my heart thunders so loud I'm surprised we haven't gotten a noise complaint from the neighbors yet. *Me? Exaggerating? Never.*

There will be no going back if we cross this line. No matter how mad I am at him, no matter how much he hurt me, if I let him kiss me… I'll let him do everything.

"You said you don't love me anymore," I remind him.

He looks conflicted. Like he's fighting an endless war within himself. Then, his eyes jerk up, their intensity telling me a part of him won the battle. But which one?

"Want to know a secret?" His gravelly voice cuts me to the bone. He stops barely a few inches away from the disaster masquerading as a harmless kiss.

His breath hits my mouth when he says it.

"I lied."

The itsy bit of self-control I thought was left in my body ditches me the second he kisses me. *Don't kiss him back!*

Annnd I'm kissing him back.

His tongue slides past my lips, tangling with mine until I'm completely at his mercy. He holds me flat against the wall, continuously working my mouth like a pro, and I can't, for the life of me, tell him to stop. *God, I missed this.* Any remnant of my reluctance turns to dust when he wraps my wet hair around his fist and releases my mouth. My body takes the reins, and my head falls back of its own accord, giving him clear access to my neck. He's quick to make me squirm, focusing all his attention on my collarbone, then the soft spot below my ear. I moan as quietly as I can, yet too loud for my liking, and I feel him grin in satisfaction. When he tugs at my towel, I'm worried he might feel my thundering heart. Even drunk out of his mind, he looks up at me, waiting for my approval. This is one of the things I always loved about him. Haze would never do something I wasn't comfortable with. He always needed more than the absence of objection. He needs a yes. *Always wait for the yes.*

I don't even realize how quickly I whisper the word he seeks. He grins and pulls on my towel, watching carefully as it hits the ground. Then like he needs a second to fully revel in it, he steps backward for a front-row view. His eyes blatantly rake over my naked body, and to my greatest surprise, I don't feel shy. Nor do I feel embarrassed. I feel empowered.

Sucking in a breath, he grunts. "You're going to kill me, Kingston."

Then his mouth is back on mine. But this time, we're doing

way more than kissing. Now, he's coming for all I have. Cupping my breasts with both hands, he twirls his thumbs around my nipples so slightly I have to keep myself from pushing into his palm. Before I know it, his hands are everywhere: my waist, my stomach, my ass, until finally he slips downward and…

I gasp when he pushes a finger inside me.

*Well, that escalated quickly.*

I moan against his mouth, my eyes closing when he begins to curl one finger in and out of me. My body is already overloaded with sensations, but it's when he adds a second finger effortlessly that I know…

I'm his.

Entirely, undeniably, and completely his.

"Fucking hell." He withdraws his fingers completely before diving back in. "Always ready for me, aren't we?" His thumb finds my clit and begins the sweet, torturous circles he mastered from day one. *Shit, he knows me.* This guy knows me, and his knowledge is dangerous. How can I be mad at him when he does this? When he can make me come undone with just the touch of a finger? How can I ever get over him when the only place I want to be is *under* him?

I brace my hands on his shoulders and grip them tightly. My nails dig into his skin as his fingers work their magic.

"Haze," I moan when he speeds up his circles. I can't help it. He's just *that* good. Don't ask me how we both end up naked on the bathroom floor—I couldn't tell you. On top of me, he stretches one of the condoms we keep in the bathroom cabinet down his shaft and teases my entrance, pulling back whenever he's too close to entering me. He's not going to stop until I'm begging, but right now, I need him.

All of him.

He's caught off guard when I spin us around and settle on top of him. My hands find his torso, and he blinks in surprise. He reaches for my breast, but I slap his hand away, trapping his wrists on each side of his head.

"I'm in charge today," I tease.

He's about to say something—that's probably very cocky—but I shut him up in a matter of seconds. I wrap my hand around his length, hold on to the bathroom counter, and lower myself onto him.

"Holy fuck…" He throws his head back with a grunt. I can deny my feelings to the end of the world, but my body missed him, no matter the stories my brain loves telling itself. The way I effortlessly adjust to his size, the warmth building up between my thighs, my reactions to his thrusting don't lie.

When firm hands cage my waist and guide me down quick and hard, my plan to be in charge is blown to pieces and swapped with pure instinct. Haze and I have always had crazy sex, but this time feels different, like a war between love and hatred. A mix between "I love you" and "we were doomed from the start."

I flitter my eyes shut and grip the counter so tightly my

knuckles turn white. I'm confident this couldn't get any better until he wraps a hand around the back of my neck and pulls me down into a horizontal position. My chest comes flush with his, and the pace isn't up to me anymore. It's all him. And he likes it rough.

"Oh my God." I can't help myself.

"Quiet, baby. Kendrick could come home any second," he has the audacity to say while he pounds into me to the point of making me forget my own name. I know he doesn't really give a shit about Kendrick hearing us, but he loves the thought of making me feel so good that I can't keep quiet.

I consider telling him that he's not coming home, but I love the intensity of this moment. Here we are, going at it on the bathroom floor like animals, and I'm not sure I've ever felt more alive in my entire life.

"He's not coming home tonight," I finally say, and Haze stops moving so abruptly my body aches for him.

He arches an eyebrow. "And you just say that now?"

*Well, damn.*

Before I can even come up with a good enough response, I'm off the floor and into his arms. My legs wrap around his hips while he slams the door open and walks into the kitchen.

"From the second we moved in here, I've wanted to take you everywhere in this room," he says in my ear. *Oh my…* This may be the second time we've ever been able to have sex outside of the bedroom, and we've lived here for months already. His hands band around the back of my thighs, and he plants me on the freezing kitchen island.

"On your back," he commands, and my heart skips a beat at his authority. He rests my leg up against his shoulder and runs two fingers up and down my entrance, as if to make sure that I'm still ready. With him, I always am. Satisfied with his discovery, he nudges himself all the way inside me with a thrust deep enough to make me see stars.

We both stop for that split, intoxicating second I've grown to love so much. That fleeting moment where we both enjoy feeling each other fully. The euphoric sensation reminding me that he's the high I never want to come down from. He begins to move again, slowly at first, then fast.

Barely a few minutes in, he snaps, "Fuck, I need more."

He pulls out and leads me down the island before we drop together onto the couch. Our bodies collide and the sudden closure, the weight of his rising chest on top of mine… it makes me more emotional than I anticipated. I was fine in the bathroom a second ago, but this… *this isn't sex*. This is so much more. Snaking his arm between us so he can rub me in rough, precise circles, he stares deeply—deadly—into my eyes.

His burning skin feels like a cure to a disease I never knew I had. Some rare illness only he can take away. He's the pain and the medicine, the addiction and the rehab. He's the defibrillator and the heart attack.

And fuck, I don't mind being sick if he's the one to save my life.

I don't mind being broken if he's the one to fix me.

He slams into me repeatedly, and I can tell from the way his body shakes in waves that he's close. I am, too. My climax begins in my toes, climbs up my legs, my thighs, until, finally, it reaches my center and my mouth drops open. I begin convulsing under him, falling apart with each thrust, and he catches on, hearing my body's message loud and clear. Grunting, he speeds up his circles and kisses me deeper, only to follow shortly after me. He rams harder until he gives in and spills into the condom.

Like I'm his safe haven, a sanctuary where only he can go, he rests his face in my neck. I can feel his heart beating wildly in his chest, but I doubt he can feel mine since he just fucked the life out of me. *I'm classy, I know.* He pulls out slowly and props himself up with both arms. Then, he presses his forehead to mine.

"I love you. So fucking much," he says in a whisper.

I don't answer, afraid—terrified—that he's just saying that because he's caught up in the moment. Or because I made him come. *Hard.*

"We're not done. Give me fifteen minutes." He presses a soft kiss to the corner of my mouth. When he gets off me, lies back on the couch, and leads me into his arms, I never want to leave them. I still love him.

*Of course I do.*

I'd take him back in a heartbeat if he still wanted me. I'd

gladly surrender my heart to him all over again if he just promised to change. It's pathetic, so pathetic it makes my skin crawl, but it's the truth. He said he still loves me. That he lied about the whole thing, and the only thought haunting my mind while I lie naked in the arms of the only guy I've ever loved is…

Please don't let me wake up alone in the morning.

# TWENTY-SIX

## One Last Try

Most days, I don't want to get out of bed. I wish I could sleep for a couple of years and wake up when the hard times are over. But today, for the first time in forever, I'm as excited as I am anxious to open my eyes. Just to see if he's still here, next to me. My body tells my mind the truth before it sees it. My hand wanders to his side of the bed—the side where he's not.

He left.

What feels like a sledgehammer swings at my heart. I honestly don't know what the fuck I expected. He was drunk, horny, and he knew he could have me. He knew I still love him.

*Goddamn it, Winter. You should've known.*

We stayed up all night having sex, and I honestly thought he was coming home. It felt like the good old days. Before my father's accident, before I found out he'd been lying. When I was oblivious and happy. I gave myself over to him completely. How could he?

Exhausted, I sneak out of bed, the icy temperature of my hardwood floors matching my soul. I couldn't fake a smile in a million years. As soon as I step into the kitchen, Waze edges his way toward me. I pet him, my mind blocking out the truth: Haze just wanted a hit it and quit it last night. I see Kendrick sitting at the table and hear the shower running. He and Allie probably came back early this morning.

"Look who it is." His eyes are packed with judgment. "Had fun last night?"

Great.

"Let me guess, you know." I slouch down on a chair.

"Yep. Saw Haze leaving when we got here this morning. He cheated on you—I'm surprised you would—"

"He didn't."

"What?" He blinks at me.

"He didn't cheat on me. I overheard the girl I saw at his apartment talking at the party. He paid her to be there."

He wrinkles his nose. "What the fuck?"

"That would be the right term." I crack a bitter laugh.

"Did you confront him?"

"That I did. Then he showed up here, fed me some shitty love confession, got what he wanted, and left."

Why am I telling him all this?

My words paint him a pretty clear picture. "He's an asshole. I'm sorry."

"Not your fault. It's mine."

"Why would it be your fault?"

"I wanted to believe him so bad that I…" *Spare him the details.* "I can't ever let him play me again." I pour myself a cup of coffee.

"You guys kept it in the bedroom, I hope," Kendrick jokes.

"Well…" I conceal my smug expression with a sip.

His eyes flash with disgust. "Winter, I swear to God, if you tell me I'm eating on a table covered in your butts…"

I can't restrain a laugh. "Relax, we didn't do it on the table." I put out his panic before it flares into a wildfire. He nods faintly, not entirely convinced, and gets up to put his dishes away.

"Can I sit on the couch?"

"It's a couch. That's kind of the whole purpose," I mock.

"No, I mean, is it clean? I don't want to sit somewhere you and Haze fucked last night."

My lips flatten.

"Oh my God! Seriously?" he snarls. "Where can I sit, then? The carpet?"

A small grin remolds my lips.

"Are you serious? The floor, too? What's wrong with you people? Are there any places you *haven't* had sex?"

I actually have to stop and think about it. We did it a lot last night—like*, a lot.*

"The balcony?" I try a joke, but Kendrick is *not* amused.

"Screw it. I'm going to my room. I can assume you guys never had sex in my bed?"

I pretend to hesitate, triggering his anger. He starts to fume, making me laugh out loud.

He's scandalized. "You freaks! I slept in that."

"I'm kidding." I throw my hands up. "We never had sex in

your bed."

Kendrick exhales in relief and carries on down the hall.

"If it makes you feel any better, we tried to clean after," I call. "Kind of."

"Clean? *Clean*?" He scoffs. "Gimme gallons of holy water, then maybe I'll sit on that couch again."

I watch him slam his bedroom door with a laugh. My eyes dart to the time on the stove. *Crap, I'm late.* I'll have to skip the shower this morning. My dad may be getting released today.

I doubt he'll want to move back in with Lauren. There's so much we've yet to figure out. He wants a divorce from Cruella, but he needs constant help and supervision until he heals completely. The doctor said he'll be in a wheelchair until his leg heals. Not to mention it should take him four months to recover from it all. He can't just slide back into his routine overnight. He called his insurance company and found out he doesn't have access to at-home care, which is another problem we'll have to tackle as soon as possible. There's no way to fix this mess, no glue strong enough to piece our broken family back together. Someone's going to have to take care of Mai and Jay. It goes without saying that *someone* will most likely be me. Now that I'm a school dropout, I'll have more time on my hands, but I also need to get a better job.

Since the house is under my father's name—pretty much everything is—I doubt Lauren will be allowed to stay there much longer. If it was up to my dad, I would've never moved out in the first place, so, safe to say that I'll still move back in after he's kicked Lauren out?

Drained, I sit on my bed and reach for my phone. I can't stop thinking about Haze and how insane last night was. I hate that it was good—okay, I hate that it was *the best.*

Waze comes strolling in through my partially opened door and hops up next to me. His waving tail whooshes a piece of paper off the nightstand. *God, I can't believe Haze told me he loved me. I can't believe he lied about something so important.*

I frown at the crumpled note I didn't notice before and bend over the side of my bed to scoop it up.

Haze's handwriting.

Three words. Nothing else.

I meant it.

## *Haze*

I've never been a good liar. Even in my player days, I'd tell my booty calls what I wanted up front to avoid getting their hopes up. Yes, I was—am—an asshole, but I wasn't a liar. Now lying is all I fucking do.

Lie to the girl I love.

Lie to my only friend.

Lie to *myself.*

I didn't even last two fucking weeks without her. Thirteen

days. That's how long it took for me to flinch and come crawling back to her. No matter how important it was for me to stay away from her, I couldn't. Last night was a mistake, but if this is what a mistake feels like… I'll make this exact mistake for the rest of my miserable life.

I can handle her hating me, but Caleb's dirty-ass hands on her? That. That I *couldn't* handle. Almost kicked his skull in right there. It hasn't even been weeks yet and he's already making his move on her. When I had to watch him take her upstairs, I honestly thought I was going to crack and kick every door down until I found them. She promised that nothing happened between them, and I wanted to believe her.

I wanted to believe her when she kissed me back.

I wanted to believe her when she bounced on my lap.

And I *especially* wanted to believe her when she came undone while calling my name. Repeatedly.

Fuck, I missed her.

I felt like actual shit when I sneaked out of bed in the morning, but waking up next to her was my breaking point. The moment I knew I couldn't keep my end of the deal. They said they're willing to negotiate if I do this one thing for them. This one thing that's way more than meeting shady people to sell them drugs in dark places the way I did most nights for the past few weeks. This something could get me killed or put in jail.

It's a job no one else wants. But no one else has something to fight for like I do.

*Lose the girl*, the douchebag repeated on the other end.

Memories flood my brain, and just like that, I'm back to begging a complete stranger not to ruin my life in an empty parking lot.

## THIRTEEN DAYS EARLIER

Pain is a part of life, my mother once said to me after my sister died. It hadn't even been weeks at this point. It'd been days at most. Still, she continued to act as though Desiree's murder was just an unfortunate event, a sad story, a bad statistic.

I didn't want to care anymore. Because all it ever did was ruin me. It destroyed me when life destroyed her. *Emotions are how you know you're alive*, she repeated. *You have to let them all in to be able to get better.* Yeah, well, what's the point of feeling if everything you love leaves you?

I closed myself off to any type of emotions until the day a five-foot-five brunette called me out on my shit in the school hallway. She made me believe that my mother might be right. That emotions did have a point after all.

But now… Now that I'm standing in front of Vic's washed-out building with a crumpled note in my hand, I sure as hell wish I didn't feel anything anymore.

*She's next.*

I keep rereading the poorly written words in the hope they'll disappear. I can't stop myself from frantically looking around as if I expect the person behind the note to have been dumb enough to stick around.

No one.

Not a single soul.

I can't believe I didn't figure this out sooner. Everything about the accident was so fucking weird. It was them. All along. It wasn't some random hit-and-run. They wanted revenge on me.

So, they took it out on the only person I love in this world.

How did they even find out that she knew? Is it because I moved out? I wasn't even the one to tell her—Caleb was—and she doesn't have a clue that I've been working with the organization for tips. They probably think she knows about them. Every bit of information spread into the world brings them a step closer to being exposed, and something tells me this twisted revenge game is something these fuckers quite enjoy.

Ricky warned me, but I didn't listen. I didn't think they were serious and now… Now, Harry is dying because of me.

*Winter's only parent is dying because of me.*

I take a deep breath and dial the last number they gave me frantically. It's a new one every week. It rings once. Twice. I hold my breath. Someone finally picks up. Not a word. Just silence. Pure and torturous silence.

"Ricky?" I say, getting inside my car and shutting the door when a family of five walks by.

"Ricky's dead."

I stop breathing.

"Why?" is all I can say.

I know I should ask what happened, but that's not what matters most right now. *Why* did they kill him?

"You know why." The voice is chilling.

"He didn't do shit."

"He helped you."

"Why are you doing this?"

"We warned his ass. Multiple times. But he wouldn't listen. Felt he owed you in some fucked-up way. Tanner might be a partner of ours, but nothing was said about his annoying little brother who risks exposing us for some piece of ass." He pauses, scoffing. "Man, I sure hope the pussy is good to be worth all this trouble. You know what, don't answer that. I guess I'll see for myself when we get her. She looks pretty tight."

Horrifying images flash in front of my eyes. Winter, touched by unknown hands. Her screams. Her tears. I will tear that guy to pieces limb from limb if I have to.

"I swear to God, if you touch one hair on her head, I'll—"

"Defensive, are we?" he laughs. "What did you expect, kid? She knows about us. You think we wouldn't cover our tracks because what… you love her?"

"She doesn't know about you. All she knows is I'm looking for my sister's killer."

"And you expect us to believe that? Give me one good reason why I shouldn't send my guys after her right now."

*Fuck, I don't have a choice.*

"I'll work for you."

He doesn't reply right away.

"Go on."

"You lost Ricky, didn't you? I can be his replacement. I've been in and out of the street fighting business for years. You could use a guy like me. I do this for you, and you leave her, her friends, her family alone. No threats. No attacks. Nothing. She's free to carry out the rest of her life unscathed."

He doesn't speak for several minutes.

"Fine."

*Thank God.*

"But you can't say no," he spits. "We call you for a job and you're here within the next hour or I'm sending my guys over to get a good fuck from your pretty little girlfriend, you hear me?"

"Yes," I say through gritted teeth.

"You start tomorrow."

I don't reply, looking around the now deserted parking lot.

"Oh… and lose the girl. You get her to stay the fuck away from you from now on."

Panic stirs up in my chest.

"Not happening."

He laughs.

"Refuse and she'll have to watch every person she loves mysteriously die one by one. You've seen what we can do. She'll think she's responsible, even believe that she's cursed. Until one day, my guys pay her a visit and show her just how right she is."

I clench my teeth to the point of pain.

"Please… don't make me do this." I can't believe he's got me to beg.

"You've got twenty-four hours. Tick tock."

He hangs up.

## NOW

I've been staring at my phone for the past thirty minutes, debating on whether or not I should call her. Just explain everything from beginning to end. Tell her that I love her and after tonight, everything will be fine. I'll come home. I can't keep this up. I did what they said like a brainless puppet because the mere thought of seeing her get hurt drove me completely mad.

To think she believed that I could even consider, for half a second, fucking someone else. I don't think I could get a hard-on even if I tried. In her defense, I got everyone fooled. Even Vic. He tried and tried to convince me not to bring the girl back home when we went out that night. He said I had something good. Something that deserved a fighting chance, unlike him. I told him nothing happened yesterday. I'm not sure how Winter even found out I'd faked it in the first place.

When they started sending me pictures of her a bit before the cheating setup, I realized how serious they were. She went out for coffee, then grocery shopping, and they snapped a pic to let me know they were watching, that they were close. I hope they didn't see me go back to the apartment last night. No death threats so far.

They've been dangling the idea of this job like a piece of meat for a while now. If I do this thing for them and survive, I could be out of this nightmare. For good. Free to be with her, or so they said, but then again, can I trust them?

I fucking hate myself. Because even after all of this, I still want to find Marcus. It put me into this mess in the first place, it risks destroying the only good thing in my life, but I want to keep looking. I need to find him. For Des.

I dial their number for what I hope to be the last time. He picks up but doesn't speak. He never does.

"I'll do it."

Silence.

"Excellent."

"I do this and I'm free? We're free?"

"Yes."

"How do I know you'll keep your word?"

He scoffs. "You don't. That's what makes it so fun."

I want to bust my fist through the car window but talk myself out of it. I'll need both hands when I pull her into my arms tonight.

"What do I have to do?"

"Go to the usual spot at nine. I'll have someone meet you for instructions. Don't be late."

I hang up.

In a few hours, I'll be free.

In a few hours, I'll go home to her.

*I just have to survive the night.*

# TWENTY-SEVEN

## *One Last Call*

*Winter*

"I'm so sorry, ma'am. I can't help you. These are the doctor's orders."

"Doctor's orders? I haven't been able to see my husband in two days! *Two days*! This has to be a misunderstanding," I hear my mother yell from all the way across the hall. I turn the corner and a highly satisfying scene comes into view.

"I'm afraid it's not. Your husband specifically said he doesn't want to see you, and we respect our patients' wishes." The poor nurse glances around in hope of catching the eye of a coworker who could possibly swoop in and save her from my psycho mother.

"My husband would've never said that!" Lauren shakes her head in disbelief. "You have no idea what you're talking about. Bring me someone with a brain. Right now!"

Sitting with his head buried in his hands, Jaden eyes the floor and impatiently waits for this moment to be over. My dad made the decision of letting Jay hear the recording. He said he was old enough and deserved to know. We made him promise not to tell Lauren about my father's plans to divorce her just yet.

When he looks up and sees me, he rises from his seat and walks over to me with a "*Thank God.*" I give him a quick hug, which attracts my mother's attention.

"They won't let me see him! What the hell is this? Did he tell you anything?" She strides to me.

"I'm sorry, Mother, I don't know what you're talking about," I say calmly.

Light bulbs blink in her eyes.

"You. You did this. Your moron of a boyfriend told him something, didn't he? He fed your father a bunch of lies."

"A bunch of lies?" I feign confusion. "We didn't feed him anything." The fire in her stare decreases. Until I hit her with the cold hard facts. "We *showed* him."

Her face decomposes.

"Isn't technology amazing? With just the touch of a finger, you can record anything these days." I've never been so cruel to my mother in my whole life. For the first time, I'm treating her the way she's always treated me. "Now I don't think I have to tell you what this means. He knows *everything*. He knows about the affair, he knows you never loved him, and he knows you're an awful mother. Well, guess what, dear Mom? He's divorcing you."

That's her snapping point.

She slaps me so hard tears fall on cue. A wave of gasps runs around the room. This slap contained years of hatred. She couldn't do it before, but now that she's lost everything—or if she hasn't yet, she will soon—she's finally revealing her true colors.

"You psychopath," Jay shouts. The pain is there, but it seems sheer compared to the satisfaction of seeing her fall.

"You fucking brat. How dare you?" she spits through gritted teeth. "I could've given you up. I would've if it wasn't for Harry coming in at the right time. The only person who ever wanted you was that stupid boyfriend of yours. Oh no, wait, he also realized how worthless you were in the end, didn't he?"

My confidence deflates. *She's not wrong though.*

"You should probably empty your stuff from the house." I fling my arm around Jay's shoulder, and her fists roll into white-knuckled balls.

"You can't do that. You have no right to kick me out!"

"Oh, I know *I* have no right to kick you, but Dad can. And everything's in his name." I attempt to ignore the burning of my cheek. A security guard who witnessed the scene decides now is a good time to get involved.

"I'm sorry, ma'am. We're going to have to ask you to leave," he tells her. Dude, you couldn't do that *before* I got slapped?

Infuriated, yet helpless, Lauren glares at me one last time and rushes toward the exit. Sure, this isn't over. My father has to file for full custody of Maika, and the process might take years, but with the recording, we may stand a chance. Nothing is going my way these days: Haze's left me again, I don't have the slightest idea of what I want to do with the rest of my life, but this is the one thing no one can ever take away from me. In the evil mother department?

I won.

## *Haze*

Delivering a truck full of cocaine to a warehouse in a ghost town. Not exactly my idea of a fun night. "*Be at this address at ten. We'll have a truck waiting for you.*" This is the last thing their new errand boy said to me. They didn't even have the decency to tell me who I'd meet there, who I'm delivering to. Told me the strict minimum and sent me on my way.

One thing's certain: we're far from delivering weed to low lives. A full truck? This could be prison for me. But I don't have a choice. Go big or go home, they said.

How ironic that I'm doing this *specifically* to go home.

To her.

To the love of my goddamn life.

The instructions were clear: deliver the merchandise to destination, don't get caught, and get the hell out of there. I can't help thinking that this sounds too easy. There's a reason they called it my "final" job. A reason they're willing to let me go if I make it out alive. Something bad is waiting for me down this path, I'm sure of it, yet, here I am, driving toward disaster.

Shortly after I called them to accept the job, I grabbed the first pen I could find and wrote two letters. One for Winter. The other for the police.

Winter's letter contains everything I wish I'd told her, including the goodbye I won't be able to give her if something happens to me tonight. I stopped by Vic's job and told him to deliver both letters if I don't make it home. If tonight goes south, who knows if anyone will ever find my body. I doubt the people I'm meeting will deliver it to the authorities and send flowers to the funeral.

If this goes wrong, I need Winter to know why I did this. So that I won't be an asshole in her eyes.

*Well, I'll still be an asshole, but I'll be an asshole with a purpose.*

The second letter holds all the information I've gathered on the organization: every place I went to, every person I met, every single job I did as their puppet, it's all in there. If something happens to me, I won't be able to protect Winter anymore. This is the police's best chance at stopping them.

She's been texting and calling all day. I couldn't bring myself to pick up knowing there was a chance it'd be our last conversation. How do you tell the girl you love that you may not live to see another day? I'm doing this for us. Because there's no way I can keep seeing her unless I end this once and for all. If there's one thing Harry's accident has taught me, it's that this, them, it's bigger than me.

I've been driving for a few hours now and racking my brain for a way out—didn't find any. We could run. But for how long? And what's to say they wouldn't just take it out on everyone Winter loves instead? Jay, Allie, Kendrick, Maika?

Maybe we could go back to Florida, but just as many dangers are waiting for us there. I've got my share of enemies: Ian and his fighters, *my* ex-fighters… my own brother. Plus, something told me they'll find us anywhere. The prefer their loose ends dead.

The GPS informs me that I'm less than ten minutes away, but the automated voice is muffled by my phone ringing on the passenger seat.

*Unknown Caller.*

Shit, they're probably calling about a change of plan.

I pick up.

"What?" I snap.

Silence.

"Hey, little brother."

I almost swerve off the fucking road. I know his voice. Even after all this time, I know it's him.

"Tanner?" I can't believe it.

It's been months since I've had any contact with my family. We haven't talked once since the night I discovered Jacob was his kid. I changed my number, tore down every possible bridge still linking us. I literally left the country for fuck's sake. I doubt I could've made myself clearer.

"It's quite a mess you got yourself into, Haze."

"How do you know about that?"

A small laugh erupts down the line.

"What? You think because you move to Canada, I'm going

to stop watching over my baby bro?"

I'm speechless.

"You may hate me, Haze, but we're family. I've been trying to make sure you're okay for months now. You haven't exactly made it easy on me, by the way. You really need to let go of your Marcus fantasy and just be happy be with your girl, man."

"What do you want?"

"I want you to stop torturing yourself."

I glance at the GPS.

*Six minutes.*

"Listen, I'm sorry for what I did to you. I'm sorry I destroyed our relationship. If it was lonely before you were gone… let me tell you, family dinners are fucking miserable now. I messed up everything, I know that. With Riley, with Jacob, with you."

"Don't forget Winter."

"Yeah, her too," he admits.

"Do you have a point?"

*Five minutes.*

"My point, brother, is that you're going to stop the car right now."

"What?"

"You heard me. You're going to pull over, get out of this car, and walk away before it's too late."

"Walk away?" I scoff. "Do you really think it's that easy?"

"It is that easy. If you have the right people on your side."

"What the hell does that mean?"

"I took care of it, Haze. You don't owe them shit. No drug deliveries, no jobs, nothing. You're free. You have a chance to be happy with Winter. Don't waste it."

*Two minutes.*

I hit the brakes and pull over on the side of the road.

Shock makes it hard to speak. "What did you do?"

No reply.

"Tanner, what did you promise them?"

"All you need to know is they will never bother you again. I made sure of it."

"Why did you do that for me?"

"I'm not going to let my little brother ruin his life for a piece-of-shit murderer. There's a train station ten minutes away. You're going to get on a train, go home, and get your shit together, understood?"

"I'm not sure there's even something to get back to..." I whisper.

"I don't believe that for a second. You two will make it work. You always do. And you need to stop this crazy hunt for Marcus. Des wouldn't want you to live like this. I promise your obsession with revenge will bring you nothing but pain."

Images of Desiree invade my mind. Her toothless smile, her small body lying in a pool of her own blood...

"I... I don't think I can." I choke.

He sighs.

"Then, for what it's worth, I looked deeper into it and I think you were on the right track at the motel."

He doesn't need to say more for me to know exactly what motel he's referring to. I always had my doubts about the place but never went back to check.

"And just some brotherly advice…"

He's not the same Tanner I left behind all those months ago. Even the way he talks is different.

"If you want to continue to hunt him, keep her out of it. She's never going to be happy as long as you seek revenge. Let her go. She's already been through hell and back. She should be enough, Haze. *She deserves to be enough.*"

His words hit me harder than I thought possible.

"And I know it might be difficult for you to believe but…" He pauses. "I do love you, brother. I hope you find everything you're looking for."

He ends the call.

His words haunt me as I walk away from the shittiest of trucks. *She should be enough.* Ironic that, in the end, my psycho brother turned out to be wiser than me.

He's right. As long as Marcus is free, enjoying life after he stole Des's, I can never give Winter Kingston the love she deserves. I can never treat her the way I should. She needs a man who can close his eyes without seeing a murder on replay. She needs someone who isn't a threat to everyone she loves. Someone who would never be the reason for her father nearly losing his life. For the first time since I've met her, it dawns on me, *really* dawns on me. One day, I'm going to lose this girl. One day, I'll have to let her go.

But that day…

Is not today.

# TWENTY-EIGHT

## *Confession*

*Winter*

Walking toward my apartment with Waze on a leash, I curse the new theme song of my life: *Silence.* It's become a usual sound for me during these past few weeks. Every time it's broken, it feels odd. Sure, Allie and Kendrick come over to the apartment sometimes, but the majority of my days are spent alone with Waze. The thought makes me sad. Silence should never be a "forever." Silence should only be a "sometimes."

Tonight is the exception. My dad was finally released from the hospital, and since we weren't sure if Lauren would be waiting to ambush him at home, he and Jay settled into my guest rooms. After we ordered food, they both passed out, exhausted from all the emotions the day had brought upon us. Maika will be visiting with Harry's parents in a few days.

I had to help my dad get around in his wheelchair and do basically everything tonight. Jay and I switched tasks every once in a while, but it only went to show how helpless we'd be in the instance that we couldn't afford help for him. I stopped by the house to get some clothes for them, and I was angry, but not surprised, to see Lauren's stuff still there. But that's a problem for another day. I have more than enough drama with my disappearing ex-boyfriend already.

Still no sign of him. Not even a phone call. *I meant it.* Part of me knows that's his way of telling me the "I love you" that made my heart beat again wasn't a lie.

But then why did he leave?

Why isn't he calling me back?

I don't know how much more shit I can handle. I want to go back. Forget the moment he made a deal with Kendrick at the beginning of it all. Time travel to when we first met and run the other way before we made eye contact in the hall.

Forget I ever loved him.

"Let's go home," I tell Waze as we head back inside the building from his walk. It's close to eleven already. I lost track of time. As soon as the elevator doors open, I pick up Waze and huddle him up to my chest. I find myself daydreaming about Haze being home when I turn the corner, but…

The person at my door isn't Haze.

It's Caleb.

Leaned back against the wall, he's on his phone.

"Caleb?"

"Winter, hey." He looks up and moves out of my way. I unlock the door the best I can with Waze in my arms.

"What are you doing here?" I ask.

"Al told me about your dad being released today and this

whole thing with your mom. I wanted to check up on you."

"Oh. That's... sweet." I push the door open. I'm really not in the mood for company, but I feel bad. He came all this way just to show his support, and we did make up at the party. Halfheartedly, I invite him in.

"How are you?" he asks when we sit down on the couch a few minutes later. Waze jumps in next to me and makes himself comfortable. I'd recognize the look on Caleb's face with my eyes closed.

Pity.

"Al also told you about Haze, didn't she?" *This girl.*

"Yeah. Sorry. She told me he left without a word. So, it's really over? You're really done with him?" he questions.

I attempt to convince myself. "I guess so."

How long am I going to let this guy walk in and out of my life whenever he feels like it? I *have* to be done with him. Out of self-respect. I *have* to never want to give him another chance.

This *has* to be over.

Maybe if I repeat it enough, I'll believe it.

"Listen, Winter, I..." He shifts uncomfortably.

I can hear the bomb explode before it's detonated. The way he leans closer makes his intentions crystal clear.

"I... I thought I could do this." He rubs the back of his neck. "I knew I at least owed it to you to try and reunite you with Haze because your happiness is all I want. But... when we got closer at the party, it did something to me, and I couldn't help but think that you felt it, too. I waited for you to come back from Florida for so long, and if you're telling me you're done with him, that you're ready to let his lying ass go, I have to be up-front with you."

*No, no, no.*

*Don't do this to me.*

"I still have feelings for you, Winter. I tried to meet someone else, and I promise I had nothing but good intentions at the party, but… I lied. I'm not over you. I think we should give this relationship a try. At least once."

"Caleb, I'm so sorry, I don't feel the same." I inwardly cringe.

He dismisses me. "Come on, deep down, you know you love me, too. That's why you let me flirt with you at the party, isn't it?"

He starts to lean in, and I would've pushed him away. I would've slapped him without question. He's wrong. I don't see him like that. I never will. But the sound of the floor squeaking behind us interrupts me.

I jump and turn around, only to see Haze.

Standing in the doorway with flowers in his hand.

Betrayal spreads across his face.

*Shit.*

Don't tell me he thinks…

When he drops the bouquet and takes off, I bounce. I throw my boots on and run right after him. I run and I run, not giving a single fuck that I might catch a cold the moment I step outside.

I don't have a coat on. Or a scarf. It's snowing like crazy—because of course it is—but I can't stop.

Conflicting thoughts spin around in my brain. He can't be mad at me. *He* abandoned me. *He* completely destroyed me. So what if *I* had kissed Caleb? He ripped my heart right out of my chest. He pretended to cheat on me. Then came back only to sneak out after we slept together. Why am I chasing after him?

"Winter, wait!" Caleb shouts from inside my apartment, but I pay him no mind. The elevator closes on Haze two seconds too soon, and I have to run like a crazy person down the stairs I've literally never used since I moved here.

I *just* told Caleb I was done with Haze. And I know if we keep this up, I'll have to be. But the story isn't over yet. I rush out of the building, the cold breeze wrapping me up, and spot his distant silhouette through the snow. How'd he get this far so quickly? *Maybe it's your lack of cardio.*

"Wait, please!" My voice strains with pain. He keeps walking. "It's not what you think." I have a hard time accepting that I'm the one justifying myself. This man will be the death of me.

I catch up to him, and he has no choice but to turn around when I grip his shoulder. I tug on his arm so hard that I almost slide over a thick hidden patch of ice.

"Wait!" My eyes are teary. Snowflakes spread over my lashes, freezing my mascara within seconds.

"Caleb? Seriously?" he snarls, but the rage in his eyes fades when he takes a look at me. "What the fuck? Where's your coat?

You're going to freeze."

"I'm not going in until you listen to me."

"Get back inside," he insists.

"I said no!"

I can't believe what he does next.

He curses under his breath, removes his coat, and drops it on my shoulders, no questions asked.

Even when he's pissed at me, even when he thinks I just made out with another guy, he's still Haze. And this, *right there*, is why I can't let him go.

He's the one freezing now, snowflakes multiplying on his black T-shirt with every passing second.

"I don't need it." I attempt to give it back.

"Winter, don't you dare," he warns.

*Damn, okay, Hazie.*

"Nothing happened. He was at the door when I came home. Said he wanted to check on me. Then he confessed his feelings and I rejected him, but he still made a move on me and I swear I would've pushed him away. You just happened to walk in at the wrong time. I'm so sorry." I pause, realization washing over me. "No, I take that back. I'm *not* sorry. You want to know why he was worried about me? Because I was miserable. I was a mess because you left. *Again*. I've never needed you as much as I did today and you…" My tears turn cold before they can stream down my cheek. "So, you know what? Fine. Leave. If that's what you want, just go. I'm sick of chasing you. I'm sick of loving someone who doesn't love me enough to stay. You suck."

*Man, did I really have to add the you suck at the end? Way to ruin the dramatic effect.*

My speech only heightens his anger. He steps forward until he's so close, I have to crane my neck.

"Is that what you think? That I don't fucking love you?" he snaps, the anger in his blue eyes sending shivers down my spine. "Of course I do. I love you more than it should be allowed to. You think I didn't want to be with you today? Winter, it's *all* I wanted to do. It's all I've wanted for weeks now."

"Then why didn't you?" I'm all sorts of emotional. "Just tell me why."

He debates on my request, silent for a short moment.

"Tell me or let me go."

Like my words just slapped him in the face, he steps back. He seems to actually be considering his options, and it terrifies me. *He can't be considering it.* Panicked, I get on the tip of my toes and slam my mouth to his. I kiss him with all I have, and in the middle of this semi snowstorm…

He kisses me back.

He's angry—no, he's furious—but he doesn't push me away. It feels like I can breathe again. Our lips dance together, equally desperate for this moment. His hand jumps to my back, and he pulls me flush against his chest. We're both freezing our asses off, kissing like idiots in a snowy parking lot.

I break away from him. "I love you, goddamn it. Can't you

see that? It's you. Not him. *You*," I say through frozen tears. When he sees the wreck that I am, pain and anger flee his gaze.

He believes me.

"What the hell are you doing? Get back inside." Caleb's voice makes us turn around.

*Ugh.*

We see him running out of the apartment complex with my coat hanging off his arm. He doesn't stop until he's next to me.

"Put your coat on. What are you? Crazy?" He hands it to me, and I give Haze's back. "Come on." Caleb captures my arm to drag me back inside. Haze's hands clench into tight fists the second Caleb touches me, and I know punches will be flying soon. I whisk my arm away from his hold.

"Caleb, I need you to go."

He stops, surprised. "What?"

"I made it clear. Multiple times. I don't feel that way about you, Haze or not. I told you I didn't want this, but you still made a move on me up there. Just go, please."

Haze's fists unfold as he watches Caleb's expression fall to the ground. I don't mean to hurt him. We used to be close friends, but no is no. Haze motions to walk to his car, which I do. I feel sorry for Caleb, but I know, from this day forward, he can't be a part of my life anymore. He's always going to want more than I can offer. I climb inside Haze's car, and he starts the engine. Just before we drive off, he rolls the window down to say something to Caleb.

"Thanks for the coat though."

We disappear down the street in a roar. I look at him in disbelief. *Savage much?*

"He tried to force himself on my girlfriend. Trust me, he deserved worse." He intertwines our fingers.

My mind lags behind on the word *girlfriend.*

He's back.

*We're* back

I have no idea where we're going. But I know we're going somewhere better. We're on the right track. I gave him a choice. Tell me or let me go. And, for once…

He's chosen right.

"WHERE ARE WE GOING?" I ASK, looking out onto the empty and silent streets. The snow decided to disappear as soon as we stopped standing in the storm, and I'm not even surprised. That's just the universe mocking me. *The usual.* Getting into Haze's car felt like the right thing to do at the time but now? I'm very aware of my father needing my presence. I called Jay to make sure he could handle my dad for the night, and thankfully, he was awake. *Okay, I woke him.* He groaned and hung up, but I know that was his way of saying, "Yes, Winter, of course I'll take care of Dad."

"We're going to the only place I can get you alone. Vic's." Haze takes a turn. It feels unreal. That we're actually good right now—and by good, I mean that we might stand a chance if he sits his pretty ass down and explains everything from beginning to end.

"Maybe we should go back. My dad needs help and—"

"I promise we'll be there to take care of him first thing in the morning, but I want you to myself for one night. Just one. Is that a crime, Officer?" he teases.

I find myself fighting the butterflies in my stomach. I know I should be requesting an explanation. I should've done so when I got into the passenger seat, but I haven't been this happy in a while. We come to a red light, and Haze turns his head to look at me. That's all he does: stare. Of course, with his *oh so famous* panty-dropping grin and a lock of hair dangling in front of his eyes.

I don't know if it's the intensity of his gaze or the fact that I'm just overall an idiot, but I can't help word vomiting. "Well, technically, we have around six hours before we have to be back, and so we won't get a long enough night of sleep because we've been on the road for thirty minutes to get to Vic's place and…"

I shut myself up when his smile grows wider.

I tuck a strand of hair behind my ear. "What? Is there something on my face?"

He shrugs. "No. Is there something on mine?"

"No?"

"Because there should be." His stare drops to my lips.

I frown. "What should be on your face?"

"You."

Oh my God.

*Did he just…*

I burst out laughing, and he joins, proud of himself.

That's why. Why I'm a fool for him.

Somewhere along the way, I heard him laugh at his own joke and I knew I wanted to spend the rest of my life laughing with him.

"You can't just drop a line like this on me like nothing happened. We still have so much to discuss. I—"

"And we will. I promise." His voice is soothing, reassuring. Thinking of what happened last night reminds me of how much pain he put me through recently. I can't let these events slide. I need an explanation before we can even start *thinking* about making this work. We step into Vic's silent apartment and slip out of our coats. Haze was right. Vic's car isn't out front. We're alone.

"Haze, we can't go on like this," I say once our eyes lock.

He steps closer.

"Hold that thought."

"Wha—"

He swirls me up and throws me over his shoulder like I'm weightless. Here I was, full of good intentions about having a mature, serious conversation, yet here I am, laughing my head off as he kicks open the door to the guest bedroom.

"What are you doing?" I wiggle around.

"What do you mean? That sounded like the beginning of you

leaving. I'm not taking any chances."

I laugh even harder. Next thing I know, I'm lying on the uncomfortable pull-out bed in Vic's guest room with Haze atop me. He presses his lips to mine, and I kiss him back without blinking. This guy has got many types of kisses. The "regular" kisses and the "I'm going to strip you down in a few minutes" kisses. I know he's not kissing just to kiss. This isn't happening. As much as I want it to, there's so much left to resolve…

When he lowers his head to my stomach and scatters kisses all over my skin, I know my goodwill might not be enough.

*Winter, what are you doing? Stop!*

He needs to explain.

He needs to explai…

He needs to expla…

He needs to ex…

*And we're naked.*

WE HAVEN'T MOVED A MUSCLE FOR at least twenty minutes. Tracing circles on Haze's bare torso, I concentrate on his heartbeat. This has to be hands down my favorite sound on the planet. *Except for when Mr. Rory, my high school math teacher, told me I'd passed. I swear, I cried.*

Haze's smile quirks when my stomach grumbles. "Are you hungry?"

"I'm good." I am starving, but it would require moving, which is something I strictly refuse to do right now.

He nods. My stomach grumbles again a few minutes later, and Haze sneaks out of bed without a word. I groan, rolling over. "What are you doing?"

"I'm making sandwiches. You're definitely hungry."

The thought of him making me a sandwich butt naked is enough motivation to pull me out of bed. After I've thrown one of his oversized T-shirts on, that is. I may be comfortable with him, but I'm not *walking around naked* comfortable. I make sure to grab him a pair of sweatpants at the same time. He might be making sandwiches now, but we might end up discussing more serious topics, and I doubt I'll be able to listen with his junk out.

I sit around the table and stare at him. I don't know what I'm drooling over the most: his ass or the sandwich. Let's call it a tie. Unfortunately, he takes the hint when he sees I brought him clothes and puts his sweatpants on, sliding a plate over to me and sitting down. I glance at the clock on the wall. It's past 2:00 a.m.

"We should talk," I begin once we've eaten.

"I know…" He looks down. "I don't even know where to begin."

I grab his hand, and it seems to boost him with the needed strength to carry on.

"I told you it all started that day at the airport. Remember the call I got?"

I nod.

"The man who called to tell me about Marcus wasn't just

some guy I knew back home. He tipped me off from beginning to end. He was part of… something bigger than I could've ever imagined. They call it the organization. They worked with Tanner in the past, which is why they helped me. They owed him. They've been giving me tips to help me find Des's killer since day one. They just had one rule: no one could ever know about them." He squeezes my hand. "It doesn't excuse that I lied to you, I know that. Nothing does. But maybe it can help you understand why I did what I did. When Caleb told you the truth on your birthday, it set them off. They wanted to make me pay for risking to expose them. They knew the only way to truly hurt me would be to hurt the person I love most… You."

*Argh. Stop, heart.*

He pauses, dragging a long and deep sigh. Why do I feel like it's about to get worse?

"What happened to your father wasn't random."

Panic takes ahold of me.

"They targeted you and your family specifically to make me their puppet. The only way they wouldn't harm any of you was if I worked for them and we weren't together anymore. That's why I had to pretend to cheat."

He scoots his chair closer to mine and motions to get on his lap. I don't move, tense as a rock. He has to tug on my hand for me to oblige. Once I'm seated, he wraps his arm around my waist.

None of it is registering.

*Haze* is the reason my father almost died?

"They told me to stay away from you, and as you can tell from what happened last night…" He chews on his lip. "I failed."

By the time he finishes his story, I'm barely holding it together. *That's* why he did all this. He had no choice but to leave me. I want to burst into tears because what happened to my father has something to do with Haze, and I hate that this link even exists. I don't want to see my father suffer and think of my boyfriend.

"I'm so, so sorry. My hands were tied. I thought I was keeping you safe. Then it just… spiraled out of control."

I bury my face in his neck and inhale his scent.

God, we're so broken.

*We're a goddamn tragedy.*

"I just want you to know, I was coming back home to you that night." I know exactly what he's referring to. The day where I waited for him for hours. "They called and threatened to hurt you, and I lost it. I was an idiot for thinking I could keep you in the dark."

The obvious question catches up to me. "Wait? How did you get out of it? You're here now and you just told me everything so… is it over?"

"Yeah. It's over." He runs a hand through my hair and leans in to kiss my cheek. "They gave me a job tonight. I had to do this one huge thing for them to let me out of this shit deal. I had to do this so that I could be with you again."

"How bad was it?" I wince.

He draws a sigh, "Listen, all you need to know is that it was bad. Really bad."

"What happened?"

"Nothing. I was about to do it. But Tanner called."

My mouth drops. "Tanner? As in your brother?"

*Way to go, Captain Obvious.*

"I know, I couldn't believe it either. He told me he was sorry for everything. That he'd handled it. He said that I could go home to you."

I'm surprised. "No strings attached?"

"None. He said he promised them something. Something big, I just don't know what. A shit ton of money is my guess," he says softly. "Do you hate me?"

His eyes are red, crippled by guilt.

"For what happened to your dad?"

I know I have to think of it from his perspective. They were basically holding him at gunpoint. Come to think of it, I'm actually relieved he did all this because he *had* to. Not because he wanted to. But I can't help thinking that his hunt for his sister's killer is the reason for all of this.

The source of all our problems.

If he hadn't been looking for Marcus, he wouldn't have lied, he wouldn't have had to pretend to cheat, and my father would've never been in a coma. I'll have to ask him the dreadful question soon.

*Are you going to keep looking for him?*

I've tried to accept it. I did everything I could to support his need for revenge because he lost his baby sister. He had to watch her die, when he was nothing but a kid himself. But I want him to stop looking. I can't live like this, wondering if he's going to make it home or who's going to get caught in the crossfire next. Not after I almost lost my only parent. He escaped this time, because he got lucky, but his brother won't always be there to save his ass. We don't speak for a few minutes, lost in each other's arms. It's inevitable. I need to know what his plans are. But not now. Right now, we're happy. I just want one night.

One night before I ask him.

# TWENTY-NINE

## *Back Together*

*Winter*

"What are you doing?" I heave a chuckle when Haze kicks my bedroom door shut and backs me up into a corner.

"We've been unpacking for three hours. I want a second alone with my girlfriend. Sue me." He snatches the cardboard box from my hands and drops it on the desk next to my bed. He's right. We've been emptying the back of his car for so long we've barely had time to say a word to each other all day.

When we woke up for what would be the last time in our apartment, we had no idea how busy the day ahead would be. Moving back into my childhood home to help my dad recover from the accident seemed like a good idea last night. I apparently failed to remember how mind-numbingly exhausting moving was the first time around. We dropped Waze at Vic's for the day because a crazy pup doesn't exactly make the moving process easier.

It did break my heart to empty our apartment. This was our first home, and we could've technically continued to live there since we're back together, but we'd already severed the lease and the landlord said he has a bunch of people lining up to rent the place. Not to mention that my family has never needed me as much as they do right now, and I could hardly see myself living away from my father after what he went through.

We barely got two hours of sleep last night. Turns out we had a lot to say since getting officially back together—our bodies mostly did the talking. *Cue the wannabe seductive wink.*

I couldn't handle how happy I was when I woke up in Haze's arms at Vic's two days ago. It'd been so long. It felt like, for the first time in forever, everything was right in the world.

No words can describe how relieved we were when we walked inside the house and saw that most of Lauren's stuff was gone. Looks like she decided to do the decent thing for once, but I know better than to think this is the last we'll be hearing of her. She won't give up Maika's custody without a fight.

"We should go back downstairs to help."

"Uh-huh." He completely ignores me, angling his head forward to kiss me. I welcome his lips with a need only he gives me. Here we are, making out in my childhood bedroom, and I have a feeling it might be hard to get some privacy once Haze moves in here to help me watch over my dad.

I break the kiss before it gets too heated. "We have like ten minutes tops before Allie and Kendrick realize we're missing."

His lips upturn into a grin, his fingers traveling down to my stomach. "Give me five." He rubs me through the fabric of my leggings, and I emit a small involuntary gasp.

"For crying out loud! You see this? That's why I won't miss

living with them," a voice flares outside my door.

Kendrick's.

I hear Allie sniggering in the hall and wonder how long they've been standing there. We were so engulfed by our make-out session we didn't even hear them come up.

"Come on, you pervs. Food's here," Kendrick calls. We hear them stride down the stairs. Haze places a quick peck upon my cheek before grabbing my hand and dragging me out onto the hallway.

Harry's parents should arrive with Maika any minute now. They've been taking care of her throughout this whole nightmare. Of course, she got to visit our dad at the hospital, but we tried to keep her as far away from this heart-wrenching situation as we could. Until the trial can occur, my dad will have no choice but to share custody of Maika with Lauren. They will each get one week with her. That is, of course, if Lauren is able to provide Maika with a stable and loving environment now that she doesn't have my father's money to pay for everything. I know she recently got a part-time job as a hairdresser. She may want to reconsider the *part-time* aspect of it. As for Jaden, he's old enough to choose who he lives with. Plus, Lauren has no legal right over him in case of a custody battle as he is not biologically hers. He's Harry's son.

"Where's the pizza?" I groan as I enter the kitchen.

Kendrick, Jay, Allie, Haze, my dad, and I all gather around the table and dig into the large pizza boxes. We're halfway through mocking Kendrick for how whipped he is over Allie when the home phone rings. My father's face loses all tint. It's his insurance company. It's got to be.

He's been waiting for their call since he got released. He needs constant help until he can go back to work. They promised to follow up as to the possibility of providing him with a home nurse. Haze stretches his arm and grabs the home phone to hand it to my father.

"Wish me luck," my father whispers before he picks up.

It doesn't require more than five seconds. It's not looking good. The way his eyebrows furrow tells us the answer we dreaded is exactly the one he's getting. After arguing back and forth for a few minutes, he hangs up.

"It's a no."

"I'm so sorry, Dad." I place my hand atop his on the table.

"It's okay, kiddo," he says, discouragement lacing his tone.

God, these next few months are going to be tough. My dad has savings, which will thankfully allow us to support ourselves for a little while, but he doesn't have enough to pay for a full-time nurse.

"We'll be there to help you. Jay will take care of you at night when I go to work, and I'll be here during the day," I say, and he offers me a warm smile. I restrain a wince. I do have to find a job first. I'll also have to take care of Maika when she's here because there's no way I'm leaving her with Lauren full-time, and my dad won't be able to watch a five-year-old by himself.

"I'll be there to help, too. No matter what," Haze chimes in, and my heart expands five sizes. I'm so grateful for him.

"I shouldn't be your problem, pumpkin. I shouldn't be a burden for any of you. I'm so sorry." Guilt stabs me in the guts. He's apologizing when Haze is the reason for all of this. God, I can't stand it.

A knock on the door interrupts our sappy moment.

Maika.

We all drop our pizza slices and gather around the door to welcome her home. Kendrick opens up. My dad's parents immediately bombard Harry with questions about his well-being. As for Maika, she starts running toward his wheelchair, then she freezes, reminded of his fragile state. She gives him a light, delicate hug, as though she's convinced that squeezing will lead to his shattering. She won't let go, tiny arms wrapped around him.

"It's all right, sweetie. I'm okay."

"I love you, Daddy," she murmurs.

*Dirty mind, go away.*

When she backs away from him, I expect her to run to Jay or me. But she doesn't.

"Hazie!"

*Are you fucking kidding me?*

One more girl lost to Haze Adams's charms.

He seems just as surprised as we are, but he lifts her up into his arms and gives her a quick twirl, which amplifies her laughter.

When he puts her down, it sinks into me that Maika's the exact same age as Haze's little sister was when she died.

Images of Maika in Desiree's place horrify me.

"What about me? Playing favorite much?" I pretend to be offended. *Let's be real, I'm offended a little.* She runs to me with a giggle. I bend down for my hug. I can tell she missed home just as much as it missed her. Maika runs back to her bedroom to find the toys she missed in the past few weeks. Nothing unusual… except that she brings someone along with her.

And by brings, I mean drags.

And by someone, I mean Haze.

"We're playing dolls, Hazie." She doesn't ask, just states the facts. Haze's eyes call for help, which only makes us laugh.

I stick my hands up. "Price to pay for being the favorite, babe."

## *Haze*

I shoot Winter a "help me" glance over my shoulder, and she bursts out laughing. I can barely tear my eyes away. I missed this. I missed seeing her happy, hearing that laugh.

"Price to pay for being the favorite, babe," Winter says from behind me. As Maika drags me toward the staircase, I catch a glimpse of the TV in the living room. More precisely of the news. On the screen are headlines that confirm the fears that have been haunting me since I got out of the truck full of cocaine last night.

**Drug deal gone wrong. Young man found dead.**

"A tragedy occurred yesterday at around midnight on the site of an abandoned factory. What the authorities assume to be a drug deal gone wrong stole a seventeen-year-old young man's life away. He was found massacred and shot fifteen times next to an empty truck at 8:15 this morning. We don't have any more information at this time."

Then she names the address where the gruesome murder took place. Shivers scamper down my spine, my bones, my whole body. But that's not even the worst part. The worst part is the picture that comes up on next. The truck I was driving. Completely wrecked by gunshots.

That's where I should've been last night.

It could've been me.

It *would've* been me.

If Tanner hadn't called and told me to get the hell out of there. He saved my life.

They must've found some other kid to do the job. Had plenty of poor fellas terrified to lose their loved ones on hand. I'm a hundred percent confident now that they would've never let me out of the deal. This was probably a targeted delivery, a way to get a nasty job done and get rid of me all at once. I'm guessing they thought my chances of getting out of there alive were pretty slim. I don't know who the fuck was waiting for that cocaine, but it sure wasn't Mary Poppins.

"Come on," Maika urges, pulling on my hand to get me to

walk faster. She noticed me slightly slowing down to listen to the reporter. I try to push the unwelcomed thoughts aside and follow her up to her room. The first thing she does when she walks in is empty a large box of her toys on the carpeted floor and hand me a soldier action figure.

I'm quick to text Tanner's number.

Thank you.

"There, you be the prince and I be the queen," she begins.

"Shouldn't you be a princess if I'm a prince?"

"No. Daddy always says that I'm a queen."

My smile grows wider.

"Who's this guy?" I point to the purple teddy bear scooped up in her arms.

"That's Wally. He's my best friend." She holds him tight against her chest. "He's always there to cheer me up when I'm sad."

I can't help but be amazed by this sweetheart of a little girl and how obliviously happy she is. She has no idea that her mother is human garbage. That her father almost died. She sees the good in people, even those who don't have one good bone in their bodies. Even those who don't deserve it.

She's just like her.

*She's just like Des.*

"What's wrong?" She pulls on my sleeve.

"Nothing. What makes you think something's wrong?" I

shove the painful memories into the deepest corner of my mind. She drops the Barbie and gazes at me with confused and intrigued eyes.

"You look sad."

"I'm okay. I promise," I lie.

She frowns.

"It's just… you remind me of someone," I reluctantly admit.

## THEN

"Daddy, Daddy," the five-year-old called when she heard the door that was always closed open in the distance. The office door was locked most of the times. The rule had remained the same ever since the young girl had been old enough to understand what a rule was. As long as the door was closed, she couldn't bother her father. *Maybe* if he ever opened it, she could ask, but even then, nothing was certain. Mr. Adams spent almost twenty-four hours a day into his office, leaving his daughter Desiree to play alone with the brand-new toys he and his wife kept bombarding the child with.

The blue-eyed girl ran from the living room to her father's office, her tiny feet knocking against the hardwood floor. Her older brother came running in after her. He'd been babysitting again. His parents hadn't even left for their stupid event yet, still he'd been put on Desiree duty as soon as he'd come home from school.

"Des." Haze smiled sadly as he watched his sister slip on the perfectly waxed floor. She was running so fast she struggled to stop when she made it to the office threshold. He knew exactly what answer his sister was going to get. She always got the same one. Her father was sitting at his desk, going through a few of the last files of the day. Running a business wasn't easy. That was his excuse, always had been.

"Daddy, look!" Desiree held a cookie she'd just made with her brother as high as her arm allowed her to. She pushed to the tips of her toes, aside her father's desk.

"Later, honey, I'm busy," he said, his eyes locked onto his computer screen. Seconds later, his daughter noticed the maid sweeping in the corner of room. *She* was the reason the office door was open. She'd be out of there as soon as she was done cleaning. Her father wasn't available.

"But Daddy… Haze and I made cookies," Desiree said.

Her father huffed, "Why don't you go play with your toys?"

"I don't want to. I want to play in the backyard. You promised, Daddy. Remember?"

It was true. He had promised. He'd promised when he wasn't listening and desperately needed her to stop asking. Leaning against the doorway, Haze stood with his arms crossed over his chest. Rage and disapproval twisted his face. He remembered a time when Richard played with them. Back when he only had two clinics to manage. Unfortunately for Desiree, Adams Inc. decided to invest further into real estate three months after she was born, and from that moment on, he'd become the self-centered piece of shit Haze was looking at now. His father made him so angry sometimes he wondered if he could move out on his own at fourteen.

"I'll go with you tomorrow."

His words banished every single hope and dream in the little girl's eyes to a foreign land. She glanced down at the now crumbling cookie in her palm. The maid walked out and motioned for the kid to follow, which she did, dragging her feet. The door closed, and just like that, her daddy was gone again.

"Des, come here." Haze bent to her level. "I'll play in the backyard with you."

It usually cheered her up. She usually smiled, accepted that her dad couldn't make it, and strolled straight to the swings outside. She loved her brother more than anything, looked up to him. She was usually glad he was there to play with her, but not this time. She didn't even spare a smile. She walked over to the kitchen and sat around the table in silence. Scattered all over the counters were cooking ingredients along with multiple trays of untouched cookies.

Haze had suggested cooking with his sister for her school bake sale after she'd told him she wished her parents didn't hand off bought cookies at each of her school's event. Haze knew there was nothing Desiree wanted more than to be a part of something, to show up with home-baked food on Monday, too.

Although the fourteen-year-old boy would've preferred

death over admitting it, he was a pretty decent cook for a teenager. He'd had a nanny he adored as a kid, who had been fired after Ms. Adams had suspected she was trying to seduce her husband. Eight-year-old Haze was constantly bored back then. So bored he'd end up watching the woman work in the kitchen. She'd eventually invited him to join and taught him everything he knew.

"You know Dad loves you, right? I'm sure he'll come out to play with you tomorrow." Haze almost choked on his lies. He wanted to be hateful, wanted to criticize his father. He wanted Des to know how much her dad sucked, but he couldn't bring himself to tell her. He had to let his sister believe there was a good man behind that closed office door. For as long as humanly possible. If not forever, at least until she was old enough to understand how cruel the real world could be.

"It's okay. He's busy," she said quietly.

*Busy being a waste of oxygen*, Haze thought. He offered to read her the storybook she loved so much. She accepted, running to the living room to grab said book. It cheered her up. It always did.

"Do the voices! Do the voices!" she giggled, huddling up against her big brother on the couch. He complied, sending her laughter through the roof. By the time the story was over, she'd turned back into her regular self. A bundle of joy and sunshine.

Their parents called them into the kitchen minutes later. They were leaving for some charity event they didn't care about but needed for positive publicity.

"Thanks, Daddy," Desiree said to Haze before she ushered her way to the kitchen to say goodbye to her parents. Haze cracked a miserable, faint smile. It wasn't the first time she'd called him that by mistake. Haze got up and trailed behind his sister. He asked his parents where his older brother Tanner was. His father replied, "Getting in trouble somewhere."

"You're going to be okay for the night?" Anita, their mother, asked her youngest son.

"We'll be fine, Mom. Don't you know? I'm a pro babysitter now." Haze rolled his eyes when his mother went in for a hug. Anita wasn't the coldest woman out there. She did, sometimes, display signs of affection toward her children. The problem was those signs never came when it mattered most. She'd say she loved her kids, then keep her mouth shut while Mr. Adams made awful parenting decisions. It wasn't what she said. It was what she didn't.

Desiree reminded her father of his promise to play tomorrow, to which he replied, "Yes, honey, tomorrow."

That night, Richard Adams walked right through the door of his mansion with no idea…

That his daughter's tomorrow would never come.

## NOW

"Is it someone that makes you sad?" Maika waves a quick

hand before my eyes.

I force myself back to reality. I dozed off for a second there. "Who is?"

"The girl I remind you of? Does she make you sad?"

"No, not at all. She made me very happy. I think you two could've been great friends." I smile.

"What's her name?" she asks with sparkly eyes. "Maybe she could come over and play sometimes."

My smile wavers.

"I… I'm sure she would've loved that."

I have no idea how the fuck I'm supposed to tackle on this topic. Does she even know about death?

"Oh." Realization seems to dawn upon her. "Is she with the angels?"

Good, someone had the talk with her.

"Yes, she is."

Maika zeroes in on the floor. She doesn't move a muscle for a good five seconds. Then, without a warning, she gets up, take a few steps forward, and wraps her tiny arms around my neck.

"I'm sorry, Hazie," she whispers, her small voice heavy with sadness. I smile, hoping that the wound that was just blown wide open will close itself. Praying that my already weak stitches will hold a bit longer, keep me from bleeding out, allow me to swim in this pain before I drown.

"There. You need it more than I do." She hands me her purple teddy bear.

I take it. "Well, thank you very much."

"But you have to give it back when you're not sad anymore, Hazie."

I breathe a quiet laugh. "I will, I promise."

*If that day ever comes.*

AS I WALK DOWN THE STAIRS leading to the kitchen after putting Maika to sleep for her afternoon nap, I hate that her attempt at cheering me up only made me sadder. She meant to help, but now all I can think about is Des.

And the life she'll never get to live.

"There you are." Winter's voice brings me back, makes me forget about the million emotions at war in my chest. I look up to see her staring at me, leaned back against the kitchen counter with crossed arms.

"How was the doll playing?" she teases.

I move toward her. "Would you believe me if I said amazing?"

"Nope." She wraps her arms around my neck.

My hands curl around her waist. "Where's everybody?"

"My dad is resting upstairs. His parents left five minutes ago, and Kendrick, Allie, and Jay went to pick up something at the store. I didn't really listen. I was way too busy imagining you playing Barbies." She chuckles.

I know this isn't the right moment—it literally never is with us—but when I pull her into my arms, I can't stop the thoughts creeping inside my head.

I want her.

So fucking bad.

Maybe it's because this girl is somehow the only person on this damn planet that makes me feel better when I start spiraling. Maybe it's because her ass looks like art in those jeans.

All I know is I need to feel her.

Right now.

When I lower my mouth to her neck, she turns to putty in my hands. A smirk remolds my lips. She's always been receptive to my touch, even when she doesn't want to be. My kisses are slow, light, but they're enough.

"Haze." She releases a soft moan.

Okay, fuck.

*Someone* wants to come out to play.

My fingers glide from her arm to her shirt, from her bare stomach to her nipples. She shivers.

"Here? Really?" she jokes, but I catch the desire in her tone, her trembling voice. She's all hot and bothered.

"Would you rather go upstairs where the baby and your father are sleeping?" I trace my lips down her collarbone, aiming for the sensitive spots I know drive her insane. "Don't think for a second because we're moving into your childhood home, I'm going to become family-friendly, Kingston."

When I bite her earlobe slightly, she lets herself go, but only for a few seconds. She's fighting it. Something's on her mind.

"Okay." Her hands fly to my chest, and she holds me at arm's length. Like she's afraid of what she could do if I were to get any closer. "Haze, baby… You have no idea how much I want to do this right now, but we can't."

When I see her hard nipples peek through the fabric of her shirt, I can't tame my smirk. "I think I do have an idea."

No bra, huh? She's making this even harder. Me—she's making *me* harder. I remember Harry accidentally dropping something on her shirt earlier. She was soaked. Probably threw on the first shirt she could find, then got too lazy to open up her billion suitcases to find a bra. She notices her nipples and crosses her arms over her chest with the most adorable, shy smile I've seen in my entire life.

"But that's what we've been doing since we got back together. Things escalate, we have sex, and don't get me wrong, it's been…" She flushes. "Amazing, but it's always before we can talk about our issues. I don't want to avoid it anymore."

Why do I feel like I'm in trouble?

"Avoid what?"

She inhales. "You've told me everything. Except…"

I just stand there, anxiously waiting for the bomb to go off.

She shakes her head. "Listen, I love you. You know I do. And I'm willing to look past all the things that we've been through recently, but I don't think I can take it going forward."

She pulls on my hand and sits me down at the table. So, I need to sit down for this one? *Not a good sign.*

"I can't live wondering if I'm going to lose you or anyone else ever again. I need to know. Are you going to keep looking for him?"

Her question hits me like a brick wall. I don't know what the fuck to say.

Do I?

"I don't know," I admit.

Her brown eyes darken. This can't be happening. Not when I *just* got her back.

"Winter, there's nothing in this world I want more than to move on, believe me. I want to tell you what you want to hear, but that night… it's fucking haunting me. I see it every time I close my eyes. I need justice for her."

She sighs. "And I get that, I really do. You lost your little sister. I would lose my mind if someone ever touched Maika, but…" Tears come up to her eyes.

Her tears confirm my suspicions. I *am* in trouble, and we're not just "discussing our issues" anymore. She's giving me an ultimatum. Our relationship solely depends on what I say next.

"I almost lost my dad, Haze." Her voice cracks.

Guilt surges up inside me.

"I know, and I'm so sorry, but the organization won't ever be a problem anymore."

"That doesn't mean you won't find some new problems along the way." She wipes a tear that escaped her eye. "I guess what I'm trying to say is… If you want to keep looking, I can't be around to watch you do it."

What happened to her dad messed her up. I think she'd never been more shaken up in her life, and I understand her reaction, but what the hell am I supposed to do?

As if I thought out loud, she says, "All you have to do is tell me that this is enough for you. That *we're* enough. That you can bear to let this go. That's all I need. I want this to work. I think I've made that quite clear with all the running around I've done for you."

I wish I could ease her pain, feed her the words she craves, but deep down, I know they would be lies. I won't stop looking. I can't. I open my mouth to tell her… but then I'm brought back to the night where she told me it was over. To the way I felt when she walked out of the apartment.

Losing this girl almost fucking killed me.

I can't stop looking. But I also can't lose her. I just *can't.*

"I won't," I lie. "I'll stop."

She grants the tears in her eyes permission to stream down her face.

"Really?" I've never seen her happier, and I hate myself.

*Fucking hell, Haze, the best part about you… is her.*

*Why are you doing this? Why are you so fucked up?*

"Really." I can barely get the words out. Before I know it, she's straddling me, her arms around my neck and her tongue dancing with mine. I kiss her back.

"I love you," she says in between intense kisses.

"I love you." Everything else may be bullshit, but this… this is true. It's the truest statement of them all.

We stay in this position for a few minutes until her phone goes off on the table.

"Can you get it?" she asks, and I extend my arm forward to scoop it up.

"It's a text from Kendrick. He went to the movies with Jay and Allie," I read and put her phone back down.

Her lips lift into a smirk. "Want to go have that breathtaking sex now?"

Is that even a question? My dick is already straining against my jeans from all that kissing.

"Now how on earth could I say no to that?"

She wiggles off me, pulls me to my feet, and leads the way to the first-floor guest bedroom. She tells me that no one ever uses it as she's pushing me down onto the bed. Before she closes the door, she realizes she forgot her phone in the kitchen. Mine vibrates in my pocket the instant she leaves the room. I have two new messages. From Tanner.

I eye Winter. She's standing by the table, talking on the phone. It probably rang when she went in.

> Don't thank me. I told you I'd always be looking out for you.

Listen, this guy owed me one and after our phone call, I dug a little deeper. I don't know if you're still interested, but I found this.

*Attached: Holland Motel Surveillance Video Tape 6245.*

I know what I do next is going to define… everything. I can choose to never open that video, abandon my obsession with revenge, be happy with the girl I love more than life itself. I want to make the right choice. I want to be noble. To be good. Fuck do I want to. But because I want to, doesn't mean that I can.

I glance at Winter from afar.

And click.

# THIRTY

## *If it can't be me*

*Haze*

The video takes an insanely long time to load. Nervously glancing back and forth between Winter and the screen, I battle a mini anxiety attack. *Come on.* I don't know how much time I have until she comes back. I let out a sigh of relief when the video starts.

I recognize the outside of the trash motel.

It's nighttime.

Someone walks out of the motel. The silhouette fumbles with the front lock. They must be closing up. I can tell this was recorded with the camera hanging above the door. I remember seeing it before. The stranger turns around, and nearby streetlights reveal a crooked face.

*Wait, I know her.*

This is the woman who tried to exchange sex for information about Marcus. Her phone rings. She slides her hands into her purse and pulls it out.

"I'm on my way," she says right away.

…

"What are you saying?" She sticks a finger into her ear to

hear better. “Babe, stop it. What did I tell you? You’re completely paranoid. We’re good. We’ve been good for a long time now.”

. . .

“What are you so worried about?”

. . .

“What, you mean him? Don’t be ridiculous. He’s nothing. I’m telling you, we’re good.”

. . .

“I’m leaving now. I have the merchandise. I’ll be there in twenty. I love you.”

. . .

“Hey, listen to me. Listen!” She raises her voice. “Stick to the plan. I’ll meet you at home.”

. . .

“Then where the hell are you? Did you go out to see her again?” she scolds.

. . .

“Damn it, Marc! We don’t have time for this. Go home. We’ll talk about it later.”

She hangs up. Fuming with anger, she walks off. The sound of tires screeching down the road reaches me, but all I can hear as it rumbles away is the name she spat angrily.

Marc.

*Marcus.*

No fucking way. Could it be?

Did I finally get the bastard?

"What are you watching?"

I almost jump to the ceiling at the sight of Winter standing in the doorway. I drop my phone onto the side table so quickly she chuckles.

"Let me guess." She sits next to me. "Porn."

I wish. I really wish it was porn instead of this fucking nightmare.

"Why would I need porn when I have the real thing right here?" I grin, and she rolls her eyes at my predictable line. Before she can question me further, I rise to my feet, lock the door, and slam my lips to hers. Barely minutes later, I'm on top of her, her fingers in my hair, my face in her neck while I squeeze in and out of her. *That's it.* The faster she disconnects me from reality, the faster I'll forget that we're doomed.

Because we are.

We're fucked if I keep this up. I know I have to tell her about the video. I know she deserves the truth after the promise I just made. And I will give it to her. I *will* show her the video. But I need to know if it's a dead end, first. Then I'll tell her.

Tomorrow, I'll tell her everything.

A FEELING OF WARMTH FILLS ME up when I open my eyes to find Winter's head resting on my chest. Her naked body tangled up with mine isn't too bad either. Carefully tracing circles on my bare skin, she seems trapped in deep thoughts.

"Morning, beautiful," I say, and she looks up.

"Took you long enough," she whispers with a smile.

"What can I say? You exhausted me, woman." I plant a gentle kiss on her forehead.

"We have to be up soon. Kendrick and Allie are helping me make the house more recovery-friendly for my dad today."

This is my chance. It's now or never. I have to go investigate the video. I have to find out if this is the *Marc* I'm looking for.

"Actually, I was thinking I'd hang out with Vic today. You know, since he's been having a bit of a tough time lately." I regret speaking as soon as the lie falls out.

It's a necessary lie. The final lie.

*No more after this.*

She nods. "Okay. When are you leaving?"

"After breakfast."

"Will you be back for dinner? I'm making my dad's favorite to welcome him home."

"Sure."

I bite back a grin. I love this woman, but *she can't cook*. This dinner will mostly consist of people spitting into their napkins when she's not looking.

Winter wasn't *finished*, still writhing with my face between her legs when we heard the car door close in the driveway yesterday. We had to get up, get dressed right in the middle of it, and I swear I've never seen my baby this moody. I had to take care of that when everyone went to bed. She went back to her regular self once I was done with her.

She kisses my cheek. "You hungry? I think I smell bacon."

We hear laughter downstairs. I conclude that Kendrick and Allie are already here.

"Let's go. I'm starving." She slips out of bed.

"Right behind you."

## *Winter*

"FOR THE BILLIONTH TIME, THEY'RE NOT mine," Jay shouts as Kendrick chases him around the house with a box of condoms.

"Then what were they doing in your backpack, Jay Jay?"

We're all laughing so hard we can barely breathe. We spent the day fixing up the house to make life easier for my dad. He truly appreciated the gesture, but it sucks to know whatever we do to help won't do as much good as having a professional to take care of him would. Kendrick found condoms in Jay's bag while moving stuff around.

Jay's fourteen. He obviously knows about sex at this point, but he'd rather die than admit it to my dad.

"Fine, they're mine. But it's not what you think," he pleads.

Kendrick scoffs. "Not what we think? Then what were you doing with them, Jaden? Water balloons?"

"Leave the poor kid alone." I laugh harder.

"Is that for that girl I saw you with when I picked you up from school the other day? Charlotte, is it?" My dad joins.

My brother flushes.

"Jay Jay's in love!" Kendrick gasps dramatically.

"Okay, I'm out," Jay growls and launches up the stairs.

We're still laughing five minutes later.

My dad asks us to help him get to his room shortly after. He needs the rest. This has been a long day. I decided not to cook because, apparently, no one wanted to eat my food, not that I'm surprised.

"Shouldn't Haze be here by now?" Allie reminds me when we spread across the couch.

"Uh, yeah, actually, he should." I check the time on my phone. "I'll call him."

It rings one time, two times, three times. He doesn't pick up. I've been texting him throughout the day, but he didn't answer, probably busy with his best friend.

"I'll call Vic. Haze's phone is probably dead."

It rings a few times.

"Hello?"

"Hey Vic. It's Winter. Can I talk to Haze?"

He snorts. "I mean… Don't you have his number?"

I hear in his tone that he's no stranger to alcohol this evening. I'm surprised Haze would allow him to drink when he went there specifically because he's having a hard time.

"I tried, but he's not picking up. He said he'd be back home by now."

"Home from where?" He sounds confused.

"From your place, duh."

A long silence follows.

"What are you talking about? Haze wasn't at my place today."

My lungs collapse.

"What? But… he said that you were hanging out."

"When I texted him, he said he was spending the day with you."

It slaps me across the face.

He lied.

*Again.*

Allie, who's sitting right next to me, offers me an apologetic look. No explanations are needed. She knows merely from the look on my face that something happened, and it's not a good something.

The front door opens.

A hurricane of emotions sucks me in.

He's here.

If he'd just picked up the phone, I would've never called Vic. If he'd just come home a few minutes sooner, I would've never found out about this. Is this what our relationship is going to be like? Am I going to develop trust issues, become completely paranoid every time he goes out?

I refuse to let go of the million excuses colliding in my head. Maybe he has a great, solid reason. Maybe his car broke down so he couldn't go. What bothers me the most isn't even that I don't know where he went today. Or what he did. All I care about is that he lied.

"Babe?" He shuts the door.

Kendrick comes back from the bathroom at the same time, and Allie gives him the look. The *let's save ourselves while we still can* look. She grabs his hand and drags him up the stairs to give us privacy.

"Winter?" he calls again.

I'm going to crucify him, I swear.

With a heavy heart, I head for the kitchen. He's standing near the doorway, with this unbearably beautiful smile on his face. Seeing him turns my rage into excruciating pain. He tucks his smile away when he notices the absence of mine.

"Why?" I whisper.

I don't need to explain myself. His face instantly changes. He knows. *He knows what he did.*

"I swear I was going to tell you."

"Answer the question." His false promises aren't enough to pierce through my icy exterior.

At a loss for words, he steps forward.

"Because I… I knew you wouldn't let me go."

"Go where?"

Tell me that you were preparing a surprise. Tell me this isn't what I think. Tell me you didn't go looking for the *one* person you promised not to chase anymore.

Tell me before I break for the last time.

"Winter, I'm so sor—"

"Haze, you can either tell me where you were today or leave," I snap. His face darkens, and he averts his gaze to his feet, a clear sign of his guilt.

"I received a video yesterday," he begins. "It was a video with a lead on…" He pauses, as if he knows that Marcus's name will change everything.

Say it. I need to hear it. *Please, Haze.* I need you to completely shatter what's left of me.

Maybe I'll finally understand.

"A lead on Marcus."

There it is.

"I went to check on it today."

"And you told me you were going to see Vic," I state.

"Winter, listen, I will tell you everything, just hear me ou—"

"*Go.*"

Color vanishes from his face.

"What?"

"You heard me. Go. Get out of my house." The pain beats my heart to a pulp.

"Winter, please. You're never going to believe what I found today. I think I might have him. Just—"

"But you lied about it. That's all that matters, Haze. You lied. Like you always do," I say a lot louder than anticipated. "So please… Please go."

Only then does he seem to realize how serious I am. He

opens his mouth, like he's looking for the right words to say, but none come to his rescue. He's stunned as he turns away and opens the door. *Don't go*, my heart screams. But my brain is louder. The way it should've always been.

Just as he's about to walk out, he stops and glances at me.

"What does this mean?" His voice breaks.

He can't ask me that. He can't ask me if this is over. Because I'm afraid I will say the right thing for once.

Even if the right thing completely destroys me.

Even if the right thing feels wrong.

"What does this mean for us?" His eyes are bloodshot.

God, do I love him.

I love the man who doesn't know how to love me back.

"I don't know."

He nods faintly.

Then he's gone.

## *Haze*

"Haze? What the hell are you doing here?" Vic asks when I burst into his apartment uninvited. I spent hours just roaming around town, talking myself out of driving straight to her house and begging her to take me back. It's past midnight.

"You told her, didn't you?" Rage boils inside me.

He tries to get up but quickly tumbles backward onto the couch. *Great, he's drunk*. I can't even be mad at his dumb ass. He won't remember a thing tomorrow.

"I'm sorry. She called and asked where you were and I…" He pauses, his eyes widening. "I…" He brings a hand to his mouth.

Tell me he isn't going to…

*Yep, he just puked.*

I'm grateful for the trash can next to him. I can't be cleaning up vomit after I just got dumped. Or did I? Shit, I don't know.

"And he's wasted." I crinkle my nose at the smell and plop onto his couch. He wipes his mouth with the back of his hand.

"You should've told me she wasn't supposed to know."

"You mean I should've told you I was lying to my girlfriend again?"

*It sounds so fucking bad put like that.*

Wow, she was right to kick me out…

She should've done it ages ago.

"Are you in trouble?" Vic asks.

I scoff. "Trouble? She kicked me out. I think we're over."

"Now where have I heard that before?" he mocks. "You two break up twice every five seconds, and guess what? She always takes your sorry ass back."

"This one was different. I'm telling you, she's really done with my shit."

*So is the whole world.*

"That's also what you said last time and you still ended up hooking up the night of the party, am I wrong?"

The memories invade my brain. I see Winter in a towel. The

drops running down her breasts. How much she didn't *want* to want me when I pushed a finger inside her. I forgot half of my night, but this… I could never forget.

He snorts. "You never really lose Winter, man. That's what makes Winter… *Winter.*"

His mocking tone triggers me. He speaks of her like I could do anything and she'd still take me back, like her love for me makes her downright stupid.

"Don't talk about her like that," I warn.

"Woah, chill." He puts his hands up. "I'm not mocking her. Not at all. I envy you for having a girl like that. Love so strong you'd accept even the worst things. It's almost like she loves you so much she'd choose you over herself."

I'm about to tell him he's wrong when my phone vibrates.

*What now?*

My whole body relaxes when I see the name on my screen.

Winter.

She texted me.

It feels like I can breathe again.

I'm sorry. Can we talk about it?

My first instinct is to jump to the ceiling. I want to scream at the top of my lungs. *I'm so fucking happy*. But then I read the text again. My eyes stick to its beginning. Wait…

*She's* apologizing to *me*?

Fuck…

Vic's right. Her love for me is making her stupid.

By accepting me, she's accepting that this is what she deserves. This girl may be good for me.

But I'm the worst thing for her.

Because the Winter I fell in love with, the girl who spat the truth in my face on her first day, would have never taken this kind of shit. She would've dropped me on lie number one.

I never wanted to change her.

I wanted her to change me.

"I can't believe I'm going to say this but… you're right."

"I am?" He's surprised.

I get off the couch and head over to the kitchen.

"I know it's hard for you to do right now, but use your brain, Vic. Think real hard. Where do you keep pens and paper?"

It takes him ten minutes to tell me to look into the box of stuff Bea never came to pick up—which makes it clear he really needs to throw her shit out. I sit down at the kitchen table and let my fingers create the hardest sentences I've ever had to write. An hour later, I walk back into the living room to see Vic opening another beer.

"Go to bed. I'm going to need you to clean up and get your shit together in the morning."

He doesn't bother asking questions because he's way beyond the point of giving a fuck. But if he'd asked, I know what I would've told him.

I'm setting her free.

I'm forcing her to choose herself.

Because I refuse to be the reason Winter Kingston doesn't think she's the best goddamn person in this world.

I refuse to be the reason she looks at herself…

The way I look at me.

## *Winter*

Insomnia has never really bothered me before. But that's probably because lying awake at three in the morning has never felt like *this*. Like slowly dying with every breath. I enjoy being left alone with my thoughts most of the time. But tonight is *not* one of those times. As soon as I heard his car booking it down the street, I lost it. Dropped on a chair and started crying. It's all I've been able to do since.

His scent clings to my pillows, my sheets. The memory of his presence floats around the room, a reminder of everything I want yet can't have. A lapse of judgment has me picking up my phone and sending him a message.

I'm sorry. Can we talk about it?

I can't believe *I'm* the one saying sorry after all this. Just as I was the one chasing after him without a coat in the snow a few days ago. *For crying out loud, Haze, what did you turn me into?*

No answer.

He usually answers right away. Still no answer after fifteen minutes. No answer after forty-five. No answer after an hour. I doubt he's sleeping. How could he after this? I drift off to sleep for a few hours, but as soon as 5:59 strikes, I'm right back to tossing and turning. I'm losing my mind. I spent all three hours dreaming that I got a text from him. That he replied. I kept waking up every hour to check and had to watch my hopes go up in flames on repeat.

He still hasn't replied.

Maybe this really is over.

I rub my eyes and reach for my phone that's on 4 percent battery. I forgot to charge it. Two missed calls await me. Except that they're not from the person I wanted.

They're from Vic.

I frown.

He sent me a text three minutes ago.

I'm outside.

What?

It's 7:30 a.m. What would Vic be doing here so early? No, what would Vic be doing here *at all*? In a hurry, I toss one of Haze's sweaters on to cover up my lack of a bra. That's just one of the many pieces of clothing he left behind. After all, we were supposed to move in together into my childhood home. We were supposed to be happy. But that's the key word here, isn't it? *Supposed.*

I scamper down the stairs and stop at the front door. What I see on my porch is probably worse than any scenario I could've ever come up with during this unbearably long night.

In Vic's eyes is *pity*.

In his hands… a letter.

"Winter, hey. Did I wake you?" He forces a smile. He looks exhausted. My guess is Haze kept him up last night.

"Hey, Vic." I frown. "No, it's all good. Haze isn't here if that's why you—"

"I know." He can't hide his slight cringe. "He sent me. I came to pick up his stuff."

*Heart failure.*

"Oh." My throat tightens.

He couldn't come and get his stuff himself? He had to send his friend to do his dirty work? I manage to bring down the few unpacked boxes he left upstairs without crying.

"Thanks." He shoves them into the trunk of his car. When he comes back to the door, I pray that he won't notice I'm wearing Haze's sweatshirt. I don't care. I'm not giving it back. If he's going to strip every trace of Haze Adams away from me forever, I'm keeping the damn sweatshirt.

"Oh, I almost forgot." He hands me the letter. "He wanted me to give you this."

I spent the past ten minutes trying to convince myself that he was just dropping mail on the way back to his place. That the letter isn't for me. But I can't lie anymore. He hands me the envelope, and I don't even need to open it to know what's inside.

*I just know.*

It's the end.

He wouldn't have sent his best friend if it wasn't.

"He said this will explain everything."

I stare at the envelope in my hand blankly.

"Winter, I'm… I'm really sorry," he says sincerely.

I watch him get back into his truck and speed away. I sit around the kitchen table and read the sentence on the back of the envelope.

Haze's handwriting.

*If it can't be me.*

I rip the envelope open with trembling fingers. I have never, in my entire life, been so scared of ink on a page.

*Winter,*

*You were right.*

*What you said to me yesterday was right. And receiving your text last night finally made me see clearly.*

*You apologized. After all that I've done, after all the shit* that I've put you through, YOU apologized to ME.

I was going to come crawling back to you. I was going to come begging for your forgiveness. But you made me realize that I can't.

I can't ask for your forgiveness because I know you'll give it to me.

And I don't deserve it.

I don't deserve one fucking drop of your love. I don't deserve you. I never did.

And I never will.

If you're reading this right now, it means that I've finally stopped being selfish. For once in my life, I'm going to do the right thing.

I'm done. I'm done making you suffer because of how fucking broken I am. I refuse to keep putting you in harm's way because of a sick obsession I can't shake.

I wouldn't be able to live with myself if something

happened to you, Winter. So, I have no choice.

I have to say it.

I can't stop looking for him.

I'll never be happy. I'll never be at peace until I find him. I can't give up on finding the man who murdered my sister. The man who destroyed my family and my life.

Not even for you.

And you have no idea how much I hate myself for it.

Part of me would like to believe that when this is all over and I've found the bastard, I'll find my way back to you. But I know better than to think you could ever forgive me this time. Or that you'll wait for me to come back after I've dealt with my shit. And you shouldn't have to. You shouldn't have to wait for anyone. This isn't the life I want for you.

I'm an asshole. I think part of you always knew that. From the very first day when you called me a jackass in the hall, you knew I was fucked up beyond repair. Yet, you chose to see the good in me.

And let me tell you, I've made a lot of mistakes in my days, but accidentally falling in love with you is by far the best one. You deserve the world and I want you to have it.

Even if I can't be the one giving it to you.

But if it won't be me kissing you every night and growing old with you, I do have to tell you this.

I hope you find everything you're looking for and fall madly in love with a guy who actually deserves it.

I hope he makes you wonder how you could ever live without him and pushes you to conquer your fears.

I hope he makes you want to be the best version of yourself.

Because that's what you did for me.

Even if, in the end, wanting to be better wasn't enough.

I'm so happy you followed your cousin that night. I'm so happy you got my bike helmet stuck on your head and dropped your phone into the fucking toilet to avoid talking to me.

Because it led me to you.

To us.

I love you, Kingston.

Always.

I'm so sorry it couldn't be me.

# THIRTY-ONE

## *Replaced*

"So, that's it?"

Standing in the doorway, I carefully eye the heartbreaking scene in front of me. Haze, shoving clothes into the suitcase on his bed. The shirt he's holding slips out of his hand when he sees me. He clearly wasn't expecting me. But what *exactly* did he expect? He's not the only one with an opinion on this. If this is really the end, if he's really giving up on us, I have things to say, too.

The second I finished his letter, I got up, got dressed, and stormed out of my house, no second thought. I knew I had to see him, give him a piece of my mind before he vanished from my life forever. I took a lucky guess and headed straight for Vic's place. I didn't let myself break down on the way over. Didn't shed one tear. Why? Because I wasn't sad.

I was furious.

And I knew I had to hold on to this anger as tightly as I could. Next will be the *ugly crying* phase, and I don't know how long I have. Some might say I'm only trying to have the last word here, and… to that I say, *damn right, I am.* There's no way he gets to leave with all that power. He's always the one fucking it all up. After all the sacrifices I've made for him. No fucking way he gets to think he left poor heartbroken Winter behind.

The door was unlocked, and Vic's truck wasn't out front. I'm glad I have him alone for this.

"A letter?" I hold up the envelope in my hand, and his eyes follow the movement. "I don't even deserve better than a letter?" My voice flickers.

*Shit, what happened to all that anger?*

"Winter, I—"

"Don't. You already said what you had to say. It's my turn." I fuel my courage with a deep breath.

He presses his lips into a line.

"You were right," I tell him.

Silence.

"You are an asshole."

He chews on the inside of his cheek and looks down.

"And a mess. And *oh so fucking* damaged. But you know what else you are?" I unfold the sheet of paper in my hand and reread his goodbye. "A coward."

Don't cry.

Don't cry.

Five more minutes.

"And you want to know what the worst part is?" My eyes dart to his. "I would've accepted all of it if it meant I got to be with you."

"Winter, I—"

"Haze, please. Just… Let me say it."

He clamps his mouth shut.

"I trusted you. Even after everything you put me through, after you ripped my heart right out of my chest and stepped on it, I would've taken you back without question. I was such a fool for you I accepted that you were part of the reason my father almost died and now *this*?" I can barely breathe. "You abandon me with nothing but a letter? Seriously? I mean, for fuck's sake, Haze, did you ever love me at all?" I only notice how loud I'm being when I finish speaking.

He frowns. "What? How can you even ask that? Don't you get it? I'm doing this precisely *because* I love you. I love you more than anything."

Not more than your revenge.

*Not more than you hate him.*

"I know you genuinely believe that. And that's exactly what makes it so sad. You don't. This isn't love. Love isn't destroying everything you built with someone because you're afraid. Because you'd rather just ruin everything yourself than risk for life to take it away from you. The way it took your sister… That's just what you do, Haze. You sabotage your own happiness. You'll never let yourself be happy. You can't." My throat is so sore it hurts. "*You don't know how…*"

He doesn't say a word, but I can tell my speech hurt him. I cross the remaining distance between us and rest a hand on his cheek for the last time. His eyes close at the touch, and my anger is swapped with heart-squeezing sadness.

Defeated, I let myself cry. *Really* cry. I let the tears cascade down my face uncontrollably. He winces but doesn't look away. Good. I want him to see what he did to me. What he did to us. So that one day, when he meets another girl—*the right girl*—he'll be the man I wanted him to be.

"I love you. So much." I choke on a sob. "But I'm done chasing you. This is toxic. *We're* toxic."

Saying it out loud feels just as liberating as it feels excruciating. I needed to say this for me. Not for him, not for anyone else: *me*. I needed to get these words out of my system. So that, one day, down the road, I can get him out, too.

His eyes widen. This isn't how he expected this moment to go. I bet he thought I'd come bawling my eyes out and beg him to stay. *Sorry, not this time.*

"You did it, Haze. You finally convinced me. You're right."

My hand leaves his cheek.

"I deserve better than you."

His mouth drops.

No reply, not even a word. He just steps backward like I shot five arrows straight into his heart.

Finally, a tear rolls down his face.

I turn away. Just two more steps before I reach the door. Two more steps before the end. I could never admit it to myself before, but I can now.

Sometimes, things just have to stay broken.

No matter how bad you wish they didn't.

No matter how far you'd go to fix them.

You can't give CPR to someone who'd rather drown.

And there comes a moment in life, one inevitable, heartbreaking, soul-crushing moment… where all that's left to do is drop the pieces on the ground, watch as they shatter one by one, and walk the hell away.

"So, no. You're not leaving me, Haze. Not this time…"

I open the door and give him one last look over my shoulder.

"This time, I'm leaving you."

TEN MONTHS LATER ...

"You're never going to believe what she said next." The blonde twirls her extension around her finger. Fiddling with my phone, I debate on whether or not I could get away with standing up mid-conversation and storming out of the coffee shop. *What the fuck was I thinking? Why did I let Vic talk me into this?*

When he set me up with some girl he knew, I didn't want to go, but he told her I would do it before I could say no and I felt bad. He insisted that it can't be healthy to go this long without some action, but I don't care. I don't even remember her name. Carrie? Callie? Cassie? She's beautiful, sure, but I need much more than that. It wouldn't hurt if she made me laugh. Maybe even surprise me with a snarky comeback once in a while. I'd like to feel like this conversation is going somewhere, and right now, the only place it's leading me is right out the fucking door.

We had coffee, we talked, *I* paid. Now I just have to find an excuse to leave.

"Shit, would you look at the time? It's late. I should go." I rise to my feet.

"But… it's 2:00 p.m.," she stutters, confused.

"Yeah, exactly. It's late." I force a smile. "It was great meeting you."

I begin walking away.

Don't say it.

Don't say it.

Don't say it.

"Haze, wait."

I turn around.

"Will you call me?" she tries.

Fuck.

*Remember what you said, Haze. No more lying. You've been good for almost a year. Don't ruin it, now.*

"Honestly?"

She nods.

"Probably not."

And she's offended. Awesome.

"I'm so sorry. I promise it's not you. I'm just… getting out of a relationship."

The face she makes screams, *"Warning! Warning! Damaged goods right here!"* I can practically feel her losing interest in me. Vic said this line always worked with girls back when Bea left him for someone else. But, in my case, it's expired. Been invalid for quite a while now.

*It's almost been a year, Haze.*

*You should be over it.*

*I bet she is.*

"Okay, bye now." I rush out of the coffee shop, my mind racing, and glance down at my phone to see a text from Vic.

You drank all the milk. AGAIN. Pick some up on the way home asshole.

I grin. Living with this guy has been… something. We decided to become roommates after I came back from my US trip—I still have to go back home every six months as I'm not a Canadian citizen—and move into a bigger place together. I made sure our new place was as far away as possible from, well, *the past.* I chose an entirely different neighborhood, simply because it seemed like the right thing to do for everyone.

I look up from my phone the second the pedestrian light comes on. I'm about to cross the street, but I can't…

Because my heart gets ripped out of my chest and brutally shoved back in.

My feet sink into the sidewalk.

She's right there.

The girl who's been haunting my every waking moment for ten months is *right fucking there.* On the other side of the street.

Winter.

My Winter.

*My Winter who's not mine anymore…*

She's walking out of a store, brown hair stopping at her belly button. She's wearing a leather jacket—it's starting to get cold out—and a white scarf. Her hair is longer. Much longer. And it's brown again. I did like it black, but her brown hair was always more natural to me. She hasn't seen me. I doubt that she will unless she looks directly into my direction. What is she even doing in this neighborhood?

She looks even more breathtaking than I remember. *Shit, how does she look like that?* I notice a few guys doing a double take as they pass her on the sidewalk. She doesn't even come close to noticing, so clueless, so ignorant as to how flawless she is. Same old Winter. With her hands in her pockets, she absentmindedly kicks a rock on the sidewalk. She seems to be waiting for something. What are the chances? What are the odds that I would see her again in a city crawling with people?

Maybe it's a sign.

I'm not sure why I do what I do next. But I don't need to know. I don't *care* to know. I just start walking, unable to control my feet as I cross the street with my eyes dead set on her. A car honks at me, but I'm so focused on getting to her that I barely hear it. I have no clue what I'm going to say. *Hey, how have you been? Remember me? I'm your garbage, compulsive-liar ex-boyfriend?*

My heartbeat increases considerably when I reach the sidewalk. But then…

Then it stops.

My legs deny me another step.

*Who the fuck is that?*

I watch the six-foot-something dark-haired guy who just walked out of the same store Winter did come up to her. I can't see his face from where I am. But I don't need to.

I see *hers.*

I see the way she smiles when he reaches for her hand and traps it into his. I see the way she laughs when he tells her something. I see how quickly he pulls her closer, cups her face, and kisses her. She kisses him back, pushing to her tiptoes for more.

Just like that… the shitty walls I spent a year building around myself come crashing down all at once.

They're picked apart brick by brick until my selfish, beat-up, bruised heart is left completely uncovered.

*Shit, I really lost her.*

But for some reason, it's just hitting me now, which is dumb because the year I spent without her should've made that clear already. No, the automated message I got when I called her the day after she walked out of Vic's apartment should've made that clear.

*The number you dialed is no longer in service.*

She'd changed her number.

I was a mess for a good two months after that. Drinking, going out with Vic, trying to feel something other than pain in any way that I could. But then, I had to go back to Florida for a month and ran into Will randomly. He told me that one day, when the time was right, we'd figure our shit out. That he and his girlfriend were rooting for us.

From that moment forward, I began seeing this breakup as a pause, a detour. I kept clinging to the hope that eventually, after everything, after I'd have found Marcus, we'd be together again. But seeing her right now… smiling at another guy, laughing at his jokes, kissing him…

I swear I'd forgotten it was possible to hurt this much.

God, she's so far gone.

She's… someone else's baby now.

Of course some other guy would show up and want to be with her. I mean, *look at her.* Plus, not every guy is as fucking stupid as I am. I bet she even has no problem sleeping with someone else, unlike me. I haven't had sex in ten fucking months while she's been dating someone this whole time.

I can't stand the thought of that random dude inside her. Does he know that her neck gets ticklish? Does he know that she might seem like a good little girl at first, but she can get really fucking *naughty* when she's comfortable? Does he satisfy her? Does she fake it with him?

Pulling away after a five-year kiss, they begin walking in the opposite direction, their silhouettes shrinking as the distance between us grows. I stand there, in the middle of the moving crowd, watching the memory of when I was happy disappear down the sidewalk.

I can't stop myself.

This is the answer I was waiting for.

Harry's lawyer has been calling me nonstop, asking me to testify in Maika's custody trial. The trial was delayed for months—something tells me lovely Lauren is to blame for that—but it's finally due in a few days. Harry said they weren't allowed to use the recording as evidence but that doesn't mean they can't use me and my memories of that night.

I pluck my phone out of my pocket and call back the latest

number in my missed calls log.

It rings a few times.

He picks up.

"Please tell me you changed your mind." Harry's desperate voice erupts down the line.

Yesterday, I said I'd think about it. Yesterday, I wasn't sure I should go since I knew it would mean seeing Winter again.

But now?

Seeing her again is what I want most in this world.

"I'll be there."

# THIRTY-TWO

## *New Boyfriend*

My footsteps are heavy, hesitant. Let's be real—my footsteps are scared little bitches. I don't have the slightest idea of why I'm doing this, but I do know one thing: I should probably be anywhere else right now. Memories of Winter on the sidewalk flash through my mind. *I mean, goddamn, has she seen herself? She shouldn't be allowed to look this fucking good.*

The trial is a few days away, but there's no way in hell I'm waiting that long. I need to know about the guy I saw her kissing yesterday, and I need to know now. Is it serious? How long have they been together? Are they crazy in love?

Does she love him the way she loves me?

*Loved, past tense*, a voice in my head reminds me.

I weave my way through the crowd and push the thick glass door to the tiny coffee shop open. It's completely dead. Good. The less people distract her, the more chances I have of getting what I came for.

I don't know how she's going to react to my surprise visit. It's been so long since I saw her. Luckily for me, she's quite active on social media. All it took was one look at her profiles to find out where she's working now. I must've looked like a predator when I came in looking for her yesterday. I managed to convince the barista to tell me when her next shift would be by claiming to be her friend.

*Wow, I really am a creep.*

I suck in a breath and come to an abrupt stop near the counter. With her back facing me, she's humming along to the song on the radio and cleaning a coffee machine.

I clear my throat. "How hard is it to get some service around here?"

She jumps and swivels around.

A thousand emotions cross her features at the sight of me.

"Haze?" She blinks in disbelief.

She hasn't changed one bit.

"Allie." I offer her my best *I know I broke your best friend's heart but please don't hate me* smile. Man, how desperate do I have to be to go to her for info? Winter used to say that Allie was team Waze. I guess I figured if there was one person in Winter's life who wouldn't completely loathe me by now, it'd be her.

"What are you doing here?" She raises a suspicious eyebrow. She doesn't look mad or like she's going to go key my car to defend her bestie's honor. *That's a start.*

"Can't a guy order coffee?"

She scoffs, not buying it for a second.

"Okay. What can I get you?"

I'm suddenly reminded that I have no clue what this place serves, and I don't know squat about coffee.

"Just… coffee."

*Way to go, dumbass.*

"Yeah, but what kind? All black? Do you want sugar? Cream? And what size?" A sly smile reshapes her lips. She is enjoying this way too much.

"The smallest you have. And all black."

She smiles. "Cool. Like your heart."

By the time I realize how bad she just roasted me, she's already making my coffee.

*Meh, could've been worse. I'll take it.*

She hands me a cup seconds later.

"Why are you really here, Haze?" She doesn't beat around the bush.

To hell with it.

"Honestly?"

She nods.

"Because I just found out Winter is seeing someone, and I need you to tell me everything you know so that I don't lose my fucking mind," I blurt into a crammed, quick sentence. She's shocked, stunned by my bluntness, but I don't have time for denial anymore. *Been there, done that.* All lying has ever done is ruin my life.

They say we all have that one person. That one person we'll never really lose feelings for, never really forget no matter how many months go by, no matter how many years wash the memories away. That person we'll always have a thing for no matter what.

Winter Kingston is my person.

Against all odds, Allie laughs.

"Straight to the point, I see." She shakes her head. "Let's get a table and talk. My break is in…" She glances at the large clock on the wall. "Now."

A dark-haired guy bursts through the door right then.

"I'm here! I'm here!" he says like he expects applause.

"I can see that, Coop," Allie says.

"I'm not late," he pants and disappears behind a door labeled *Employees Only*.

A minute later, I've paid and Coop is back to the front to serve the few customers who just walked in. Allie motions to sit down at a table, which I do. We stare at each other for a painfully awkward ten seconds.

"So…" She breaks the ice.

"So…" I repeat.

"You know about Matthew."

*Matthew. That's the fucker's name.*

"I do."

"How?" She eases herself deeper into her seat.

"I saw them kissing on the street yesterday."

She winces. "Ouch."

I huff a chuckle. "Tell me about it."

"Let me guess, you saw her after all this time and your heart started beating again?" she mocks and crosses her arms over her chest. I don't confirm or deny it, staring at the black coffee in my hands. "Well, Kendrick owes me fifty bucks."

I frown. "What?"

"We made a bet that you'd be back into her life one way or another. I knew you'd never really be over each other."

My heart leaps forward.

"What do you mean we'll never be over *each other*? As in…"

Could she still have feelings for me?

"What do you want to know, Haze? I only have a few minutes." She presses.

"How did they meet?" I ask.

"Winter's job. She works at a five-star hotel now."

"How long have they been seeing each together?"

She shrugs. "A few months, at most."

"Are they serious?" *Please say no.*

"God, I hope not," I think I hear her mutter.

"I'm sorry?"

"I just said they're not official yet," she retracts herself. "Anything else?"

"Have they…"

I don't need to finish speaking for her to know.

No way that I just asked her that.

"Wow, we're going there. Okay," she mocks. "Listen, I don't know. I don't think so."

She's most likely lying and just not interested in telling me. That's Allie. Winter tells her everything.

"Is she… happy?" My voice falters.

The mockery in her eyes morphs into ego-smashing pity. There's something broken about my tone. Fuck, it feels like she dumped me yesterday.

"She says she is." She nods. "But if you ask me, she's… different."

"Different how?"

"Different like she doesn't really trust anyone. I love the girl to death, but she doesn't tell me anything anymore. Truth be told, we kind of grew apart. I still see her all the time, but it's almost as though I'm more her cousin's girlfriend than her childhood best friend. She's been like this since, well… you."

"You must hate me," I conclude.

She thinks about her reply long and hard.

"I think I hate what your absence did to her more than I hate you."

I wince.

"Don't get me wrong. She's always laughing, she's made new friends, and she's been working out like crazy, but something feels off. It's like she's in denial. Like she just put her pain on pause or something. She didn't let herself be a wreck over you. As soon as you left, she just shut it off."

"Or she just moved on?" It hurts to say.

"Right." She scoffs. "Must be why she can't let Matthew touch her."

She regrets speaking as soon as the words trickle out. Her

widened eyes go *"Did I say that out loud?"*

So, they *didn't* sleep together.

A wave of relief rolls over me.

*Calm down, idiot. Doesn't mean she didn't have sex with a hundred fucking guys after you.*

"I have to go. My break's almost over." She gets up.

I wish I could ask her a million more questions, but she's clearly beating herself up over letting that last detail slip out.

"Okay. Thanks anyway."

She forces a smile and walks off. Getting up, I watch her disappear into the back of the shop and walk out of the building in a surprisingly good mood.

*So, she won't let him touch her, huh?*

*And he's not best friend approved?*

This trial can't come soon enough.

## *Winter*

"A new wife barely a year after his divorce? *My, my.* Uncle Harry is a player." Kendrick's voice echoes throughout the spacious wedding venue, and I chuckle.

"I heard that," my dad calls from the other side of the room, interrupting his pricey wedding organizer midsentence. I laugh and Kendrick joins.

My cousin does have a point. It is a bit ironic that in less than two weeks, my father will be walking down the aisle with a new woman, but my dad and Judy deserve it. They love each other as much as humanly possible, and after everything my dad has been through during the past year—fighting for the custody of Maika, recovering from the accident that wasn't an accident at all, coming to terms with the fact that his own wife never loved him—he deserves every single moment of happiness he can get.

When he burst into my bedroom earlier today to remind me that we had to go visit wedding venues, I couldn't believe I'd forgotten about something so important. Judy has been bugging me about going with them all week.

In my defense, I spent hours on the phone with Matthew last night, wondering whether or not I should wear blue or red to his parents' charity event this weekend. I fell asleep while he was telling me about the time he rescued an injured animal on his trip to Africa. He must've told me this story a thousand times, and although it really is interesting, my eyelids disagreed.

The venues we've been visiting are way too expensive. I know it, Judy knows it, my dad knows it. But he claims money is the last thing on his mind, and he isn't going to hold back on the *second* best day of his life.

"Is this it? That's like the hundredth place we've seen," Kendrick whines.

"It's the fourth," I mock. "Why? You eager to go back to your girlfriend? Oh wait, you can't."

"Shut up," he groans.

Allie has always been the world's worst liar. She's never been good at keeping things to herself—especially surprises—but she still loves to try and pull them off anyway. This year, to celebrate Kendrick's birthday and their one year together, she decided to skip the secret part and straight up tell him that she's organizing something for him. After five weeks of begging, she managed to convince her loaded uncle to let her throw Kendrick an epic birthday party on his massive boat. Downside is, between her job and the time-consuming party planning, she hasn't been able to see Kendrick once in four days.

"Who invited him to visit venues anyway?" I whine.

Kendrick scoffs. "You did, dumbass."

Crap, he's right.

"Stop your bickering," Judy says. After they've finished up with the wedding organizer, she and my father march down to us. "Honey, do you want to tell them, or should I?"

My dad smiles. "You can have the honor."

"This is the one," she squeals.

"What? I'm so happy for you guys." I pull her into a tight hug. Judy is an angel sent from above. She showed up at the worst possible time in my father's life and completely turned it around. Who would've thought the nurse my father's insurance sent would turn out to be his soul mate?

I was certain things like that only happened in movies, but spending so much time together led them to a very real relationship. And, well, here we are, less than a year later, visiting venues for their wedding. He explained that almost dying put his priorities in perspective, and he didn't want to waste any more precious time. Yes, their relationship evolved quickly, but these two are the couple that could actually defeat the odds and stay together in the long run.

I vividly remember the relief I felt when my father told us his insurance company had called to rectify their mistake; they said he would have access to at-home care after all. I couldn't believe that they'd just made a mistake on something so important, but when asked about it, my father said, "Good things do happen in life, and there isn't always a catch."

"Winter, is your boyfriend still coming?" Judy asks.

"He's not my boyfriend."

"Is that why you were giggling on the phone with him all night?" my dad teases. *Oh, yeah, Judy taught my father sarcasm. I'm not sure I'm a fan. Still working on it.*

"Seal the deal yet?" Kendrick wiggles his eyebrows.

"Learn to use your brain yet?" I retort.

"Answers, please," Judy insists.

"Yes. Matt will be there," I give in, ignoring Kendrick's smooching sounds and his pretending to make out with air.

"Great." She smiles.

Kendrick snaps out of it. "You know what? Good idea, let the guy come. I bet you twenty bucks he bores everyone to death with his trip to Africa story and the guests leave early, so we can go get drunk."

Dismissing him, I pull my phone out of my pocket. I have a

shift at the hotel in two hours.

"Hi, my name is Matthew. I have rich parents who donate to charities and travel to Africa to build schools. Want to hear about the time I saved a burning village from a hurricane?" he says in a ridiculous high-pitched voice, and my dad fails to repress a laugh.

My family isn't exactly a big fan of Matt. They think he's a brag and an annoying spoilt kid, but I see something in him that a part of me has been desperately looking for: *stability*. He was very understanding when I told him I wanted to take things slow. Immediately said he would wait and didn't want me to feel pressured. We aren't officially dating, but we've been talking and getting to know each other for about three months now. We've kissed, of course, but we've never… crossed the line. I don't know when I'll be able to let him—anyone—touch me in that way again.

In the way *he* used to touch me.

So, what if Matt is a bit of a brag? He does amazing things around the world, treats me with respect, and wants a serious relationship. But most importantly… he isn't a liar.

I met him at the hotel during a painfully boring shift. He was in town with his family for a business event and came to the front desk to ask for my number. I came this close to blowing him off. It'd been such a long time since, well, *him*.

I wasn't sure I even knew how to do this anymore. Not to mention I had no idea if I was ready to get back into the dating game. But I eventually gave in, told myself that it'd almost been a year and it was time to move on. *He did.*

"You want to talk about boring people to death? How about you and Allie stop telling us how happy and in love you are every second of every day?" I fire back.

Kendrick doesn't argue, because he knows I'm right. I love them together, but these two are the insufferable couple. The couple that make out in public, call each other disgustingly cute nicknames, and talk about having kids and a home after barely a year of dating.

They're the couple we used to be.

I hate it, but their perfect relationship put some distance between Allie and me. We're not as close as we once were. I could barely stand to be around them at the beginning.

After he left.

"The trial's in two days. We have to meet up with my lawyer. Are you good to get home?" my dad asks me.

"Yep. I'll ride with Kendrick."

"All right, I'll see you tonight, pumpkin" is the last thing my father says before both he and Judy walk away.

"You have got to get a car." Kendrick gets his keys out of his pocket as we make our way to the second exit.

"Meh. One day, maybe." I shrug.

"I mean, unless Matthew's chauffeur drives you everywhere from now on," he taunts.

Sliding into the passenger seat of Kendrick's car, I

contemplate how much my life has changed during the past ten months. I certainly did not expect that my father would be planning his second wedding so soon, or that we'd find ourselves fighting for the custody of my sibling before I turned twenty. I decided to take a year off shortly after I dropped out of school, and I'm pretty damn happy I did. I needed time to figure myself out. I've been looking into psychology for a while now. For the first time in so long, I'm actually excited to go back to school, but before I apply, I want to travel a bit. Matt has been talking of going to Europe this Christmas. I could definitely use the time away.

Maybe I'll even stop looking for *him* in the crowd when I come back. Maybe I'll stop hearing his voice at every street corner.

I remember the day we broke up like it was yesterday. The few tears in his eyes, the freaking *ocean* in mine. I walked out of Vic's apartment, got into a cab, and never saw him again. Sometimes, I wonder if he's still in Canada. I have no clue really. Logically, if Marcus is here, he is, too.

"How's Waze?" I ask.

"He's so big now. You should come and see him soon," Kendrick says. It's such shame that I couldn't keep him after Haze and I broke up. With my Dad's injury, it would have been unsafe to have an excited pup running around the house. Not to mention that I was at work most of the time. Waze deserved an amazing life, owners who could take him outside every day and play with him. Kendrick and Allie could give him that—I couldn't.

"There's something I have to tell you." Kendrick's voice requests my attention.

"Mm?" I ask absentmindedly and text Matt back.

"They found Haze."

I almost drop my phone.

"I'm not even supposed to know. I showed up when you were still in the shower this morning. I heard your dad on the phone. He said something about Haze calling him yesterday."

Like my mind is dead set on rejecting any information regarding this guy, it plays Kendrick's words on repeat.

"W-What?"

"Your dad's lawyer wanted him to testify. They already asked him."

"And?" Anxiety grips me.

"He said yes."

One second you think you've moved on, that you don't care anymore, and the next? You're crumbling to pieces.

"So, he's still—"

"In Canada? Yeah. He never left."

I'm stunned, crippled by confusing emotions.

"I can't believe my dad didn't tell me," I whisper.

"I'm sure he would've tonight."

*Haze is in Canada.*

I somehow convinced myself that he moved back to the US

the day I ran out of Vic's dirty two bedroom. That maybe Marcus left maple syrup and snow behind and Haze followed. The thought of him miles and miles away made coping slightly easier. It meant I would never have to worry about running into him on the street. Although deep down inside, I really hoped that I would. I had this perfectly rehearsed scene in my head. This moment that would tell me what I always knew.

That Haze Adams was just a pit stop, not the final destination. Just a chapter, not the whole book.

He'd have another girl on his arm. He'd be holding her hand, laughing. We'd exchange awkward smiles and pass each other on the sidewalk like two strangers who were in love once upon another life.

Now I know my moment is never going to happen. I'll have to see him again in court, testifying about a time when he loved me. His presence in Canada tells me one thing: if Haze is still here, so is Marcus. He still hasn't avenged his sister's death.

*Or is it that he met another girl? One that gave him a reason to stay?* Whatever it is, I'm glad Kendrick told me before I stepped into the courtroom and came face-to-face with my ex. And, as I glance at the date on my locked phone screen, I hate that I won't see "Two days until we get Maika back" anymore. From now on, I'll read…

Two days until I see him again.

# THIRTY-THREE

## Nothing But The Truth

For months on end, I waited for this day. Waited, obsessed, nearly lost my mind, all over this one moment. I feared the outcome of this trial—found myself constantly battling this voice in my head saying, *"What if we lose?"*—but let me tell you, what I *thought* I was going to feel is absolutely nothing compared to how I *actually* feel.

And that pit in my stomach, my heart's annoying tendency to crawl up my throat? All thanks to the blue-eyed boy they'll be calling to the stand soon.

When we stepped into the courtroom earlier, I was surprised to see it didn't resemble my expectations in any way. Not sure where I picked up the high ceiling idea, but this is a rather small room, with no windows and cool white lights plastered to the ceiling.

The doors open.

Sitting with Jay, Kendrick, Judy, and Allie, I keep my gaze straight ahead of me. I don't want to turn around because I know if I do, there's a chance that I'll see him. And I'm not particularly eager to get my heart ripped out of my chest today. Allie's eyes fly to the door before it even closes. She doesn't say a word, just sends a glance my way. Her eyes apologize for something she didn't do, and the second she covers my hand with hers, I know…

He's here.

I'm thankful that I'm seated near the front. So thankful that, unless I intentionally turn around, I won't catch a glimpse of him. Not until I'm absolutely forced to. The trial begins and I force myself to focus, but I can't stop thinking about him sitting barely a few rows behind me.

As the plaintiff in this case, my father gets to present his witnesses first. It is explained that since Maika is legally under the age of reason, we decided it would be best for her to stay home with Harry's father today.

First witness up is the mental health professional that was ordered by the judge to run a psychological evaluation on both my mother and father. She goes on to speak about Lauren's poor evaluation results, how her mental health isn't at its best—what a shock. Next is Harry's mother, Claire, who recalls the night of the accident, confirms how my mother disappeared on us, talks about how she had to go retrieve Maika from a friend's house herself. So far, things are going well. The evidence pointing to Lauren being an unfit parent keeps piling up. Only a mental case would allow a six-year-old to go home with her at the end of this.

Then they call for him.

When I hear his name, I regret never taking a class to learn how to breathe like a human. My pulse goes wild in my neck, and Allie's hand finds mine. I appreciate her support more than she'll ever know. I hear his footsteps approaching, see him walk to the front from the corner of my eye.

Then he's up there.

*Shit, I can't do this.*

My head hangs low. I stare at my shoes, count the seconds until this is over. It's all I can do.

"Please raise your right hand."

Maybe if I avoid looking at him this entire time, it'll be like none of this ever happened. Like the boy who ripped me apart isn't right in front of me.

"Do you swear to tell the truth, the whole truth, and nothing but the truth?"

"I do."

My entire body contracts at the sound of his voice.

*How the fuck can a voice affect me this much?*

He handles every question like a pro, carefully detailing the awful things Lauren told him when she was wasted the night of the accident. Even if recording someone without their knowledge, as long as you are yourself a part of the conversation, is legal in Canada, the recording was still rejected as evidence. He tells them about her admission to not loving me, her own daughter, to being disgusted by my existence, the whole shebang.

Then comes the time for Lauren's side to counter-interrogate him.

"Mr. Adams, you said when you heard my client say these things, you were in a romantic relationship with Winter Kingston, Lauren Kingston's daughter, correct?"

Kill.

Me.

Now.

"I was. But we're not together anymore," is all he says.

Can I please be anywhere else right now? Like *anywhere else*?

"Is that so? Would you mind explaining why?"

"It's complicated." He shuts her off faster than a speeding bullet.

Do you think if I hold my breath long enough, I'll faint?

"Which one of you exactly ended the relationship?"

"Which time?" Kendrick snickers quietly, and Allie elbows him.

"She did," Haze says.

"When was that exactly?"

"Almost a year ago."

"Okay. Any particular reason?"

*Oh my God. Just drop it, lady!*

He doesn't reply right away. To think that if I wasn't a complete pussy, I could see the look on his face right now. Is he staring at me? Is he half as messed up by this as I am?

"We just… wanted different things."

I almost scoff.

Him: killing his sister's murderer.

Me: rainbows, unicorn and happily ever after.

"Really? Are you sure there's no other reason?"

He clears his throat, clearly uncomfortable. "I wasn't good for her."

"Is there a point to all this?" my father's barrister snaps, and the judge shuts him up with one look.

"Did you or did you not know Winter Kingston had a rather complicated relationship with her mother, Lauren Kingston, when you were together?"

"If by complicated you mean that I knew Lauren treated Winter like sh…" He retracts himself. "Very poorly. Then yes, I knew."

"And you also moved here for Miss Kingston last year?"

Lauren probably told her that.

"Yeah," he admits.

"Wow, that's a big move. Would you say you would have done anything for her? Put her above everyone else?"

A long silence.

She has no idea how ironic this is.

"Mr. Adams, I don't need to remind you that you're under oath, do I?" she presses when he doesn't reply fast enough.

He caves. "Yes. I'd do anything for her."

That's when the last of my resolve shatters.

My head jerks up.

And our eyes meet.

He's staring at me from across the room. Probably has been

since the beginning. His blue eyes…

*Motherfucking ouch.*

"Even manipulate a situation to get revenge on a woman your girlfriend had big disagreements with?"

"Manipulate? What do you mean? I couldn't have forced her to say those things."

"Objection. Leading," my dad's barrister calls.

"I'll rephrase. Mr. Adams, do you love Winter Kingston?"

An unbearably heavy silence descends over us. I squeeze Allie's hand so tight it must hurt, but she doesn't flinch.

"I'm sorry. I really don't see what's the point of this." He glances around nervously.

"Answer the question, please," the judge says.

"It's really not that hard of a question. Are you, Haze Adams, in love with Winter Kingston? Yes or no?"

He lets out a long sigh, staring down at his hands for a second too long.

His gaze finds its way back to me.

I wait for what feels like five years before he speaks again.

"Yes."

*Brain malfunction.*

"Even after all this time? After you've been broken up for a year?" she asks.

He pauses, chewing on the inside of his cheek.

"Always."

*Fuck.*

"So, let me get this straight: you moved to another country for this girl, left your entire life behind, said yourself that you would do absolutely anything for her, and just admitted to still loving her long after the relationship ended. And you're telling me you just happened to conveniently hear the woman your girlfriend had the most problems with say all these things?"

"It sounds bad when you say it like that, but it's—"

"Is anything I just said wrong?"

"You're twisting everything. I'm not—"

"Answer the question. Am I wrong?" she insists.

"But—"

She raises her voice. "Am I wrong?"

"No!" he snaps.

A crooked, victorious smile covers the woman's face.

"Thank you. That will be all." She turns on her heels and edges her way back to Lauren. My father's head drops between his hands. This is exactly what she wanted him to say. She wanted him to discredit himself, to make it seem like his claims could not be taken seriously. She wanted to reduce his testimony to garbage. And she did just that.

I've never been so conflicted in my life.

*Did he mean that?*

Haze gets off the stand, walking back to his seat, and it takes everything in me not to turn around and watch. The trial carries on. Numbers concerning Lauren are splattered onto the judge's plate: her low income, her hectic work schedule, you name it, they have it. I dare a gaze toward my mother. I haven't seen her once since my father kicked her out ten months ago. She looks composed, confident in her ability to win this, and it only allows doubt to dig deeper into my skin.

"May 12, 2002. 3:14 a.m. Winter Kingston, three years old, was spotted by a neighbor playing alone outside of the building she resided at. He called the police, convinced that her parents had lost her. He was wrong. Her mother was having a party in their one-bedroom apartment and didn't notice that her kid had walked off. Social services looked further into this and considered taking Winter away unless her mother provided her with a stable, safe, and loving environment. Which she was only able to provide when she married Mr. Gale a matter of days later. If he hadn't been in the picture, odds are Winter Kingston would've grown up in foster care. This simple fact alone should tell you everything you need to know."

The judge's face remains unreadable.

"Winter Kingston also dropped out of school to tend to her father, who was injured in a hit-and-run near a year ago. She had to care for the household when her mother never showed up after her husband's accident, which, may I remind you, is the day Haze Adams dropped by the family house and found her highly intoxicated. Leaving a fourteen-year-old kid unattended after he was just in an accident and possibly lost his father, not to mention neglecting to go pick up her five-year-old daughter, doesn't exactly scream good parenting to me. Does it to you?"

I'm trying, with every fiber of my being, to focus, but my mind is tirelessly fighting out of its cage, desperate to wander back to Haze. I can't stop hearing his voice as he says that he loves me.

He can't. He can't still love me.

I don't still love him.

I could never.

Not after everything.

*Right?*

I can't deal with this right now. No matter what he just said up there. No matter if he meant it.

Today is about Maika.

WHEN WE'RE GIVEN A MUCH-DESERVED break, I'm the first one out of the door. At the end of this wait… is the answer to our question: Will Lauren get to take Maika home?

> On my way. So sorry I couldn't make it to the first half.

I read Matt's text quickly. Not going to lie, I'm thankful he wasn't there to hear Haze say those things. He's asked me about my ex multiple times before, but I only told him the bare minimum. That Haze broke my heart. Desperate to get a bit of fresh air—and also to avoid running into Haze inside—I step out of the building and sit on the cold stone stairs. I text Matt back and decide I should head back inside when…

"Hey."

*I hate my life.*

Sensing his presence behind me, I curse under my breath and turn around. He's standing one step higher than me. I didn't get to take in his outfit earlier. He's wearing a long-sleeve button-down white shirt and a black tie. Hard, tight, sculpted body? *Still here.* Piercing gaze? *Check.* His brown hair is a gorgeous mess, his skin glowing with a natural tan. His hands slip into his pockets as he stares at me with his damn puppy eyes.

Why couldn't he just have turned ugly this past year?

"Hey," I breathe out.

"How are you?"

*Nope. Not doing this.*

"Why did you do that?" I cut to the chase.

"Why did I do what?" He plays dumb.

"You know what."

*Did you mean it?*

"You mean tell the truth when I was under oath?"

"Why are you here?" I change the topic, tossing what he just said right out of my brain. *Just words, nothing else.*

"Because this might be your only shot at getting your sister back."

"Bullshit. You could've said no. You wanted to be here. Why?"

He moves closer to the edge of the step, and his cologne reaches me.

*Get back. I don't want to remember your scent. I don't want to miss it.*

*I don't want to miss you.*

"Maybe I wanted to see you," he says huskily.

I go down a step.

He does, too.

I scoff. "After all this time? You choose *now* to want to see me?" Intending to walk away, I climb back up a step, but as soon as we're at the same level, he circles my wrist with his hand and tugs me straight into his chest.

"Winter, wait." His gaze descends to my lips. "Please."

*Oh my God, shut the fuck up, heart.*

"I really want to catch up," he says like I didn't just tell him to go screw himself. "How have you been?"

I'm careful to avoid looking directly into his eyes. "I'm good, Haze. I'm fabulous. Never been better. Now I know you didn't just come here out of the kindness of your heart. Tell me what you want?"

He arches an eyebrow. "You really want to know?"

"Yes. What do you want?"

He leans forward, his breath fanning my cheek.

"You."

I swear I almost fall down the narrow step.

"There you are!"

I've never backed away from someone faster.

"Matt. You're… here." *Why is there disappointment in my voice?*

"Hey, gorgeous." He climbs up the stairs.

"What took you so long, babe?"

*Ugh.* Did I just call him babe? I never, ever call him babe. I just said it in front of Haze to clarify that I'm dating Matt. He frowns at the nickname but doesn't question it. I kiss him on the cheek, and he wraps one arm around me for a quick embrace. All I want to do when he presses his lips to my forehead is watch out for Haze's reaction.

Haze's eyes are cold, empty. Like he's doing everything in his power to hide how he's feeling, but I know him too well to buy the fake façade he portrays. That hurt.

"Matt, this is Haze," I say politely.

"Nice to meet you." Matt holds out his hand, but Haze doesn't shake it—doesn't even *consider* shaking it. He raises a challenging eyebrow at him.

"So that's my replacement, huh?"

"Excuse me?" Matt frowns.

With a shit-eating grin, Haze says, "You downgraded."

*I'm going to kill him.*

"Haze!" I scold.

Matt's eyes light up in realization. "Is this…"

"The boyfriend? Yup. Took you long enough," Haze says.

"Ex-boyfriend," I correct. "You know the one I told you about? The guy I'm never getting back with?"

The cocky smile is instantly slapped off Haze's face.

"Really, Winter? Matthew Connor? I thought you had better taste."

"Wait… You know him?" I frown.

"Know of him. Our parents used to do business together. He's an asshole."

"We're leaving." I grip Matt's arm to pull him away but…

"Hold on. Haze, was it? I've heard that name somewhere. Wait. Haze as in Haze Adams? You're the kid Adams Inc. disowned, aren't you?"

Haze doesn't deny it, nor confirm it.

"How's it feel being rejected by your own parents?"

Baffled, I eye Matt. *Where did that come from?*

"You want to repeat that, see what happens?" Haze says through gritted teeth, going all alpha male as he steps dangerously close to Matt. The vein that always pops out in his neck when he's angry captures my attention.

"Okay. Good chat." I practically have to shove Matt back inside the building before the situation degenerates. Matt proceeds to bash Haze for the next twenty minutes.

When we we're informed of the trial picking up again, I push all Haze-related thoughts out of my head.

"I've come to a decision," the judge says.

If I thought these words were stressful in movies, I'd obviously never experienced them in real life. With my heart thumping against my rib cage, I assess the complete stranger whose next sentence will affect my entire family. Matt intertwines our fingers to display his support.

"I believe young parents can sometimes make mistakes, and

it doesn't have to define who they are for the rest of their lives. Ms. Kingston, leaving your three-year-old alone outside didn't define you."

The air escapes my lungs. Lauren's lips quirk into a smile.

*No, it can't be.*

*Don't tell me this excuse of a woman gets to keep her child.*

"What defined you is everything after."

Wait, what?

"I don't believe Lauren Kingston to be a fit parent for Maika Gale at this time and therefore give full custody to her father, Harry Gale."

He then grants Lauren visitation rights but only if supervised by a social worker. He also says there is a way to revisit the custody arrangements if my mother agrees to go to therapy weekly for a year and gets herself checked into some alcohol treatment facility, but let's be honest, that's just to be politically correct. The chances of her actually going through with it are slim. I try to listen as he lists more and more conditions, but truth be told, none of it registers. We won.

*We won.*

I hold no control over my body when Jay, my father, Judy, and I give in to the cliché family hug we see in the movies. Except that this is better than movies. This is real. And tomorrow, at Kendrick's birthday…

We'll actually have something to celebrate.

# THIRTY–FOUR

## Stuck With You

Ushering up the stairs with Matt on my heels, I count all the reasons why seeing Haze again shouldn't have felt the way it did. Reason #1: he chose revenge over me. Reason #2: he left me with nothing but a letter. Reason#3: he lied to me for months. *You can't really blame him for that. He had no choice.* I curse my inner voice. Reason #4: …

Why can't I find a fourth reason?

Ah. Reason #4: he's probably still chasing a murderer.

"What are you thinking about? You've been quiet the whole way home," Matt points out when I swing my bedroom door open.

"I'm sorry, today was a lot."

What would he do if he knew what was going on inside my head? If he knew what I'm really thinking about?

After the trial, we all went out for a celebratory dinner at my dad's favourite restaurant. Matt suggested that we watch movies at my house. His parents' charity event is in two days, and since he can't make it to Kendrick's party, we won't be seeing each other tomorrow.

As soon as we enter my bedroom, his arms are around my

waist, tugging at my clothes a bit… insistently? I'm surprised when his hands skim under the fabric of my shirt and over my stomach. He kisses me, my back hitting my closed bedroom door. I try to be into it, I really do.

But I'm not. *God, what's wrong with me?*

He keeps on kissing me, his hands on my waist hinting at his intentions. When he grabs the hem of my shirt and begins lifting it up, I can't bite my tongue anymore.

"Matt, hm…" I apply pressure to his chest. "I'm really tired."

I've never seen someone's face change this quickly.

"Are you serious?" Oh, he's pissed.

"It has nothing to do with you, I promise. I've just had a really long day." I could cringe at my own words.

"Do you even hear yourself?" He frowns. "We've been going out for months now, and you've barely let me touch you once. Why don't you want this? I really like you, Winter, but it's like… your foot's always on the brake. I'm so sick of this one step forward, three steps back thing."

I've been suspecting this moment would come from the very first time I rejected him. I just kept convincing myself that the next time he'd try, I'd be into it.

"Matt, I'm sorry. I guess I'm just not ready. I—"

"Is this because of your ex? That Haze guy? Are you not over him?" he accuses.

I open my mouth, ready to deny it, to call him insane but… I can't go through with it, and my lack of a response is enough answer for him.

He scoffs. "Fuck this. I'm done."

Two heartbeats later, he's scampering down the stairs. I call his name in vain.

Then I hear the front door slam.

MIXING UP THE FRUIT PUNCH WITH way too much vodka, I can't find it in myself to listen to the story Allie's been telling me for the past two and a half hours. She needed help to set up the party, and so we spent the entire day juggling last-minute tasks and running around her uncle's gigantic boat—or is it a yacht? I don't know. The guests should be here in a few hours. We're still waiting for the guy who'll be driving the boat all night.

I can't stop thinking about what happened with Matt. *"Why don't you want this? I really like you, Winter, but it's like your foot's always on the brake. I'm so sick of this one step forward, three steps back thing."*

I know he's right. We dated for three months without getting to second base. Truth is, I don't want to. I get massive anxiety just thinking about it.

"Okay, what's wrong?" Allie's concern makes me jump.

"What?" I look at her.

"You know what. You're somewhere else. What's on your mind?" She empties a bag of chips into a bowl.

I suck in a breath.

"Matt and I broke up last night."

A poorly hidden smile creeps its way onto her lips.

"What happened?"

I snort. "Don't pretend like you're not happy right now."

"Okay, fine. Maybe I'm not a fan of the guy, but I'm your friend. If you're hurt, I want to help."

"He wanted us to... *you know*." I shift from one foot to the other.

"Oh." Her eyes widen. "And... did you?"

"No. That's the problem. I told him I wasn't ready, and he just... snapped. Started telling me I was still hung up on Haze. Then he left."

Allie provides me with a brief "I'm so sorry," and bites her tongue not to explore the matter further.

"Spill it." I release her from the hell that's keeping her opinion to herself.

"I mean, he's not wrong," she gives in.

"What? Of course he's wrong. I don't... I'm not..." I trip over my words. "Haze and I are over."

"So?" She arches an eyebrow. "That's not what this is about. This is about you still having feelings for him. And you clearly do."

I don't bother entertaining her drivel and walk over to the mini fridge to pack it with the last beers.

She follows me. "Come on, you two were epic. You were the Juliet to his Romeo. The glasses to his Harry Potter. The—"

"Al, I get it." I laugh.

"I still think you're going to get back together. Maybe in a year. Two years. Five years. I don't know when, but you will. Which is why I might've kind of, sort of…" She pauses in anticipation of my reaction.

*Oh no.*

"Invited him to the party tonight." She winces.

"You did what?!"

"I know, I know. I'm sorry, but he was just standing there looking like a sad puppy dog watching you and Matt and I just… I felt bad for him. I always liked him, you know that."

"I don't care if you like him. He's my ex. Do you have any idea how many friendship rules you just broke?" I scold her.

"Chill. It's not like you're going to have to talk to him. I told him to bring a friend. Plus, have you seen the gigantic boat? I'm sure you won't even run into him."

I know, with my luck, it's impossible that I won't run into the one guy I don't want to see. That would go up against the universe's oath to ruin my life.

Halfheartedly, I let go of my irritation. There's nothing I can do about it.

Allie already invited him.

And I'll be seeing Haze tonight.

STANDING ON A BOAT THAT'S IMMOBILIZED and standing on a boat that's in motion are apparently two very different things. As soon as the guests arrived, we departed, and consequently, my stomach decided to flip upside down. Allie suggested that I drink a few shots to take the edge off. It helped a bit, but I still can't see myself going anywhere near the water without throwing up. With a rum and Coke in my right hand and my heart in the other, I chase off the mental images of Haze getting drunk somewhere in this crowd.

Kendrick's having the time of his life with—you'll never guess it—Alex, Will, and Kass. Allie had them flown to town without telling us. We were thrilled to see them hop aboard with gifts for Kendrick.

"Where have you been?" Allie comes close to tripping on her way over to me. She's getting *there*, all right. "What are you doing all alone in a corner?"

"Trying not to puke." I take a long sip of my drink.

"You won't. You'll be fine, come on." She drags me to the guys, and as soon as I reach the middle of their circle, what I feared would happen, happens. I don't feel well—like at all—but I breathe through the nausea. As long as I don't see the water, I should be good.

"Canada!" Will opens his arms for a hug.

"How have you guys been?" I ask Alex and Will to update me on their lives when we pull away. I've missed so much. Alex tells me about his relationship with Morgan. Kass tells me she's doing well in school, and I'm so incredibly proud of her.

"Hey, Canada, I saw your ex earlier. What's he doing here? Didn't you two break up like ten years ago?" Will mocks.

"Yes, we did." I glare at Allie, and she emits a shy giggle. "*Someone* invited him."

"I'm telling you, you'll never find something like this again. If anything, you should be thanking me." She glances at Kendrick, requesting his support. I snort in anticipation of his disapproval and take a sip of my drink.

"She's right, you know," Kendrick says.

I choke on my rum and Coke.

"E-excuse me?" I say through a few coughs.

Am I hallucinating?

"The guy's not perfect—like, far from it—but he loves you. You heard what he said yesterday. It's been a year, and he'd still do anything for you."

"Are you sure you're feeling okay?" I lift the back of my hand to his forehead to check his temperature. He slaps my fingers away. "Since when do you support me dating Haze?"

"Since I haven't seen you smile the way you did when you were with him in a year."

I wince.

*If my heart could speak, it'd be cussing Kendrick off right now.*

What the hell is everyone's deal? Why is every person on the planet dying to push me into the arms of the one guy I spent a year trying to forget? Thankfully, the conversation drifts to lighter topics, but I'm interrupted by yet another rush of nausea on subject number one. I tell them I'll be back and tumble inside the cabin. I push the bathroom door open and stare at my reflection in the mirror.

You know that moment at a party when you only realize how fucked-up you are when you're alone in the bathroom?

That's what's happening right now.

I pull my phone out and see a text from Allie. She's asking if I'm okay. I text back that I need a breather and not to worry about me. Stepping out of the bathroom, I head for the stairs leading back to the deck and stop dead in my tracks when I hear a voice I know all too well.

"You've had enough, Vic."

Haze.

My heart sinks.

As in literally… because I'm on a boat. Get it?

*Shut up, Winter.*

"For real though, are you at least invited to the wedding?" Vic cackles.

"You know I'm not," Haze says quietly.

"Well, you should be. As far as I'm concerned, Harry should give you some credit. Make you best man or something."

I frown.

"I might've gotten his new girlfriend into the house, but I didn't create what they have. They did that all on their own."

Wait, what?

Haze got Judy into the house?

"Stop being so modest, man. If it weren't for his home care, Winter's dad would still be a single pringle. And I mean… you paid for it."

My jaw falls to the floor.

At first, my brain attempts to convince itself that I heard him wrong. But then, the truth completes a puzzle I didn't even know was missing a piece.

Haze… paid for my dad's care?

I always wondered about the insurance company's sudden change of heart. My dad never gave me a real explanation. Does he know that Haze paid for it? *Shit, that must've been so expensive.* I can't believe it. Haze is the reason I didn't lose my mind while my dad was healing. Without Judy, I would've been alone to take care of him, Jay, and Maika full-time.

On autopilot, I step out of hiding and expose myself to a very drunk combo. They're both leaned back against the wall, drinking beers.

"What the hell?" It comes out way louder than intended.

Haze's face collapses at the sight of me.

That's Vic's cue.

"I… I'm going to go see if they have any food." He disappears up the stairs in a hurry.

An intolerable silence sits between us.

Haze speaks first.

"How long have you been listening?" he sighs.

"Long enough."

He begins to say something, but I can't hear him, thanks to the loud music upstairs. Irritated, I act on impulse and snatch his beer from his hand. I finish it in one gulp and throw it into a nearby trash can. Then, I grab his arm, lead him into the guest bedroom Allie assigned to me, and shut the door.

Kendrick, Alex, Will, Kass, Allie, and I will be sleeping inside the boat tonight. It's coming back to the shore at around 3:00 a.m. for the guests to leave, but we decided not to bother arranging for a designated driver and will be sleeping at the marina. I flick the light on and wait. I don't even know what I expect him to say.

"When?" I try to convince myself that he did it when we were still dating. Just so he won't be a saint who paid for his ex-girlfriend's family for months.

"The day after we broke up."

*Damn it.*

"Why?" I'm overwhelmed. "Why would you do that? You… You didn't owe me anything."

"Are you kidding? I owed you *everything*. Your dad was in a wheelchair because of an accident I caused, and you refused to admit it, but there was way too much on your shoulders. I knew if I couldn't be there to help you, someone else had to."

"D-Does my dad know?"

Haze nods. "Yeah, he called me the day he found out he'd get a nurse."

"But how did he connect the dots?"

Haze runs a hand through his hair. "I went to visit him when he was in a coma."

It comes back to me. My dad told me a while ago that Haze came to see to him alone at the hospital.

"I felt so fucking guilty, I… I told him I'd do anything to make this right. I guess he heard me, and from there, he put the pieces together."

My head starts spinning. This is so much to take in.

"So, he knew all along? All this time, he knew you'd paid for us?"

"Yeah, but I made him promise not to tell you. You wanted nothing to do with me anymore, and you were right… back then."

*Back then?*

As in I'm not right anymore?

"I didn't want you to think I was trying to sway your decision because I wasn't. And you were right. You deserved someone better."

*Again with the past tense.*

His blue eyes cut me with every glance.

"Are you mad at me?" he worries.

Mad at him? Thankful is more like it. He spent so much money on helping his ex's family—hell, he practically saved it. And he didn't think I'd ever find out.

My voice softens. "Of course not."

Hesitant, he steps forward, as though he's testing the waters. I don't stop him. He gets closer. And closer. And closer. Until we're mere inches apart. I can't move. He pushes a strand of hair off my face with the back of his hand, and I curse myself for shivering at something so little. I can't believe I'm going to say this, but… in this moment…

I want to kiss him.

I know I shouldn't. I know crossing this line would mean completely destroying one year's worth of efforts, but I really, really, really *fucking* want to kiss him. I eye his lips. It's been forever, but I vividly remember how breathtaking it was. So, before I make the mistake of falling all over again, I walk out of the room.

No, I *try*.

But the door won't open.

It's locked.

*No!* Allie talked about going down to lock the bedrooms sometime during the party in case some of the guests wandered around and wrecked her uncle's boat. He said one scratch on his "baby" would lose Allie access to his boat for five lifetimes. She'll unlock them all when she goes down to sleep later.

"We're stuck," I say and explain the situation to him. I triple text Allie, call her four times. No reply. Same goes for Kendrick. They're probably drunk out of their minds, making out somewhere. I try Alex, Kass, Will—everyone. Not a single peep.

Panic takes over me.

"Relax. It's just for a few hours," Haze says, unbothered.

"*Relax*? How am I supposed to relax?" I prowl around the bedroom, my breathing unsteady.

"Winter, calm down."

"I can't," I say, strangled.

"Yes, you can."

"No, I can't!" I continue to drag myself deeper and deeper into an anxiety attack.

He snatches my wrist into his hand. "Winter, stop. What are you so afraid of?"

"I'm afraid to be alone with you!" I almost scream.

Stunned, he stares at me in silence.

I take my wrist back.

After a few seconds, I let it all out.

"Don't you get it? I was fine with my decision. Up until yesterday, I was completely, one hundred percent fine with never seeing you again, but then… then you had to show up in court and fuck with my head and…" My voice wavers with emotions. "I need to get out of here."

I make my way to the door—I swear I will kick that door down if I have to—but he grabs my waist with one arm and spins me right around.

My breath hitches in my throat. His chest, hard as rock, welcomes mine, and he cups my face firmly with both hands. I squeeze my eyes shut to avoid eye contact. *If I don't see it, it's not real. If I don't see it, it's not real.*

"Why can't you be alone with me?" he whispers.

He knows. He just wants to hear me say it.

No reply.

"Winter, tell me why."

Tears build up behind my eyelids, threatening to fall the second I open them.

"Because you hate me?" A twinge of vulnerability lingers between every word.

I peel my eyes open.

And surrender.

"Because I don't hate you at all."

His lips part.

He stares at me in shock for what feels like forever.

The room is so silent you could hear our beating hearts.

Then he slams his mouth against mine.

No warning, not a word, he just kisses me. Hard.

I'm confident my heart is on a countdown to self-destruction when I return the kiss. His tongue pushes past my lips. He's such a good kisser it's almost painful. Painful to think that I went without this for a year. But what hurts even more… is how quickly he pulls away.

He presses his forehead to mine. "I missed you every second. Every day. Every single fucking minute since that night."

I'm speechless, but he doesn't expect me to muster a reply. Just pulls me into his arm and hugs me. Long and hard. The gesture is overwhelmingly sweet, excruciatingly heartwarming. The way he wraps me up and holds me tighter than ever before. This is so much more than lust. *This* is missing someone. I want to fight the current, the wave of feelings washing over me, but as I stand here, head against his chest, I think I'd rather let it sweep me away.

He breaks away from me, and suddenly… I can't think of one single reason not to kiss Haze fucking Adams.

*You deserved someone better*, he said.

And I know.

Right here.

Right now.

There's no such thing as someone better.

I lurch forward and kiss him again. He grunts in relief at my initiative. His fingers run through my hair; mine run *everywhere.* He lifts me up into his arms and bands my legs around his waist. He squeezes my ass, plastering me to the locked bedroom door. A whole year and it still feels natural, as necessary as breathing, laughing with your friends, making mistakes, and trying again. As essential as being alive. When he yanks my shirt over my head, I know exactly why I kept on rejecting Matthew.

I didn't want to sleep with Matt.

I wanted to sleep with Haze.

My bra is off within seconds. His mouth latches onto my nipples, my neck, my earlobe, and I'm so sensitive to his touch I could cry. He tugs at my leggings, resting me down to render their removal easier. I'm the one undressing him now. We never stop to discuss what's going to happen next. That would require thinking, and we're operating on pure instinct.

We're both only in our underwear by the time I'm back up

into his arms, bare skin against the freezing door. Impatient, I slide his underwear down with my feet, or at least try to, and he laughs. *God, I missed that laugh.* He tosses it down his legs and kicks them off with one move. Then he slips my underwear to the side and slides his length up and down against my center.

*Holy fuck. I can't believe this is happening on the second time I've seen him in a year.*

We're both so eager, desperate, that I can't help but wonder if it's been as long for him as it has for me. I haven't had sex once since we broke up. Has he? He toys with me, just relentlessly teasing my sweet spot and watching our bodies connect with a smug grin on his face.

Then he puts me out of my misery.

He grips a fistful of my hair and jams himself inside me with a calculated, powerful thrust. I almost cry out at how much I missed this, and from the look on his face, he feels the same. He doesn't move, just groaning as he kisses me deeper, like he wants to relish in every single detail, every sensation this moment unfolds. Like he's been waiting for this forever. And he has.

We both have.

When he begins to move, I wonder if someone standing outside could hear our bodies slapping against the door.

"Fuck, I'm not going to last," he immediately admits, working my neck. I let out a loud moan unintentionally, and he grins, covering my mouth with his hand as he continues to squeeze in and out of me. I almost forgot there was a party raging upstairs.

Quickly, he swaps the hand on my mouth for his lips, and I kiss him back. *Of course I do.* With every quiver and moan his mouth blocks, he thrusts harder. Until eventually he breaks away from me and searches my eyes for an answer. What's the question? I don't know, but the blue of his eyes is all it takes to send me spiraling.

*Fuck, I still love him.*

*I never stopped.*

"I love you." He lifts my right leg higher and plunges back into me. I swallow a moan.

I don't say it back.

I can't.

I physically *can't.*

My body won't let me. It screams, *"Don't you dare."*

"You don't." My throat tightens.

He thinks he does. But he doesn't.

"Yes. I do." He stares dead into my eyes, drawing back entirely for a torturously long moment before he fills me all the way again. *Shit.* With his mouth hovering right next to my ear, he whispers the words that destroy the poor excuse of a wall I spent a year building around myself. "I fucking love you, Winter Kingston. I don't care if you don't want to hear it. I don't care if it's wrong. I love you and I'm always going to love you. Even when you don't feel the same. Even when you don't want me to. Even when I shouldn't. I'm going to love you. *Always.*"

*No, no, no.*

*Don't you dare, Winter.*

*Don't you dare say it.*

*You know what happens when you say it.*

*You know how much it hurts.*

"I love you, too," I practically sob.

Relief, disbelief, and happiness spread onto his perfect features, competing for a spot.

"You do?" his voice is thick with emotions.

"Of course I do." I choke. "I don't think there will ever be a day where I won't."

He brings his lips back to mine, his hand dropping downward as he pumps faster and faster. I nearly fall apart when he starts rotating his fingers precisely where I want him to. He touches me as though he's going to reward me for what I've just said, and my eyes roll back.

*Oh my God.*

My stomach clenches in bliss, and he groans. He always hated when I clenched around him. Said it made it impossible for him to last. But I can't stop. We're both at each other's mercy, losing what's left of our sanity. It's not long before he begins to tremble. I'm next in line. The pressure in my stomach rips me apart.

"I love you," he grunts as his features twitch in pleasure.

"I love you more." I say it again. One more time. *One last time?* I'm gutted by just how true that is.

I do love him more.

No matter how much he thinks he loves me, no matter how many times he says it. If he'd loved me half as much as I did him… he would've chosen us.

I don't even realize how irresponsible we are not to use a condom when he finds his release and I follow, coming undone in an outburst of spasms. We've never *ever* gone without a condom before.

Breathing heavily, he slams his palm against the closed door he's got me pressed up against and nestles his head in my neck, still deep inside me. I'm glad he doesn't see the tear rolling down my cheek. Is it a tear of joy? Sadness? Anger? Maybe all of the above. All I know is this single tear calls me stupid in five different languages. It tells me I was dumb to think I was going to fall for him again.

Dumb to think I ever *un*fell for him in the first place.

# THIRTY-FIVE

## *Polaroid*

I've never run out on Haze before. I've never woken up, seen his adorable sleeping face, and snuck out. He's always been the one sneaking out on *me*. Lying naked next to him, I consider my escape routes and rate each of them from easiest to most likely to get caught. Sleeping safe and sound, Haze holds me tightly against his chest. So tightly I'm terrified the tiniest move will wake him. His embrace is warm, reassuring, and it pains me to have to leave it.

Last night was out of this world. Breathtaking, incredible, intoxicating. But because it was amazing, doesn't mean it changes anything about the year we spent apart. Because I admitted to still loving him, doesn't mean we can get back together. He's still searching for Marcus. Why else would he have stayed in Canada? He's chasing his revenge, that's why.

In other words, we're still a lost cause.

I have a shift at the hotel in a few hours. If I'm lucky, I'll be able to catch a cab home and shower before work. Hopefully, I won't run into Allie or the others when I go up. Pressing one last, soft kiss to Haze's cheek, I struggle out of his hug and throw my clothes back on as quietly as I can. I walk to the door, pushing down the pain associated with the mere thought of leaving him behind. I can't go through this again with him. I won't. And I might've let myself forget about the colossal bump in the road to our happy ending when we went at it against the door last night, but it's time to face the music.

And our song?

It sings to walk away.

"ARE YOU SURE YOU WANT TO do this?" Allie stresses, parking her car in front of the oldest of apartment complexes. When I asked her for a ride, I had no idea she would end up making this harder for me. I love this girl with all my heart, but she's even more nervous than I am, and it's driving me nuts.

She buried me under a mountain of questions about Haze the instant I got into her car. I didn't tell her a thing about what happened last night, but I didn't have to. Turns out, she knew we were in there when she locked the door. She heard us talking when she came down. She even told Kass, Will, and Alex not to take my calls. I considered murdering her for five minutes, then decided I needed a ride more than a dead best friend.

"Yes, I'm sure," I breathe out. I understand where she's coming from. Me? Purposefully getting anywhere near Lauren Kingston after what she did? If you'd told me I'd find myself in front of her new place a few days ago, I would've laughed in your face. But after I got out of work early, I met up with Judy for a bridesmaid dress fitting. We talked about everything and anything. Somewhere along the twists and turns of our conversation, she convinced me to confront my mom about an issue that's been gnawing at me my whole life.

My biological father.

Hearing Lauren bring him up on Haze's recording only increased my curiosity, and the woman may not be a part of my life anymore, but if there's one thing she owes me, it's a goddamn name.

"Thanks for the ride." I reach for the car door.

"Do you want me to wait out front? I can drive you back to your dad's after," she offers.

"Would you? It shouldn't be too long."

"Of course. I'll be right here." She nods.

I smile gratefully. Our friendship is slowly but surely getting back on track.

"You're the best." I climb out of her car and walk toward the building hesitantly.

My phone goes off in my pocket. I don't recognize the number.

> I can't believe you left me butt naked and asleep. Kendrick found me. Not cool, Kingston.

The dopiest grin of all time spreads across my face.

How did he even get my new number?

I do feel bad about leaving him like that, but I couldn't have been there when he woke up. If I'd so much as seen his smile, heard his voice, kissed him, I would've wanted to stay, for good, and the last thing I need is to get sucked into this vicious circle with him again.

Without texting back, I shove my phone inside my pocket and enter the unlocked building. *Apartment 11*, I repeat to myself as I drag my feet down the hall. I come to a sudden stop in front of mommy dearest's door and knock.

Maybe she's not home.

I consider running back to Allie for a second. Then noises flare on the other side.

I hear her distant groan. "Just a minute."

*Someone's in a good mood.*

The door swings open and a complete stranger comes into view. The woman before me is merely a shell of the person I knew, a pale copy. My once perfectly neat mother is wearing an oversized, stained gray T-shirt and joggings. Her hair is a mess, and a cigarette dangles off her lips. Since when does she smoke?

"Winter," she says coldly and draws the lit cigarette away from her mouth. "What are you doing here?"

I notice an empty liquor bottle on the low table in the living room from over her shoulder. So much for getting sober to win Maika back, huh?

"Just thought it was time we had a chat."

She raises an eyebrow. "About what?"

"Can I come in?" I'd rather not have her tell me about my biological father in the middle of the hallway.

She doesn't seem too pleased by my request but grants it anyway, sidling aside to let me in. Her apartment isn't doing much better than her appearance. Don't get me wrong, it's well decorated, just so incredibly messy that I debate on asking her if her roommate is a fifteen-year-old teenager. She beckons to sit at the kitchen table. A cigarette butt holder containing at least five packs lies in the center.

"If you're here to gloat and relish in my misery, don't bother. You've already ruined my life."

I bite back a scoff. *I* ruined *her* life? What about my miserable childhood? When do I get that back? How about my mommy issues? When do they go away?

"I'm not. I'm here to ask about my dad."

Her face hardens.

"Don't waste your breath. I'm not telling you anything."

I sigh. "After everything you've put me through, after I spent my entire childhood feeling bad for existing, don't you think you at least owe me that? I'm not asking for the moon here. I'm not even asking for a biography. Just his name."

Unconvinced, she remains silent.

"Do this for me and you'll never hear from me again."

These seem to be the magic words.

She curses under her breath and gets up, venturing into one of the rooms of her tiny, clustered apartment. I hear her rattling through stuff.

Five minutes later, she's back.

"Michael." She hands me a faint, old-looking picture with writing on the back. "Your father's name is Michael. But everyone called him Mike."

I assess every inch of the photograph carefully. It's a Polaroid, which I'd say was taken at some sort of fair from the colorful lights in the background. On the right is a laughing sixteen-year-old Lauren. Next to her is a smiling, brown-haired guy with dark eyes. He looks so obliviously happy, admiring my mom while she laughs her heart out. Man, they might have been young, but I would've believed any guy loved me too if he'd looked at me like that.

He's a good-looking guy with unique features, not one of those people whose faces get lost in the crowd.

*Crazy to think I come from him.*

"He's probably dead, if you ask me." She shrugs. "He loved getting in trouble. Could've made it a profession."

"Did he ever contact you again? After he left?"

"Not once. His friends just said he disappeared one day. Packed his bags and left town."

"And his family?"

"Never met them. I was just a summer fling, remember?"

I nod.

"Thanks." I mean it.

I rise up and hand her the photograph.

"You keep it. I never want to see his face again."

I nod and walk over to the door. Sliding the picture into my coat pocket, I tell her goodbye—although what I really mean is *farewell*—and exit her apartment. I check my phone as I walk down the hall. Numerous texts await me.

> Winter?

> Please don't do this. You can't just ghost me after last night.

> I meant what I said. Every single word.

> Fuck, text me back.

> I'm not giving up on us. Not this time.

His last messages hit the hardest.

> I'll be at the park where I gave you Waze tonight at eight.

> Meet me and we can figure this out.

> Don't… and I'll never bother you again.

# THIRTY-SIX
## Wake-Up Call

"Judy, you okay in there?" I ask, crossing my arms over my chest and leaning back against the wall. Alone in the wedding venue's never-ending hallway, I tug at my low-cut lavender bridesmaid dress. Judy wanted me to wear it for the rehearsal dinner. "Judy?" I knock on the bathroom door when she doesn't answer.

"Just a minute," she calls. Turns out, my future stepmom couldn't care less that this isn't the real wedding. She needs her makeup to be on point either way. I'm surprised that she didn't insist on wearing her wedding dress tonight.

"Your makeup was already perfect," I say, and she laughs.

"Thank you, sweetie, but my sister's supposed to be giving the toast, and I'm pretty sure I'm going to need waterproof mascara."

With a chuckle, I pull my phone out of my cleavage—what? This dress doesn't come with pockets—and eye the date featured on my locked screen. The wedding is tomorrow.

"We should go down. They're waiting for us," I say.

"I'm almost done," she assures me.

Unlocking my phone, I select the text conversation I've

probably read an unhealthy number of times in the last three weeks.

Meet me and we can figure this out.

Don't... and I'll never bother you again.

I never showed up that night.

Well, technically, *I did*, but Haze didn't see me. When 7:30 struck, I gathered every single drop of courage in my body, got into a cab, and headed for the park where Haze gave me Waze. It'd just started pouring outside—because of course it had—and when the cab slowed down across the street, my heart broke in six. I saw him. Sitting alone by the water fountain. He didn't budge, just let the rain soak him to the bone. I tried, Lord knows I tried, but I couldn't bring myself to get out of the car. I told the driver I'd changed my mind, and we sped down the street in a roar. I started bawling in the back seat and sent him a message.

I'm sorry.

Albert Einstein said, the definition of insanity is doing the same thing over and over again and expecting a different result. Going back to Haze would've been exactly that: insanity. We've been here before, with our hearts on the line, our heads filled with false hopes and promises, and *every single time*, without exception… it ended in tears and heartache.

Losing him once almost killed me.

Losing him twice definitely would have.

During the week following Kendrick's party, I felt a bit guilty about how things ended with Matt. After all, I slept with Haze barely one day after we called it quits, but my guilt was cut short when I saw a picture of him at his parents' charity event online. He was all smiles, kissing another girl. Good for him. He deserves someone that's not hung up on their ex.

"There you are." I see Allie striding my way and assess her as she walks: her gorgeous pale pink dress, her long, curled hair. I have a hard time believing that, one day, she might be the one freaking out over her makeup at her rehearsal dinner. In a few years, she might be marrying Kendrick. "What's taking so long?"

"She's waterproofing her makeup." I chuckle.

"We thought you got lost on the way here or something."

"We almost did." I recall our hunt for the bathroom. "This venue is huge."

"I know, right." Allie makes it rain imaginary dollar bills with her hands, and I laugh. We hang outside of the locked bathroom for a good ten minutes, mocking Kendrick's complete incapacity to wear a tie. He can't stand it, constantly fiddling with it. Judy walks out of the bathroom the next second, and we hurry back downstairs.

"DEAR LORD, WHERE DO I EVEN start?" Margo,

Judy's older sister, says, wrapping a shaky hand around the microphone. She's already fighting tears. Sitting around a beautiful rose-petal-covered table with Jay, Kendrick, and Allie, I eye the near-overflowing champagne glass in my hand. "A year ago, I told my sister she worked too much. That I was worried about her becoming a cat lady." The audience laughs. "She told me that you don't find love—love finds you. Even if you don't want it to, even if the timing isn't right, even if the odds aren't in your favor. She used to say what's meant to be yours will always find you, so you might as well stop running. I'll admit I laughed in her face. I said how can you possibly meet someone when you're working so much? And well, because that's what Judy does, she just had to go and prove me wrong by meeting her husband at work."

She proceeds with a tear-jerking speech. By the time she's done, there isn't a single dry eye in the room.

"A toast to Harry and Judy, who defeated all the odds and will continue to do so for the rest of their lives."

We all get up, clapping, as Judy wipes her face and embraces her sister. I bring the champagne glass to my lips, but just before I can take a sip, my phone rings in my breast—literally never thought I'd say that in my entire life. I forgot to put it on silent.

The whole room scowls at me.

"Sorry," I mouth. Plucking my phone out of my dress, I peek at the caller, just in case it's important. No caller ID. I motion to Allie that I've got to take the call and slip out of the reception room. By the time I step into the entrance hall, I've already missed the call.

Luckily, a new voicemail pops onto my screen the next second. I dial my voicemail password and stick the phone to my ear.

"You have one new voicemail," the automated voice informs me.

*Beep.*

Static.

A male's voice.

"Hi, this message is for Winter Kingston. This is Dr. Reegan. I'm just calling to tell you about the results from the tests we ran last week."

I've been feeling *bleh* for a week now, could barely keep anything down. My dad forced me to go to the doctor to run some tests.

I nibble at my bottom lip anxiously. What do I have? The flu? Some viral virus? A serious disease?

Am I going to die?

"I double-checked the results myself, and you couldn't be in better health. You're not sick at all."

*Thank God.*

"What you are is pregnant."

My vision goes blurry.

"Congratulations."

*End of voicemail.*

My full champagne glass slides right out of my hands and

crashes against the carpeted floor.

A piece of broken glass digs into my foot, but I don't blink.

Did he just say…

Because it sounded liked he said…

I'm…

No, I can't be. It's impossible. I've always been safe. I've…

Memories knock my soul right out of my body.

Haze.

Me.

Against the door.

*No condom.*

Fuck.

Fuck.

Fuck.

Fuck.

I'm not on the pill anymore. I didn't see the point after we broke up. I just thought I'd take plan B. I took it two days after. I completely forgot about it the next day and… I knew the success rate wasn't as good past the first twenty-four hours, but I didn't think I could…

*Oh my God.*

I watch the spilled champagne at my feet, the stained carpet. Thank the universe I didn't drink that. All I can do is stand there in complete and utter shock. I'm pregnant. Me, the dumbass who can never find her other sock, is creating a whole new human. There's a person growing inside of my body at this very moment.

A person made of Haze and me.

*I think I'm going to faint.*

I stare at my phone blankly. I have no idea what this means... But I know one thing: I need to tell him, so I call back the number he used to text me.

He doesn't pick up.

Not on the first call. Not on the fifth.

*Pick up, damn it.*

On call number eight, I give up and settle for Vic. I have to get his number directly from my contacts log since it's been so long. He's Haze's best friend. Maybe he knows something.

"Yeah?" a voice says.

"Vic, hi. It's Winter."

"Winter, long time."

"Tell me about it. Hey, I really need to get a hold of Haze, but he's not picking up his phone. Do you know where he is?"

"He's not home, that's for sure."

I frown. "How do you know?"

"He's my roommate. I just got home, and his car isn't out front." I hear motion down the line. "Wait..."

"What?"

"There's a note on the table."

"What does it say?"

It takes him an irritatingly long time to answer.

"Tell her I'm sorry."

Fear slams against my rib cage.

"The place is a fucking mess. It looks like he left in a hurry," he states. "What do you want with him anyway? Didn't you break his heart three weeks ago?"

A raw edge of regret cuts through me.

"I'm pregnant."

A beat of silence.

"It's his," I add.

"Oh," he says in realization.

"Do you have any idea where he could've gone? Can you, I don't know, remember any of the places he went to while looking for Marcus? If you could just give me *something*, I'd—"

"Wait… he didn't tell you?" He sounds surprised.

"Tell me what?"

"For crying out loud, Adams, you can be so slow sometimes," he mumbles under his breath.

"What, Vic? What didn't he tell me?" I press him.

"He's not looking for Marcus, Winter. He hasn't been looking for a year now. He stopped when you broke up with him."

My heart drops to my stomach.

"What?"

This makes no sense.

"Then why did he stay in Canada?"

He scoffs. "What do you think?"

It hits me.

He stayed for me, didn't he?

Because he thought, one day, we'd find our way back to each other.

"But… why didn't he just tell me that? That's all I ever wanted."

"He said it wouldn't have made a difference."

I'd love to deny it, but deep inside, I know he's right. Even if he had come up to me and said he was going to stop looking for Marcus, would I have been able to believe him? To trust him again? Would I have taken him back after my father's accident, the lies, the letter, the toxic behavior? We were broken beyond repair. Not to mention that, if I hadn't left him for good, he might've never stopped looking in the first place. Maybe he needed that push, to really lose *everything* to want to change.

"He said one day he'd be someone who deserved you, but first he had to get his shit together. He couldn't do that if he lived in the past."

Judy's sister's speech crawls back inside my brain. *You don't find love—love finds you. Even if you don't want it to, even if the timing isn't right, even if the odds aren't in your favor. What's meant to be yours will always find you, so you might as well stop running.*

I've been running from this, from *us*, for so long. I don't want to run anymore. I want to let him catch me.

"Did he say anything weird to you recently?" I'm grasping at straws at this point.

He stops to think.

"He did say one thing yesterday."

"What?"

"I think it really hit him that you weren't getting back together last night. He got drunk and said if he'd really lost you, he had some unfinished business to take care of. He talked about a lead he never followed up on. Something about a motel, I think."

*The motel. Of course.*

"Thank you."

I hang up and type the name into the internet search bar. I remember it like it was yesterday. *Holland Motel.*

The address pops up.

There.

This is where I have to go.

## *Haze*

The establishment in front of me clashes with the faded memories I have of it. The large window by the door is shattered, and the Holland Motel sign isn't lit up, nor is the inside of the building. *What the hell happened here?* The parking lot is empty, has been since I got here thirty minutes ago. There's a sign on the door.

It reads Closed Permanently.

Tanner was right: the motel was abandoned. For good.

But why?

A few days back, when I realized I had nothing to lose anymore, I flinched and called him. Winter didn't show up that night. She couldn't have made herself clearer. She doesn't want me. I decided to look into the leads Tanner has been sending me for months.

At first, it was the leaked surveillance tape. The day I went to look into it and lied to Winter about hanging out with Vic, I rolled into the parking lot only to find it completely deserted. On the front door was a sign that read Closed until further notice. It was suspicious. Almost made me wonder if they somehow knew that someone was onto them. Maybe they'd found out about Tanner's guy hacking their system. My brother used to say that sometimes the best thing you could possibly do to save yourself is nothing.

Straight up *nothing*.

He said if things got too hot, it might be good to disappear for a while. *Time heals almost everything, brother. Play dead. Just make them forget. They always forget.*

A bit ironic that I once had to take Winter to my family's lake house in my hometown precisely so that *he* would forget about wanting her head—my own brother. Yet, there I was, following a lead the very same bastard had given me. After he saved my life and got me out of a dangerous drug operation, might I add.

When Winter broke up with me, Tanner started sending me more and more tips. This wasn't just a "senseless" revenge obsession to him anymore. It was like he knew we were actually getting somewhere this time. The day I called Winter and found out that she'd changed her number, something died in me—something broke.

And I told him to stop sending me tips.

He listened.

Until he texted me, four months later, to tell me the motel had been reopened. Whoever didn't want that surveillance tape found thought four months was long enough for us to forget.

They were wrong.

I almost went back on my word right then. I came so close to continuing my investigation. But then I thought of her. And talked myself out of it. *You've come too far to regress to your old ways, Haze.*

But now, it's closed again.

Has been for around three days according to my brother. He told me to come prepared, that something definitely went down between these walls and that someone could still be hiding inside.

And if we're lucky…

That someone is Marcus.

It's a long shot, I know. But this was the last place he was ever tracked back to, and everything about it is so fucking sketchy. This *has* to be the answer. I glance at the gun lying on my passenger seat from the corner of my eye.

It wasn't too hard to get my hands on one. All I had to do was go back to the shady guys I met up with when I was the organization's little bitch.

I exhale a long breath and reach for the weapon next to me. I curse myself for forgetting to charge my phone before coming here. What dumb fuck forgets to charge their phone in a moment like this? *This dumb fuck*. It's almost dead. I had to turn it off in case I need to make an emergency call.

Slipping the gun inside my coat pocket, I stalk toward the entrance of the beat-down motel. The front door isn't locked, nearly coming off its hinges. It opens with a screech, and as soon as I walk into the dark building, the absolute most horrendous smell I've ever experienced in my life guts me. I slap my palm on my mouth with a gag. What the fuck is that?

The very same lobby I once stood in has been turned upside down. The furniture has been knocked to the floor, some snapped in two, some wrecked. I grab the flashlight I brought and turn it on as I venture deeper into the dark corridors. The farther I get, the more awful the smell. I cover my mouth with the inside of my shirt as I pass countless rooms, my eyes watering to the point of blindness.

That's when I hear it.

The sobs.

They're faint, almost inaudible.

But real.

Somewhere, in one of these rooms, there's someone crying. I follow the noise, which seems to grow along with the awful smell, all the way down to the end of the hall.

**Room 25.**

The sobs are clearer now. They're deep.

This isn't a female.

This is a man.

I reach for the knob. My hands are shaking.

*One, two, three.*

I swing the door open.

The smell hits me a million times harder when I walk in. It's so fucking strong that it takes me a second to focus on what's in front of me. *Who's* in front of me.

Two windows illuminate the room, but the sun will be setting soon. I shine the flashlight directly onto the scene, and my stomach flips over.

Sitting on the carpeted floor with his legs cradled up against his chest is a forty-something man holding a bourbon bottle. Brown hair, crooked nose, dried tears on his face.

Every single hair on my body stands on end.

The picture I saw so long ago returns to me. He still looks the same. Just older.

Marcus.

I don't know how the fuck to feel when our eyes meet.

We just stare at each other in silence. He seems surprised to see me, at first, but quickly, the shock dissipates. Like his emotions just said, *"Meh. Never mind."* He blinks at me. I blink at him.

I gaze downward and stop breathing.

There's a puddle of blood on the carpet.

But that's not the worst part.

The worst part is the lifeless body lying next to him.

I instantly recognize her. The woman I talked to when I came in looking for information. The same woman that was on the stolen video tape.

She's dead, wounded to the stomach.

And from the smell of this place, not to mention the looks of her rotting corpse, she's been dead for a while now.

Heaven only knows how I manage not to vomit right then. Has he been sitting here with her decomposing body this whole fucking time? The guy looks distressed, disconnected. This woman was special to him, probably his girlfriend. I remember hearing her call him babe on the video.

"If you're here for revenge, don't bother. They already took everything from me," he says blatantly. For a second, I think he knows who I am. That he remembers me from the night he broke into my house. But the vacancy in his eyes proves me wrong.

"You don't even recognize me, do you?" I scoff.

He takes his time to answer, clearly wasted.

I notice the tremble of his body, the lack of color in his face. I know an addict when I see one. He's not that big of a guy, most likely shorter than me. God, he seemed so fucking scary when I was fourteen. So terrifying when he forced a tape onto my mouth and tied me to a chair. Now? I could take him in a heartbeat.

"You're that kid who came lurking around here searching for me, aren't you?" He takes another sip from the glass bottle, unbothered by my presence. "I assume that means I did something to you, and you want revenge." He cracks a laugh. "I suggest you get in line."

My fists clench on their own.

"That all you recognize me from?" I can't believe I'm actually talking to him right now. That, after all this time, I've found him. I guess I never thought about what would happen once I did. He arches an eyebrow at me, thinking long and hard, and nods to confirm my suspicions. Rage boils within me.

"Five years ago. Colton Gate. You broke into my house."

As soon as the words leave my mouth, his eyes widen in realization.

"No…" he says in disbelief. "It can't be."

"I assure you it can." I step forward.

Suddenly, the once careless guy is paler than his dead girlfriend.

"I'm not going to lie. You were pretty hard to find. Took me a long time to track your murderous ass." I move closer to him, and fear finally seems to settle into his wrinkled eyes.

"Listen, kid," he babbles and drunkenly rises to his feet. "I'm not a killer. I'm a thief, a drug dealer, a piece of shit, I admit, but… that little girl…" His hands fly up as if he's begging for mercy as he steps backward. "That little girl was the worst mistake of my life."

That does it for me.

*A mistake?*

"That little girl had a name!" I shout, and he jumps. "Did you ever think about that?" I keep stepping closer. "Did you even wonder what her name was?"

He remains quiet, scanning the crass motel room as though he's searching for a weapon of some sort. He's scared of me.

*Good.*

"Desiree Adams. Brown hair, blue eyes."

The murder seems to unfold in front of him.

"You shot her in the stomach. She bled out on the carpet."

"I-I'm so sorry," he says in a crammed, desperate sentence.

"She was five years old."

"It was an accident, I swear."

I'm not sure when or how I throw the first punch.

I must black out for a few minutes, running on rage, because by the time I come back to my senses, he's bleeding all over. His mouth, his eyebrows, his cheeks—everywhere. He spits out blood while I pummel his face with a strength I've never let myself use before. Tanner always used to tell me there was a clear line between fighting to harm and fighting to kill. Right now, I'm crossing that line. I'm fighting to kill.

And it scares the shit out of me…

Because I can't stop.

I push him to the floor, and he groans in agony. Yet, I kick him in the stomach over and over and over. Nothing is too far.

"Get up," I belt out. When he fails to do so, I lift him by the collar and force him off the ground.

All I can see when I look at him is the end of her life. Her body in my arms. Her funeral.

*Her small casket.*

If I thought I'd seen him scared before, I was wrong. Nothing, and I mean *nothing*, compares to the look that covers his face when I get the gun out of my pocket with a shaking hand.

I point it at him.

Tears fog my sight.

"Please, don't. I'm begging you." He puts his hands up.

It all happens too fast.

"Stop!" a voice screams from across the room.

I jolt around.

And see her.

In the doorway.

Eyes full of tears. Fear.

Her gaze travels to the floor.

To the decomposing corpse. She gasps in horror, her hand flying to her mouth.

*What the fuck is she doing here?*

*No, no.*

*She can't be here.*

The rapid pumping of my heart echoes in my ear. Then the

bloody mess on the ground speaks.

"Winter?" he chokes.

I frown.

She arches an eyebrow, just as confused as I am. Marcus's lips quirk up into a smile. He's happy. The bastard is actually happy that she's here.

Why?

His smile seems to trigger something in her.

Life drains from her eyes.

Trembling fingers sneak into her coat pocket, and she pulls a piece of paper out.

A picture.

Her eyes sway back and forth between the waste of oxygen and the photograph in her hands.

Then she says something straight out of my worst nightmare.

"D-Dad?"

# THIRTY-SEVEN

## Last Chance

*Winter*

"What?" Haze's voice echoes in my head.

I only realize how tightly I'm squeezing the Polaroid when it shrinks into a crumbled ball. I can't move a muscle, just staring at the bloody man in front of me.

"This isn't happening." I step backward.

This guy is not my dad.

*Haze's sister's killer cannot be my biological father.*

The man gives me a faint smile, his teeth painted with blood.

"What the hell is going on?" Haze turns to me.

"I…" No words seem appropriate for this moment.

"Did you just call him Dad?" Haze's horrified.

I try and regain my composure.

"No." I chase my breath. "This is a mistake. He's… He's not my dad." I close my eyes while I say it. Like I'm hoping it'll shield me from the look on Haze's face when I tell him. "A few days ago, I… I went to see my mom. I asked her about my biological father. She gave me a picture."

I hand him the wrinkled photograph.

Silent, he scans the picture.

One second is all it takes.

I can see it in his eyes: how fast he realizes what I'd go to the end of the earth to deny.

"But… she said his name was Mike. This doesn't make any sense. He can't be my dad," I convince myself.

"She's right," Marcus cuts in.

Haze's furious eyes dart back to him.

"My name isn't Marcus. It never was."

None of us speak, blink, move.

This is too much.

"I was nineteen when I started working for the organization. Just like your boyfriend here." He motions to Haze with his chin. "They got my name wrong. Thought I said Marc and just assumed it was short for Marcus. I didn't correct them, and it stuck with me."

"No." Haze shakes his head. "There's no fucking way. Out of all the people in the world, you're… *Fuck*." Haze jams his fist right through the shitty hotel wall, and I yelp, eying the hollow hole he left behind. "This isn't real. You… You can't be her dad." He holds his head in his hands and paces around the room obsessively as if he's waiting for another explanation to come to him.

"I can't believe you're finally here. In front of me." Marcus—shit, *Mike*—smiles at me, and it sends Haze over the edge.

"You're not her fucking dad!" Haze shouts at the top of his

lungs and grips Mike's collar. He takes a powerful swing at him, near having a mental breakdown. Mike collapses onto the floor with a loud thud.

"How do you know about the organization? How do you even know we were dating? You said you didn't know me!" I've never seen Haze this furious. "You're going to explain everything. Right fucking now. Am I making myself clear?"

Mike wipes blood from his mouth and leaps off the ground with a groan of pain.

"The day you came looking for me, I knew the organization had sent you. It was the only thing that made sense. But I just figured you worked for them. Then, I found out you were Winter's boyfriend. I didn't know you were that little girl's brother, I swear."

"How?" I raise my voice. "How did you find out we were together?"

His eyes soften when he addresses me. "By watching you. My daughter. I've been watching you for a while now."

*What the fuck?*

"Did you really think…" He looks at Haze. "That it would be that easy? You never found it weird that I just happened to be in the same city as you when you were searching for me?"

Haze's jaw drops.

*Of course.*

The chances of him being this close were practically nonexistent. There's a reason he was here this whole time. He chose to stay here. But why would he put himself in danger like that?

"Why would you watch me? You never gave a shit about me!" I snap.

"You're wrong! So wrong." He speaks rapidly.

"Tell that to my mom. Remember her? Lauren, the girl you abandoned when she was pregnant?" I'm getting emotional.

"Winter, you have to understand… When I got your mom pregnant, I owed the organization a lot of money. I was just a kid. A scared, broke, stupid kid. I didn't leave your mom because I didn't love her. I left because I did. Every minute I spent with her put her in danger. The day she told me she was pregnant… was the worst day of my entire life. That's when I knew I had to disappear."

"Bullshit!" I belt out. He's just messing with my heart to save his own ass.

"It's true!" he insists. "I just… panicked and left the country. Then I met…" His gaze drops to the rotten corpse, reminding us that there's a dead body right fucking there. "I met Greta, and she helped me out. Said if we paid back my debt, I'd be fine. That's why I started stealing, breaking into loaded pricks' houses." He glances Haze's way, knowing damn well that, in this case, the loaded pricks were his parents. "At first, I just wanted a normal life… To go back to you and your mom."

"Liar!" I yell.

"I promise you everything I just told you is the truth," he

says like his promises mean shit to me. Yet, his words afflict me. I can't help seeing a sick, twisted similarity between Haze and the damaged man in front of me. Leaving the girl to protect her? *Because I haven't heard that before.*

"When Greta and I moved back here for the first time in years… we opened this place. Mostly for money laundering, a bit of drug dealing on the side. I just couldn't help myself. I had to find out what happened to your mom. I went to check up on her. Up until then, I'd always convinced myself that she'd gotten an abortion. That she couldn't have possibly raised the baby alone. But Winter… the second I laid eyes on you, I knew you were my kid."

I want to scream, puke, hit him, run away. I'd do anything to change the truth.

This man is my father.

*This man is my fucking father.*

"What the hell happened here?" I motion to Greta.

Tears of rage spill down Mike's face. He wipes them off.

"I-I was on the move for so long after they traced me back to the motel, never staying in the same place for over a day, but I still… I still continued to watch over you. Greta warned me, she begged me to stop, but I kept coming back. I wanted to see you, even from a distance. It's all my fault. I led them right to us." He assesses the lifeless woman at his feet. "I lost everything, kid," he tells Haze. "There's nothing else you can take away from me."

Haze is the definition of conflicted, blue eyes drifting between me and his sister's killer repeatedly.

"There's still something," he says and points his weapon back at Mike.

But this time...

He cocks it.

My heart stops.

"Haze, don't!" I scream and step right in front of Mike.

"Winter, get out of the way!" he yells, but I can see how distressed he is.

"You're not a murderer. You don't want to do this!'

"It doesn't matter what I want. I have to do it." A tear rolls down his cheek. "*For her.*"

"No. You're wrong. Don't you see? You're not doing this for her, Haze. You're doing it for *you*. Because you're angry. Because you're hurt. And you have every right to be. No one should ever have to go through what you went through. But you can't change what happened to Desiree. You'll never be able to. The one thing you can do is send him to jail for the rest of his miserable, pathetic life."

He doesn't reply, but his clenched jaw, the tears streaming down his face, they tell me I'm getting through to him.

"What do you expect to happen, huh? Once you've shot him? Do you think it's going to make you feel better? Bring you peace? Do you think you'll finally be able to breathe again?" I shake my head. "You won't. It'll feel good for a second. Then you'll realize what you've done. Killing him won't make you happy, Haze. But you know what it *will* make you?"

I pause.

"A murderer."

Color spills from his face.

"You'll go to jail. And you'll never have the long and happy life Desiree wanted you to have. He already took her life. I'm begging you, please… *please don't let him take yours.*"

He's shaken up by my speech, but he fights it.

"Why do you even care?" Haze clenches his jaw. "You gave up on me, remember?" Pain emanates off every word.

"I care because I love you!" I blurt.

His lips part.

He blinks at me in shock.

A long, heavy silence ensues.

"No, you don't."

"Yes, I do. I love you, you idiot," I repeat.

"Then why didn't you show up that night?" he sounds so broken—so hurt—that it destroys me.

"I did show up!"

He frowns.

"I showed up, but you didn't see me. I… I never got out of the cab."

It takes a second for the information to sink in.

"It fucking killed me, you know that?" His voice cracks.

The ache in my chest spreads to my entire body.

If I'd just gotten out of that cab, we wouldn't be here right now. He changed his ways for me. He was finally the man I wanted him to be. All he needed was for me to tell him we still stood a chance.

I sniffle. "I know, and I'm so sorry. I was just scared. So scared that if I opened up to you, you'd break my heart again, and I…" I'm full-on sobbing at this point, crying so hard it's hard to speak. "I… I didn't think I could survive you losing you a second time."

His face softens, but he's still so angry. At me, at Mike, the whole damn world. The words come out of their own will.

"Haze, I'm pregnant."

He doesn't react right away, completely baffled.

Like his brain is rebooting, he opens his mouth to speak, then closes it, then opens it again, all to no avail.

"What?" he whispers.

"I'm pregnant." I cry harder.

"But… how?"

"Remember three weeks ago? At the party."

His eyes grow in realization.

"And I have no idea what the hell I'm going to do from here, but I know one thing: I need you by my side to do it. I need you to stick with me. So, we can figure this out, okay? Together. If you pull that trigger, you won't get to see the first steps. You won't get to hear the first word. Or the first laugh. And for what? For him? Just look at him." I point at Mike. Haze's eyes follow the motion. "You're going to throw everything away for this guy? Our future together? All of it? Please. If not for me, do it for mini Haze." I bring a hand to my belly. "Please don't be like your father. *Be there.*"

He squeezes his eyes shut, tears pouring uncontrollably down his face for the longest wait of my entire life.

Then…

He lowers the gun.

Drops it on the ground and kicks it away.

As cliché as it may sound, in that moment, it feels like the world stopped turning. Like time slowed down for us. I don't think. I just run straight to him.

He's chosen to have life.

He's chosen us.

His arms curve around me, holding me so closely it's difficult to breathe. We're both suffocating each other, but… what's a little asphyxia when you've just gotten everything you've ever wanted?

"We're going to have a baby?" he says in a trembling voice. I nod, my heart swelling with joy, fear, panic, and love all at once. I'm so caught up in the moment I almost forget Mike is right there, witnessing our heartfelt reunion. It isn't long before his voice pulls us away from each other. Haze glares at him, probably considering kicking his teeth out for interrupting. But… there's something different about the man in front of us. He seems just as emotional as we are.

Haze's fists contract when Mike dips his fingers into his dirty clothes' pocket, in search for something.

"What the fuck do you think you're doing?" Haze warns.

Mike looks at me. Then at Haze.

"The right thing," he exhales. "For once in my goddamn life."

In his hands is a phone.

In his eyes… regret.

Mike dials the number right in front us, and I somehow know not to stop him. I grip Haze's bicep before he can spring into action and snap his phone in two.

The room is so quiet we can hear the first ring.

"911, what's your emergency?" a distant voice says.

He sucks in a breath.

"My name is Michael Walker."

And holds my stare.

"I want to confess to the murder of Desiree Adams."

I'm not sure how long Haze and I stayed in each other's arms after that. I'm not even sure if we spoke at all after the police took him away. All I know is we cried. And smiled. And kissed. The aftermath is a bit of a blur, although it might have something to do with the fact that I was sobbing so hard I couldn't see.

Looking back, I do remember one sentence.

One specific, unforgettable moment.

"I love you more than anything," Haze whispered into my

neck while I bawled into his shirt.

He'd said that to me once before.

But this time was different.

Because this time…

I believed him.

# EPILOGUE

## SIX YEARS LATER

I've never pictured myself doing a gender reveal.

The whole "pierce a balloon" slash "cut a cake" slash "kill your loved ones with suspense" thing has never really appealed to me. Don't get me wrong, I understand why people do it. I just always thought when the time came, I'd tell my family up front and get it over with, quick and easy.

But that was until Auntie Allie had a say.

"It's a girl!" Kass squeals.

"What?" I exclaim, my gaze jumping to Haze as he cuts the cake. We come to the same realization at the exact same time.

The inside is pink.

Pink.

Pink as in not blue.

Pink as in *this is the wrong cake.*

The sixty-five-dollar gender reveal cake that I had to run all over town to get, almost dropped five times on the way inside our house, had to go above and beyond to make sure my daughter didn't eat. That cake… is the *wrong color.*

And this, my friends, is why I didn't want a gender reveal.

"Are you freaking kidding me?" I whine, and a deep, quiet

laugh flares on my right. Strong arms—one tattooed, one not—wrap around my body and atop my huge baby bump from behind.

"Picked up the wrong cake, huh?" Haze mocks. "Way to go, babe."

"I didn't! There must've been a mix-up at the shop or something. I can't believe it." I pout and Haze smiles, leaning in to peck my cheek. He releases me from his embrace too soon.

"So… it's a boy?" Kendrick states the obvious.

"No, it's an alien, dipstick," Haze says.

"What's a dipstick?" a small voice asks.

My eyes jump to my baby girl seated next to her uncle Kendrick.

*Shit.*

Haze just had to say that in front of Desiree, didn't he?

Her soft brown hair trickles down her face, concealing parts of her blue eyes—guess who she got them from. I really need to cut her bangs soon.

I glare at Haze, and he slaps a hand on his mouth overdramatically. I bite back a grin. *Idiot.* That's just what Haze does. You'd think teaching our six-year-old all the wrong words is a passion of his.

"It's hm… something you use to check the oil on your car, honey." Haze tells her with a shit-eating grin, and Desiree nods, but I know she has no idea what he's talking about.

"Back to the point, please. You're having a boy!" Kass is the first to hug my whale-ass—I'm due soon and so big I'm sure you can see me from outer space—then comes Alex, Maria, Kendrick, my brother Jaden, the whole party. Congratulations come flying left and right, and by the time I've hugged everyone, I want a nap. *Pregnant woman problems.*

I can't believe Allie couldn't be here for the gender reveal after she planned the whole thing and invited everyone. She said we had to make up for the gender reveal party we *didn't* throw for Desiree. She even stayed up until midnight to finish decorating our backyard last night.

Part of me knows if she'd been there to see the pink cake, she would've insisted on driving it back herself and getting a refund immediately, but she had to go pick up her son earlier than expected. I know Des will be over the moon to see him. She and Nathan, Kendrick and Allie's kid, are just one year apart and pretty much inseparable.

I expected Kass to bring her twins, but she said she needed a break. She left them with their godfather Ethan and hopped on a plane to Canada. I get it. Can't be easy raising two kids by herself. It sure doesn't hurt that she's got a lawyer wallet to do it. As for Judy and my dad, I assume they're sipping margaritas on a beach somewhere. One of my dad's past investments paid off out of the blue and let him retire early last year. He and Judy hopped on a plane to Hawaii two weeks ago to celebrate their six-year wedding anniversary.

Meanwhile, Maika is at Lauren's. Crazy, I know, but in the

past six years, Lauren completely turned her life around. The billion conditions she had to respect to win back shared custody of Maika? Well, after I visited her asking about my dad, she started following each one to a T. She even went back to school for a better job, and after a year of therapy, she was allowed near her daughter again.

I thought I was going insane when she showed up at our door one day. Haze nearly chased her off our porch, but I decided to hear her out. She hugged me—I repeat, my mother, who's never touched me unless she absolutely had to, *hugged me*—apologized, and asked me if she could possibly meet her granddaughter. I let her hold Desiree for a good two minutes—which is impressive considering my major trust issues. I think we both know we'll never be close, or at least not in the way that a mother and daughter should be, but we're on *okay* terms now, which is more than I ever thought possible.

"Do you have a name for the little dude yet?" Kendrick asks.

"Yeah, we're going to name him Harry." I smile. Haze circles my shoulder with his arm and pulls me into his chest.

Kendrick nods. "Oh, for your dad?"

"No, for the guy in One Direction. We're big fans," Haze deadpans, and Kendrick looks like he doesn't know if Haze is serious or not. Haze breaks into laughter, and Kendrick rolls his eyes, elbowing him in the stomach. They start wrestling each other like kids, and I smile. These two are best friends now. They watch sports together every week, hang out just to hang out.

To think they used to be sworn enemies.

"We're starving over here. Can we eat the cake?" Jaden and his boyfriend Dan come up to me. I have to crane my neck to glimpse at my brother's features. He's gotten so tall. He's a man now. Still, I don't think there will ever come a day where I won't look at him and picture my greasy-haired little bro.

I give in, surrendering my wrong-color sixty-five-dollar cake to my hungry guests. They're quick to dig in, lining up for a piece. When they point out that there aren't enough utensils, Kass offers to get more. I watch her enter the house and decide to follow her, asking Haze to watch Desiree for a bit.

Walking in a minute after Kass, I stop dead in my tracks at the sight of her staring blankly at the utensils she just pulled out of a drawer. Her back is facing me, but I don't need to see her to know exactly what's going on.

I hear her sniffling.

I don't say a word and step closer. She jumps, noticing my presence and wiping her eyes quickly.

"Hey." She acts as though she wasn't just crying. "I'll be back out with the forks in a second."

I don't budge, arching an eyebrow. She doesn't have to pretend with me. I know her.

Defeated, she lets her walls hit the ground. "I'm sorry. I know today's your big day. I'm just being a baby."

"No, you're not." I offer her a hug, and she walks straight into my arms. "I miss Will, too," I whisper, and she comes apart, crying into my shoulders.

"I just wish he was here," she admits.

"I know, honey, I know."

I hug her for a few seconds longer, my huge belly smashed down by our embrace, until she dries her tears and pulls away.

"I should probably bring those out before the guys start eating with their hands." She motions to the forks she's holding, and I chuckle.

"Good idea."

I watch her slide the patio door aside and walk back into the party. My attention wanders around our cluttered kitchen. It's still a work in progress as we haven't gotten around to repainting the hideous green walls and renovating yet. When Haze and I bought this house last year—right after Haze got his Canadian citizenship—we promised to make it home, but Haze's house flipper business has been doing so well lately he can't even focus on our own. I'll be done with my psychology degree in a year, which means I'll have way more time and money to pour into renovations, but for now, nauseating green walls it is.

"There you are," a voice I know by heart says. "Admiring our ugly house?"

I peek over my shoulder, only to see the most beautiful man I've ever laid eyes upon smiling at me.

*Damn*, I still can't believe I scored Haze Adams.

"Admiring how far we've come," I correct.

Six years ago today, we were standing in a dark motel room,

watching Mike be taken into police custody. I remember it so clearly: I'd just found out I was pregnant with Desiree. I remember how scared I was, dreading what life had in store for us.

Now I know the best was yet to come.

"Did you hear?" Haze asks, and I connect the dots.

"Yeah." I nod and turn around. Haze wraps me up into a warm embrace, resting his chin on top of my head. I listen to his heartbeat and inhale his cologne.

Mike passed away two days ago. Heart attack. The police called me at home since I was his only relative, but we were too busy trying to convince Desiree to take a bath to pick up, so they left a message. Haze and I heard it at different times.

Since Mike was sentenced to life in prison, some could say he was lucky to escape his sentence early. Still, when I found out, I felt a bit… sad? I beat myself up over it. *His confession doesn't change what he did*, I repeated to my heart.

Then I realized that while his surrendering to the police didn't change the past…

It sure as hell changed the future.

Haze picked himself off the ground and built himself back up after that night. He even got in touch with his family. They're not what one would call close, but they're on speaking terms. In a way, that one awful day opened the door to a million beautiful ones.

"Hey, where's Des? I told you to watch her," I realize.

"She's playing with Nathan. Allie just got here. You should've seen her face when she saw him," Haze remarks. "I swear if he grows up to break her heart, I don't care if he's Allie's kid, I'm kicking his ass."

I laugh and plaster my lips to his. He kisses me back, gripping my waist and lurching my body as close to his as the big bump sticking out of me allows him to. This still feels like the first time. Like the night he first kissed me on that beach all those years ago. My meteor shower tattoo has been a bit stretched out by my pregnancies, but I wouldn't trade it for the world.

"Hey, Kingston?" He pulls away.

"Yeah?"

"Any reason you didn't tell your family about me proposing to you last night?"

I grin. We were cleaning up in the kitchen after we put Desiree to bed yesterday. I asked him to hand me a clean glass so I could get myself some water.

He did just that.

He handed me a glass.

But… with a wedding ring at the bottom. Want to know what the worst part is? My dumb ass didn't even see it until the glass was almost empty and I was this close to swallowing it whole. Haze yelled to stop and saved me from certain death by choking on jewelry.

Then he got down on one knee.

"Yeah, about that. I changed my mind," I tease.

"Did you now?" he smirks, smoothing his hand up and down my arm. Shivers erupt over my skin.

"I'll tell them soon, I promise." I kiss the tip of his nose. "I just wanted this day to be about our little guy."

This seems to be Haze's cue to sprinkle my stomach with kisses and talk in a ridiculous high-pitched voice to his unborn son. I'm smiling so wide my face hurts.

"We should probably pick a venue," I say once he's done conversing with my belly.

"And a date," Haze adds.

"And write our wedding vows."

"I don't need to write my wedding vows. I've got them all right here." He taps his forehead.

"Really?" I cross my arms over my chest. "Go ahead. Let's hear it, then."

He clears his throat and picks my hand into his. "When I was in high school, I met a girl. She called me out on my shit. We fell in love. After six years of me pestering her, she finally agreed to marry me."

"That's it?" I mock.

"I didn't say it was long."

He draws a laugh out of me and grins, proud of himself.

"Jerk," I tell him.

"Prude," he says right back.

**Thank you so much for reading Haze and Winter's story!**

## WHAT TO READ NEXT?

**Next in line is Will & Kass's forbidden brother's best friend romance! Make sure to follow Eliah on Instagram (@eliahgreenwood) and sign up to her Newsletter (https://www.eliahgreenwood.com/subscribe) to be the first to know when Forgotten Rules is available to binge!**

# ABOUT THE AUTHOR

Eliah Greenwood is a Canadian author who started writing books online when she was fifteen years old. When her book "The Bad Boy's Rules" and its sequel gathered up to 30,000,000 reads on the internet, she decided to give her loyal readers what they'd been asking for and self-publish. She's currently working on the fourth book in the Rules series. It is expected to come out in early 2020.

# ALSO BY ELIAH GREENWOOD

Forgotten Rules *(Will & Kassidy's story*, Book 4 in The Rules series) **AVAILABLE EARLY 2020**

Forsaken Rules *(Will & Kassidy's story,* Book 5 in The Rules series) **AVAILABLE EARLY 2020**

Heartbreakers For Hire (Book 1 in the Heartbreakers series)

**AVAILABLE LATE 2020**

Enjoyed the book? Please consider leaving a review for **Unbroken Rules** on Amazon!

# ACKNOWLEDGEMENTS

To my beautiful, amazing readers… thank you. I can't believe we made it this far. I'm forever grateful for your time, support and love. This series would've never been finished if it weren't for you. Waze would have remained an idea in my head.

To my boyfriend, thank you for knocking some sense into me when I needed it. God knows I almost discontinued this series, and the world also owes these pages to you. You were there from day one, there to cheer me up when I felt as though this writing thing was a waste of time. I love you so much. Always.

To Sandra, my editor, thank you for dealing with my tired brain and its weird tendency to mess up the same words on repeat. Thank you for the hilarious memes at the plot twists. Thanks for loving Waze as much as I do. You're the best.

To my father, thank you for being curious about every single thing I do and asking me about my books every time I see you. I couldn't have asked for a better dad. Thank you for believing in me.

It all started with you.

Printed in Great Britain
by Amazon

59446439R00331